COURTING ANNA

"How will you get to the firehouse?" he asked.

"I don't know. This is Emily's Saturday at the restaurant, and my *aenti* has too many children to keep an eye on."

"I could take you if you want."

"You would?" Her eyes shone. Then she looked troubled. "But I can't leave the children with my *aenti*. All three of them have to go along. And you . . ."

Anna's sympathetic look melted him. She must be remembering his reaction to Ciara and his story about Jonah.

His words, which stuck in his clogged throat, came out gruff. "It's all right." He tried to correct his tone. "I'd be happy to take all of you."

Anna glowed like a girl who'd just been given a special present. "*Danke*. That would be wonderful."

Levi's heart overflowed with joy. She'd said yes. Not to his original plan to spending time together. Instead, his invitation had been for all four of them. So maybe her excitement stemmed from having a chance to eat barbecue or to entertain the children, who definitely appeared to need some cheering up.

Perhaps this was God's way of reminding him to be patient. . . .

Books by Rachel J. Good

HIS UNEXPECTED AMISH TWINS

HIS PRETEND AMISH BRIDE

HIS ACCIDENTAL AMISH FAMILY

Published by Kensington Publishing Corp.

His Accidental Amish Family

RACHEL J. GOOD

ZEBRA BOOKS
KENSINGTON PUBLISHING CORP.
www.kensingtonbooks.com

ZEBRA BOOKS are published by

Kensington Publishing Corp.
119 West 40th Street
New York, NY 10018

All Kensington titles, imprints, and distributed lines are available at special quantity discounts for bulk purchases for sales promotion, premiums, fund-raising, educational, or institutional use.

Special book excerpts or customized printings can also be created to fit specific needs. For details, write or phone the office of the Kensington Sales Manager: Attn.: Sales Department. Kensington Publishing Corp., 119 West 40th Street, New York, NY 10018. Phone: 1-800-221-2647.

First Printing: December 2020
ISBN-13: 978-1-4201-5046-9
ISBN-10: 1-4201-5046-4

ISBN-13: 978-1-4201-5047-6 (eBook)
ISBN-10: 1-4201-5047-2 (eBook)

10 9 8 7 6 5 4 3 2 1

Printed in the United States of America

Chapter One

Anna Flaud wheeled herself down the ramp and to the mailbox out front. The spring sunshine warmed her body but not her heart. Purple crocuses and yellow jonquils lined the walkway. In the flower beds, small green shoots fought for room beside spindly tendrils of onion grass. On days like this, *Mamm* would be tending her plants, but now weeds sprouted everywhere. The garden missed *Mamm*'s loving attention as much as Anna did.

She still couldn't believe *Mamm* was gone. Each day of the past three months had been harder than the one before.

Blinking back the moisture blurring her vision, Anna tugged the mailbox open. A pale blue envelope peeked out from between bills and circulars. Anna pulled out the mail, set the blue envelope on top of the others, and shut the box. Her cousin Emily used that color stationery, and the return address of Ronks, PA, confirmed she'd sent this one. Anna hoped Emily's newsy letter would cheer her.

Anna rolled herself back to the lonely house. How she missed *Mamm* humming as she stirred soup on the stove. After fixing a ham and cheese sandwich, Anna pulled herself up to her spot at the table. If she avoided looking at the empty chair, she could pretend *Mamm* had joined her. *Mamm* loved hearing Emily's updates on the family.

This letter wasn't Emily's usual circle letter. The relatives all took turns adding a new page or two before sending the thick envelope on to the next recipient. When Emily came for *Mamm*'s funeral, Anna had asked her to keep an eye on one special person in her town. Would Emily's report be good or bad?

With trembling fingers, Anna opened the letter and withdrew the single sheet of paper inside.

Dear Anna,
    Mamm *talked to your brother Merv. He agrees you should come to stay with us.*

Anna wasn't ready to live in her *onkel*'s busy household. They always had several foster children in addition to Emily's three younger siblings. Although the house here seemed much too silent without *Mamm*, Anna preferred peace and quiet. If she were honest, she had a different reason for wanting to avoid her *onkel*'s home.

Emily's older sisters had new babies, and Anna's *aenti* often fostered infants. Being around them reminded Anna that she'd never have children of her own. The accident that had landed her in the wheelchair had taken that from her.

An ache blossomed inside. To force her mind away from her grief, Anna returned to the letter.

Your brother wants a larger house for his growing family, so he could move into your parents' house, and you could stay in our dawdi haus *now that* Mammi *is gone.*

Anna leaned back in her chair. She'd have some privacy in the *dawdi haus*, but she'd also have family nearby when she grew lonely. And the one-story house had been adapted for *Mammi* after rheumatoid arthritis confined her to a wheelchair. But staying there would also remind Anna of the grandmother she'd lost several months before her *mamm*.

It might also bring her closer to her dream, depending on what her cousin had discovered. Emily had a friend in the nearby Bird-in Hand *g'may* who'd promised to report on Anna's questions. She braced herself in case the information dashed her dreams.

> *In other, more important news, you have nothing to worry about. He attends singings and is friendly to everyone, but he's shown no interest in dating any of the girls. Even though several have been trying to get his attention, he pays them no mind.*

Did that mean he truly did intend to keep his promise? She'd worried that after all this time, he'd have forgotten her and found someone else. If she moved to Ronks, she'd be near him.

Anna pushed aside the doubts that often plagued her. All that time and *he* was still faithful? Could it be *he* was God's will for her future?

Emily continued:

> *The Community Care Center in a town nearby has equipment and programs that could help with your rehab. Two children from our g'may travel in a van to special schools. The van is wheelchair-accessible,*

*and the nurses who drive them could pick you up
and take you to the center.*

Only her cousin knew of Anna's secret promise—the
reason why she'd been working so hard at rehab the past
seven years. Why she needed to continue her rehab.

Emily's closing lines tugged at Anna's heart.

*I'd like to have you nearby. I miss spending time
with you. And you'd also be closer to HIM. If he's
been faithful to you all these years, I'm sure he'll
keep his promise.*

Being around her cousin would be fun. Anna wasn't so
sure about the rest. For all these years, she tried not to
dream because he could fall for someone else. Someone
who could help him on the farm. Someone who could give
him children.

He'd agreed to wait for her answer. It seemed as if he
was still waiting. If so, she needed to let him know soon.
And she could only do that when she could walk.

Anna sorted the rest of the mail, tossing the *Englisch*
circulars and ads into the trash and gathering the bills into
a tidy pile to pay. She placed those and the *Die Botschaft*
on the desk in the kitchen. If only she could go through
the mail now, but she had a little *redding* up to do before
Nancy arrived. She'd already cleaned earlier today, but she
wanted the house spotless.

Although Nancy had been her best friend since their
buddy bunch days, when they'd taken baptismal classes
together, Anna dreaded seeing her. On Sunday, though,

Nancy had said she had news to share. Anna couldn't refuse her request to get together.

She'd finished her cleaning and was pulling a pan of brownies from the oven when Nancy knocked. Stomach in knots, Anna wheeled herself to the door to find her friend standing on the porch with a baby in her arms and a three-year-old clinging to her apron.

Nancy shifted the baby to one arm and bent to give Anna a one-armed hug and a *poor-you* smile. "*Vi bisht du?*" The pitch of her voice when she asked how Anna was sounded like an adult talking to a toddler.

Anna struggled to keep from mimicking Nancy's tone. "Come into the kitchen. I just made some brownies." She led the way and headed over to cut the brownies on the low counter her *daed* had installed.

Nancy plopped Katie on the bench and scurried over. "*Ach*, let me help you with that."

Anna waved her away. "I can do it."

Nancy shifted from one foot to the other as if wishing she could snatch the knife from Anna's hands. "Are you sure?"

Rather than pointing out that she'd managed to cut most of it already, she tipped her head toward the table. "Maybe you should check Katie." Nancy's daughter had wriggled partway off the seat and dangled over the edge.

While Nancy rushed over to rescue Katie, Anna padded her lap with a thick dish towel, set the brownies on it, and wheeled over to the table. She'd set plates and silverware out earlier, so Nancy wouldn't feel obligated to help.

"You said you had some exciting news?" Anna said as she passed around the brownies.

"You're the first one to know, except for John, of course."

"Of course." Anna certainly wouldn't have expected to know before Nancy's husband.

Leaning closer so Katie couldn't hear, Nancy whispered, "I'm having another baby. Being so soon after this one"—Nancy jiggled her four-month-old son in her arms—"it was a surprise, but we're both delighted."

"Th—that's *wunderbar*." Anna tried to infuse cheer into her voice, but her eyes stung.

"*Ach*, Anna. I didn't mean to hurt you. It's just that I can't tell many people, and you're my best friend. . . ."

Anna had never told anyone, except her parents, she couldn't have children, so Nancy had no idea of the pain she'd inflicted.

Nancy set a hand on Anna's arm. "I'm sorry. I wasn't thinking about you not being able to marry and have—"

Anna waved to interrupt before Nancy said *children*, a word that would pierce Anna's heart. "Actually, I have news too. I'm moving to the Bird-in-Hand area because I'm planning to get married." *If he even remembers me. If he still plans to honor his promise. If he . . .* She pushed away her doubts. Emily had given her hope. She needed to cling to that.

"Oh, Anna, I'm so happy for you." Nancy leaned over again to envelop her in another brief hug. Then she pulled back and fixed Anna with a searching gaze. "Wait. Bird-in-Hand? Near Lancaster? Isn't that where—?"

"*Jah*, it is." Anna tried not to squirm under Nancy's scrutiny. She didn't want her friend to know how tenuous her plans were. "I'll be sure to invite you to the wedding." *If there is one.* No more *ifs*. She needed to take her future into her own hands.

The sooner she got to Bird-in-Hand, the faster she could do that, and the happier she'd be.

Chapter Two

Levi King took his brother's hand and helped Jonah into the Community Care Center on Saturday morning. They stopped by the wall charts hanging in the hall to review his activities for the day.

"Can you show me which is your chart?" Levi asked.

His twelve-year-old brother ran a finger over the names at the top of each chart. He slid right past his own name.

Levi stopped him. "Wait a minute. Did you see 'Jonah' in that row?"

His face creased in puzzlement, Jonah turned in his slow, ponderous way to look at Levi. "Jonah is here." After pointing to his chest, he glanced behind him. "Not in a row."

Suppressing a sigh as well as his guilt, Levi waved a hand toward the papers on the wall. He should have phrased his question more precisely. Jonah took everything literally. "Do you see your name on any papers on this wall?"

Jonah squinted at the section Levi indicated. "Nooo . . ."

"How about here?"

His brother's face lit up. "Yes."

"Let's read your activities for the day." Levi slid a finger along under each word as he read aloud, hoping Jonah might recognize some of them.

When Levi pointed to the words in the first box for the morning, Jonah brightened. "Craft room," he echoed after Levi said it twice.

Jonah bounced on his toes but stretched out a hand and pressed his palm to the wall to maintain his balance. Levi's stomach clenched as it did whenever he watched his brother struggle. This was all his fault. If he hadn't . . .

Cutting off those thoughts, he concentrated on the daily plan. He read the other blocks in order. Not that Jonah would remember, but an aide would keep him on track throughout the day while Levi worked. In fact, he needed to get his brother settled so he could attend to his own schedule.

"Let's go to the craft room now," Levi suggested, and Jonah shuffled down the hall beside him, mumbling "craft room" in a low, excited voice.

Once Jonah had greeted the aide, he lowered himself onto a chair, and the Mennonite volunteer explained they were tearing newspaper into strips to stuff into water-proof tarps stitched together to make mattresses for the homeless.

Levi had volunteered to deliver the completed mat-tresses to the Tabitha Truck, a mobile mission that fed and assisted the homeless. He loved that his brother was part of this project to help others. Levi tamped down the thought that if it hadn't been for his mistakes, his brother could be doing so much more to assist the community.

After Jonah began awkwardly, but enthusiastically, tear-ing pages, Levi smiled at the aide, patted Jonah's shoulder, and headed for his own list of appointments.

Saturdays were usually busy. Not much time to fit in all those who needed exercise plans. *Hmm, a new name on his list. Anna Flaud.* She'd be coming at one o'clock. Right after Jonah's lunch. With his packed schedule, Levi barely had time to breathe, let alone find out more about the new girl on his list.

At lunchtime, he joined his brother to help him with small motor tasks. Levi peeled up a small corner of foil on the yogurt container and then encouraged Jonah to pull it off. Levi kept a firm hand on the bottom to prevent Jonah's hard, clumsy tugs from sending yogurt splashing across the table. When he succeeded in opening it, Jonah beamed up at him.

"Good job," Levi said with a genuine smile, but inside he railed, *Why, God? Why does Jonah have to pay for my carelessness?* Although both of his parents had accepted the accident as God's will for their son, Levi never stopped questioning. Mainly because he'd been responsible.

He concentrated on wiping the yogurt smeared on his brother's face and mopping up spills. Questioning God was not the Amish way. Everyone else around him seemed to take the changes and challenges in stride, but shame and self-reproach festered inside Levi, burning a hole in his gut. No matter how hard he tried to compensate for his childhood mistake, he could never erase the consequences.

Concentrate on your brother instead of wallowing in your guilt, a small voice whispered. And Levi jerked his attention back to Jonah.

Despite hurrying his brother along, by the time they finished lunch and Jonah went off with his aide, Levi was a minute late for his one o'clock appointment. He rushed into the room to find a pretty, dark-haired young woman facing the door and skidded to a stop.

Readjusting his mental picture of a small girl, he tried to sound professional rather than breathless. "Anna? I'm Levi King. Sorry I'm late."

Her tinkling laughter did strange things to his insides.

She gestured to the battery-powered clock over the doorway. "One minute? I wouldn't consider that late."

"I usually try to arrive before the children do. I mean, you're not a child, but . . ." Heat rose from under his collar and splashed onto his face.

A pretty shade of pink colored her cheeks. "Is the center only for children? I thought my cousin said—"

"No, no," he hastened to assure her. "We welcome both adults and children." Adults usually came during the weekdays, though, when the children were in school.

Her slow exhale sounded uncertain. "You're sure?"

"*Jah.* We help all ages." He cleared his throat. "I don't know why, but when I read your name on the schedule, I pictured a six-year-old. But you're definitely not six. I mean—" Levi stopped before he blurted out she'd been a pleasant surprise.

Her bell-like laughter interrupted the awkward pause. "I can act like I'm six if you want."

"*Neh, neh.* I'm happy to have you act your age." *Get a grip, Levi. You're making a fool of yourself.*

Dimples peeked out from her cheeks. "You expect me to act twenty-four? I'm not sure that's possible. *Mamm* always said . . ."

A glimmer of tears drew his attention to her brown eyes. "Are you all right?"

"It's just that *Mamm* passed four months ago. I still miss her."

"Of course." His mother had been gone for several

years, but the pain remained fresh. "Maybe we should get started."

Blinking back the moisture in her eyes, she nodded.

Forcing his attention to the equipment instead of her lovely face, Levi gestured toward the corner of the room. "If you back your wheelchair between those bars so you're facing me, we can work on upper-body strength."

"*Neh*, I want to learn to walk."

"Walk?" Levi stood there stunned.

"In rehab, I managed to stand at my last session. I want to keep going. I have to move ahead because, well"—she pressed her lips together—"just because."

The steel in her voice revealed she had a strong motive. One she didn't feel comfortable sharing.

"The doctors told my parents I'd be bedridden all my life." Anna waved a hand toward her wheelchair. "I've already proved them wrong. They never believed I could walk, but I will. I have to." Desperation underlay her final words.

Levi wanted to ask why, but they'd already frittered away five minutes of her session. "To walk, you'll need upper-body strength to support you on crutches." At least he assumed she planned to use them. "Why don't we do some of those exercises first, then we'll work on standing?"

"Not standing. Walking."

"All in good time. It's a large transition. We can take it slowly."

Besides, he wasn't a trained therapist. Being Amish, he couldn't be licensed. *Jah*, he'd worked as a physical therapy volunteer in a hospital for five years after he turned sixteen. He wasn't allowed to have hands-on contact with the patients, but he observed everything they did. And he still read and studied techniques. He also asked the licensed Mennonite therapists who worked here for suggestions.

"You don't understand. I need to walk now," Anna said in a firm voice. "Right away."

The last thing Levi wanted to do was discourage her, but he needed to be realistic. No sense in contradicting her, though. He pinched his mouth shut. She'd discover the truth soon enough.

Anna didn't want to act disagreeable at her first appointment, but she needed him to understand how important walking was to her. When he turned his charming smile her way, some of her fight dissipated.

She'd start the session doing things his way, so he didn't think she was uncooperative. Or a troublesome six-year-old. A smile played around her lips, and she almost shared her thoughts with Levi.

He waited while she crossed the floor. "Let's see what you can do without my help."

She'd already done a lot of upper-body exercises. Once she'd finished those, she'd get him to discuss walking rather than standing.

To show him she was used to the equipment, she rolled over and wheeled around quickly. *Clang!* Her handle bumped into a metal bar.

"It's all right," he soothed.

Anna's cheeks burned. So much for impressing him with her competence. "*Ach*, I thought I had more room." Did that sound like she was making excuses?

"You'll get used to the layout."

She hoped so. Maneuvering more carefully, she completed the turn and backed into place.

Levi's smile broadened. "See, you did it."

Of course, she had. Getting into position hadn't been that difficult. Maybe he was used to encouraging children. Actually, if she hadn't been concentrating so much on him and on showing off, she'd never have misjudged the space she had to turn.

Levi gestured toward the metal bar just overhead. "Why don't you start by pushing this bar up and down?"

Anna bit back her impatience. She'd done exercises like this before. She wanted to move ahead as rapidly as possible. She did as he asked and also lifted the additional weights he added. Then she did armchair push-ups. She waited until ten minutes into the session before saying, "Can we work on walking now?"

Levi's brows drew together. "I'm not sure . . ."

"I am." He might not be ready, but Anna definitely was. "The whole reason I'm coming here is to get back on my feet."

"I understand."

His attempt to placate her only increased Anna's frustration. She had to get him to realize the urgency. "You promised we could devote some of the session to walking." He hadn't said that exactly.

"You're really determined, aren't you?"

"Very determined," she replied.

Was that a gleam of admiration in his eyes or only a trick of the light? Anna couldn't be certain.

A small hiss that might have been frustration vibrated his lips.

She hadn't come all this way, moved from her childhood home, and scheduled these rehab sessions to be deterred from her goal. "Please?"

His resigned look signaled she'd won this skirmish. "You stood at your last session?"

"*Jah*." Only for a shaky second, but surely that counted.

"Why don't you show me?" He bent, flipped up the footrests on her wheelchair, and stepped back.

All the cockiness drained from her, and a wave of fear flashed through her. What if she couldn't do it again?

She gripped the chair arms. Her muscles, exhausted from exercise, refused to work.

"Take your time." Levi's calm voice penetrated her panic. "It's a huge step. Let go of the chair for a minute and flex your fingers."

Anna uncurled her hands. Wriggling her fingers eased some of the tension.

His voice light and teasing, Levi suggested, "You might also try breathing."

Laughter bubbled up and burst from Anna's throat. Then she inhaled a deep breath and glanced up. A big mistake.

His eyes expressed approval, and his smile radiated encouragement. Anna ducked her head and pretended to study the floor in front of her. Never before had she had such an odd reaction.

"You might also want to shake out your arms. Release some stiffness in your muscles."

Anna obeyed.

"How about some head circles?"

Until he said it, she hadn't realized her neck had cramped. So had her jaw. Levi seemed to know every spot in her body that held anxiety. Well, except for her insides.

"Ready now?" he asked.

Not really. A lot of her courage had leaked out as she released her tension.

"Take your time," he advised.

Once again, she curled her fingers over the arm of the wheelchair. She clutched hard and pressed upward to lift her body from the seat. Inch by inch, she raised herself, arm muscles quivering.

"That's it. You're doing fine."

Levi's reassurance increased her determination.

Anna pushed harder. Almost upright. She struggled to lift herself a little higher. Squeezing her eyes shut, she willed her body to cooperate. Once her legs dangled in position, she lowered herself a few inches on wobbly arms until her feet touched the floor.

Concern flashed across Levi's face. He held his arms out to catch her if she pitched forward, but he didn't touch her. She appreciated him being there after her arm muscles gave out. Rather than falling into his arms, though, she collapsed back into the chair, her forehead and the nape of her neck damp.

"That was amazing." Levi's proud smile warmed her, but it couldn't take away the sting of her failure.

How long would it take to stand, to take steps, to walk, to reach her goal? How much longer would Gabe wait for an answer?

Chapter Three

It took all of Levi's willpower to remain in place while Anna struggled to stand on her own. He could reach out to support her, help her to her feet, hold her up. But she needed to do it on her own. He wished he understood the driving force behind her insistence. He admired her persistence, though.

Anna slumped in the wheelchair as if most of her confidence and energy had seeped away.

"Getting to a standing position is difficult. And you did it." Levi wanted to cheer her up. "It's natural to feel tired."

With a grimace, she pushed herself upright. "I'm not tired. Well, maybe a little." She lifted her chin and squared her shoulders. "I'm ready."

"For what?"

"To do it again."

Evidently, nothing would stop her from succeeding.

"Why don't you rest awhile first?"

"I can do it." Anna's tone brooked no argument.

Even though Levi had given in a few minutes ago, he was supposed to decide the timing and exercises. Anna had a strong personality, and she might not like it, but he needed to take the lead in their sessions.

"I don't want you to overtax your muscles. They need a chance to recover."

Anna shot him a glare, then softened it. Her eyes sparkled, making her even more attractive. The overhead lights glinted on the glossy brown hair exposed by her *kapp*, and Levi had an unexpected urge to reach out and brush back the two damp curls on her forehead. He thrust his hands in his pockets. Time to concentrate on exercises. "Let's do a few cooldowns."

"I don't want to cool down. I want to stand again."

"Do you want to be stiff and sore tomorrow?"

"*Neh*, but if I don't keep going, I'll be in worse pain."

"What?" That didn't make sense.

"It's just that I . . . Never mind." Anna turned her head away. "I didn't mean physical pain."

Were those tears in her eyes? What kind of pain was she talking about? And why did she so desperately want—or need—to walk? This seemed much more than the usual desire to recover. He wished he could ask, but they were still strangers. Perhaps once she got to know him, she'd confide her secret.

Anna wanted to power through another try, but with her muscles tight and strained, her nerves taut and shaky, her arms heavy and useless, she struggled to prepare herself. This shouldn't be so difficult. During the day, she lifted herself into bed and onto chairs. She had to push herself up much higher to stand. Yet, the minute she decided to push herself up, her body rebelled, her muscles weakened, and her brain refused to cooperate.

Maybe if she rested a bit as Levi had suggested, she could try again. Stand longer. Show him she was ready to walk.

First, she had to gather more strength. She let Levi talk her through the cooldown, and the gentle stretching relieved some of the stiffness and aching. But the more she was around him, the more he drew her interest. If only he had cooldown exercises for her nerves.

They finished five minutes before her session ended. Enough time for one more try. She planned to make one more attempt. Even if she failed.

With a smile, Levi asked, "Would you like to—"

Before he could suggest more cooldown exercises, Anna burst out, "I want to stand one more time." As soon as she said the words, her stomach fluttered as doubts surfaced. What if she collapsed again?

"We didn't set up your future sessions yet."

Was he trying to distract her? If so, he was doing a good job of it with his caring eyes and sincere smile.

With the exception of the members of her *g'may*, who'd known her for years, few strangers, especially men, looked her in the face. Usually, once her wheelchair caught people's attention, they averted their eyes. Moving down the streets in town, she might as well be invisible.

Levi had been trained to help people who came here. He'd learned to concentrate on each individual he assisted. Still, his smile appeared genuine and appealing.

After he headed across the room for a folder, Anna shook her head. Some *Englisch* girls in rehab got crushes on their physical therapists. Anna never had, and she'd always dismissed those girls as silly when they batted their eyelashes at a male therapist or pretended to swoon when he walked away. But maybe that was only because her therapists had always been *Englischers*, so they hadn't attracted her interest. She'd never worked with an Amish man.

"My schedule is pretty tight." Levi's deep voice startled her.

"What?" Although he couldn't possibly know what she'd been thinking, Anna's cheeks burned.

He walked toward her. Tall and broad-shouldered, he carried himself with self-confidence, but he exuded humility. A very attractive combination. Not that he appealed to her, of course. Her mind should be on another man.

Levi hadn't grown a beard, and she couldn't help wondering why he wasn't married. Surely, he was courting someone. Not that it was any of her business. But Anna was curious. She pressed her lips together to keep from blurting out the question.

"How often did you want to come?"

"Huh?" *Ach*, once again, her mind had flown into forbidden territory. She had to answer his question. "Every day."

"You are eager, aren't you?"

For a second, Anna thought he was referring to being around him. She almost slipped and answered that question instead. "*Jah*, very eager"—she caught herself just in time—"to learn to walk," she added quickly, hoping the heat creeping up her neck wouldn't reach her cheeks and give her away.

She pulled her thoughts away from that danger zone. She needed to concentrate on her reason for learning to walk instead of getting sidetracked by a handsome and personable Amish man.

* * *

"If walking is your goal," Levi said, "you should rest between each session." How could he convince her to slow down, take care of her body, to stop pushing herself so hard?

Before he even opened his folder and flipped to the monthly schedule, Anna had snapped out an answer. "How about Monday, Wednesday, Friday?" She leaned forward. "Will those days work?"

Levi examined his schedule. Most of his slots were filled. Someone else could work with her in the early evening, but he didn't want to give up working with her. "If you can come at five o'clock, we can do a session."

He hoped his *aenti* wouldn't mind having supper a little later. Jonah arrived on the van from his special school around three-thirty to take classes here until five. Levi had to be sure the aide who worked with Jonah after school would be available until the sessions ended.

Anna tilted her head as if uncertain. "Doesn't your day end then?"

His face flushed. "It's all right. I can make time for you." He shouldn't have added *for you*. That made it sound too personal.

"I don't want to keep you after hours."

He didn't want her to think he was doing something special just for her. Even if he was. "The center is open into the early evening, so it's no problem." He rushed out his words, hoping he'd convince her.

"If you're sure?"

He was sure. Very sure. He wanted to say he'd be delighted to do it, but he tempered his words and kept his voice neutral. "It's no problem."

"I don't know. I don't feel right. Are there any other . . ."

Neh, don't ask about the others. He didn't want to tell her about the two part-time therapists.

Anna finished her question. ". . . times you have open?"

She wanted to work with him. Though he tried not to show his happiness outwardly, his smile broadened. "I do, but my openings are scattered." He knelt beside her chair and tilted his schedule so she could see the openings. "Here's what I have. None on Monday."

With a sigh, Anna traced her finger over the full day on Monday, then moved on to the three empty blocks—two on Tuesday and one on Thursday. "I see."

"I can do those two days in the early afternoon, if you want."

Anna hesitated. "I suppose I should take those."

She sounded so disappointed, Levi returned to his earlier offer. "Seriously, I don't mind doing the five o'clock appointments. My brother never wants to leave, so I'm sure he'll be happy to stay longer."

"Your brother works here too?"

Levi tried not to wince. "*Neh*. He's twelve. He comes here."

He prayed Anna wouldn't pry more. But she seemed so straightforward, he expected questions. He wasn't ashamed—at least not of Jonah—but he was ashamed of his own part in the story. He'd rather not answer questions about how his brother ended up at the center. That was a story he never wanted to tell.

To distract her, he said quickly, "Actually, I've been thinking. If you really want to learn to walk, you might be better off with one of our trained therapists."

"You're not trained?"

"I don't have a degree, if that's what you mean. I can't

take the certification. I'm mostly here to supervise basic exercises. If you'd prefer someone with a license, the office can schedule you with one of our Mennonite therapists."

Anna looked thoughtful. "I'd rather work with you for now, if that's all right."

"So, should I put you down for Monday, Wednesday, and Friday at five?"

"Only if you're sure it'll be no trouble." She looked up as if waiting for another confirmation.

"I promise it won't be." Not when his spirits were soaring.

"*Danke* for doing this," she said with a smile that filled his heart with sunshine.

Danke *for agreeing to work with me*, he almost said. Instead, he managed a polite "You're welcome." And hoped she hadn't seen his huge grin before he reached for his pencil.

Humming, Anna went out to meet the van. Although she'd rather have daily sessions, working with Levi three days a week would be fun. Something inside her stirred when she was around him, and of all the rehab appointments she'd had over the years, this one had been the best.

She'd always worked with *Englischers*, so she could never quite relax. She'd been a little more comfortable around the Mennonite workers, but Levi made her feel at home. Perhaps because he was Amish. Although the bond between them in this first session seemed deeper than that. Almost as if . . .

Anna jerked her thoughts away. She had no right to be

pulled toward another man. Not when she intended to walk to Gabe.

Gabe. That's where my heart and mind should be focused. No other distractions.

Although she dragged her mind from the vivid pictures of Levi, she could hardly wait for her next session. She hoped she hadn't been too pushy or overeager. But she needed to reach her goal. And soon.

The van pulled up, and Anna stepped back to let the nurses help two children first. Once they were settled and belted in, the driver lowered the wheelchair lift for Anna.

Over the idling engine and the drone of the lift, an excited voice carried across the parking lot. "Levi, look. Look at this."

A boy who looked to be eleven or twelve waved a paper in front of the man beside him. *Levi.* He clasped the boy's hand and looked down at him with tenderness. His brother? Levi had mentioned he had a twelve-year-old brother.

When Levi squatted and took the paper, that joyful smile that had warmed Anna during the session spread across his face. Her heart picked up its beat.

Their heads bent close, Levi examined the paper as the boy pointed out things on it. Then putting an arm around his little brother's shoulders, Levi hugged him.

The hug brought to mind Nancy's one-armed hug. Hers had been snide and accompanied by an *I'm-so-sorry-for-you* smile. By contrast, Levi's was warm and generous, and his face beamed. Anna would love to be the one getting a hug like that.

The nurse cleared her throat. Anna's face and neck burned. They'd all been waiting while she ogled a man. A man who was only her therapist. A man who'd thoroughly distracted her. A man she had no business looking at or longing for.

"Sorry," Anna mumbled and tore her gaze from the parking lot. She maneuvered her wheelchair onto the lift and pretended she was staring straight ahead as the nurse strapped the chair in place. But her attention remained on the side mirror reflecting the touching scene between Levi and his brother until the van pulled away.

Anna answered the nurses' cheery questions about her first day at the center, but she wished they'd chatter to the other two children and let her daydream. She looked forward to getting home, where she could be alone to review her session.

Before they reached the house, Anna said, "From now on, I'll be doing sessions at five on Monday, Wednesday, and Friday."

The nurse pulled out her scheduling book. "Hmm, let's see. Could you go in earlier? We have several after-school pickups at three and three-fifteen. We could get you after that. Two of the children are done at six, so you could ride home with them."

"That would be fine."

It gave her more time at the center. More time to watch Levi. No, she wouldn't peek into the room while he was working. She could stroll by casually, though. And maybe, with her being the last appointment of the day, he might have time to talk after their session before the van picked her up. Why did that make her heart sing?

Chapter Four

Anna enjoyed working with Levi three days a week, but he'd been right. Advancing from standing to walking took weeks.

One Wednesday, after she'd finished her warm-ups, Levi turned to her. "What about trying the parallel bars today?"

Anna almost cheered out loud. Now she'd move ahead. "*Jah!*"

Levi motioned for her to move in front of the two waist-height metal bars. She moved to the spot he'd indicated, positioned her chair facing forward, and pushed her wheel locks.

After he bent to raise her footrests, he handed her a long strip of webbed fabric. "That's a gait belt. Wrap it tightly around your waist. I'll hold the ends to help you keep your balance when you stand."

Fear mingled with excitement as she adjusted the canvas belt. Today she'd actually start walking.

Levi knelt and pointed her toes toward the ceiling. "Now your feet will be in the correct position when we pull you upright." He stood and placed a leg against her right ankle. "This is to stabilize you."

Anna wasn't so sure how stable she'd be with sparks shooting up her ankles from his touch. Trying to ignore those flashes of electricity and the fluttering in her stomach at being so close to him and to reaching her goal, she concentrated her attention on his instructions.

Taking the belt ends, he said, "Slide to the edge of your chair."

She wriggled forward until she feared she'd pitch out on her nose. What if she splatted onto the mat below? Would he pick her up? She'd enjoy that, but would it be worth looking foolish? She tilted back a bit.

As if sensing her fear, he spoke to her in a soothing voice. "Don't worry. I won't let you fall."

She trusted him, but it didn't stop her insides from quivering.

"Lean forward a bit and grasp these bars." Levi patted the parallel bars that were close to her chin level. "On the count of three, I'll hold the belt ends to help you stand. You'll need to do the same arm push-ups you do when you stand by your chair. Ready?"

Not really. But she'd never get over her trepidation if she didn't do this now. Gripping the bars with all her might, Anna leaned forward and waited for the countdown.

Dear Lord, please help my muscles to support me.

"One . . . two . . . three."

Anna pushed. The belt tautened. Her bent feet slapped the mat. She was upright almost a foot from her wheelchair. She'd done it.

Levi stood so near, she could reach out and touch him, if she weren't gripping the bars. She pushed that thought from her mind.

Tears of joy welled in her eyes. "I'm ready to walk."

"Oh, Anna." Levi squeezed his eyes shut as if he were in pain. When he opened them again, he said in a gentle tone, "This is only the first step in a series of exercises we'll do together. We need to strengthen your Y-ligament, so eventually you can use crutches."

Eventually? Her eyes stung as the tears of joy changed to tears of frustration. "How long will it take?"

Levi avoided her question. "You're a fast learner. Let's see how your body responds."

"How long?" she repeated, intent on getting an answer.

This time Levi looked straight at her. "The only one who can answer that question is you, Anna. If you work hard, it may go quickly."

Quickly was not the answer she wanted. A day? A week? Surely not more months of waiting.

"Why don't we get to work?" Levi suggested. "The sooner we practice, the sooner you'll be walking."

He ran her through a series of exercises—finding her center of balance by swaying back and forth until she ended in the proper position with her hips ahead of her ankles, then shifting side to side, and finally doing arm push-ups on the bar. Levi explained what muscles she was strengthening, but Anna barely heard him.

Her mind raced in circles, worrying about how long it would take to walk. Then the aching set in. Gritting her teeth, she finished another set of push-ups. If they didn't stop soon, she'd lose her grip on the bars.

Maybe she'd collapse into Levi's arms. He was near enough to catch her.

"Anna?" His voice broke into her daydreams. "Are you too tired to continue?"

She hadn't realized she'd been swaying in his direction.

How embarrassing. Hoping he'd think her cheeks had reddened from exertion, she straightened her arms and lifted herself into another push-up.

"What about trying side push-ups?" Without letting go of the belt ends, he nodded to each bar in turn. "One arm at a time. That'll get each arm strong enough so you can hold on to the bar with only one hand."

"Let go?" Anna's grip tightened. If she did, she'd tumble.

"Not yet," Levi assured her. "Right now, keep both hands on the bars. Just lean to one side and lift your body. This'll also prepare you to move forward when you're on crutches."

Anna's chest and arms ached, but she persisted. Why had she assumed she could just walk from one end of these bars to the other? Her face and dress grew damp, but when Levi suggested returning to the chair five minutes before the end of the session, she begged to keep going. The faster she learned, the sooner she'd walk.

Levi sighed. "Anna, if you strain your muscles, you won't be able to do anything for the next few sessions." At her downcast eyes, he added, "I wish everyone who came here was as motivated as you. But you have to take care of yourself."

Anna relented. Levi explained how to lower herself back into the chair, and she listened and obeyed his instructions. The few seconds between letting go of the bars and flopping onto the edge of the chair were terrifying. Every muscle tensed. Her stomach plummeted. Her only safeguard was Levi, who held the belt ends. Although she trusted him to guide her, she tensed, expecting to miss the chair.

When she hit the seat, she expelled a huge breath. She'd made it safely. She wanted to hug Levi. Instead, she wriggled herself back in her chair and whispered a demure *danke*.

Levi grasped the bars to keep from reaching out while Anna settled back in her chair. He could say he was trying to help her. When he worked with two of the children, he held their waists as they lowered themselves into their chairs. He couldn't do that with Anna. Although he had to admit, he'd like to.

"Let's do some cooldowns," he suggested, and she grimaced. His insistence on cooldowns always made her unhappy. But he didn't want her to end up with a strain or a sprain. Those could sideline her for a long time.

Over the next two days, Levi's mind stayed on Anna. He could hardly wait until she came for her next session. He wanted her to succeed in her goal as much as she did, but he wished he could help her understand and accept how long and involved the process would be.

All day, the clock hands moved slowly toward the afternoon. As they ticked off the minutes, his impatience grew. At five o'clock, he adjusted the parallel bars for Anna's height and waited for her to appear.

Her familiar tap at the doorjamb set his heart racing faster. He rushed over to greet her. Although he tried to control his lips, they widened so much, his muscles hurt. Was he grinning like a fool?

He needed to get his reactions under control. But Anna's answering smile touched a chord deep inside him. He hoped her joyful expression meant she was as happy to see him as he was to see her. Or was she only looking forward to walking?

Concentrate, Levi. She's here for a session, not a friendly visit. And definitely not for courting. He struggled to smooth his face into a businesslike expression. An attempt he suspected was unsuccessful.

"Ready to try some new exercises today?" he managed to say.

"Walking?" she asked, her eyes filled with hope.

Levi hated to dash her dreams. But he had to keep her realistic. "Anna . . ."

Her shoulders drooped. "I know." Then she brightened. "I practiced the side-to-side push-ups using my wheelchair arms yesterday and today. I'm already getting stronger."

"I'm sure you are." No sense in telling her two days of practice would be only a small part of the work she'd need to build her muscles enough to use crutches. Better to keep her sessions upbeat.

"So, how long until—"

He forestalled her usual question. "We'll add more exercises as we go along. Once you've mastered all of them, you can practice using crutches."

"But how long will—"

He motioned toward the clock to interrupt her again. "Why don't we use our time to work?"

"Good idea." Anna wheeled over to the parallel bars.

Once again, she wrapped the gait belt around her waist, and they did the prep work to help her stand. Levi held the ends of the canvas and counted down. At *three*, Anna lifted herself upright.

Close enough to be in his arms. Levi closed his eyes and tamped down the longing to hold her.

"Are you all right?"

At Anna's soft question, Levi's eyes popped open. "Fine." Or as fine as he could be while fighting his feelings.

He changed the subject. "Let's run through the exercises you did last time."

Anna found her center quickly and repeated all the other exercises perfectly. Levi introduced the dipper, explaining how to bend forward and press herself up to develop her triceps.

Although Anna looked winded, she completed it and asked eagerly, "Are there more?"

Next came the exercise that scared most people—letting go with one hand. Knowing Anna, though, he expected she wouldn't even blink. And he was right.

Her eyes sparkled as soon as he said it. "That's close to real walking, isn't it?"

"You definitely need to be able to let go if you want to move forward on these bars or on crutches. And you need to be strong enough to support all your weight on your other side," Levi said as he demonstrated how to position her body for the exercise.

Levi admired the set of Anna's lips and tenseness of her body, which revealed how intent she was on succeeding. She was amazing.

After following Levi's directions for placing her hands, Anna took a deep breath and squeezed her eyes shut. She had to get this exactly right. This was one of the big keys to walking.

She tilted herself a little at a time until her right side bore all her weight. Her right arm muscles trembled. Would they hold her? Now all she had to do was to lift her left hand.

"Good job," Levi encouraged. "Looks like you're ready. Now try lifting your left hand."

As hard as she tried, she couldn't loosen her grip. If she did, she'd collapse in a heap and need Levi's help to get up from the mat. In some ways, that sounded appealing, but she refused to act helpless. If she did, Levi might make her backtrack and redo other exercises.

"Try wiggling your fingers a little," Levi suggested.

But Anna's left hand stayed rigid, locked into position. "I can't."

Levi had lectured her once about never saying "I can't," and she braced herself for another correction, but he surprised her.

"It can be pretty scary. I know you can do it."

His voice, gentle and persuasive, gave her a shot of courage. If he believed in her, she'd do it. She lifted one finger and wiggled it. Her right arm ached. If she didn't move her left hand soon, her other arm would give way.

After a quick prayer, she lifted her hand a half inch. Then she grabbed the bar and balanced her weight evenly.

"Great job. Let's give your body some rest," Levi suggested.

Anna was too exhausted to protest. She sagged back into the chair, her chest heaving. She gulped in air and blinked back tears.

"That was great for a first attempt."

All that effort, and she'd barely lifted her hand. If she couldn't get over her fear of letting go, she'd never be able to move. She'd never cross a whole room. She'd never walk to Gabe. And she'd never get married.

Anna hung her head and clenched her still-shaking hands in her lap. A failure. A total and complete failure.

Levi squatted in front of her and placed his hands on the arms of the wheelchair. If only she'd left her hands there. Would he have covered them with his if she had? His touch might have given her some comfort. And maybe something more. Something she had no business wishing for.

"Hey, look at me." His tone soothed some of her shame. "You did fine."

"You probably say that to all the six-year-olds." Bitterness and disappointment crept into her tone.

Levi laughed. "You're not six, remember?"

That drew a giggle from Anna. "But I'm acting like it."

"Not at all. You have to work up to it."

"Are you saying I'm not in condition?" After all the weeks of armchair push-ups, all the practice standing, all the extra work she'd done at home?

"*Neh*, Anna, you've been preparing well every step of the way. But you can't do everything in a day."

"It wasn't only one day," she snapped, and then wished she hadn't. Levi had only been kind and caring. "I'm sorry."

"I think you understand what I mean. It took time for you to stand. Now it'll take more time for you to trust yourself enough to let go. Give your body time to adjust."

"But I don't have time. I've wasted too much already."

"Do you want to tell me why you're in such a hurry?"

Anna met his eyes for a second, then glanced away. He'd probably think her foolish for trying to walk to a man she hadn't seen in seven years, hoping to accept a marriage proposal.

Levi had seen her at her worst. Sweaty, exhausted, grumpy, irritable, frustrated. Would he wonder, like she did, if that man—or any man—would want her?

"You'll find I'm a good listener. And I know how to keep secrets."

How could she admit any of this? But she'd come to trust Levi, to admire him, to . . .

Don't go there, Anna.

She focused on the far wall so she wouldn't look at his caring expression. If she did, she might blurt out the truth. "You wouldn't understand."

"Try me," he said.

What could she say to stop his probing?

With a huge sigh, she admitted a small part of the story. "Someone asked me a question a long time ago. I promised to give them an answer when I could walk across the room. But I need to do it soon." *Before he finds someone else.*

Chapter Five

All this work to answer one question? Levi wanted to ask. It must be a very important question. Should he push for more information?

She had a sad, faraway look in her eyes. When she realized he'd been studying her, she shuttered her expression.

Now wasn't the time to press her. If and when she was ready to tell him, she would. Perhaps it was too private.

They didn't have much time left in today's session. And she hadn't come here for counseling. He needed to do his job.

"Listen, Anna. I won't pry anymore. But I want you to know, if you ever want to talk about this or anything else, I'm here." He rubbed his hands together briskly to signal a change of subject. "Back to your session."

She looked up at him, her eyes wide and startled.

"Don't worry. I'm not going to have you do any more exercises on the parallel bars today. Your muscles need to recover from such an intense workout."

"But I want to keep going."

"I know you do. Right now, we'll do some cooldown

exercises. Then I want to talk about the next session with the bars and how you can get ready." Part of today's mishap was his fault for not giving her time to prepare. She'd seized up.

He worked through her cooldown and then pulled a chair over so they'd be close to eye level. "You might be unhappy with your progress today, but you actually did well."

Anna stared down at her hands, resting in her lap. "You don't have to make me feel better."

"I'm not." Well, maybe he was a little. But she had done well. Not by her standards, but by his. "Most people freeze up when it's time to let go for the first time."

"I was petrified," she admitted. "I wanted to lift my hand, but I was afraid I'd collapse."

"I could tell. Next time, you'll be more relaxed. If you have someone to work with, you can do the side push-ups. The more you trust each arm to hold your body weight, the easier it'll be to lift your hand."

All she needed to do was trust her strength. She'd been working on that for so long, she should be able to do it. He had no doubt she'd succeed at the next session.

"I can't let fear stop me. Could I try those side push-ups again now?" Anna's old *I-can-conquer-anything* confidence had returned.

A smile tugged at the corner of Levi's lips. She never gave up. "You could."

For the rest of the session, she did the one-armed chair push-ups. When their time together ended, she headed for the door. "The only problem with this is that the chair is there to catch me if I make a mistake."

"True. But if you get your muscles used to the feeling, you'll be able to do it on the parallel bars next time."

"I don't know." She chewed on her lower lip a moment.

"Being on the bars frightens me because I don't have anything to catch me."

"That's why I'm there," he said softly. "I'd never let you fall."

And if he could, he'd go through life protecting her so she'd never fall. Not ever. Not in any area of her life.

Anna wheeled past Levi so he wouldn't see the tears forming in her eyes at his gentle tone. She'd been on her own since *Mamm* died. Sure, Emily and her *aenti* helped from time to time, but she had no one to depend on except herself.

Levi had only meant he'd assist her here, but his words brought up a deep yearning to have a man she could depend on, one who'd support her and encourage her the way he did.

Would Gabe do that?

Anna scolded herself. She had no right to compare him to Levi. Gabe had been gentle and kind after the accident, but she always suspected he stayed with her out of guilt. And despite Levi's kindness, he cared about her like he did the many others he helped each day. She shouldn't read anything more into it.

"Have a good weekend," Levi called after her.

"Same to you." As Anna reached the door, it opened. Holly Musser smiled at her but leaned around her to talk to Levi.

"Hey, Levi, we need a volunteer to do tours tomorrow during the Stop and Shop fundraiser at the school next door. Would you be available?"

Anna couldn't resist one last look at him before she went out the door.

"Sorry," he told Holly, "but tomorrow is my Saturday rotation, so I have appointments until two in the afternoon."

"Aww. I was hoping you could do it. Sharon called in sick a few minutes ago, and everyone else has left."

"What does a volunteer have to do?" Anna asked. She had many lonely hours to fill. If Levi would be here all day tomorrow, she wouldn't mind being here too.

Holly turned toward Anna with an eager expression. "They show people around the center. Explain what we do in the different rooms. Answer questions about the facility. Hand out brochures. Invite visitors to sign up for our newsletter."

"Would I be able to do it?"

"Of course. We'd be happy to have you."

"Anna would be a great choice," Levi said. "She's friendly and cheerful."

Levi's comments warmed her, and she smiled at him. From his shining eyes, it almost seemed as if he was as enthusiastic about having her at the center as she was about being there. Maybe that was only wishful thinking.

"You can talk about your experiences here," Levi said.

"I know a lot about the torture in this room." Anna flashed him an *I'm-only-teasing* smile, and he responded with a laugh.

"When you bring visitors in here, I'll be sure to tell them what you've done."

Anna sucked in a breath. Was he serious? From his expression, it seemed so. What if he told them about her collapse today? Or of all the other times she failed? How she hadn't reached her goals?

"I'll let them know how you've overcome obstacles to

become one of my star students." Levi's cheeks reddened when Holly studied him closely.

Then she glanced from one to the other, tiny frown lines beside the bridge of her nose as if trying to identify the undercurrent flowing between Anna and Levi. Anna smiled to herself. If she couldn't figure it out, she doubted Holly would.

But one thing she knew for sure: Levi's eyes captivated her, and she tried unsuccessfully to look away. Holly's voice startled Anna back to the room, back to the secretary's questioning eyes.

"If you follow me to the office, I can give you some information," she offered, "so you can read about the various things we do. Then you'll be prepared for questions."

Reluctantly, Anna tore her gaze from Levi's and trailed Holly down the hall.

"I'm so grateful you're willing to volunteer." Holly pulled a few brochures and booklets from her desk drawer. "I'll set up a table in the lobby before I leave tonight. I really appreciate you doing this. I have a family wedding tomorrow. Otherwise I'd be here."

"I'm happy to do it." *More than happy*. Anna reached for the small stack of materials, grateful to have a place to go tomorrow and something to read tonight. As long as she could keep her mind on the words rather than the handsome man in the exercise room, she could keep her heart safe.

After Anna and Holly left, Levi whistled as he cleaned the equipment and straightened the room for tomorrow's sessions. Tomorrow, he'd get to see Anna again. All day. He could hardly wait.

As much as Levi warned himself not to fall for anyone he worked with, Anna did strange things to his insides whenever he spent time with her. She drew him more than any other woman he'd ever met. He'd never had time for dating because, from the time he turned sixteen, he started volunteering at the hospital and taking EMT training. He'd held two jobs ever since to support his family.

Now that he'd met Anna, he'd like to make time. He'd been attracted to her from the first day he met her, and the more time they spent together, the more she appealed to him.

But he had no idea if she already had a boyfriend. Or even a husband. He needed to find out those important details before he let himself fall for her. Actually, it was a little too late for that.

Levi woke before dawn on Saturday, eager to get to work. Doing chores and helping Jonah dress took some of the time, but he still had extra time to kill before he left.

"Want to go over early?" he asked Jonah more than an hour before their usual time. "People will be setting up for the Stop and Shop."

"Stop . . . and Shop?" Jonah appeared puzzled.

Used to Jonah's loss of short-term memory, Levi explained, "People set up tables with things to buy. And they have food. Want to go?"

Jonah's eyes brightened, and he clapped. "*Jah.*" He plodded out to the barn with Levi and bounced up and down, getting in the way, while Levi tried to harness the horse.

"Why don't you stand over here?" Levi put an arm around Jonah's shoulders and led him to a safer spot before he backed out the buggy. His brother could still watch but stay out from underfoot.

Jonah kept asking questions, sometimes repeating himself, but Levi answered each one. When the horse had been hitched up, Levi helped his brother in.

"Can I get food?" Jonah bobbed up and down on the seat.

"If they're set up when we get there, you can have a snack." Levi hadn't packed their lunch boxes today, because he planned to treat Jonah to barbecue. But he'd wait until his brother finished his morning sessions to tell him. Otherwise Jonah might get overexcited.

Levi had enough problems with his own overexcitement. This would be the first time he'd ever seen Anna outside of work. *Jah*, they'd both be working today, but he hoped to catch her before she went inside.

When they reached the parking lot, Levi had trouble finding a space to park. Crowds already milled around the packed parking lot. A funnel cake stand did a brisk business, and the scent of cooking pork wafted from the barbecue stand. Although he'd just had breakfast, Levi's mouth watered. Some Amish vendors were still carrying crafts into the school building.

Jonah bobbed up and down, pointing from one thing to another. "What's that?"

A girl, her arms full of huge vases of flowers and grasses, headed for the entrance. The greenery hid most of her face.

"A lady with flowers," Levi answered.

"She's scary."

"That's because you can't see much of her face. Look

there. See her eyes?" Levi pointed to brown eyes peering through the blooms.

Jonah squinted. "The flowers have eyes?"

"*Neh*." Levi wondered how much to explain, but another vendor caught his brother's attention.

"Babies," Jonah squealed, pointing to a young mother with two toddlers clinging to her dress, staggering under a huge container of dolls and homemade clothes. She looked about to collapse.

"Not babies. Dolls," Levi corrected. "Stay in the buggy," he commanded and jumped out to tie up the horse. "I'll be right back."

He dashed across the parking lot and approached the woman, who looked exhausted. "Let me get that for you."

She looked reluctant to let go, but when he reached for the heavy box, she released it.

"*Danke*," she said, out of breath and red-faced. "I should have packed it in smaller boxes, but it's hard for the children to make many trips back and forth."

"Do you have more to get?"

"One more."

Levi followed her to her assigned table and set the dolls down. "I'll get the other one. Which buggy is yours?"

A teenager came rushing up. "Sorry I'm late."

"This is my sister," the young mother told Levi. "Lizzie, can you watch the kids and start setting up, while I get the rest of the stuff?"

Lizzie bent down, unfastened tiny hands from her sister's dress, and clasped them. "You can help me set up," she said cheerfully. The two little ones followed their aunt behind the table.

Levi accompanied the mother to her buggy. He'd just started back with her when Anna's van pulled into the parking lot. She waved, but then glanced from him to the woman, and her smile dimmed. Did she think he and this stranger were a couple? He'd need to clear that up. But her reaction added sunshine to his day. Perhaps that meant she was as attracted to him as he was to her.

Chapter Six

Anna spotted Levi across the parking lot, and her heart skipped and jumped. The van had come for her early because they had several other stops that morning. She'd hoped she'd get to spend time with Levi. But he had a woman beside him. They were walking close together, and he was carrying a box for her. Were they dating?

What difference did it make? She had no interest in Levi. She planned to marry Gabe. Once she could walk across the room. It wouldn't be long now. Or at least she hoped not.

Yet, she couldn't stop the twinge of disappointment.

By the time the van found a clear space to pull over and let her out, Anna had lost much of her anticipation. Maybe it was for the best. She'd been spending too much time with Levi.

Across the parking lot, Levi exited the school building alone. Despite her resolve not to think about him or react to him, her pulse paid no attention. It thundered even more when he headed in her direction, his grin warm and friendly.

She certainly couldn't ignore him, so she smiled back.

Her lips might have stretched a little too wide. Her eyes might have been overly bright. So much for curbing her attraction.

He waved. "Hey, Anna, I need to get my brother, but I'll be right there." He strode toward the building, and though she shouldn't, she trailed after him.

When he reached a nearby buggy, he skidded to a stop. "*Ach*, where is he?" Levi looked frantically from side to side.

Anna rolled up beside him. "What's wrong?"

"I told Jonah to stay in the buggy so I could help that woman. Now he's gone."

That woman? He wouldn't speak about his girlfriend that way. Hope flashed through her. But right now, he had to find his brother. "Can I help?"

Levi stared at her in surprise. "You know what he looks like?"

"I, um, think so." A flush of heat rose from her chest and splashed across her cheeks. She couldn't tell him she'd stared at him and his brother in the van's rearview mirror.

Worry lines etched into Levi's face. "That would be great."

Anna wanted to reach out and smooth away those lines and to reassure him. "I'm sure he's fine. Didn't you say he's twelve?" Most of the crowd was Amish, so he'd be safe.

"But he's more like a kindergartner."

Even a child that young would be all right, but the distress on Levi's face warned her his was not an ordinary worry.

The whole while they'd been talking, Levi's eyes had been darting around the clusters of people.

"Why don't I go this way?" Anna gestured toward the food stands. If Jonah was a typical boy, he'd probably go there first.

"He doesn't have any money." Levi grimaced. "That wouldn't stop him, though. I'll go this way." He rushed off in the opposite direction.

Anna mostly stared at people's backs; she couldn't see over heads. She tilted her body to one side to peer around the long lines at the food stands. Lemonade and iced tea were doing a brisk business. The barbecue stand hadn't opened yet, but a pig was roasting on a spit, sending out waves of a crispy meat aroma. Several people gathered around the long counter, chatting with the owner.

The heavy scent of sugar and oil drew her toward the funnel cakes. She'd been so nervous about doing this volunteer job today—and if she were honest, about seeing Levi outside her sessions—she'd barely eaten much breakfast. Her stomach growled, but she couldn't stop now. Not until they found Jonah.

Trying to wheel through the masses of people filling the parking lot proved challenging, but Anna kept searching. Only one more food truck stood between her and the school entrance. The entrance Levi had gone in with that woman.

She pushed herself forward, scanning the long lines. There! That young boy staring longingly at people walking away eating pretzels. Wasn't that Jonah?

Pretty sure she'd identified him correctly, Anna maneuvered her chair through the lines to reach him.

"Jonah?"

The boy looked at her, startled. Then he studied her curiously. First, her face. Then, her wheelchair. He seemed to be trying to place her.

"I'm Levi's friend Anna. Your brother is looking for you."

A guilty look crept over Jonah's face. "I wanted . . ." He gazed over at the pretzels hanging on a round rack.

"You wanted a pretzel?"

He nodded.

Anna would have offered to buy him one, but Levi had appeared so upset, she needed to make sure the two brothers reunited. "Why don't we find Levi? And then I'll come back here to get you a pretzel."

Jonah's face glowed. "*Jah!*"

"Stay with me now," she told him, but she needn't have worried. Her promise of the pretzel kept Jonah close to her side.

They traversed the parking lot in the direction Levi had gone. When he looked up and saw them, his face registered relief, and he jogged toward them.

"*Danke.*"

The gratitude in Levi's eyes warmed her. It more than repaid her search. A search she'd have been happy to assist with for no reward.

Then he knelt in front of his brother and set both hands on Jonah's shoulders. "You know the rules. It scared me when I couldn't find you. You could have been hurt."

Jonah hung his head and scuffed the toe of his shoe on the ground. "Sorry."

"Next time I tell you to stay in the buggy, I want you to obey. Do you understand?" Levi stared Jonah straight in the eye.

Jonah nodded, but bowed his head.

"I'm not angry with you. I just want to keep you safe."

"I know." Then Jonah peeked over at Anna. "Can I have my pretzel?"

"Pretzel?" Levi looked at her with a question in his eyes. "You bought him a pretzel?"

"Not yet, but I promised him one after we found you."

Levi laughed. "You make it sound like I was the one who was lost."

Anna grinned back. "We both know the truth." She wasn't so sure Jonah understood how he'd worried Levi. And he probably hadn't considered himself lost. He'd been right where he wanted to be. In front of the pretzel stand.

"Do we have time?" she asked. "The line is really long, but I hate to disappoint Jonah."

"I'll get the pretzels. It's the least I can do. You found Jonah, after all."

Anna wasn't sure how she felt about letting him buy her food. It seemed almost, well . . .

Before she could protest, Levi stood. "Stay here with Anna," he said to Jonah. "I'll be right back."

A few minutes later, Levi returned, carrying three hot pretzels.

"How did you get through that line so quickly?"

"I have my ways." Levi raised his chin and pretended to look haughty. "I shoved everyone out of the way."

"I don't believe you."

With a cheeky grin, Levi confessed, "Friends of ours from church own the truck. I avoided the long lines and knocked on the door."

"I see." Anna smiled her thanks and bit into the hot pretzel. She closed her eyes to savor the thin, crisp outside and soft, squishy inside and the salty tang it left on her tongue.

When she opened her eyes, Levi was studying her. "You really enjoy your food, don't you?"

"I didn't have much breakfast." She tried not to sound defensive. "And this tastes delicious."

"I wasn't criticizing you. It's great to see someone who appreciates the little things in life."

Was he complimenting her? The appreciative glow in his eyes made Anna uncomfortable. If she didn't watch herself, she could easily fall for Levi. And that was wrong. All wrong.

Levi wished he'd been more cautious. Had he given away his feelings for her? The wary look in her eyes warned him he'd stepped over a line. He had no idea if she was married or courting someone, so he had no right to be thinking about her this way.

But how could he resist? Her face lit with pleasure as her pink tongue darted from her mouth to lick the last bits of salt from her lips. Lips that looked soft and kissable. With an effort, he tore his mind from that thought.

Think about business, Levi.

"Um, if you need any help getting set up today, I could do that before my first appointment."

Tension lines appeared around her mouth and eyes. "I've been so busy enjoying this pretzel, I almost forgot about that. I hope I can do it."

She looked so nervous, Levi wanted to reassure her. "I'm sure you'll be fine."

"I stayed up later than usual last night to memorize all the information Holly gave me, but I'm worried people will ask questions I can't answer."

"You can give them the brochures. If those don't have the answer, you can take their names and contact information so Holly can call them."

Anna visibly relaxed. "I've been so concerned about making mistakes, I hadn't thought about that."

Levi shot her a reassuring smile. "Most people are just curious to see what we do here. The ones who are interested in the programs will call."

"True. You've made me feel much better. *Danke*."

"Should we go inside and see if anything needs to be done before the visitors start arriving?"

For the first time since he'd handed Jonah his pretzel, Levi glanced in his brother's direction. Jonah popped the last bite in his mouth, but his gaze remained fixed on Anna. Not that Levi blamed him. He had the same problem.

"Are you ready to go in, Jonah?"

His brother held up his hands, slick with melted butter. "Sticky."

Actually, they were greasy rather than sticky. And Jonah's soaked napkin would be little help.

"Would you like this?" Anna held out her napkin. When Jonah extended his hands, she gently cleaned each finger and his palms while he stared at her adoringly.

Her kindness plucked a string deep in Levi and set his heart vibrating. The more time he spent around her, the more taken he was with her.

After she finished, Jonah stood there, unmoving, his attention on Anna.

"What do you say?" Levi prompted.

Without taking his eyes from Anna, Jonah said, "You're nice."

Anna beamed. "That's the nicest *danke* I've ever heard."

Jonah's chest puffed up, and thankfulness filled Levi, expanding until his own chest ached with gratitude for Anna's kindness to his brother.

Many people ignored or discounted Jonah, and Anna

probably had similar experiences. That's one thing Levi appreciated about the center. All the staff there respected Jonah and treated him like an important individual. And right now, Anna had just proved herself to be equally as caring.

"Maybe we should go in now." Levi seemed to have repeated that several times already, but he'd gotten sidetracked by his brother and Anna. If he didn't start concentrating on business soon, he'd have trouble keeping his thoughts from straying to Anna all day.

She wheeled to his side, and Jonah followed her. Levi motioned for them to go first so he could keep an eye on both of them. He unlocked the center door and relocked it after they entered. A few curious people glanced in the window, but seeing the sign posted with the hours, they backed away.

"Oh, good." Anna went straight to the tables in the lobby. "Holly said she'd set everything up." She pointed to the array of pamphlets, printed information, and sample newsletters. "There's even a sign-up sheet." She sounded relieved.

"So, all you have to do is show people around." Levi checked out the paperwork on the table. "And with your cheerful personality, you'll be great at that."

Anna shot him a questioning look. He'd said something similar yesterday, and she'd seemed to doubt him then too.

"You don't believe me?"

"You've seen me grumpy and frustrated and . . ." She shook her head.

"When people work with me, they're struggling. Often, they're in pain, and I push them hard." Although to be truthful, Anna usually pushed him harder than he pushed her. "I judge everyone by the personalities they have when they come into the room. You've always been sunny and smiley."

Levi pretended to arrange a stack of newsletters. If he looked at Anna, his eyes might reveal more than admiration of her personality.

Anna's "I see" sounded uncertain, as if she didn't believe him.

He kept his back to her. "I can count on you to work hard and do your best. And you never complain."

She giggled. "Except when I'm pestering you to let me do more."

"Wanting to move ahead is positive."

Anna's tight smile revealed her nervousness over doing the tours.

Levi wanted to help her feel sure of herself. He had no doubt she'd do fine, but she didn't seem convinced. Perhaps after she'd shown a few people through the building, she'd come to realize it.

If Anna hadn't been so nervous, she might have appreciated Levi's compliments, but right now she could barely take them in. Maybe that was for the best. The last thing she needed was to like Levi more than she already did.

"I'd better check the exercise room to be sure everything is ready. Do you need help with anything else?" Levi seemed reluctant to leave.

"I'll be fine." At least she hoped she would be.

"Come on, Jonah." Levi beckoned to his brother.

Jonah shook his head. "Want to stay with Anna."

"He's welcome to stay with me until his aide comes. I don't mind."

"You're sure?"

"Of course." Having Jonah here might keep her calmer as she waited, although she couldn't be sure how much of the fluttering in her stomach was related to the upcoming volunteer work and how much was connected to Levi's presence.

She tried unsuccessfully to drag her gaze away from Levi's back as he walked down the hall, but she didn't turn around until the door to the exercise room closed behind him. Then she directed her attention to his younger brother.

"Do you like your classes here, Jonah?"

His head pumped up and down in a vigorous yes.

"Which one is your favorite?"

Jonah's smile broadened. "All of them."

If Levi wanted an example of an upbeat personality, he could use his brother.

Two women knocked on the glass doors. Anna recognized one from the center, so she hurried to the door and leaned forward to push on the bar.

"Thanks. You're Anna, right?" Without waiting for a response, she rushed on. "Holly told me you'd volunteered to be the tour guide today. I'm Leanne. I'll relieve you for an hour at lunchtime."

The younger woman with her gave Anna a shy smile.

"This is Addy," Leanne said. "She's in my first class of the morning, so she'll help me get everything ready." Leanne unlocked the front doors, tested both metal push bars to be sure they worked, and then strode past Anna. With a quick wave and a "Hey, Jonah," Leanne disappeared down the hall with Addy.

Soon, various other teachers and students entered, some accompanied by parents, others in chattering groups, a few alone. Jonah's aide claimed him, leaving Anna alone in the lobby. No one showed up for the first hour, so Anna sat and reread the brochures and leafed through a few newsletters. She fought the urge to peek into the exercise room.

By the time several *Englischers* showed up, Anna was so relieved she forgot to be nervous. She greeted them with her brightest smile. "Would you like a tour of the building?"

When they agreed, she offered them brochures and led the way down the hall. She described each room they approached, then tapped at the doors, and let the visitors enter. The staff had already prepped the children they were working with, so after a brief glance at the newcomers, they returned to what they'd been doing.

The next door led to the exercise room. Anna forced herself not to look through the window as she went through her spiel. But when she turned to knock at the door, she stopped with her hand raised because her eyes met Levi's.

His special smile held her in place, and the visitors beside her disappeared. No one existed except for him. And her. The two of them alone in the universe. Suspended in time and space.

Behind her, someone cleared his throat. Anna jumped, and heat flashed to her face. What was wrong with her? She had a job to do, and Levi should never be a distraction.

"I'm sorry," she mumbled, and wrenched the knob. She pulled the door open and motioned for the *Englischers* to enter. To hide her burning cheeks from Levi, she stayed behind them.

As if sensing her distress, Levi took over. "Welcome, everyone. I'm Levi, and this is Deirdre, who's nine. She's working on upper-body strength." He had her demonstrate some of the equipment.

Anna had no need to see because she'd done the same exercises, but she moved to the side to focus on Levi. His back muscles rippled under his blue shirt as he assisted Deirdre. Though Anna's conscience nagged at her, she couldn't look away.

When he turned back to the group, Anna spun her wheelchair toward the door. She'd better not stare at him again.

"Let's go to the next room," she said to the visitors. Although she'd thanked the other teachers, she feared speaking to Levi would reveal her interest to the *Englischers*. And to him.

Anna completed the tour with no further mishaps and returned the visitors to the lobby, where she found another group waiting. Each trip went more smoothly than the previous one, and she even relaxed enough to joke a little with Levi whenever she brought people to the exercise room.

At noon, Levi surprised her by asking if she'd like to stroll around the Stop and Shop, and then have lunch. "Jonah begged for your company."

Anna checked with Jonah to see if he had. His beaming face revealed the answer. If only Levi were equally enthusiastic. Maybe it was better he wasn't, or she might make a fool of herself.

She schooled her face into a neutral mask before she joined the two of them. They wandered around the school auditorium filled with tables. Amish women, many with children, sat or stood behind their wares.

Jonah bounded from one item to the next. "Look at this. And this. And this."

Anna could barely keep up. He grabbed her hand and tugged. "Come on."

Levi set a hand on Jonah's shoulder. "Slow down a little. Anna might be tired after her busy morning."

She loved how protective he was of her. She made the

mistake of smiling up at him in thanks. And once again, the hustle and bustle of the room crowded with people disappeared, and she was lost in his eyes.

If Jonah hadn't tugged on her hand, drawing her back to reality, how long would she have been frozen there?

Anna forced her attention back to Jonah. And to the table of baked goods beside her. She inhaled the chocolatey whoopie pies. Beside them lay rows of homemade cookies, cupcakes, and donuts.

Jonah picked up a cupcake with rainbow sprinkles. "Look."

"Would you like that one?" Anna asked him.

His starry eyes told her the answer.

"You don't have to do that." Levi reached for his wallet.

Anna held out a hand to stop him. She brushed against his skin, and a jolt shot through her. Stunned, she drew back. Had Levi felt it too?

"I'll pay for it." Her voice shaky, Anna fumbled for the money she'd tucked in her pocket. Too afraid she'd be disappointed at his reaction, she didn't look up at Levi.

Jonah danced on his toes. "*Danke! Danke! Danke!*" He started to unwrap the cupcake, but Levi stopped him.

"Better save that for after lunch," he said. "Why don't we get some pork barbecue now?"

Jonah's slight frown turned to a rapturous grin. Then he headed for the door without waiting for either of them.

"We'd better catch up before we lose him." Levi took the handles of her wheelchair. "Is it all right if I push?"

Anna nodded. Until he took over, she hadn't realized how exhausted her muscles were. She'd been pushing herself back and forth all morning. Levi rushed through the crowd until they reached Jonah.

"You need to slow down a little," Levi told his brother. "We can't keep up."

Jonah's mouth quivered.

"I'm not upset with you. It's only that Anna and I can't move as fast as you can."

Levi could hustle as quickly as his brother. He was trying to save her from embarrassment with his excuse. Although she could move rapidly when she had a clear space, trying to weave through crowds proved tricky. She might still be fighting her way out of the building if it hadn't been for Levi.

Jonah's head remained down. He didn't even look at his cupcake.

Anna wanted to help. "You must like barbecue." She accompanied her words with a wide smile.

"I do." Jonah lifted his head, his glum face now beaming.

Levi leaned close to whisper, "You're good with children. Maybe you should think about working at the center."

His warm breath heated her skin, and Anna shivered. Her nerves zinged throughout her body.

Levi studied her with concern. "Are you all right? Do you need a sweater?"

On a May afternoon? With the sun beating down?

"*Neh*, I'll be all right." Outwardly, the quivering subsided. But inwardly, it increased. At least Levi hadn't figured out what had caused that response.

"Why don't you get in line?" Levi said to Jonah. "I'll push Anna over to one of the tables, and she can save us a place."

He headed for the numbered church benches inside a canvas tent. "Or would you rather be outside?" He waved toward some picnic tables in the schoolyard.

Anna would prefer the privacy. But with her insides still trembling, she'd be safer around chattering gaggles of people. "The tent is fine." She managed to keep her answer steady.

Levi situated her at the end of a table. "I'll be back as soon as I can."

Anna pulled out some money, but he refused to take it.

"This will be my treat. You bought Jonah's cupcake." Before she could protest that he'd paid for the pretzels, he hurried off, saying over his shoulder, "I don't like to leave Jonah alone for long."

When the two of them returned, Jonah carried one take-out box, and Levi balanced two. Jonah set his in front of her. How could she turn him down? Had Levi done that on purpose?

They settled one on either side of her, and Anna, who'd been expecting only a sandwich instead of a full meal, held out several more bills. Levi waved her hand away and bowed his head for prayer.

Sighing, she tucked the money into her pocket and lowered her head. After they'd prayed, she tried again.

"*Neh.* You were kind enough to keep Jonah company this morning and buy him a cupcake. It's the least I can do."

Letting a man buy her a meal made Anna feel uncomfortable. She noticed that he'd only mentioned Jonah, not himself. She couldn't help feeling a little disappointed. Had he asked her for Jonah's sake rather than his own? Maybe he'd sensed her reaction to him and was making it clear he had no interest.

He needn't have worried. She planned to marry someone else. Anna concentrated on Gabe instead of the appealing man beside her. But Gabe couldn't hold her attention for long. Not when she had two real-live lunch companions.

As the three of them shared a lively conversation and lots of laughs during the meal, Anna couldn't help wondering: If she were here with Gabe, would she be having fun like this? Somehow, she had trouble picturing Gabe rather than Levi. Spending time with Levi was dangerous. Very dangerous. She needed to walk so she could give Gabe her answer soon. As soon as possible. Before she started falling for another man.

Chapter Seven

After weeks of work, both of Anna's arms could now support her full body weight. She'd worked on cruising down one bar, first sliding her hands along, then lifting them briefly as she moved them along.

When Levi introduced the last exercise, a hip hike that required her to shift her weight off the leg she'd be moving, he said, "Once you've mastered this, we can work on walking. You just need to put all these exercises together."

Anna beamed, and the answering smile he returned added to her exhilaration. With her spirits soaring like a balloon, she tried to tug at the string by reminding herself of her purpose. Walking to Gabe. But whenever her eyes met Levi's, she let go of the balloon string and her emotions, and the balloon bounced into the sky again.

Think about Gabe. Not Levi. Anna sobered.

Soon, she needed every ounce of concentration and energy to do the exercises. Combining the hands and the legs proved challenging.

"Think of them separately," Levi advised. "Rather than trying to walk, just balance your weight on one side. Then lift the other hand and move it forward. Even a little bit is fine."

Anna did what he said.

"Great. Now try the hip hike. Shift to that side." He pointed to her right side. "Next lift and move that leg."

Focusing all her attention, she managed to shuffle her leg forward.

"*Wunderbar.*" Levi gave her a reassuring look. "Can you do the same on the other side?"

Anna inched her hand along, and her leg followed.

"You know what you just did, right?" Levi asked her.

Salty sweat stung Anna's eyes. All her muscles trembled. The only thing she knew was that she'd just completed the most difficult set of exercises ever. The exertion had drained so much from her, she couldn't speak or even nod.

Levi's eyes shone. "You just walked your first step."

Her first step. She'd walked.

She might be worn-out, but she wanted to do more. Urging her weary muscles to continue, she repeated the set of exercises and moved forward another step. Then another.

After traveling a few feet, her arms wobbled. If she didn't stop, she'd crash.

"Hang on." Levi ducked under the bars, grabbed the wheelchair, and pushed it behind her. "Brake's on."

He popped up in front of her and grabbed the ends of the gait belt again. "Ready?"

Her body sagged, but she clung to the bars, unwilling to let go.

"The wheelchair is in the right position. Loosen your grip and lower yourself back into the chair." Levi guided her down with the belt and a proud smile.

Anna glowed inside. She'd only walked a few steps, but now that she had the idea, she'd make rapid progress. And Levi's thrilled expression added to her joy.

Levi could hardly believe how well Anna had done. After the first set of movements, she'd kept going. He probably should have stopped her sooner, but he wanted her to enjoy her triumph. A triumph that made him as happy as it made her.

He needed to end the session with information. Anything to get his mind off her beaming smile. "Next time, if you plan to walk along the parallel bars, you'll need a different gait belt."

"What do you mean?"

"From now on, you'll have a belt that buckles, and I'll be walking behind you, rather than standing in front of you."

Was it his imagination, or did she look disappointed?

There was no mistaking the frown that followed. "Behind me? What if I fall over?"

"We'll adjust the belt so there's some slack, and I'll hold on to it. You're already fairly steady. I'll only be here as a backup."

"I see." Anna sounded less than enthusiastic.

"I thought you wanted to walk?" Her reaction puzzled Levi. He'd expected her to be eager and enthusiastic.

"*Jah*, I do. But it's easier doing the exercises when I'm walking toward you. I mean . . ." she stammered, and lowered her eyes. Her face flushed a becoming shade of pink. "It's just that . . . you encourage me to move ahead."

"That won't change. I promise I'll still nag you to keep going."

"Nag?" Her gaze flew to his face. "You don't—" Her rosy cheeks deepened to crimson. "*Ach*, you're teasing."

"Don't be so sure about that. Plenty of people tell me I'm mean because I ask them to do exercises that scare them or make them sore."

"You're only trying to help." Anna's indignant tone matched her concerned frown.

Levi loved having her defend him. "Not everyone believes that. Some people see this room as a torture chamber."

"I don't believe you."

"That's because you're always so eager to do more than I ask. Doesn't it bother you when I tell you it's time to stop?"

"Well, *jah*, but I don't get upset with you."

"You don't?" Levi could recall many times when she'd resisted doing cooldowns.

"All right, I guess I do sometimes." She stared down at her lap. "It's not you I'm upset with. I just don't want the session to end. I mean—"

Levi knew exactly what she meant. He never wanted her sessions to end either. Although his longing was for a different reason than hers.

Through the broiling hot summer months, Anna persisted. She did her exercises at home and with Levi. She could now walk the entire length of the parallel bars without needing Levi's help, although he walked behind her with his fingers in the gait belt to steady her and prevent a fall. He also kept one hand behind her shoulder.

Anna had seen him do the same for children, but that didn't stop the tingles every time his fingertips grazed her back. At least having him behind her meant he couldn't see her thrill at his touch. Over time, she'd trained herself not to react outwardly, but she had no control over the internal shivers.

One Monday, just before July sweltered into August, she entered the exercise room dripping wet from the waves of heat rising from the parking lot.

Across the room from her, Levi held up crutches. Anna stopped dead in the doorway and stared at him, speechless.

Crutches!

He thought she was ready for crutches.

She'd waited so long for this moment. Tears welled in her eyes. Tightness choked her throat. And her heart exploded in joyous fireworks.

Good thing the temperature outside had sapped her energy, or she might have been tempted to wheel across the floor and hug him. Only out of excitement, of course. Not for any other reason. At least, she tried to convince herself of that truth.

Maybe she wouldn't have been so enthusiastic if she'd realized how much work lay ahead.

Levi crossed the room to her. "Do you want to start from here?" He held out the gait belt.

With shaking fingers, Anna wrapped it around her waist, threaded the belt into the buckle, and made sure she left enough room for Levi's fingers before winding the canvas strip through the other loops to lock it. With the children, Levi adjusted the belt, but he always avoided touching her.

Once she'd secured the belt and scooted forward in her seat, he showed her how to put her arms through the crutches.

"Now for more practice," he said. "You need to learn to pull yourself to a stand."

How could she balance on such small rubber tips? Impossible. No bars to grab if she tipped. Only air on either side of her.

"It's all right," Levi soothed as if he'd read her mind. "It's hard when you have all this empty space around you."

"What if the crutches can't support me?" Anna's words came out breathless and squeaky.

"They will. And I'll be here to help." Levi's usual encouraging smile did little to reduce her fear. "Right now, I want you to get used to letting the crutches and your arm muscles support your weight."

If she fell using the parallel bars, she'd land on a thick blue gym mat. Here, she had only linoleum to break her fall. Anna murmured prayers for courage. She added a silent plea that she wouldn't slip and embarrass herself in front of Levi.

He positioned her crutch tips. "Now I'm going to steady you until you're ready to stand on your own." He reached out and grasped each side of the gait belt at her waist.

Anna froze. His hands didn't quite touch her, but they were close enough. . . .

If she breathed out a bit more, she might brush against his fingertips. How would she ever concentrate?

"Can you stand?" Levi studied her with a look of concern.

"I—I'm not sure."

"Your crutch tips are in the right place. Your feet are

positioned correctly. All you need to do is use the crutches for support the way you use your chair arms or the parallel bars."

When he said it in such a matter-of-fact tone, it sounded simple. But he'd be pulling her toward him. If her crutch slipped or if she pushed her upper body too hard, she might fall into his arms. Actually, that wouldn't be so bad.

Anna scolded herself. She had no business thinking of Levi like that. She tried to picture Gabe, but his image eluded her. Besides, right now, she needed to concentrate on Levi's instructions.

"Once you're balanced," he said, "I'll stand behind and to one side. That'll allow you to move forward."

She couldn't even think about moving. All she wanted to do right now was to stand, propping herself up with the crutches.

"Ready?" Levi waited for her nod. "Let's try it on a count of three."

"One."

Fear curled in the pit of Anna's stomach.

"Two."

She had to do this. She just had to.

"Three."

Her movements jerky, Anna lurched to her feet. Levi's hands on the belt steadied her.

She'd done it. She was standing. With Levi's help.

He eased his grip, and most of her weight sagged onto the crutches. Despite the cushioning, the metal band encircling her forearm bit into her skin.

"Use your hands to support yourself more."

Anna wobbled. Levi reached out to help her again. She sucked in a breath and held it until she stopped swaying and he let go.

"You can do it," Levi encouraged.

She managed to stay upright.

Levi flashed her a delighted smile. "Why don't we try that several times until you feel confident you can get out of the chair alone?"

With his assistance, Anna sank onto the edge of her chair. Her arms ached. So did her jaw because she'd been clenching her teeth. Would she ever be able to do this by herself?

"Relax a bit first. Try some head circles." After she did those, he had her shake out her arms and flex her fingers. Then he reached for the belt. Anna took shallow breaths and tried to still the rapid pounding of her pulse.

"On three." This time Levi seemed almost as tense as she was.

Despite her stiffness, she lifted herself a little more smoothly. And balanced alone for a slightly longer time.

"Good job. You're doing well."

For most of the session, she practiced standing. When she'd done it several times in a row, Levi suggested taking a step.

"If you're ready," he added.

For once, Anna didn't snap back with a confident answer. Now that she was so close to her goal, anxiety and uncertainty gripped her. If she succeeded in this, she'd have to walk to Gabe and give him an answer.

Would he be the same person he'd been all those years ago? They'd both probably changed a lot since then. What if they had nothing in common? What if he'd changed his mind?

"Anna?" Levi's quiet question reminded her he'd been waiting for an answer.

"Sorry. This is a big step." In more ways than one. It held her whole future.

"We can wait until next time if you're not ready."

"*Neh*," Anna burst out. "I want to do it now." If she waited, she'd only come up with additional excuses and frighten herself more.

"You're sure?" Levi's doubtful look increased her determination.

"I'm certain." Not about succeeding at this, but about the fact she couldn't wait.

"I'm going to move behind you to hold the belt. Like I did for the parallel bars."

Anna managed to stand while Levi moved into place. She forced herself not to flinch when he slid his fingers under the belt.

Then he moved to her right side, but slightly behind her. "Try lifting this crutch." He motioned to the one on the right.

Anna did as he asked. Her whole body swayed. Levi's grip on the gait belt kept her from tipping over.

"Remember how you shifted your weight on the parallel bars? Do the same with the crutches."

"But they were strong enough to hold me. This is only a little rubber tip." A tip that might slide and send her tumbling to the ground.

"They're sturdier than they seem."

Levi's assurance didn't convince Anna.

If she didn't do this, she'd never keep her promise. Never walk to Gabe. Never answer him. Never marry.

Nancy's pitying smile loomed in front of Anna's face. That was enough to keep her going.

"Keep shifting your weight from one crutch to the other until you're positive they'll hold you."

That might take forever. Anna did what Levi suggested, and just before the end of the session, she started trusting the crutches to hold her.

She set the tip of her forearm crutch a few inches in front of her. Taking a deep breath, she tried to appear confident as she moved her body slightly forward.

"You did it." Levi cheered beside her. "Can you keep going?"

Anna's muscles were already trembling. Her arms ached, and the drops of sweat sliding down her forehead blocked her vision. Levi still supported her, and all she wanted to do was lean back against his strong arms.

Stop it, Anna. Don't give in to weakness. For over seven long years, she'd worked toward this moment. She'd taken her first step today. After the buggy accident, the doctors had warned her she might never walk again, but she'd refused to give up. Whatever it took, she'd do it now.

Lord, please help me.

"Are you all right?" The concern in Levi's voice forced Anna to steel herself against the pain.

With a nod, she pushed aside her anxiety and doubt. After enduring all the years of rehab, she could do this. Besides, she had no choice.

Once she remained as steady as possible on her feet, Levi spoke softly. "Come on, Anna."

One step. All she had to do was take one more step. That's all Levi had asked of her. Anna had planned to do more and surprise him, but now she wasn't even sure she could manage to inch her way forward again.

"You can do it," Levi repeated.

Gritting her teeth, Anna shuffled her stronger foot forward. Then she supported herself on one crutch and lifted the other. Red-hot needles shot through every inch of her body. She'd suffered every day since the accident, but this was torture. She couldn't go on.

Wishing she could rub her blurry eyes, Anna planted the crutch and forced herself to take her next step. The padding pressed deeply into her forearms, and she gripped the handles so hard, her fingers numbed as much as her legs. All her muscles shuddered. Rivulets of sweat trickled down the back of her neck.

Anna squeezed her eyes shut. *Please, Lord, give me strength.*

Only one more step. Just one more.

Visions of Gabe floated through her mind. With God's help, she'd take her next steps toward Gabe.

Gasping for breath, Anna steeled herself. Then she moved the crutch forward and swung her body that tiny distance. She'd done it.

Her whole body longed to collapse.

She turned pleading eyes to Levi, whose wide, generous smile stretched across his face. The laugh lines around his eyes crinkled. "You did it! Your first steps!"

Anna managed a nod, though every muscle in her body ached beyond endurance. "Could . . . we . . . stop for . . . the day?"

"Ordinarily, I'd encourage you to finish the session, but today's a special day. And you reached your goal." Still beaming, Levi assisted her back to the wheelchair.

She sank into the chair. All the adrenaline shooting through her body trickled away, leaving her limp and worn. This time, the moisture in her eyes came from more than sweat. She blinked to clear her vision.

Anna's patience had worn out, and it wasn't fair to keep Gabe waiting any longer. This journey had been long and hard. She'd come so close today, but she still had a long way to go. Would she ever be able to cross a room?

Levi seemed to sense her discouragement. "Look how far you've come. You've made remarkable progress since we started working together."

The confidence shining in his blue eyes gave her hope. And his words renewed her courage and determination. No matter how long it took, she'd conquer this. With God's help and Levi's.

Chapter Eight

A month later, Anna smiled to herself as she curled up in bed. She'd done it. Crossed the room to Levi several times in the past few days. Now she was ready to repeat her triumph. This time, in front of Gabe.

According to a recent ad in the *Die Botschaft*, his store stayed open until seven on Thursday nights.

"Tonight's the night. Could you take me after work?"

Emily didn't ask what Anna meant. She understood. "He might be at that big event out at the Graber farm. Didn't you read about it?"

Anna sighed. "I forgot that was tonight." Since she'd woken that morning, she'd spent so much time gathering her courage. If she had to wait until next Thursday night, all her bravery would leak away.

"Want me to take you to the event?"

"*Neh*, I can't walk to him or say what I need to say in front of a crowd." For that, she'd need privacy.

"That's true."

"Besides, the ground at the farm will be uneven. It'll be too difficult for me to walk there. He'll either be at the store or at home afterward. We may have to try both places."

"I don't mind. The store would be easier access," Emily pointed out. "Let's pray he'll be there."

Neither spot would be comfortable for Anna. She'd be taking a huge risk with her heart.

This week's therapy sessions had been grueling, and she hadn't had the extra stress of dealing with her roiling emotions. Or the trauma of the past. But she'd need to deal with all that when she faced Gabe.

And would she be able to walk across the room?

If only she could have Levi there for support. He'd become so attuned to her every movement, he knew when she needed his support, when he should step back, and when she needed encouragement.

Once again, she brought herself up short and forced herself to concentrate on Gabe.

The rest of the day as she did her chores, she kept pulling her mind from Levi to Gabe. How had he changed since she'd last seen him? Would she even recognize him? Was Emily right that he'd remained faithful? Would he still want to marry her?

As doubts crept in, Anna turned to prayer. *Dear God, help me to accept Your will. You know how much I want to be married, but I will leave all this in Your hands.*

Praying calmed her nerves the rest of the day. Anytime she started getting agitated, she'd turn the situation over to the Lord. But after Emily returned and they'd finished supper, the food in Anna's stomach curdled. What if Gabe rejected her the way she'd rejected him all those long years ago?

Dread settled over her as Emily helped her into the buggy. After Emily handed her the crutches, Anna set them beside her and clutched the metal so hard, her hands ached. She forced herself to loosen her grip, so she didn't tire out her hands. She'd need all their strength to take the long journey across the floor. If only she could unloosen the invisible hands clenched around her stomach.

Deep breathing didn't help. Willing herself to relax didn't help. Remembering successful walks to Levi didn't help.

But picturing Levi's smiling face helped. A lot. Reminding herself she was in God's hands and whispering a prayer proved even more effective.

By the time they pulled into the store parking lot, Anna's nerves and stomach both buzzed. But her mind was clear and calm.

Two buggies sat in the parking lot. Gabe must have a customer. Anna would rather not walk to him with other people staring at her, but waiting for the customer to leave would drain too much of her strength. She couldn't back out now.

"I don't recognize that buggy." Emily pointed at the nearest one. "But I'm pretty sure that's Gabe's."

He was here. What if she couldn't speak, couldn't answer? She hadn't come this far to quit. Murmuring another prayer for courage, she collected her crutches.

Emily helped her from the buggy and to the door. A sign about the event at Graber's farm blocked their view through the window. Emily tilted her head to ask if she should open the door.

"Go ahead," Anna whispered. "He must be here."

As much as she longed to get back into the buggy and gallop away, she needed to do this.

The door swung open and hit the wall like a gunshot.

Anna's heart stopped, then exploded into rapid banging. Not only from the sudden noise but also from seeing Gabe.

Across the room, he jumped back at the loud crack. Now, he stared at her, his eyes wide, startled, uncertain.

In the seconds before the bang, an image had seared itself into Anna's mind. Gabe, at the counter facing her, with his gaze fixed longingly on the petite blonde standing in front of him. Standing so close, the girl could almost be in his embrace. Perhaps she had been.

Gabe's face drained of color. "Anna?" he choked out. His hands, which had been on the girl's arms, dropped to his sides.

She fumbled with her crutches in the doorway, trying to steady herself. Emily kept a firm arm around Anna's waist until she'd balanced herself. As soon as Anna nodded for Emily to let go, her cousin stepped back.

"I'll wait in the buggy." Emily turned to leave.

Please stay with me, Anna wanted to beg, but she had to do this on her own. She'd planned to do it without any help from anyone. Anyone except God.

But she'd expected Gabe to stand across the room from her the way Levi did, with a smile of encouragement and his eyes like a lifeline, keeping her from drowning when waves of fear crashed over her. Always ready to catch her if she fell.

Gabe only stared at her with the same uncertain, worried, and guilty expression he'd had during their school days when the teacher called on him to recite and he'd forgotten to do his lesson. Like he was waiting to be scolded. Or even worse, punished.

Her insides ached as if they'd been wrapped with rope, and the ends pulled harder and tighter, squeezing her heart, cutting off her circulation, choking her breathing and her voice.

She'd made a mistake. A terrible, terrible mistake.

Levi had missed Anna today at work. Ever since he'd met her, his days had seesawed from mountain to valley. Her presence brightened his Mondays and Wednesdays and Fridays, making those his peak days. On Tuesdays and Thursdays, his spirits plunged downhill. Although on those evenings, remembering he'd see her the next day cheered him. Weekends passed like a long, hot drought.

As he drove home from work with Jonah sitting silently beside him, God kept bringing Anna to mind. She'd mentioned having an important meeting this evening, something connected to her desire to walk, so he prayed for her multiple times.

He wished he knew more about her burning desire to walk. Who had challenged her to do this? A family member? A friend? And why? If only he could be there to encourage her, to support her if she faltered, to catch her if she stumbled.

Levi swallowed hard. Imagining her stumbling, wrapping his arms around her soft, warm body, brought up other fantasies. Her face tilted up. Her lips sweet and inviting.

He stopped himself. He had no right to be imagining scenes like that. For all he knew, she could be dating someone. But the pictures came unbidden.

When he reached the driveway, ten-year-old Daniel drove all thoughts of Anna from Levi's mind. His brother waited at the end of the driveway and flagged him down.

"Levi!" Daniel dashed toward the buggy.

Pulling the horse to a stop, Levi waited for his brother to reach him. "Something's wrong with *Aenti* Betty."

"What?" Immediately on alert, Levi leaped from the buggy and twisted the reins around a nearby fence post. *A heart attack?* That's what had killed his *daed* ten years ago. *Daed*'s death and Jonah's near-drowning had prompted Levi to take emergency training with the EMTs. He prayed he had the right training to help Betty.

"She's crying so hard, she didn't even hear me come in from school."

"Crying?" Not a medical emergency? The rush of adrenaline slowed, and Levi unwound the reins. He'd take care of the horse and then hurry in to see what was wrong. "Maybe she got some bad news."

"It must be really, really bad. She's still crying with her head down on the kitchen table."

"You mean now?" Levi did some quick calculations in his head. Daniel got off at three, and it was past 5:30. Had someone in the family died?

"*Jah*, she hasn't stopped. Not even when I try to talk to her. It's like she doesn't hear me."

The quietest of his three brothers, Daniel always spoke softly. Betty, who was slightly hard of hearing, often had to strain to hear him. Maybe he hadn't raised his voice enough.

Levi unhooked the buggy reins as quickly as he could. Then he handed them to his brother. "Can you take care of the horse while I check on Betty?"

Without waiting for a reply, Levi jogged toward the back door. Before he reached the porch, Betty's sobs drifted through the screen door. Daniel had been right. Levi had never heard his stoic *aenti* cry like that. Something terrible must have happened.

Levi rushed into the kitchen and set a hand on her shoulder. Betty started and lifted her head.

"Levi?" Her voice thick with tears, her eyes swollen and bloodshot, she stared at him as if in a daze. Then she shook her head and shot to her feet. "If you're here, it must be almost suppertime. I—I haven't fixed anything yet."

With quick, nervous movements, she swept pages of a letter into a neat pile, folded them quickly, and tucked them into her pocket. But not before Levi spotted a tearstained, half-written page in his *aenti*'s handwriting. He hadn't been able to read the words.

"What's wrong?"

"N-nothing for you to worry about." She turned toward the stove, keeping her back to him. "I'll heat up some spaghetti soup. You teach a class tonight, right?"

"*Jah*, but . . ."

His *aenti* waved him away. "Let me get supper." She headed down the basement steps to the canning shelves and soon returned carrying quart jars of soup and applesauce.

When she saw Levi still standing there, she jerked to a stop. "Go wash up," she ordered in a brisk tone that didn't match the sadness in her eyes.

Levi crossed his arms. "First, tell me what upset you."

Sucking in a deep breath, she walked past him to the stove. "Let it go. It's a private matter."

"Did someone die?"

Betty turned startled eyes in his direction. "What made you ask that?" Then her expression grew shuttered. "Of course not. Please just leave it alone."

Only twice had Betty ever cried in front of them. The first time was ten years ago in the living room while she and *Mamm* hugged in front of *Daed*'s casket. By the time people arrived for the viewing, she'd greeted them with dry eyes and a matter-of-fact voice.

She'd stayed on to help *Mamm* care for newborn Daniel and the other three boys. At times, muffled whimpers came through her door late at night, but whenever his *aenti* emerged in the morning, she showed no sign of sadness or distress.

The only other time Betty shed tears was the day *Mamm* died of cancer three years later. As she had before, Betty dried her eyes before the viewing, and they'd stayed dry ever since. Since she'd taken over raising the four of them, Levi had never heard her cry, not even at night.

That meant something was wrong. Very wrong. And Levi had no intention of letting this go until he discovered the truth.

Wavering on her feet, Anna stood in the doorway of Gabe's store. She'd worked so hard and waited all this time to walk to him, to answer him. But she hadn't counted on finding him with another woman.

Should she go ahead with her plan?

Please, Lord, direct my words and steps.

As soon as she prayed, God wrapped His loving arms around her. His presence gave her strength. She'd made an agreement with Gabe. She had to fulfill it. No matter how difficult. No matter how heart-wrenching.

If only Levi could be here, standing in Gabe's place, so she could walk to him. He'd be smiling at her. A quiet contrast to Gabe's startled and unsettled expression.

Anna planted one of her metal forearm crutches in front of her and swung herself forward.

"You're not in a wheelchair." Gabe stared at her when she stopped to catch her breath.

"Neh, I promised one day I would walk to you."

"You don't have to do this." He took a step toward her.

"Don't." She sharpened her tone to prevent him from moving any closer. She wouldn't let him diminish this walk after she'd tortured herself for months. Years, actually.

She lifted the other crutch, set it in place, and moved ahead. Her arms trembled. Sweat prickled her forehead. Before taking her next step, she closed her eyes and inhaled a deep breath.

"Please." Gabe sounded distressed. "I can come to you."

"Neh." No matter what, she'd go to him. With renewed determination, she opened her eyes. But the woman beside him stood tense and wary, watching Anna's slow crawl with pity.

How Anna hated pity! And it was even worse to see it in a woman who'd edged much too close to Gabe to be a casual acquaintance. Anna had no idea what was going on between the two of them, but it looked like Gabe had found someone else.

After all her struggles, Anna wouldn't be married after all. She blinked to clear away the moisture welling in her eyes. She didn't want either of them to see her cry, but teardrops trembled on her eyelashes, and her damp eyes probably gave her away.

To protect herself from their pity, she laced her words with sarcasm. "Maybe I didn't need to do this after all."

The woman beside Gabe shifted from one foot to the other and glanced from Anna to Gabe. "I'll go now, Gabe," the blonde said. "We can talk about the speech some other time."

"Wait, Priscilla. This is Anna, my girlfriend, um, fiancée, from—"

Priscilla? Gabe infused the girl's name with tenderness. A sharp pain pierced Anna's heart as Gabe's tongue tangled on her own name. Then again on "girlfriend" and "fiancée." To Anna's ears, both words seemed tinged with regret.

Priscilla's face went ashen. She glanced up at Gabe, her eyes wide and betrayed. Clearly, Gabe had never told her about his proposal.

With a strangled "Nice to meet you," the woman rushed for the door.

Anna couldn't look at Gabe. She didn't want to see his reaction to the woman's departure. Her imagination supplied enough details. She'd rather not have them confirmed.

Silence, uneasy and uncomfortable, stretched between them. Anna teetered, then righted herself. She'd been standing much longer than she ever had when she'd worked with Levi. And this time, rather than walking toward his encouragement, she was moving toward a man who looked as if he'd rather be anywhere but facing her.

"Sorry I interrupted you," Anna said. "I hope I didn't mess anything up." She tried to act indifferent and unfazed, but she followed her words with a nervous laugh. A hollow, pain-filled noise that reverberated around the huge warehouse, mocking her, embarrassing her, branding her as awkward, insignificant, and unwanted.

Gabe winced. "No, Anna, you didn't interrupt. You have every right to be here."

If Anna had possessed enough energy, she'd have shaken her head to deny his words. But she couldn't waste any strength if she hoped to make it across the room. Inside, though, she railed at his falsehood. She'd seen that girl's face. Something had been going on between the two of them.

Gritting her teeth against the agony in her body and her heart, Anna took another shaky step.

"Let me get you a chair." Ignoring the wooden chair nearby, Gabe started toward an open door, a room that looked like an office.

"Stay there!" Anna didn't want his pity or his help. She had to prove she could do this on her own. "I told you I'd give you an answer when I could walk across the room to you." He owed her this chance to fulfill her pledge, no matter how agonizing it was for both of them.

Her arm muscles aching, she pulled herself closer. Each *click* of the crutch, each swing of her leg, each slow shuffle forward echoed in the cavernous space around them. Each step increased the irregular pounding of her pulse, the dread sloshing in her stomach.

Fists stuffed in his pockets, Gabe stood rigid, his face a mask of pity and pain. He pressed his lips together as if holding back words.

Anna stopped several times to rest and catch her breath between wobbly steps. Perspiration stung her eyes, soaked her neckline, trickled down her back. She planted a crutch only a few yards from him and looked him in the eye. "I wondered if, after all this time, you'd find another woman . . ."

Guilt flickered in Gabe's eyes, but he met her gaze. "The promise I made still stands."

What good was that long-ago promise if his heart wasn't in it?

This was all her fault. She'd made him wait eight years.

Eight long years with no communication. She never should have issued such a foolish ultimatum. "We were seventeen, Gabe. Much too young to make life decisions."

He closed his eyes.

To hide his thoughts? To block her out? To avoid the truth?

Anna sucked in a shaky breath. *I will not cry. I will not cry*, she repeated like a litany. She had to control her tears. Block off her emotions. Not let herself feel anything. Anything at all. Not yet. Not until she left.

Concentrate on those last few steps. Give him an answer. Finish this.

When her crutch clicked on the floor close to him, Gabe's eyes popped open. He studied her with compassion.

Anna cringed inside, imagining herself through Gabe's eyes. Her overheated face, soaked with perspiration, her clenched jaw, her uneven gait . . .

She must have looked like this to Levi too, but his eyes had mirrored only triumph and joy.

Gabe shifted uncomfortably. "Please let me get you a chair."

"*Neh*." The word exploded from her lips. Then she pinched her mouth into a tight line and forced herself to take one more step. Then another.

Gabe's eyes filled with sadness. "I'm sorry. Will you forgive me?"

Anna was too winded to speak. She tried to bob her head, but it came out as more of a shake. From Gabe's expression, he'd interpreted it as a no. Perhaps that answer was more truthful. Right now, she didn't feel forgiving. Maybe once she was alone, she'd pray for God to change her heart and mind.

With one final step, she stood directly in front of him.

Drawing in a raspy breath, she tried to soothe her achy, constricted lungs, but nothing could relieve her trembling legs or quivering heart. She had to make a statement, one he'd understand as final. "Look at me, Gabe. I want your full attention when I say this."

When he met her eyes, Anna used every last ounce of her willpower to hold back tears and say the words she'd never dreamed would leave her lips. "My answer to your question is NO." The word rang around the room. "I don't want to marry anyone who would rather be with some-one else."

"Anna, that's not—"

Had he been about to say it wasn't true? Had he stopped because he knew it was a lie? She'd seen the longing on his face when he gazed at Priscilla.

"Look me in the eyes and tell me you don't love her," she challenged.

Gabe avoided her eyes. Anna read the truth in his fidgeting.

Their relationship had died. So had her future.

She stood, numb and shell-shocked, as all her dreams came crashing down. She'd never marry. She'd never have a husband. She'd never have a family.

Chapter Nine

Anna's whole body trembled, threatened to collapse. *Why, God, why? All I've ever wanted is to be a wife and mother. Why did You plant this dream in my heart and soul, only to deny it?*

Gabe was the only man who'd ever marry her. Other Amish men, if they'd even consider her, would want children. Something she could never give them.

That series of blows knocked the breath from her lungs. "I'll take . . . that chair . . . now."

Gabe rushed toward the office, but she stopped him. Sitting here with him would only prolong her agony. What would they talk about? Priscilla?

She had to get out of here. "Better yet, why don't you help me out to the buggy?"

Gabe hurried to her side to support her. Being this close, knowing they'd never be together, increased her unsteadiness. Ice edged her heart, sending chills from her core to her limbs, until she could barely stand.

She took one shaky step and hissed out a long, quavering breath. "I'm not sure I can make it. Maybe I should sit for a while."

"I can carry you."

He'd done that many times when she was in rehab. He'd lifted her from the bed and set her gently in the wheelchair. Then he'd pushed her up and down the halls or along the outdoor paths. Even now, she could smell the lilacs, the roses, the lilies as they'd circled the gardens month after month. Until the day she told him not to come back.

Gabe bent to pick her up.

"No, no." If only she could wave her hand or her crutch to stop him, but her balance was too precarious. "You don't have to do that. I'll be all right after a rest."

Gabe ignored her protest and scooped her into his arms. She stiffened. How much longer could she hold herself together?

He waited until she'd transferred her crutches to one hand. The last thing she wanted to do was touch him, but she had to hold on as he lurched forward.

To prevent tears from falling, Anna closed her eyes and imagined Levi's arms closing around her, cradling her. Her daydream became so vivid, Gabe disappeared, and Levi took his place.

"Levi," she murmured, soft as a cat's purr.

"Did you say something?" Gabe asked.

Anna's eyes flew open, and her face flamed. Had she really done that?

Levi had never held her this way and never would. What had even made her think of him like that? He'd always been kind and friendly. Too many shocks had addled her mind.

They reached the buggy, and Emily stared at her with concern. "Is everything all right?"

"I got overtired, and Gabe helped me back." Anna lowered her lashes, hoping to prevent tears from leaking out.

Emily slid over to open the door. She moved back so

Gabe could set Anna on the seat. The crutches slipped from Anna's nerveless hands and clattered to the floor.

Gabe picked them up and settled them beside her. Then he met her eyes. "I'm so sorry. I never meant to hurt you. The offer—"

She touched his arm to stop him. She couldn't bear to hear the words. Not when they were empty and meaningless. Her voice thick, Anna managed to respond. "I know. I'm sorry too."

Just before he slid the door shut, Anna prayed for God's mercy and grace. Then she lifted her head and met his eyes. "I do forgive you, Gabe. I should never have made you wait this long for an answer." She stared down at the floorboard. "Remember I told you no in the hospital and in rehab? Many times. You should have listened."

"I didn't believe you."

"I know," she said in a choked voice. "That's why I pushed myself to walk."

"*Ach*, Anna, I didn't mean to make you suffer like that."

She had to be honest. If it weren't for her determination to walk across a room to him, she might still be bedridden. "I'd never have learned to walk again if it weren't for you."

His sickish expression revealed his guilt.

"We should go." Anna turned her head away, her eyes misty. Without looking at him, she pushed polite words from her lips. "I wish you two the best."

No one but God would ever know the heroic effort that took.

Now all Anna wanted was to flee. She kept her face averted from him, but Emily could see the tears.

"Are you all right?" her cousin asked softly.

"Just go, please." Anna had to get out of here. To be alone. To hide until she could deal with this crushing blow.

Emily flicked the reins to hurry the horse into a trot. Gravel flew from under his hooves. Fear normally gripped Anna when a horse sped up, but all she could focus on was escaping her humiliation.

Why had she bothered walking to him? To show off? To prove something? That's what had gotten her into this mess. Years ago, she'd wanted to beat Nancy in the buggy race to show who had the better boyfriend. Anna squeezed her eyes shut. How foolish she'd been. As if winning a race could prove anything. And she'd paid dearly for her mistake.

Today, pride had led her to make another mistake. She could have answered Gabe years ago. Instead, she'd set almost impossible conditions for both of them.

She stared straight ahead, her neck muscles stiff and tense. *Don't look back, Anna.* As the buggy turned onto the street, she ignored the inner warning and craned her head for one last glimpse.

Gabe stared after them, his shoulders drooping. Did he look sad? Sorry? Or was that her imagination? Most likely his look wasn't regret, but pity.

Emily took the curve in the road too fast.

Anna sucked in a breath. "Slow down," she begged.

"Sorry." Emily, who understood Anna's fears, pulled the horse to a walk. "I thought you wanted—"

"I did." Anna shouldn't blame her cousin for trying to help. "I—I didn't want Gabe to know . . ." Know what? That she'd lied? That she'd planned to say yes? That she'd wanted to plead with him to keep his promise?

Emily echoed her question. "To know what?"

Anna had no answer. Or perhaps too many answers. She needed time to process everything. To make sense of what she'd seen. To make sense of what she'd done. If she'd said yes, would Gabe have given up that girl? A girl he obviously loved.

He had a strong sense of duty. Most likely, he'd have kept his promise. At least she thought he would. But did she want him to?

Neh, she'd done the right thing. If they married, she'd never know if he'd done it out of obligation. Or out of pity. Even worse, she'd never know if he still pined for another woman.

Levi headed home from the firehouse community room after leading another Water Safety class. He'd started training as an EMT when he turned sixteen and now volunteered when guys went on vacation, but his main duty was instructing parents, teachers, and caregivers about drowning prevention. That was his passion. He never wanted another family to live through that terrifying experience. Jonah was a constant reminder. And Levi's motivation for teaching.

But tonight, his mind was on his *aenti*. What news had she received in that letter? If it had been a death in the family, she would have shared it and made plans to attend the funeral. But she'd only bustled around the kitchen making dinner, her eyes the saddest he'd ever seen them.

He pulled into the driveway, surprised to see the propane lamp still on in the kitchen. Class had run later than usual, so he'd expected everyone to be in bed. His two younger brothers woke early to do their morning chores before school. And at fourteen, his brother Zeb had finished eighth grade, so he was working at a neighbor's farm on the days he didn't have German or vocational school. Levi should be in bed too, because he needed to get up before dawn. Betty rose before all of them to fix breakfast. She never stayed up this late.

Levi rushed through caring for the horse and headed for the back porch. Betty sat at the kitchen table, where he'd found her crying earlier that day. Papers spread on the table before her, she held a pen in her hand but stared off into the distance.

He didn't want to startle her, so he eased open the screen door. The hinges squeaked when he opened it.

Betty jumped and turned toward the sound, pressing her free hand to her throat. "*Ach*, Levi, you startled me."

"Sorry. I didn't mean to."

Her eyes red and puffy, she scrambled to pull the pages together into a semi-neat stack. When Levi sat on the chair beside her, she dropped her pen and spread her hands across the top sheet, blocking it from view.

"What's going on?" He pinned her with a gaze.

"Nothing you need to know about. It's a private matter."

Since when did his *aenti* have private matters she couldn't share with him and the rest of the family? This was so unlike Betty, who prized honesty and openness. She always said, "Never do anything you can't do in front of your whole family."

Levi was tempted to quote her words back to her, but he couldn't be disrespectful to the woman who'd raised him. She'd taken over when *Mamm* had died and done her best to mother all of them.

With quick, nervous movements, Betty gathered the papers and folded them haphazardly. She fumbled as she hugged them against her, and several sheets cascaded onto the table and floor.

One drifted under Levi's chair, and he bent to pick it up. He shouldn't have read it, but he couldn't mistake his *aenti*'s careful handwriting.

Dear Vern,
     It was so good to hear from you. I'm sorry to
hear about Liz. I understand how hard it is to raise
little ones. I've done it myself. I wish—

The rest of the sentence had been scribbled out. A few more sentence fragments dotted the page, also with parts blacked over with heavy, dark pen marks that looked as if they'd been slashed into the paper.

Betty leaned over and snatched it from his hands. While he'd been reading, she'd collected the rest of the loose sheets. She tapped them into an orderly pile.

"Who are Vern and Liz?"

His *aenti* sucked in a sharp breath. "You know better than to read other people's mail." Though her tone was firm, her lips quivered. She turned her head away, but not before he'd glimpsed her eyes shining with tears.

Betty pressed her lips together as if she had no intention to reply. But Levi kept his steady gaze on her until she answered.

Lowering her eyes, she said in a choked voice, "A man I used to court."

Levi had never seen her date anyone in the ten years she'd lived here. Had she gone out with someone before that? She'd been twenty-one when she arrived to help *Mamm*. His *mamm*'s family all lived in New York State. "Someone from Fort Plain?"

"*Jah.*"

"And Liz? Who is she?" Another friend from the past?

It sounded as if Liz might be unwell. Maybe that's what upset Betty.

Her words dull and flat, Betty said, "His wife."

Wait a minute. His *aenti* was writing to a married man. A man she'd once loved. Levi reined in his runaway thoughts. Maybe he'd written to tell her about Liz. "Is she all right?"

"She's dead."

No wonder Betty had been crying. Levi's heart went out to her. "I'm sorry. Will you be going to the funeral?"

"*Neh*, she died more than a year ago."

"And you just found out?"

Betty shook her head. "My sister mentioned it in a circle letter when it happened."

"Then why were you crying?"

"I told you. It's private." She headed from the kitchen.

Levi turned out the lamp and trailed behind her up to bed. How would he get her to confide her sorrow?

After Emily and Anna reached the *dawdi haus*, her cousin stopped near the front porch. "Why don't I run inside and get the wheelchair?"

Too exhausted to answer, Anna barely managed to tip her head up and down. *Thank you, Lord, for Emily.* She always seemed to sense what Anna needed. Levi did the same.

Emily looped the horse's reins over the porch railing and scooted inside. A short while later, she hurried down the ramp and helped Anna into her chair. As she pushed her up the ramp, she asked, "What happened?"

Unable to keep bitterness from seeping into her voice, Anna forced the truth from her lips. "He has a girlfriend."

"I saw," Emily said softly.

She'd held open the door, so she'd seen the same thing Anna had. Gabe and the girl gazing into each other's eyes. To be honest, the girl—What had Gabe said her name was? Priscilla?—had her back to the entrance, so Anna hadn't seen Priscilla's eyes. She didn't need to. Their closeness and the way Priscilla's head tilted up, her hands outstretched as if to stroke Gabe's arms, left no doubt of their feelings for each other.

"Do you want me to stay with you tonight?" Her cousin trod the fine line between sympathy and pity. "I can come over after I help *Mamm* get all the little ones in bed."

Anna should be helping too. She usually went over during the day before her sessions with Levi. And in the evenings, she helped with diapers, pajamas, and prayers.

"Don't worry about it tonight. I'll explain . . ." After a quick glance at Anna's pleading eyes, Emily continued. ". . . that you're tired?"

"*Danke.*" Anna was exhausted, but she also wasn't ready to face the family's questioning. For now, she wanted to keep her anguish to herself.

Sitting alone while Emily bathed her foster brothers and sisters and tucked them into bed, Anna's whole body went numb. Her walk to Gabe and their conversation slid into soft focus, like wisps of a dream, halfway between imaginary and real. The kind of dream where you long to waken.

When Emily came back to keep Anna company, she brought a bowl of buttered popcorn and a listening ear. "Want to talk about it?" she asked.

Anna shook her head. If she could keep floating in this

cottony, cushiony cocoon, she wouldn't have to feel, react, or accept the truth.

The next morning at breakfast, Betty's puffy face, reddened eyes, and quiet sniffles while she hunched over the stove all signaled she'd wrestled with sorrow throughout the night.

Levi wanted to hug her, find a way to comfort her. But when he touched her shoulder, she stiffened and drew away.

"I'll be all right."

"But what's wrong? What did Vern say in his letter that made you cry?"

"Can't you just leave it alone?" Betty scraped the bottom of the cast-iron skillet harder than necessary to turn the eggs.

"Not until you tell me what's bothering you."

"If I tell you, will you promise to leave me alone and not talk about it ever again?"

"All right." Levi hoped he wouldn't regret agreeing to those terms.

"Vern asked for help caring for his children."

Levi's mind started putting together facts into a pattern. A widower, struggling to raise his kids alone—at least that's what the letter implied. "He wanted to send them here?" But why would that make her cry?

A violent headshake. Tears trickled down her cheek. "He wants to marry me. I'm turning him down."

"Why?"

"I can't leave you boys alone. Vern thought maybe you'd be married by now, so you could take care of your brothers. But . . ."

"But I'm not." He hadn't even considered courting anyone. Well, except maybe for his flights of fancy about Anna. He hardly knew her, but she intrigued him. And she was off-limits. He shouldn't date anyone who came for sessions.

His brothers hurried into the kitchen. Betty dried her eyes and shooed them all to the table.

Levi studied her carefully while she bustled around the kitchen and set bowls of eggs and applesauce and platters of toast in front of them. Would she do the same thing she'd done following his parents' deaths? Stop her crying and go on as if everything was normal?

He'd promised not to talk about it again, but he wasn't sure he could keep that promise.

Chapter Ten

After a lonely, sleepless night, Anna could barely get out of bed in the morning. Every inch of her body ached. She'd had sore, tired muscles after intense sessions with Levi, but never this bone-deep exhaustion. The gray clouds outside the window mirrored her mood.

Emily peeked into her bedroom. "Are you getting up today? I brought some breakfast back for you, but I need to go and help *Mamm* with the laundry."

Anna dragged herself into clothes and into her wheelchair. She forced her weak arms to pull her hair back into a bob at the back of her neck and tie on the kerchief she wore when she did housework. Then she wheeled into the kitchen.

Although her stomach rebelled at the greasy odor of bacon, she couldn't ignore childhood warnings to eat everything on her plate. With a sigh, she picked at the scrambled eggs.

Emily stared at her with compassion. "Eat what you can."

Her cousin was encouraging her to break a rule?

Before Anna could ask, a loud knock on the door interrupted her. Emily hurried from the kitchen to answer it.

"Gabe?" Emily's voice wavered.

Anna's fork clattered onto her plate. What was Gabe doing here? Had she dropped something in his store last night?

She tried to calm the negative charges zipping through her whole body. Gabe would give the item to Emily, and she'd close the door, shutting him permanently out of their lives.

"I'd like to talk to Anna." Gabe's words penetrated the kitchen wall.

Neh. Wildly, Anna looked around for an escape. Could she make it into the bedroom and shut the door before Emily brought him in here?

"I don't think that's a good idea." Emily's tone rang with finality.

Anna relaxed in her chair, filled with gratitude toward her cousin for protecting her.

"Please?" Gabe's plea hung in the air.

Say no, Emily, Anna mouthed. But her cousin didn't receive the silent request.

"Stay here and I'll check." Emily scurried into the kitchen. "Gabe's here," she whispered, "and he wants to see you."

Unable to speak, Anna shook her head violently. *Neh, Neh.* She formed the words with her lips.

Emily nodded and returned to the front door. "Anna doesn't want to see you, and she doesn't want you to come here again."

Anna hadn't added that last part, but her cousin was exactly right.

"I'm not leaving until I talk to her." Gabe used the same stubborn *I'm-not-going-anywhere* tone he had in the hospital whenever she'd told him to leave.

"Please just go," Emily pleaded. "Anna's exhausted and not up to having company today."

Emily had never dealt with Gabe when he'd made up his mind. She'd find it hard to get rid of him.

"I'll just sit here until she's ready to talk."

"Suit yourself." Emily clicked the door shut and hurried into the kitchen. "He's sitting on the porch. I'm going over to the house to do wash, but I'd suggest you stay inside for a while. He'll soon get tired of waiting and leave."

Anna wasn't so sure. Gabe had outwaited her many times in rehab. But she had bedding to change, dishes to wash, and floors to mop. That would keep her inside for a while. Perhaps by then, he'd have left.

Anna was finishing the last of her chores when Emily called out from the backyard, "It's over, Gabe. Just leave her alone."

"I want to tell her one thing."

Emily's loud sigh carried through the open window. "I'll let her know you're still here." An empty laundry basket in hand, she stomped through the door. "He's still on the porch." She kept her voice low. "I tried getting rid of him, but . . ."

"I heard." Anna resigned herself to seeing him. That would be the only way to get him to leave. She didn't want him coming here to reopen old wounds or to inflict new ones. "Give me a few minutes to get ready."

Emily waited until Anna had smoothed her hair, pinned on her *kapp*, and splashed cold water on her reddened eyes, and wheeled herself into the living room. Then her cousin walked to the door.

As soon as Emily turned her back, Anna pinched her cheeks to give herself some color. It was vanity, but she didn't want Gabe to see her wan cheeks and think she was pining for him.

She wasn't. Not really. She was pining for the lost opportunity to marry. All she'd been aiming for was to be a wife. And he'd been her only chance. Was that even fair to Gabe?

If she had to make a choice, the only man she'd want in that role was Levi. But that could never be. Levi would never be interested in her. And who would want a wife who couldn't have children?

Emily opened the door and led Gabe into the room. When he saw Anna in the corner, he winced before his eyes, brimming with guilt and pity, met hers.

He stood in the center of the living room, his hands clasped. "I have only one thing to say," he said. "I'll honor the promise I made to you, Anna."

The Gabe from her past always did what was right. No matter the consequences. It seemed that hadn't changed. But one thing had changed. She'd never questioned his love. Now that she thought of it, he'd never once told her that he loved her. And even more importantly, she'd never prayed about her decision to marry. Had he?

"I have some questions for you." Anna pinned him with her gaze. "First of all, have you prayed about this? You're sure it's God's will to marry me?"

Gabe hung his head. "*Neh*, I haven't prayed about it. I've always assumed God wanted me to take care of you."

"Take care of me? That's why you asked me to marry you?" Anna's voice rose. "I'm perfectly capable of taking care of myself."

"I didn't mean you couldn't. It's just that . . ." He stopped as if searching for the right words. "I cared about you."

"Care for me. Cared about me." That made her sound

more like a burden than a cherished wife. She wished she
hadn't started this line of questioning. But now she had to
know how he really felt about her. "Did you love me? Or
did you pity me?"

Gabe ran a finger around the back of his collar and appeared uncomfortable. The fact that he hadn't answered
right away told her everything she needed to know. Gabe
was kind and wouldn't deliberately hurt anyone's feelings,
but his hesitation dealt another blow to her already-fragile
heart.

Before he could answer, she hurried on. "I have one
more question. If you knew I loved someone else, would
you still want to marry me?"

His eyes widened as if she'd caught him off guard. "Of
course not."

I am interested in someone else. Anna stopped herself
before she let the words slip out. Although it rang true—
Levi had definitely caught her interest—Anna had learned
her lesson about bragging. Pride had been behind the
buggy race that had paralyzed her. Pride had been behind
her boast to Nancy, who would now be expecting a wedding invitation. An invitation that would never come. She
wouldn't make the same mistake with Gabe, who might
press her for the man's name. A name she couldn't supply.

But Gabe really did have someone else. Someone he
loved.

Anna gazed off into the distance, her heart heavy. She
could accept his proposal and reach her dream of being
married. For a brief moment, she was tempted. They'd
always gotten along well, they had common goals, and
most importantly, they shared the same faith. Couples who

started marriage as friends, and without romantic love, often made good lives together.

Jah, marrying Gabe would be easy. But could she live with pity rather than love? With knowing Gabe loved Priscilla rather than her?

Anna had never opted for the easy way out. All her years of rehab had proven that. And she wouldn't take that route now.

Gathering her courage, she blurted out what was on her mind. "I don't want a man who pities me. A man who sees me as needy. A man who believes marrying me is his duty. And I especially don't want a man who loves someone else."

Gabe stared at her as if her every word had been an arrow aimed straight at his soul. She'd hit her mark. Now it was up to him.

Anna sat up straight and waited for him to respond. To contradict her. To deny her accusations.

Instead, he stayed silent. After a while, he bowed his head. "I'm sorry, Anna. You deserved more from me."

"I'm sorry too." Anna was sorry. For him. And for herself. She was sorry they couldn't work things out. Sorry to say good-bye to the man who'd prodded her—whether he knew it or not—to get out of bed every day. To claw her way back to walking.

And most of all, she was sorry to let go of her only opportunity for marriage.

But she had to do it.

Levi hummed as he prepped for his last session with Anna on Friday. She always brightened his days. He hoped her meeting had gone well. She would have done a good job of walking after she'd done so well here. He couldn't wait to hear her good news. After her triumph, she'd be glowing.

The day crawled along. Each session seemed to last hours until finally five o'clock arrived. He waited near the door to greet her.

But when she arrived, her shoulders slumped, her expression glum, Levi longed to hug her. If she'd been one of the children, he might have. But Anna?

He couldn't help wishing he could comfort her. Although if he did, it wouldn't resemble the encouraging hugs he gave the little ones. The gentle *I'm-here-for-you* or *I-know-you-can-do-it* hugs. Or even the cheery *you'll-be-all-right* hugs. His hug for Anna would encompass all of those, but he worried it might turn into an *I'm-falling-for-you* hug. Or, if he wasn't careful, a promise of much, much more.

Levi clutched his suspenders to keep his hands in place. Hugging her would be wrong on so many levels. He wished she really was the six-year-old he'd originally expected her to be, because she could definitely use a hug. But he wanted to let her know he sympathized.

Should he ask what was wrong, or would she prefer her privacy?

"*Vi bisht du?*" he asked.

She winced and lowered her lashes.

All he'd done was ask how she was. He'd said something wrong, but he had no idea what.

Her eyes still on her lap, Anna mumbled an "all right." She remained in the doorway rather than wheeling herself into the room.

"You don't sound all right." Maybe he shouldn't have said anything.

"I'll be fine." She answered so quietly, he could barely hear her.

He'd skip asking about the special meeting that had made her so eager to walk. It must have gone badly. But he was unprepared for her next words.

"I guess this is good-bye." Anna choked out her words. "*Danke* for helping me learn to walk, but I won't need any more sessions."

No more sessions? He'd never see her again? If she'd whacked him over the head or punched him in the gut, it would have hurt less than this blow.

Had he done something wrong? He'd touched her during some of the sessions. Always accidentally. Maybe she'd sensed his growing interest and needed to put a stop to it.

"Why, Anna?" As hard as he tried, Levi couldn't keep the anguish from his words.

She twisted her hands together in her lap and didn't raise her eyes. "I—"

Jonah barreled down the hallway, shouting at the top of his lungs, "Levi, Levi." Panting to a stop behind Anna's wheelchair, he yelled, "Come!"

"I can't right now. I'm working," Levi said.

The boy's face crumpled. "We need you."

Anna waved over her shoulder toward Jonah. "If you need to help your brother, that's fine."

"But you didn't get your—" He'd almost said "session." But she'd come to tell him she didn't plan to work with him anymore.

Levi wanted to find out why, but first he needed to take care of Jonah. He turned to his brother. "Where's your aide?"

"On the floor."

"The floor?"

Jonah pointed down the hallway. Anna backed her chair from the doorway and gasped.

Levi peeked out to see Diane crumpled on the hall floor. As he dashed toward her, a few staff members rushed from their doorways, but he arrived at her side first.

"Anna," he called over his shoulder, "could you ask the van driver to take Jonah home when you leave?"

"Of course" floated to him as he reached Diane's side.

"Did someone call nine-one-one?" he asked as he knelt.

A *yes* sounded behind him. "I also called her husband."

A small crowd gathered. "Did she have a heart attack?" someone asked.

Levi didn't answer. He concentrated all his attention on the woman sprawled before him. Putting one hand on top of the other, he interlocked his fingers and pressed on Diane's sternum. After each compression, he waited before pressing again. Thirty times.

He tilted Diane's head back and pinched her nose. Two breaths. Then he returned to compressions, repeating the breath-compression sequence until the ambulance arrived.

A hand descended on his shoulder. "Hey, Levi." One of his friends from the firehouse squatted beside him. "We'll take it from here."

Levi moved aside so they could handle it. Once they had Diane stabilized and on the stretcher, Levi followed them to the ambulance.

"Wanna ride along?" Ron asked as he headed for the driver's door.

"*Jah.* I'll stay with her until her husband arrives."

"Anyone notify him?" Ron asked before Levi climbed in.

"One of the women did."

When they arrived at the hospital, Diane's husband was

pacing by the emergency entrance, and she was awake, but disoriented. Her husband rushed over and took her hand.

Ron clapped Levi on the shoulder. "If you wait around until we're done here, we'll drive you back to the firehouse. Then I can drop you at the community center on my way home."

"That'd be great." Levi had been so focused on Diane, it hadn't even occurred to him he'd have no way back to the center.

"No problem, man."

Doing CPR had also forced all thoughts of Anna from his mind. Now they came rushing back. It had been kind of her to take care of his brother. He had no doubt she'd made sure Jonah got home safely.

But what about Anna herself? She'd looked so sad, so forlorn. Why had she decided to stop her sessions? He needed answers. But how would he get them if she never returned to the center?

Chapter Eleven

Anna sat paralyzed as Levi rushed down the hall. She stared at his back as he knelt by Diane and started CPR. He never hesitated. His competence made her certain Diane would recover.

Levi was someone you could trust. With your feelings. And with your life.

Everyone around him let out a sigh of relief. Staff members began herding children and adults back into the classrooms. A few aides escorted children down the hall to meet their rides.

That jolted Anna back to her duties. She'd promised to take care of Jonah. He stood beside her, rigid and fearful.

Anna reached out and took his hand. "Diane will be all right," she assured him. "Levi knows what to do to help her."

Jonah turned toward her. "Levi will help," he echoed. But his shaky voice belied the confident statement.

Anna should get him away from this scary scene. "Let's go out to the parking lot to wait for the van."

"I want Levi."

So do I. Anna stopped herself before she said the words aloud. "He'll come home soon."

She wheeled her chair around and reached for Jonah's hand. He turned and clasped hers hard. She gave his fingers a quick squeeze, hoping to reassure him. Before she turned into the lobby, Anna couldn't resist one last look down the hallway.

She admired his broad shoulders, his command of the situation. Tears blurred her vision. He'd taught her so much. Not just how to walk, but about how to live. She couldn't bear to think she'd never see him again.

Good-bye, Levi, she whispered silently.

Jonah squeezed her hand back. "Don't cry. Levi will make Diane all better."

"You're right." Anna swiveled her head to face the door, leaving Levi behind. Forever.

Anna wheeled herself slowly to match Jonah's uneven gait. An aide escorted a small girl to the sidewalk outside the building. When Anna wrapped an arm around the frightened child, Jonah leaned against Anna's other side, and she hugged him too. She held them tight as the ambulance screamed away. The van arrived a short time later.

The nurse emerged. "An aide called and asked us to come early. So, we'll be taking you home tonight, Jonah, eh?"

He looked at Anna, his eyes uncertain.

She nodded. "If you have enough room. He can have my seat, if not."

"We'll be fine," the nurse assured her as she buckled the small girl into her seat.

Jonah clung to Anna's hand the whole way home. When they arrived at his house, a woman rushed out to meet the van.

"Is everything all right? Where's Levi?" The woman's puffy face and tear-filled eyes revealed a deep sorrow.

She looked too young to be Levi's mother. His older sister, perhaps?

"Levi's fine, Betty." The nurse hopped from the passenger side and rounded the van to let Jonah out. "He stayed to help with an emergency."

Jonah refused to let go of Anna's hand. "This is my friend. Anna."

"Nice to meet you." The woman leaned in to smile at Anna. "I'm Betty. Jonah's aunt."

Anna returned her greeting, then extricated her fingers from Jonah's. "Good-bye," she told him as the nurse turned him over to Betty's care. Jonah's *aenti* started to lead him toward the house.

He stopped and turned to wave at Anna.

"I'll see you later," she called as she waved back. Then she cringed inside. She'd just told a lie. She'd forgotten she wouldn't be going back to the center ever again.

That thought occupied her mind the rest of the way home. When the van pulled in front of her house and turned on its flashing red lights, a car idled in the driveway. Anna's *aenti* came rushing toward her, holding a small boy, as the nurse opened the van door and undid the straps.

"Anna, I'm so glad you're here." Her *aenti* cradled the boy in her arms. "Rowan's sick, so I'm taking him to the doctor, and Emily isn't home yet." Her words came out in a rush. "Can you watch the children until she gets here? That way, I won't have to take the other children."

"Of course, but isn't Sarah here?"

"*Jah*, but she's too young to watch the foster children."

Anna crinkled her forehead. "Too young?" Sarah was nine and took good care of her younger siblings.

"Although there's no law that sets a minimum age for

watching foster children, I don't want to do anything that might get the children taken away. *Englischers* usually leave their children only with a teen or adult."

"I see." How odd. Most Amish children were capable of caring for themselves and doing household chores unassisted by age six, and they often cared for infants and toddlers.

Her *aenti* must have seen her puzzled expression. "Most *Englischers* don't trust God's will for their children the way we do. They won't leave children alone or let them cook or do major chores."

Anna wheeled beside her *aenti* toward the waiting car. That was true. *Englisch* customers often seemed shocked when eight-year-old Anna handled their purchases in their family's farm store years ago.

"You're here alone?" they'd ask, glancing around in dismay as she counted out their change.

They also couldn't believe she could drive her pony cart by herself to a friend's house at that age.

It was strange how *Englischers* hovered over their children and never let them do things alone. *Aenti* Miriam was right. They didn't seem to have the same belief that whatever happened was God's will.

"I need to go, or we'll be late." Miriam opened the car door and strapped Rowan into a baby seat.

"I should be back in an hour or so," Miriam called as she got into the passenger seat. "Sarah and Hannah are making chicken corn soup for supper. I asked them to give the children a snack because we'll be eating so late."

"I'll be praying for Rowan." Anna waved and headed up the ramp to the *dawdi haus*. Then she hurried along the wooden walkway to the kitchen of the main house.

"Hi, Sarah," she called as she reached forward to open the door.

Her cousin's faint response came from upstairs. "I'm changing Xavier. Be right down."

Seven-year-old Hannah was shredding carrots for the soup. Several small children sat around the large farmhouse table, banging spoons impatiently while six-year-old Naomi dished out bread pudding for their snack.

A few minutes later, Sarah descended the stairs with a toddler balanced on one hip. She plopped him on the long bench and passed him a bowl and spoon. Then she joined her sister at the counter to chop celery to add to the soup, while Naomi rushed around the table, wiping faces, cleaning up spills, and settling arguments.

"Can I help with anything?" Anna asked. Her cousins seemed to have everything under control.

A faint wail came from the cradle in the corner of the living room. "Baby Quinn needs to be changed," Sarah answered. "*Mamm* just filled that cabinet with several stacks of diapers. Quinn uses the smallest size." She pointed across the room. "Naomi can get her bottle ready."

Naomi grabbed a bowl of bread pudding and shoveled it into her mouth. "I'll do that," she said around a big bite, "as soon as I finish my snack."

"I'll get her out of the cradle for you." Hannah set down the grater and wiped her hands on her apron. She hurried over and lifted the little girl from the cradle.

Patting Quinn on the back, Hannah waited until Anna had set the changing pad, diaper, and wipes on a low counter. Then her cousin handed over the baby.

Anna hugged the baby close and breathed in the scent of baby shampoo and lotion. An ache started deep inside.

She squeezed her eyes shut, praying no tears would spill onto her cheeks. This was as near as she'd ever get to a baby. Swallowing back the sadness clogging her throat, she laid the small girl on the makeshift changing table.

Quinn wailed as Anna removed her diaper.

"Sorry, sweetie. I know these wipes are chilly." Her misty eyes made it hard to see. And it took two tries to get the tabs in place on the squirming baby.

She wiped her hands with an antiseptic wipe before snapping Quinn back into her sleeper. Then she held the baby and rocked her to lessen her cries.

Naomi ran over with a bottle. "Here." She smiled down at Quinn and held out a finger for her to grasp. "Did you want me to feed her, Anna?"

"*Neh*, I can do it." Anna didn't want to give up this precious chance to hold and cuddle an infant, something she'd never get to do as a mother. With a heavy heart, she shifted Quinn to one arm and took the bottle with the other. As soon as she slid it into the screeching mouth, Quinn's lips clamped tight, and she stopped screaming.

Behind Anna, some shrieks accompanied scuffling. After propping the bottle against her body to keep it in Quinn's mouth, Anna turned her chair around to see Iris and the boy next to her in a tug-of-war over a blanket.

"Mine," the boy insisted.

Iris yanked hard, almost toppling the boy off the bench. He let go of the small piece of green velour clasped in his hand and grabbed at the edge of his seat to keep from falling. With another rapid jerk, Iris claimed the blanket.

Naomi intervened. "Iris, that's Xavier's." She unwound the blanket from Iris's hand. "Yours is blue. You left it up-stairs after your nap."

Iris bawled. With a sigh, Naomi lifted the little girl and propped her on one hip. Iris was half Naomi's size, and overbalanced, Naomi tilted to the side, but she soldiered on, plodding up the stairs to find Iris's blanket.

By the time Iris returned cuddling her blanket, toddling beside Naomi and holding her hand, Hannah had swept the carrots and celery into the soup pot, wiped all the children's hands and faces, and assisted a four-year-old with sweeping under the table. Sarah chopped the chicken into bite-sized pieces and put them in the pot with the vegetables and chicken broth.

Once it was set to simmer, she took Quinn from Anna and tucked her into the cradle. Anna's arms and heart ached with emptiness.

She needed to accept her loss of motherhood and marriage as God's will. She regretted being so critical of *Englischers* for not trusting God with their children. How was she any different if she refused to surrender to God's leading over remaining single and childless?

I'm sorry, Lord. Please help me to be obedient and grateful for whatever Your will is for me.

Little fingers poked at her. "Is you sleeping?" Xavier, clutching his green blanket, stood staring up at her.

"*Neh*, I was praying."

"Pwaying? What's that?"

"Talking to God."

Xavier tilted his head to one side. "Like when we eat?"

"*Jah*. Then we're thanking God, but we can also ask Him things."

"Like when's Mommy coming back?"

Ach, the poor boy. She'd been so focused on her own

losses she hadn't thought about these little ones who were separated from their families.

Anna held out her arms to Xavier and lifted him onto her lap. When she wrapped her arms around him, he cuddled close. "You miss your mommy, don't you?" she asked.

His eyes filled with tears, he nodded.

"Let's pray for her." Anna wished she could ease his pain. She had no idea why his mother had to give him up—drugs, abuse, jail time—so it wouldn't be wise to pray for a rapid reunion, which might give him false hope.

She bowed her head until her chin rested on his soft curly hair. With him leaning back against her and her arms encircling him, she folded her hands, and he did the same.

"Dear God," she prayed in a low, soft voice, "please help Xavier's mommy."

"Bwing her back fast, pwease, God."

Anna choked up. *Lord, if it's possible, grant his request.*

Xavier opened his eyes and twisted his head to look up at her with shining eyes. "God heared me. Mommy's coming soon."

Anna hugged him tight and hoped he wouldn't be disappointed.

She might not be a mother, but she'd just showed a child how to pray. Perhaps God had already answered her prayer. Small children like this boy needed care. Instead of feeling sorry for herself, she could make herself useful. When Miriam came home, she'd ask about getting certified to be a foster parent.

The whole way home from the hospital, Levi couldn't get his mind off Anna. He answered Ron's questions without thinking much about his answers because, in the back of his mind, he was busy trying to puzzle out what had happened to change Anna so much.

He hoped he hadn't done something to scare her off. He ran through Wednesday's session again. She'd walked across the room and back alone. And she'd left with a huge smile on her face.

She mentioned having a big meeting on Thursday night. The meeting she'd worked so hard to get ready for. Had she seemed nervous? Excited? Levi closed his eyes, trying to picture her face. *Anticipation mixed with a little fear.*

"Hey, Levi, you okay?" Ron's voice jolted Levi from the past.

"Um, sure."

"You seem so far away. You worried about that woman?"

How had Ron guessed?

"She'll be fine. You kept her going with the CPR. I can call to see how she's doing if you want." Ron pulled out his cell.

Oh, he means Diane. "She seemed to be all right. I'll check later." They kept a black box at home so Levi could get emergency calls from the firehouse.

"So, what's with you? It's not like you to drift off in the middle of a conversation." Ron's searching look made Levi tense.

He didn't want to talk about Anna, afraid he'd give away too much. And knowing the guys and gossip at the firehouse, he'd never live down the teasing if Ron told them Levi had a crush. They'd all badger him for more information. Information he could never give because his feelings were one-sided.

"Just thinking about one of my sessions," Levi said.

"Must have been a pretty bad one." He grinned. "Or judging from your frowns and grins, maybe it was a good one? You ever get any good-looking Amish girls in there?"

"I suppose. I never paid much attention." Not until Anna arrived.

"Hmm. You're not interested in women?"

How did Levi answer that one? If he said no, he knew exactly what rumors would fly around the firehouse. But if he said yes, Ron would bug him until he confessed.

Ron laughed. "Aha. Your face just gave you away. Who's the special girl?"

Levi waved a hand. "Lots of nice girls. No one special." At least, there wouldn't be anymore. Anna wasn't returning to the center.

"Looks like she broke your heart."

"Are you watching where you're going?" Levi pointed to a man who'd just stepped off the curb.

Ron swerved to avoid the pedestrian. "I can watch your face and drive at the same time."

"Maybe," Levi muttered. "But if I hadn't pointed out that man, you might have run him over."

"Nah, I saw him. You're just trying to change the subject."

Ron flicked on his turn signal. They'd reached the center parking lot. Levi had never been so happy to leave a conversation with Ron before.

"I'm right over there." Levi pointed to the lone buggy in the parking lot.

"I already figured that out." Ron slowed and pulled in near the buggy. Before Levi got out, Ron leaned over and touched Levi's arm. "Hey, man. I was just teasing about the woman, but I have one piece of advice. You're a nice guy. Make sure this chick, um, woman, is worth a broken heart."

Ron's words echoed in Levi's mind as he crossed the parking lot. Was Anna worth a broken heart?

Only one answer came to mind. *Jah*, she was worth any sacrifice he had to make.

Chapter Twelve

When Miriam got home, Anna approached her about becoming a foster parent.

"Are you sure?" Her *aenti* looked harried. "It's a lot of work. And you don't have much freedom. You're still young. Maybe you'll decide to date."

Anna had blown her only chance for courting and marriage this morning when she turned Gabe away. That opportunity would never come again. "It's not like I have anyone dying to court me," she pointed out.

Miriam winced. "You never know what God has in store for you."

"I helped Xavier pray today, and God touched my heart. I really want to do it."

"It's a long process. You might get emergency certification in thirty days, especially if I vouch for you, and the *dawdi haus* can be considered an extension of this one."

"Supper's ready," Sarah called.

"We'd better go in," Miriam said. "But let's both pray about it. If you want a small taste of what it might be like, they're bringing an emergency placement in a few hours. I'll let the baby stay with you and Emily tonight."

Anna smiled. "That would be great."

Miriam's sympathetic smile should have served as a warning, but Anna welcomed any distraction from Gabe and Levi.

After supper, Anna sat in the living room with her *aenti* and Emily while the social worker discussed baby Ciara's situation. Miriam reached for the screaming baby. She paced the room, patting the baby's back as Millie spoke.

"Ciara's six months old." Millie raised her voice to be heard over the baby's shrieks. "But she's developmentally delayed."

Poor little girl. Anna wished she could hold and comfort Ciara, but most likely, her *aenti* would do a better job.

"Her mom was caught with crack and arrested," Millie explained. "The mom has priors and will probably be charged with child abandonment, so she may be in for a while. Ciara was diagnosed as a crack-addicted baby at birth, which means she'll be irritable and jittery and cry a lot."

"Does she need to be fed?" Miriam asked.

The social worker pulled some cans of special formula and vitamins from the bag beside her. "She's malnourished and underweight, so the doctor who checked her suggested using this formula. She also needs these extra vitamins."

Emily took the containers from Millie and headed for the kitchen. "I'll fix her a bottle and be right back."

"Neighbors complained Ciara screamed most of the night," Millie continued. "Some of that might be lack of care. We received reports the mother left her alone much of the night while she went out partying."

Anna couldn't understand how anyone could do that

to a tiny baby—God's precious gift to parents. The poor mother must not have had family to help her or teach her right from wrong.

"The mom wasn't home when we checked. Turns out she was at the police station. We're not sure how long Ciara was by herself. Looked like she hadn't been changed or fed for a long time. She has a bad diaper rash, so you'll need to keep an eye on that."

"Poor thing," Miriam said, still striding back and forth with the screaming baby. Emily returned with a warm bottle. At first, Ciara wailed and turned her head away when Miriam tried to feed her. But once she latched on to the nipple, she sucked greedily. Miriam sank onto the nearest chair.

"Ciara will need a lot of extra care." The social worker directed her comments to Miriam, but Miriam pinned Anna with a searching gaze that Anna met with a steady look.

What difference did it make if she stayed up all night? Unlike Emily and Miriam, she had nowhere to go in the morning and nothing to do but basic household chores. Those she could do in her sleep.

Now that she no longer needed to spend time practicing, hoping to impress Levi or to walk to Gabe, she could help Miriam more and care for this baby.

You're sure? Miriam mouthed.

Anna nodded, positive she'd be up to the challenge.

By the time Levi arrived home, the dinner dishes had been washed, and his *aenti* had her head bent over a letter again.

When he walked through the door, she jumped up. "*Ach*, Levi, have you had anything to eat?" She bustled over to the stove. "I didn't know how long you'd be, so I kept the chicken pot pie hot."

"Sorry I'm so late, but we had an emergency at the center."

"So I heard."

Levi washed up and started to sit at the table. Betty rushed over and snatched the papers at her place.

"We need to talk about that," Levi said.

His *aenti*'s face stiffened into a stoic expression. "About what?"

"About what you're going to tell Vern."

"Levi, you promised." His aunt's voice held the stern note she usually used for giving his youngest brother a serious scolding.

"I did, but I can't let you ruin your life for us. I never knew you had a boyfriend." In all these years, she'd never once mentioned leaving someone behind in Fort Plain.

"A fiancé," Betty corrected.

"Fiancé?" Levi stared at her back as she ladled the noodles and broth into a bowl. "You broke your engagement to come here?"

Betty turned her back and stirred the pot on the stove, but her shoulders heaved.

"Did you ever tell *Mamm*?"

Without turning, his *aenti* shook her head. "She had enough problems to handle. Widowed with four young boys. She needed help."

"But how could you leave him?" Levi may not have a fiancée, but even with his feelings for Anna, knowing he wouldn't see her again devastated him. If they'd been engaged, nothing could have kept them apart.

"It wasn't . . . easy." Betty's tear-clogged words made it

clear she still felt that pain deeply. She sniffled quietly before she carried the bowl to the table. "Let it go, Levi."

When she set the food in front of him, Levi reached for her hand and held her there for a moment. "I can't let it. I won't stand in your way of happiness."

He motioned to the chair beside him. "Please let's figure this out."

"There's nothing to figure out." She stepped back. "Eat your pot pie before it gets cold."

"Wait." Levi pushed out the chair with his foot. "You still love him. And he must still care for you."

She started to turn her back, but Levi dropped his bombshell. "I've found a girl I want to marry." The only problem was that she had no interest in him.

Betty whirled around. "You have? Who? Why haven't you said anything before this? Are you courting someone? Where did you meet her?"

"If you sit down and stop asking me so many questions, maybe we can talk this out." He took a bite of her pot pie, and the homemade noodles and hearty broth slid down his throat, warming his stomach. "First, I want you to promise me you won't tell Vern no."

"You didn't keep your promise, so I don't have to keep mine." Betty crossed her arms.

"Please, Betty. I don't want to be responsible for destroying your relationship with someone you love. Especially not now, when I know what it's like to fall in love."

"Who is it? When did it happen?"

"I'm not ready to share it with the world."

Betty sucked in a sharp breath. "Are you accusing me of being a gossip?"

Levi shook his head. "Not at all. It's just that I want to keep it private." So private, even Anna didn't know.

Betty traced circles with a fingertip on the tabletop. "I understand. I've always been the same way."

"I have an idea." Levi hoped she'd agree. Once she did, he had a feeling she'd never want to leave Vern. "Why don't you plan a trip to Fort Plain? Stay with your cousins. I can handle things here for a week or two. Make sure you still have the same feelings for Vern."

From the glow that lit his *aenti*'s eyes, Levi had no doubt they'd rekindle their love.

Betty stared off into space. "I could make meals ahead of time. And you can open some canned soups and meats on the basement shelves. I'll leave instructions." Then she sobered. "But what about cleaning and laundry and—"

"The boys and I will handle it as best we can. If we get in trouble, I can ask—"

"Your special friend." Betty's smile broadened. "Of course. I'm sure she'd be happy to help. And I can do extra cleaning when I return."

Levi had been about to say he could ask somebody at church for help. He'd be happy to pay them, but he didn't correct his *aenti*. He wanted to reassure her they'd be all right while she was gone. "We won't make that much of a mess while you're gone."

Betty laughed. "I don't know about that, but it'll be good for your girl to see what she might have to take on when she marries you."

His *aenti*'s words were like daggers to his heart. He wanted to correct her, but how did he explain the girl he wanted to marry had no idea of his interest?

After the social worker left and Ciara had been fed and changed, Anna swaddled the fussy baby into a baby carrier against her chest and headed for the *dawdi haus*. She had a few diapers, a clean outfit, and some baby shampoo, soap, and diaper cream tucked into a bag beside her. Emily and Sarah followed, carrying a cradle that swung on a stand, which they set up in Anna's bedroom.

"Will this height work for you to get Ciara out?" Emily asked.

Anna rolled over to the cradle and unwrapped the kicking, screaming baby. She lowered her into the cradle. It took a bit of stretching to get her out again, but it was doable. "It'll be fine," Anna assured her.

"I hope it goes well tonight," Sarah said as she headed out the door.

"I'm sure it will." Emily tried to sound encouraging, but doubt seeped into her words. "I'll be back after I help *Mamm* with the bedtime routines. And I'll bring all the other supplies when I come." She shut the door behind her, leaving Anna alone with the baby.

Anna rocked Ciara, then tried putting the baby over her shoulder and patting the little one's back, but nothing soothed her. Warm weather made some babies cranky, and everywhere Ciara's head rested soon grew damp and sticky.

Emily returned with a wicker basket filled with bottles, formula, baby food, wipes, and a small stack of fresh clothes. "You both look so hot. Want me to give Ciara a bath?"

"I can do it. Maybe that'll cool her down so she can sleep." Anna took Ciara to the kitchen and slid her wheelchair in under the sink, grateful that *Mammi*'s kitchen was accessible. She could easily bathe Ciara here—that was, if she could get the little girl to stop squirming. Switching the crying baby to her shoulder, Anna turned on the water, trying for the perfect mix of lukewarm.

Her cousin collected soap, shampoo, and a washcloth. The minute Anna slid the baby into the water, Ciara's body stiffened. But her crying quieted.

"She seems afraid of the water." Anna didn't want to frighten her, but Ciara needed a bath.

"Why don't you keep on holding her since she seems to be getting used to you, and I'll wash her?" Emily wet the washcloth. "I'll save her hair until last. Most babies hate that."

"Poor little one," Anna cooed. "Look at that diaper rash. That must be making her uncomfortable."

With Emily washing and Anna soothing, they managed to get Ciara clean.

"Now for her hair." Emily pointed to the yellow scaly patches on Ciara's head. "She has terrible cradle cap. I brought over a soft hairbrush. That might help."

Ciara's eyes widened as Emily rubbed shampoo on her scalp, but when Anna tipped her back and Emily poured rinse water over her head, Ciara arched her back and shrieked. She fought and wriggled so hard, Anna feared she'd drop her.

"Hurry and get her rinsed," she said as she struggled to hold on to the slippery, screaming baby.

"I'm trying." Emily filled another cup of clean water and started to pour, but Ciara flailed and squirmed. Despite Emily's hand shielding Ciara's face, half the water poured into the baby's eyes. Some went into her mouth. She sputtered and choked.

Anna lifted Ciara onto her shoulder and patted the baby's back, soaking her dress. She was starting to see why her *aenti* had been so hesitant when Anna wanted to get certified.

And they were only getting started. They still had to face the long night ahead.

Once Ciara stopped coughing, Anna put her back in the sink to finish the hair rinsing. Then she wrapped her in a towel and used the hairbrush to loosen some of the flaky skin. Ciara cooed as Anna brushed.

"Does it feel good to get that off your head?" Anna whispered close to Ciara's ear. Maybe she was getting the hang of being a foster parent.

"Was getting your certification hard, Emily?"

"Not really. You have to take some classes like First Aid, Water Safety, and CPR."

CPR. Her mind flooded with pictures of Levi. How she wished he could teach her. Would he have to demonstrate the technique? She pictured him giving her mouth-to-mouth resuscitation. Would his lips be—?

"Anna," Emily snapped, her voice sharp.

"Huh? What?"

"You've been brushing the exact same spot on Ciara's head. You'll rub her scalp raw."

Anna turned her attention to the baby. "Sorry," she muttered, keeping her head down so Emily couldn't see her warm cheeks or wistful eyes. "I was daydreaming."

"I could tell." The note of curiosity in her cousin's voice indicated she wanted Anna to share.

But Levi was one secret Anna planned to keep to herself.

Chapter Thirteen

Levi tossed and turned all night. Partly out of guilt for letting his *aenti* believe half-truths, but even more from wishing that those fantasies could turn into reality.

At dawn, he got out of bed, intending to find out what had upset Anna yesterday and, if possible, discover why she'd decided to give up her sessions. He also wanted to thank her for getting Jonah home safely yesterday.

He didn't have to work today, but he always took Jonah to the center on Saturday. Maybe he could stop by Anna's after that. He didn't need to get back to the center until noon for Jonah's lunch, so he and Anna'd have a little time to talk.

Since she'd missed yesterday's session, maybe he could even talk her into working with him during the afternoon if she had time. She'd said she didn't want to continue, but she had shown up for her Friday appointment. At least, he could offer.

When he entered the kitchen, Betty had her back to him, stirring scrambled eggs. And humming.

Levi had never heard her hum before. Had she spent all her years here brokenhearted and pining for her lost love?

Perhaps she'd be embarrassed to know he'd heard her. He slipped out of the kitchen and made some noise before entering. Sure enough, her humming stopped.

When she turned, her huge smile gave her away. "Breakfast is almost ready. Can you call your brothers?"

Levi headed outside to notify Daniel and Zeb before he went upstairs to help Jonah finish dressing. Then Jonah clomped downstairs and out to the table.

During breakfast, Daniel and Zeb both kept studying their *aenti*, as if puzzled by the difference in her. All the gloom and sadness of the past few days had disappeared, and a new person sat in Betty's usual place. Even her voice had become bright and chirpy. It went well with her dazzling smile.

When they bowed for prayer, Levi added a petition that Vern and his *aenti* would rekindle their love. He longed to include a similar request for himself, but that seemed wrong. He had no idea if Anna had a husband or a boyfriend. Until he learned whether or not she was single, he had no right to ask God for a future with her.

As soon as breakfast ended, Levi hustled Jonah outside, eager to get his brother to the center so he could stop by Anna's. But when they arrived, Levi stopped in the office first.

"Have you had any news about Diane?" he asked Holly.

"She's doing well, thanks to you. She'll be out for several weeks, though. I'm working on lining up a sub for her, but I don't have anyone for Jonah today. I'm really sorry."

Levi had been so focused on visiting Anna, he hadn't considered that Jonah might not have an aide. What could he do now?

Holly stood and headed to the door. "I'd do it, but I

need to substitute for someone else who's out sick. You're welcome to accompany Jonah, if you have time."

"I wasn't planning to stay. I had an errand to run this morning."

Jonah stared at him. "No Diane? No school?" He looked about to cry.

A little girl came through the door, and Holly waved hello. "I have to meet Tabitha, but you can bring Jonah back later if you want."

"I'll do that. Thanks." Levi would have to take Jonah with him to Anna's, but first he notified the teachers that Jonah wouldn't be attending the morning sessions.

Levi squatted so he was eye level with Jonah. "Listen. I wanted to stop at Anna's today." Would his brother even remember her?

"Anna?" Jonah clapped. "Go see Anna?"

She must have made quite an impression. "Yes, we'll visit Anna, and then I'll bring you back to the center."

Jonah bounced along beside Levi and they headed for the buggy. Anna had mentioned living with the Flauds. He'd driven by their farm several times but had never seen her. He hoped she'd be home today.

He knocked at the front door and asked the little girl who answered if Anna was around.

She pointed to the *dawdi haus*. "Anna lives over there."

"*Danke.*" Levi helped Jonah from the buggy and headed across the lawn. It was a bit unusual for someone so young to live in the *dawdi haus*, but once he reached the ramp, it made more sense.

All morning, he'd anticipated this visit, but now as he climbed the ramp, nerves tensed his stomach. Maybe he shouldn't have come. Would she read something more into his visit? Maybe having Jonah along would make it seem more like a friendly gesture.

He hesitated before knocking. Inside, a baby howled.

No. Levi's stomach churned. Anna was married and had a baby. He should never have come. All his dreams dissolved.

He started to turn away, but Jonah pounded on the door. Someone called, "Come in." And before Levi could stop him, Jonah opened the door and walked inside.

After being up all night with a screaming baby, Anna could barely drag herself out of bed that morning. She'd put on her oldest housedress and work apron. The one that was faded and stained. The one she wore for messy chores.

And taking care of Ciara had proved to be extremely messy. Anna had changed her own nightgown three times last night, and Ciara needed fresh clothes five times. Spit-up, diarrhea, a leaky diaper. One after the other, while Anna sleepwalked through the baby's care. In between, Ciara startled herself awake and screeched at the top of her lungs.

Emily had gotten up twice to relieve her, but her cousin had to go into work later today, so Anna took over most of the night duty. She could see why her *aenti* had suggested moving the baby over here. Ciara's shrieks would have woken the other children. Nobody would have gotten any sleep.

They'd already run out of fresh clothes for Ciara, so Emily had taken the laundry to her *mamm*. Ciara sat on Anna's lap, clad only in a diaper, waiting for Emily to return with another stack of outfits.

Anna spooned cereal into the baby's mouth. Ciara ate

eagerly, but as she clamped down on the spoon, cereal sprayed over both of them and dribbled down Ciara's chin. Anna had tried putting Ciara in the wooden high chair Emily had brought over, but Ciara fought so hard, she'd almost flipped herself onto the floor.

Warm wetness seeped onto Anna's lap. *Ach!* Another leaky diaper. They'd run out of the small size, and Anna couldn't get the next size tight enough. Emily had volunteered to run out to the store after breakfast, but for now Anna would have to make do.

A loud knock on the door startled her. Why didn't Emily just come in?

Anna didn't bother turning around. "Did you get the diapers and extra clothes?"

"A baby," a boy squealed.

Whipping her head around, Anna spotted Jonah. And right behind him, Levi. Her face flamed. She hadn't put her hair in a bob yet, her kerchief was askew. Her dress and apron were soaked, and she'd been up all night. She looked worse than last week's leftovers.

Even worse, the house was in disarray. She couldn't imagine what Levi thought of her or her housework. She was so stunned, she hadn't even turned to greet them. Now she didn't want to. What he could see was bad enough.

"I'm sorry." Levi's red face probably matched hers. "Jonah opened the door and walked in. I didn't mean . . ." He stopped and stared at her.

For the first time, he seemed to be taking her in. "Are you all right?" he asked gently.

"As well as I can be after no sleep all night." Her attempt at humor came out sounding pathetic.

"Sorry," Levi repeated. "I didn't know about, um, the

baby. I shouldn't have come." He reached for his brother's hand and backed toward the door.

"It's okay." Any other time she would have been overjoyed to see him. But right now . . .

Levi had been so stunned by the fact that Anna—his Anna, his future dream wife—had a baby, he couldn't come up with a coherent thought.

He must have stammered "sorry" several times already, but he wasn't quite sure why he was apologizing. For barging in on her? For including her in his dreams of the future? For not realizing she had a home, a husband, a family?

Jonah broke free of Levi's grasp. "A baby. I want to see." He rushed through the archway to the kitchen and sidled up to the table beside Anna.

"Wait." Caught up in his regrets, Levi didn't react fast enough. "We didn't mean to intrude."

Jonah extended a gentle hand and touched Ciara's cheek. "Soft," he said, his tone reverent.

Ciara stopped whining and stared up at Jonah.

He smiled at her. "Pretty baby."

"She is, isn't she?" Anna stared with adoration at the tiny baby in her arms.

Levi's heart clenched. The sight of her with a little one made him ache inside. Even with tired circles under her eyes and her hair in disarray, she was the most beautiful angel he'd ever seen. Her heavenly smile. Her shining eyes. Her . . .

Stop, Levi. She belongs to another man.

"Jonah, she likes you," Anna whispered.

Her quiet voice slashed at Levi's heart. If only he had the right to bend down and . . .

He straightened abruptly. He had to get out of here. Now.

"Jonah, you need to leave for the center." Levi's voice came out harshly. He squeezed his eyes shut and tried again, hoping for a neutral tone. "You wanted to thank Anna, remember?"

"For what?" Anna turned startled eyes in Levi's direction.

He looked away before their eyes met. "For being sure he got home last night."

"That was no trouble. The nurses took care of it." Her brows drew together. "How is Diane?"

"Holly says she's doing well, but she won't be back to work for a few weeks."

"You did a wonderful job of helping her."

The admiration in Anna's eyes set Levi's spirits dancing. Just as quickly, they plummeted. Pulling his gaze away, he concentrated on the wooden floorboards under his feet. "It's what I'm trained to do."

"I should probably ask you about CPR classes."

"You're planning to take them?"

"I need to in case something happens to the children." She gestured with her chin to the baby in her arms.

She had more than one child? The thought made him even sadder.

Anna turned back around to face his brother. "Ciara hasn't cried once since you've been touching her, Jonah. Would you like to hold her?"

Jonah's enthusiastic "*jah*" startled the baby, and she whimpered.

Neh. Levi didn't want Jonah getting attached to a baby. Or, even worse, holding one. "I don't think . . ." He snapped his mouth shut at the sight of his brother's starry eyes.

Maybe with Jonah's troubles with short-term memory, he'd soon forget about the baby. And about Anna.

An advantage Levi didn't have.

The living room door banged open.

Anna turned her head to find Emily standing in the entryway with a box of diapers and a pile of clothes. "Oh, you're here. Jonah would like to hold the baby, but she needs to be changed first and so do I."

"Jonah?" Emily stared from one to the other.

"This is Jonah." Anna nodded toward the boy beside her who remained enraptured by Ciara. "His older brother, Levi, was my therapist at the center." She tilted her head in his direction. Technically, he wasn't certified as a therapist, but he seemed as knowledgeable about her recovery as her therapists at rehab. And he'd helped her walk.

Levi stood awkwardly in the living room, looking as if he wanted to flee. Maybe babies made him uncomfortable.

Emily greeted both of them, then reached for Ciara. "Why don't I change her while you get cleaned up?" She glanced from Levi to Anna's hair, the tangled waist-length chestnut hair that hung down her back.

Anna understood her cousin's shock. The wheelchair back hid most of her hair, but still, it was unseemly to be out here with a man alone and with her hair down. Good thing her *aenti* hadn't seen her, or Anna would have endured a lecture.

As soon as Emily scooped Ciara from her arms, the small girl thrashed and screamed. Jonah stepped back, his eyes wide and frightened.

"It's all right." Anna tried to comfort him. "Ciara cries a lot. She's a sick baby, but we hope she'll get better." She didn't know how else to explain the problems of babies born to crack addicts.

Leaving Emily to calm and change Ciara, Anna rushed back to her bedroom. "I'll be back soon," she called over the baby's screams.

She was grateful she had no mirror in her bedroom to reflect her rat's nest of hair and stained dress. Splotches of cereal and spots of dampness dotted her apron. Anna washed up quickly and donned a clean outfit. Then she brushed out her hair, pulled it into a bob, and pinned on her *kapp*. Feeling fresher, she wheeled back out to the living room.

Levi's eyes lit with appreciation. But the abrupt way he turned his head away and focused his attention on Jonah hurt Anna's feelings.

He'd always been so generous with his smiles. Now, he almost seemed to be avoiding her. Perhaps she'd hurt his feelings by telling him she wouldn't be doing any more sessions.

"I promised Jonah could hold Ciara," Anna told Emily. "The baby really seems to like him." She motioned to Jonah. "Why don't you sit on the couch?"

"I'm not sure this is a good idea." Levi paced nervously. "He's pretty young to be holding a baby."

"I'm sure he'll be fine." Emily's matter-of-fact tone dismissed Levi's worries. "My younger sisters do fine with babies."

"But Jonah's never been around any. And he's only twelve."

"Time for him to learn. He'll be a father someday. Or an uncle." Emily shot Levi a speculative look.

He lowered pain-filled eyes and thrust his hands into his pockets.

Anna longed to reach out to him and ease his hurt. His sadness seemed so fresh and raw. Had he broken up with someone recently? Her heart ached for him. She'd just been through the same devastation.

Calm down, Levi. Nothing bad will happen. Jonah will sit on a couch with an adult nearby. The baby will be fine. Jonah won't hurt her. He's calm and gentle.

But facts didn't lessen fears. Levi had been the same age as Jonah when . . .

The old nightmare swirled around him, trapped him, sucked him into its depths. Water closed over his head. He couldn't breathe, couldn't reach his brother.

Save Jonah. He repeated it to himself over and over.

"Levi?"

Anna interrupted the terrifying memories. He struggled to return to the room. When he did, her concerned expression only added to his heartache.

She looked like she cared. About him.

He shook his head. He'd already read too much into the special glances they'd shared as they worked together. Hers had been friendly. She'd been joyful over her success. His had held admiration for her determination. And so much more.

Emily helped Jonah settle back on the sofa and sat beside him. She lowered the whining baby toward Jonah's arms. Levi clenched his hands into fists in his pockets and forced himself not to interfere.

Babies were such fragile creatures. One tiny mistake and you could ruin them for life.

Then Emily cupped Jonah's hands around Ciara and supported him for a minute before withdrawing her arms.

Levi sucked in a silent breath and prayed as his brother cradled the helpless baby.

He'd been so worried about a possible disaster, he hadn't noticed Anna headed toward him until she touched his arm, shocking him.

"Is something wrong?" she whispered.

The gentle brush of her fingertips jolted him, and Levi jerked away. How did he answer her question? Should he say everything was wrong?

Anna cuddling a child had dashed all hopes of a future together. And Jonah holding that baby raised deep-seated fears about putting a child in danger.

Her fingers on his arm had delivered the final blow. If things had been different, he would have reveled in her touch, but now his reaction shamed him. He had no right to feel like this about someone else's wife.

Chapter Fourteen

Anna wanted to reach out to Levi. After all he'd done for her, he didn't deserve to suffer so much distress. If only she had a way to reach him. Touching him had been a mistake. He'd jumped back as if he'd been bitten by a poisonous snake.

He'd always been so friendly and talkative. Now he seemed aloof. He hadn't answered when she asked if something was wrong. He'd just retreated further from her.

"We need to go," Levi said through clenched teeth, his back rigid, his gaze fixed on Jonah.

"I need to go too. I have to meet my ride for work." Emily set a gentle hand on Jonah's shoulder. "You're doing a great job. Ciara's almost asleep."

The baby's eyes kept drifting shut. Anna prayed they'd stay closed. After being up all night, Ciara needed to rest.

"Could Jonah keep holding Ciara until she goes to sleep?" Anna turned to Levi to see if he'd agree.

His eyes wide and worried, he sucked in a sharp breath as Emily slipped off the couch, careful not to disturb the baby.

It didn't seem like Levi had even heard her question.

Something was wrong. Very wrong. Anna yearned to comfort him. Didn't he trust Jonah with the baby? Or did he dislike babies?

Maybe she should take Ciara. She wheeled closer to the couch. Ciara's chest rose and fell in an even rhythm, and her eyes remained closed. "I think she's sleeping already."

Anna pushed her concerns about Levi from her mind and concentrated on the baby. One jiggle could disturb Ciara and start her bawling.

"Can you lift her very, very gently?" she whispered to Jonah. "And then pass her over to me?" She positioned her wheelchair near him and held out her arms.

Levi stepped nearer, hovering over them, his arms outstretched as if to catch a falling baby. But Jonah inched Ciara up toward Anna's waiting hands so slowly, Ciara didn't stir. With a soft sigh, Anna cuddled the still-sleeping baby close.

Beside her, Levi let out a long breath. Anna had forgotten about his tension. She wanted to find out what had upset him, but first she needed to put Ciara in her cradle and hope she took a good nap. Maybe Anna could rest too.

"Let me put Ciara in bed, and I'll be right back to see you out." She spoke quietly so she didn't disturb the baby.

"You don't need to do that," Levi answered, his voice husky. "We'll let you go."

"Please wait," she begged. She couldn't let him leave without knowing what was bothering him.

Praying the jostling wouldn't disturb Ciara, Anna switched the baby to her left arm, and began the awkward, one-handed pushing to wheel herself back to the bedroom.

"Wait." Levi hurried over. "Let me help." He took the

wheelchair handles and pushed her toward the kitchen. "Which way?"

Anna tipped her head to indicate the door to the right side. He leaned over to open the door and eased her into the room. He stopped for a moment before wheeling her over to the cradle.

"*Danke*," she whispered as she lowered the sleeping baby into the cradle and covered her with a light blanket.

"Should I take you back to the living room?"

"*Jah*. That would be great." Ordinarily, she'd prefer to wheel herself, but today she was drained and exhausted.

She appreciated Levi asking her rather than assuming he knew best. Some people just took over without waiting to find out if she wanted or needed assistance. Others ignored her struggles when she needed help. Levi seemed so attuned to her needs.

Anna broke off her thoughts. She had to stop thinking about him like that. He sensed the right things to do because he had so much experience, not because he was paying special attention to her.

"I wish I could keep you here," Anna said to Jonah when they entered the living room. "You seem to calm Ciara. Maybe with you as a babysitter, I could get some sleep."

Jonah beamed. "I can stay with you."

"I'd like that." Anna's lips curved into an answering smile. He was such a sweet boy. It would be nice to have his company. And Levi's.

His brother punctured that fantasy.

"We need to go," Levi said stiffly. "Jonah and I only stopped by to thank you." He paused and stared off into space. "And I was going to ask why you'd stopped your sessions, but I can see why." He nodded toward the bedroom where Ciara slept.

All night long, caring for Ciara had prevented her from thinking about the debacle at Gabe's store. But Levi's words tore open the wounds Gabe had inflicted. Anna squeezed her eyes shut as the pain washed over her in a flood.

Levi stared at Anna in alarm. "Are you all right?"

He couldn't help wondering if she'd need CPR. Which brought up other, more troubling thoughts. He yanked his mind away from the picture of his lips on hers.

"I'll be fine."

Her weak answer did nothing to reassure him. His emergency training kicked into high gear. "Maybe we should stay for a little while to be sure."

Reluctance flashed in her eyes to be quickly replaced by longing. She looked almost desperate for . . . For what? Company? A listening ear?

"You can go. I know Jonah needs to get to the center."

Levi couldn't meet her eyes. She'd caught him in a lie. Lately he seemed to be tangling himself in half-truths. Time to be honest. "The center isn't expecting him back until lunch."

"But you said . . ." Anna stopped, the surprised look in her eyes changing to puzzlement.

This was why you didn't lie. Because eventually you had to admit what you'd done.

"I, um, wanted to leave because I felt uncomfortable."

"I'm so sorry. I didn't mean to make you feel unwelcome."

"It didn't have anything to do with you." Another fib. "I mean, it wasn't your fault. It was mine." The flush of heat in his neck crept up toward his face. His collar felt tight, and he shifted from foot to foot. *Please don't ask me why.*

Her brows drew together. "You looked upset when Jonah held Ciara. You don't like babies?"

"*Neh, neh.* That's not it at all." At least, she hadn't stumbled on his main reason for feeling awkward and upset. "It's a long story."

Jonah tugged at his pant leg. "Can I play with toys?" He pointed to a small wicker basket in the opposite corner of the living room that held some baby toys.

"Of course," Anna said.

His brother sat on the floor beside the basket and pulled out a box that had buttons with animal sounds. He pressed each button, and his face lit up when it made a sound.

Anna smiled and returned to their conversation. "It looks like you might have time to tell your story after all."

Ach, he hadn't intended to dredge up the past. But Anna's color had returned, and she appeared eager to hear his tale. He couldn't disappoint her. "I don't want Jonah to overhear."

"Why don't we go into the kitchen? Would you like some coffee cake or shoofly pie or lemon bars?"

"All those choices?" How did she have time to bake all that with a fussy baby? She was amazing.

As usual, Anna's laugh strummed a chord deep inside him. Levi cautioned himself to control his reactions, but how did you stop yourself from falling for someone, even if you knew it was wrong?

Plates clinked as Anna took them from a low cupboard. "I was so nervous on Thursday, I spent all day baking. Emily took a lot of it over to their house for the kids."

Thursday. That was the day she had an important meeting. "How did it go?"

Anna bit her lip. "Let's just say I shouldn't have wasted my time."

"On the baking or the meeting?"

"Probably both. But I meant the meeting."

"Wasn't that the whole reason you were so determined to walk?" Levi wanted to confront whoever had dashed her dreams.

She turned to set the plates on the low counter by the sink. "*Jah.* Seven long years of recovery for nothing."

Seven years? Levi had no idea of how long she'd worked before he'd met her. "You'd been working for more than six years before you came to the center?"

"*Jah.*"

That word held a world of agony.

Anna recovered quickly. "What dessert would you like?"

She wanted to change the subject, but Levi wasn't about to let her. "Coffee cake sounds good."

"What about Jonah?"

"He loves lemon bars." And he could eat them with his fingers, so Levi wouldn't need to supervise his brother.

He decided to wait until she'd served everyone before bringing the conversation back to her recovery.

Anna poured a glass of milk to take out to Jonah. "Milk or coffee for you?"

He would have preferred coffee, but he didn't want to wait for her to brew it. He wanted to hear what happened on Thursday. "Milk, please."

She placed everything on a tray and wheeled it to the table. Once she'd set their food out, she took some to Jonah. After she returned, she pulled herself up to the table.

Levi took a bite of coffee cake and savored the cinnamon and sugar crunch. "This is delicious." Her husband was a lucky man. A beautiful wife. A dedicated mother. A good cook. And best of all, a caring heart.

He wanted to know who had hurt her and why. "So, what happened on Thursday?"

Anna choked on her pie. Her face turned so red when she coughed, he worried he might need the Heimlich maneuver. Tears streamed from her eyes, and she sipped some milk.

"Sorry," she said, when she could talk again.

Had the choking been meant to avoid the question? Levi kept staring at her until she answered.

Putting her fork down on her plate, she kept her head down and blinked several times before answering. Although Levi couldn't see her eyes, her slumped shoulders spoke of defeat.

If he had the right, he'd reach out to lift her chin and take her hand. Instead, he clenched his jaw and the hand in his lap.

Her words, when they finally came, carried a heavy hurt. "I did it. I walked across the room, thanks to you."

"No, Anna," he corrected. "Thanks to you. You did it by yourself. Your determination is the reason you succeeded." That victory belonged to her, and her alone.

Anna picked at the molasses layer of her pie to avoid Levi's eyes. His faith in her touched her aching heart and soul. He'd always been there for her, encouraging her, supporting her. Many times, since the other night with Gabe, she'd wished she'd been walking across the floor to Levi.

"You made it the whole way, huh?" Levi speared another piece of coffee cake and waited for her answer.

"I did, but . . ."

"But what?"

She'd rather not explain about Gabe's promise or his girlfriend. Or that she'd expected to be Gabe's fiancée. The word still wounded. But it had been her fault. Even Levi might think her foolish for making Gabe wait so many years. "Let's just say the person I walked to wasn't as encouraging as you."

Ach! Anna couldn't believe she'd just said that aloud. "I mean, I didn't get the response I'd hoped." She swallowed hard and hoped no tears would fall.

"Whoever it was should have been grateful for your effort."

"They weren't. Now I wish I'd never made the promise. Why did I even try to walk?"

"You don't walk for other people. You do it for yourself."

Levi's wisdom sliced through Anna's self-pity. "You're right," she said softly.

Who had she walked for? All these years, she'd set her own goals, but her motivation had always been to walk to Gabe. She wanted him to admire her, not pity her.

When she'd crossed the room to Gabe the other night, he hadn't appreciated her hard work and strength. His eyes had reflected only guilt and pity.

Silence stretched between them. Levi broke it. "Is that why you decided not to continue your sessions?"

Anna hung her head. "*Jah.*" It hadn't seemed worth it. She'd reached her goal. One of them, that was. Her other goal—marriage—was no longer an option.

"Look, Anna, it's not my business, but I don't think you should let one person's opinion stop you."

It had been more than an opinion; it had been her whole future. But why deny herself the chance to work with Levi, which she enjoyed? And if she planned to take in foster children, walking would be helpful.

"I know. I just felt so, so discouraged." That was putting it mildly. She'd been totally blindsided. "I'd like to keep coming, but now with the baby, well . . ."

Levi grimaced, reminding her she'd planned to ask him about why he'd been so upset earlier. And now would be a good time to change the subject, before Levi probed more about Thursday night.

"You said you'd tell me something once Jonah couldn't hear." Anna took a bite of the shoofly pie she'd massacred.

"Oh, that." Levi glanced out the window, but his eyes revealed he'd gone to a time and place far from here. A place of deep distress. "My *daed* died when I was twelve. *Mamm* had just had my baby brother, Daniel. Jonah was two."

Anna did some quick calculations. That would make Levi twenty-two. Two years younger than her.

"My *aenti* came to help out and asked me to take my brothers outside to play so *Mamm* could get some rest. I took Zeb, who was four, and Jonah to the creek to fish."

Levi's face screwed up in anguish, and his fingers clenched his fork, but he didn't eat his last few bites of cake. Anna clasped her hands in her lap to keep from reaching out to touch his hand. She wished she hadn't pushed him to tell this story if it caused so much suffering.

"I gave Zeb my rod and showed him how to fish, and he sat on the bank, patiently tossing his line and reeling it in. But I took *Daed*'s fishing pole for myself. It made me feel grown-up. Something I needed to be, if I wanted to help *Mamm*. I hoped fish for supper would stop her crying."

Anna pictured Levi as a young boy. He might have looked like Jonah, except with bright, mischievous eyes and a perpetual grin. And a much-too-long fishing rod.

"My *daed*'s death left a huge hole in our family. One I needed to fill. I had to be the man of the house now, so I needed to cast like my *daed*. Catch fish like my *daed*. Provide for the family like my *daed*."

Poor Levi. To lose his father at such a young age. Anna's heart went out to him. A young boy trying so hard to take a man's place.

"But I struggled to handle that pole. I'd finally hooked something, so I ignored some splashing downstream."

Anna bit her lower lip. From the deep lines of grief on Levi's face, she suspected what was coming next.

Levi no longer sat in the kitchen with Anna. Instead, his mind had pulled him so deeply into the past he relived every second, every minute, every hour of the tragedy.

Water rushed past him as he stood on the bank of the creek, lonely and desperate for his *daed*. The too-big rod slid through his grasp as he fought to reel in the flopping fish. He dug his heels into the muddy ground while the tip of the rod arced and bent. His line jerked and pulled, dragging him closer and closer to the edge.

The fish broke the surface. Silvery scales sparkled in the sunlight. He'd won.

Zeb screamed and pointed.

Jonah! Facedown in the water.

Levi dropped his rod. Raced toward his brother. Waded through ankle-deep water. Slipped and slid on rocks. Lost his balance. Struggled to drag his body and waterlogged clothes from the creek holding him captive.

"Jonah!" he screamed, praying his baby brother would lift his head.

Please, God, please let him still be alive.

Wading through calf-deep water, Levi reached the spot where Jonah lay sprawled. Levi lifted his brother's head from the water. Jonah's eyes remained closed, his body limp.

"Zeb," he yelled, "help me!"

Levi tugged at the heavy weight of his brother's soaked body. Then Zeb was beside him, untangling Jonah's pant leg from the tree branch trapping him, so Levi could pick Jonah up.

How long had Jonah been in the water? Was he dead?

Levi couldn't tell if his brother was breathing. As soon as Zeb freed Jonah, Levi cradled him close and raced to the house. His chest burned from exertion. And from terror. Had he killed his baby brother?

Chapter Fifteen

Anna's stomach clenched at the horror on Levi's face. He sat at the table, silent, staring off into the distance as if lost in a nightmare. She had to reach him, bring him back to the room.

Reaching across the table, she set a hand on his fist, which still clenched the handle of his fork. "Levi?" She kept her tone soft and gentle so she wouldn't startle him.

He jumped. He blinked several times and then gazed at her with a puzzled frown. He seemed to be trying to figure out who she was. "Anna?"

"*Jah*, I'm here."

"Sorry. When I remember the past, I go to a dark place."

Anna had experienced those dark places. "I understand. But it's over. You've moved past it." She'd discovered the best way to rid herself of those old memories was to remind herself she'd survived. And to thank the Lord she no longer had to go through that misery.

Levi's brittle laugh made her ache for him. "You don't understand," he said. "I have to relive that accident and my carelessness every day of my life. Every time I look at Jonah, I remember it's my fault."

Anna hadn't heard the whole story and would never ask him to repeat it. Not after she'd seen the damage it did to Levi's soul.

The fork clattered onto his plate. He glanced down as if surprised to see the last of the coffee cake in front of him. "I was so wrapped up in my own activities, my brother almost drowned. I neglected to keep an eye on him. Because of me, he suffered brain damage."

"He's alive. You should be grateful to God for that."

"But he could have had a much better life if it hadn't been for me." Levi picked up the fork and pressed it into the remaining cake crumbs.

"God has a purpose for Jonah being just the way he is. He's a wonderful and special boy."

"*Jah*, he is." Levi lifted the crumbs to his mouth. "I still can't believe God wanted that to happen, though. Why did He allow it? Jonah was innocent."

"We don't always know why, but we can trust Him. He has a reason."

Levi shook his head. "I do trust Him for everything else. But I struggle with this."

Would she offend him if she suggested a new way to look at this? "Perhaps it's not God you don't trust, but yourself."

Anna had lived through those self-doubts. And she still sometimes confronted them.

Her idea penetrated deep into Levi's soul. How had she read him so well?

He sent her a smile to convey the depth of his appreciation. Her answering smile reflected back the spark lighting his soul. Their wordless connection flamed into an intense understanding and unity. A spiritual bond that transcended time and space.

In the living room, Jonah pounded a drum. The tempo echoed the rapid beating of Levi's heart. Then reality crashed over him with a thud.

He broke their gaze. He had no right to think of Anna this way. For a moment, he'd forgotten about her husband, her baby, her family. Guilt mired him down.

He stood so abruptly, he almost tipped over his chair. "We should go."

"Already?"

She sounded so hurt, Levi couldn't look at her. He must seem rude after gobbling down her cake and pouring out his pain. "Let me get the dishes."

He reached for his plate and hers. She held out a hand to stop him. He evaded her touch. The last thing he needed right now was to have that captivating current coursing through him when he was wrestling for control of his emotions.

"I can do them if you need to leave," Anna said.

"It's the least I can do." Levi rushed to the sink and set the plates in it. "I'll just get Jonah's." He hurried into the living room.

Jonah gave Levi an odd look as he picked up the plate. Levi rarely helped with the dishes at home. But he'd need all the practice he could get with Betty leaving soon.

By the time he returned to the kitchen, Anna sat at the sink, putting soap into the water.

Levi slipped the plate he was holding into the sink. "I said I'd do it."

Anna ignored his protest and started washing the dishes.

"Can I at least dry?" Without waiting for her answer, he picked up a dish towel hanging on a nearby rack.

"You don't have to do that."

Levi picked up the plate and wiped it. "Where does it go? I'll put it away."

"I can do it."

She must think he doubted her ability to keep house. "I'm sure you can, but after you listened to my long story . . ."

"I didn't mind." With her head bent over the sink and the water running, Levi could barely hear her.

But he minded. He'd only intended to give her a quick sentence or two of Jonah's history. Not his own. But he'd fallen into an abyss. Drifted back to the past. And she'd had to pull him out of the pit.

"I didn't mean to go into such detail." He hadn't even mentioned the reason why Jonah holding the baby had upset him. "I just wanted to let you know why being around babies makes me nervous. And seeing a twelve-year-old holding a little one gives me chills."

"I can understand that." Anna's words came out flat.

She'd lost her earlier luster. All his fault. She'd sensed his interest and backed away. That was for the best.

Anna scrubbed extra hard at the plates, pretending she didn't notice Levi's closeness. If she extended her arm, she could touch him. Not that she ever would. He'd made it clear how he felt about her. He saved his brilliant smiles for the exercise room. He'd only intended to encourage her to do her best. She'd misinterpreted his friendliness. And read more into his long gazes.

For a few brief moments, Anna had been in heaven. A divine presence had descended over both of them. And she'd hoped and dreamed . . .

Anna tossed her head back and forth, trying to dislodge the feelings overwhelming her. She'd made a mistake with Gabe. No way would she let herself fall for someone even more unattainable. Someone who had no interest in her.

They finished washing and drying the dishes in silence. Now all she had to do was get through the good-byes. She could break down once the door closed behind them. Pinching her lips together, she drained the sink and took extra time wiping it clean.

Levi set the last plate on the shelf and hung the towel on the rack. If only this could be her daily reality. The two of them working together in the kitchen. But she'd never experience this with a spouse. Never.

Heavyhearted, she turned from the sink. Levi averted his eyes, increasing her loss.

"*Danke* for the coffee cake." The stiffness and formality of his voice widened the gap between them. All their old comradery had vanished, and they'd become two strangers exchanging polite words.

He headed for the living room. "Jonah, it's time to go. What do you say to Anna?"

Jonah looked up at her. "I love you." He paused for a minute before adding, "A lot."

Anna's eyes brimmed with tears. She'd been feeling so lost and lonely. Jonah's affirmation touched her heart.

She could barely choke out her response. "I love you a lot too."

The sunshine on Jonah's face shed rays of sunlight into what had been a depressing week. Anna kept her attention on him and basked in the warmth of his smile. What a special boy he was.

Levi may not understand why God had allowed the

tragedy to happen, but He'd given Jonah a special gift. Jonah's purpose was to share God's love with everyone around him.

Sometime—if she ever saw Levi again—she'd point that out to him. The rest of the world could learn so much from Jonah about Christ's love.

Her heart overflowing, Anna expanded her joy to encompass Levi, only to encounter a stone-cold face. Although his response cut her deeply, she refused to let him dim her happiness.

Levi broke their gaze and motioned to the toys on the floor. "Can you put those away?" he asked his brother.

Jonah's expression dimmed for a moment before returning to his usual cheerfulness. He dropped all the toys in the basket and lumbered to his feet. Levi took his brother's hand, and a lump formed in Anna's throat.

What would it be like to feel Levi's strong fingers close around hers?

Without looking in her direction, Levi asked, "Do you need help with anything before we go?"

Although he had withdrawn from her emotionally, he remained polite, but distant. He'd ask the same of an elderly neighbor.

For some reason, his offer of assistance didn't grate on her the way her friend Nancy's did. Nancy pitied Anna and acted as if she were helpless. Levi didn't discount her abilities or try to rescue her. He accepted her as capable.

"I'll be fine." Or as fine as she could be after suffering two rejections in the past few days. Levi hadn't been asking about her life, so her answer was true as far as it went.

"If you're sure." He hesitated. "You have help with the baby during the day?"

"I can always go next door to my *aenti*'s. That's not a problem."

Laying a hand on Jonah's shoulder, Levi steered his brother out the door, but paused on the doorstep. "Anna," he said, a serious note in his tone, "I hope you won't let one person's opinion or actions stop you from progressing."

Anna had only one reason for learning to walk. That reason had vanished.

When she didn't respond, he continued. "I'd be happy to continue your sessions, but I understand if you'd prefer to work with someone else."

Was that his way of letting her know he'd rather she went elsewhere?

Anna wasn't sure she could ever go back to the center. Not feeling this way about him. Maybe if she could get her longing under control. But a sharp pain shot through her at the thought of never seeing him again.

Jonah tugged at her apron. "I love your baby too."

She smiled down at him. Every time she was close to tears, he lightened her spirits. "Ciara loved you too. You did such a good job with her." She gestured toward the bedroom. "This is the first time the baby has slept more than an hour since yesterday."

Anna had no idea how long this quiet would last, but she appreciated every second of peace.

A proud smile swept across Jonah's face.

"Wait here a minute. I'll be right back." She wheeled into the kitchen and packed up the lemon bars. After a quick debate, she added the coffee cake to the package. She wanted to give Levi a gift to repay him for all he'd done for her.

Hurrying to the porch, she handed the snacks to Jonah. "This is a present from Ciara."

Jonah peeked into the bag. Once he saw the lemon bars, he bounced up and down. "*Danke. Danke!*" He threw himself at her and hugged her hard.

"Careful there," Levi warned as he untangled Jonah's arms and took the bag that had almost been squashed in the process.

Her eyes wet with tears, Anna stared after them as they walked past her *aenti*'s house to the driveway. Then they disappeared from view. She went inside and closed the front door, but she parked herself where she could see their buggy drive down the road and out of her life.

Chapter Sixteen

When they left Anna's porch, Levi tried not to let the dragging on his heart slow his steps. He needed to accept his defeat and walk away with dignity. Anna belonged to another man. He'd made a mistake in not finding out about her relationship before he fell for her.

For the rest of the afternoon, he had to keep pulling his attention back to Jonah. When the day ended, Levi exhaled a long, slow sigh. For once, he didn't have to teach any classes. Usually, his one Saturday off each month from the center meant all-day sessions at the firehouse. After chores, he'd go up to his room rather than sit around with the family. He needed time to heal.

At home, Jonah helped with the horse after Levi un-hooked the buggy. Then his brother snatched the paper bag from the seat and rushed into the house waving it.

"Look, Betty," Jonah called as he banged through the back door into the kitchen.

Levi trudged along the walkway in time to hear Betty questioning Jonah.

Betty peered into the bag. "Your favorite snack. Where did you get these?" She raised questioning eyes to Levi.

The spicy smell of meat loaf greeted him. Instead of answering her question, he headed to the sink to wash up for supper.

Jonah was more than happy to answer. "Anna gave it to me."

"Anna? The girl who brought you home the other night?" His hands soapy and water still running, Levi froze. "You know her?"

"*Jah*, and I must say I approve of your choice. Jonah does too. He couldn't stop talking about her."

Levi needed to rinse his hands and stop wasting water, but his racing thoughts kept him stuck in place. How much did his *aenti* know about Anna? Had they had a chance to talk? What if she'd asked about Anna's family? What if they'd talked about him? What would Anna say?

Betty never would have asked Anna if Levi was her special friend. Sanity returned. He rubbed his hands to remove the last of the soap and snapped off the water.

"She's a sweet girl," Betty said to him. "And she was so kind to Jonah."

Levi thought so too. He loved everything about her. Except for one thing. She'd never be his.

"You don't know how happy this makes me. I really worried about Jonah adjusting to a new female, but he seems to love Anna. I can go to Fort Plain with a light heart."

Intending to tell the truth, Levi turned from the sink. But at his *aenti*'s glowing face, he choked back the words. If he said Anna wouldn't be helping them and that she'd never be his girlfriend, Betty would insist on staying here.

All evening, his conscience pricked him. Several times, his mind drifted off as he wrestled with being honest or ruining Betty's romance.

* * *

As soon as Levi was out of sight, Anna had slumped in her chair. If only those few minutes when they'd gazed at each other had been real. She'd never experienced such a soul-to-soul bond. Had it all been her imagination?

Maybe she'd conjured it up because she was overtired. Perhaps, after a nap, she'd be more clearheaded. Anna wheeled into the bedroom as quietly as she could to avoid waking Ciara and lifted herself onto the bed.

She stretched out, but her mind raced. Resting during the day seemed lazy. She'd never questioned if other young mothers napped, but somehow she couldn't picture them neglecting their duties . . .

Hand in hand, she strolled down to a riverbank with Levi. Jonah rambled along behind them.

A shrill siren split the air.

Had that been a loud splash? Had Jonah fallen in?

Frantic, Anna searched the water for him as the shrieking grew louder.

She startled awake, her body on high alert, her heart pounding against aching ribs. Where was she? What was that noise?

Why was she in bed in the middle of the day? For a moment, the nightmare strangled all coherent thought. She was still in the hospital.

Then the bedroom came into focus around her. And the screeching beside her turned into Ciara.

How long had she been sleeping? And how long had the baby been crying? If they found out she'd neglected the small girl, Anna would never get certified.

The last vestiges of the dream still lingered. She wanted

to stay in that fantasy world where she could walk. One where Levi held her hand.

But Ciara needed to be changed, fed, and comforted. Anna heaved herself into the wheelchair. Sleeping during the day made her mind too fuzzy to concentrate. She needed to keep a clear head to care for a baby.

Wheeling over to the cradle, she picked up the crying baby. Ciara arched her back and fought being held. Anna feared the baby would flip out of her arms and land on the floor. How would she pick up Ciara if that happened? And what if the baby hurt herself and Anna couldn't reach her?

Clinging tightly to the flailing baby, Anna wheeled to the low dressing table shelf they'd set up as a makeshift changing table. She grabbed a diaper and fresh clothes. She applied a thick layer of cream on the raging diaper rash and managed to redress the squalling baby.

Then clutching Ciara close, Anna headed into the kitchen to warm a bottle. For once, Ciara's lips closed on the bottle, and she sucked greedily.

Anna nuzzled her while she drank. "That's the way, little one. You're safe and loved here."

Once Ciara had finished her bottle, Anna burped her. Singing a low, soft hymn, she rocked the baby. A tiny frown between her brows, Ciara focused on Anna's moving lips and snuggled closer to Anna's vibrating chest.

"Hasn't anyone ever sung to you, sweetie?" Anna began another song.

The front door clicked open.

"Anna?" Emily called softly. "Is everything all right?"

Reluctant to disturb Ciara's concentration, Anna didn't answer. She hoped her cousin could hear the singing.

Emily entered the kitchen, and her brows shot up. "She's quiet."

"Jonah got her to sleep, and she just woke up." At least Anna prayed that Ciara hadn't been crying long.

"I hope you got some rest."

Although her cousin wouldn't judge her, Anna was reluctant to admit she'd slept too. She glanced at the clock. "I had a two-hour nap. Ciara slept even longer than that."

"Terrific. I hope she'll do that tonight and let you get some sleep."

"Me too. I wish I could keep Jonah here to hold her. He seems to have a calming touch."

"*Jah*, he sure did. That was the quietest Ciara's been since she arrived." Emily set a steaming casserole dish on the counter. "*Mamm* made extra. She figured you might be exhausted after being up all night."

"*Danke*." Anna hadn't even thought about supper. Not that she was hungry. The pie she'd eaten earlier lay in her stomach like a leaden lump.

"What's the matter?" Emily asked. "You look so sad. You thinking about Gabe?"

Anna shook her head. Dreams of Levi had driven all thoughts of Gabe from her mind. If she confided that, would her cousin consider her fickle?

Emily's right brow arched. "No? Maybe that handsome guy from this morning caught your attention. I know he caught mine."

"Emily!" Anna spoke much too sharply. But the idea of her cousin and Levi . . .

Her cousin giggled. "Gotcha."

Sometimes Emily sounded like the *Englischers* she worked with at the restaurant. Anna couldn't meet her eyes.

"Seriously, Anna, I'm not interested in him. But I could tell you were."

"You could?" The leaden lump in her stomach grew

into a heavy rock. No wonder Levi had turned so cold and distant.

"Don't worry. I'm positive he didn't notice." Emily's tone turned teasing. "Besides, he appeared as fascinated with you as you were with him."

"He is not," Anna burst out, close to tears. If anything, he'd backed away fast.

"Don't be so sure about that. Not with the way he kept staring at you when you weren't looking." Emily made mooning eyes at Anna.

"That's not true," Anna snapped. Then she hesitated. "Is it?"

"All I know is what I saw."

"Did you really?" Anna sounded desperate, but she didn't care. Was it possible?

"Would I lie to you?"

"*Neh*, but—"

Emily put her hands on her hips. "But what?"

"You do like to tease."

"*Ach*, Anna, I'd never tease about something so important." Her cousin leaned over and hugged her.

Caught between them, baby Ciara squawked, then wailed.

Emily sighed. "So much for the peace and quiet."

Anna didn't want the baby's screams to interrupt their conversation. She wanted to know what Emily had seen. "Can we talk in the living room for a while?"

"You mean can we screech at each other over that noise?" Emily rolled her eyes in Ciara's direction and raised her voice so she could be heard. Her rueful smile made it clear the baby's crying didn't upset her. "I have to get back for dinner. Not much else to tell. Levi kept sneaking glances at you in the way guys do when they like you."

Anna stayed in the same spot, jiggling Ciara and murmuring soothing words that did little to calm the shrieking. But she barely heard the racket.

Emily's words echoed in Anna's mind. Her cousin had a gift for reading people. Had Levi really shown an interest in her? If so, what had happened?

When their eyes met, she'd been sure they'd connected deeply. But soon after that, he'd grown cold. Had she done something to scare him off?

The next morning, Levi avoided additional questions as they got ready for church. The service and meal kept them apart, but Levi hoped Betty didn't share her happiness about Levi and Anna. If she mentioned Anna's last name, someone in the community was sure to know her or her uncle's family.

But Betty climbed into the buggy to go home, her face aglow. "Everyone is so excited for me. I can't believe I'm leaving tomorrow."

Levi sighed and relaxed. She must have spent all of her time in the kitchen talking about her own plans rather than his.

"Several ladies offered to help you if you need it, but I told them your special friend would be fixing meals and cleaning. They were so surprised to hear that."

"Wh—what did you tell them?"

"Don't worry. I know how private you are. I only said you're dating someone from the center."

"But I'm not—"

Betty talked right over him. "I didn't tell them her

name. Besides, I only know her first name. I didn't want to admit I didn't even know her last name."

The hurt look in his *aenti*'s eyes made Levi feel awful. But the light in her eyes would go out completely if he told her the truth. He took a deep breath. "Betty?"

"*Ach*, Levi. Can you believe I'll be leaving at five tomorrow morning? I didn't tell Vern I'd be coming. Just in case something went wrong."

Something like him telling her he had no special friend?

"I packed my suitcase yesterday. When we get home, can you carry it down to the porch? I want to be ready before the driver arrives."

With his *aenti* looking as giddy as a schoolgirl, Levi couldn't bear to give her bad news. Would it hurt to wait and save the truth until she returned? He could always ask someone from church to come by to help if he and his brothers couldn't manage the cooking and chores.

Betty chattered the rest of the way home, so Levi had no chance to tell her anything. Or was that just an excuse to hide his hurt?

Betty had already left when Levi woke at dawn on Monday morning. She'd put a breakfast casserole in the oven and a note on the table.

I'm so happy you've chosen to court a lovely girl. This will be a good chance for her to see what's it like to clean up after all four of you. At least I know she's a good cook. That coffee cake is delicious. I'll be praying for all of you while I'm gone.

Levi stood in the kitchen, holding the note and imagining what it would be like to have Anna stopping by to cook and clean. To see her every day.

He slammed a wall down in his mind to block off those thoughts. But even by reminding himself Anna was off-limits, he couldn't wall off his heart.

Concentrate on other things. Keep busy. He raced through doing chores, serving breakfast, packing lunches. But nothing kept images of Anna away. Worst of all, washing and drying dishes brought back Saturday in vivid color.

Jonah tugged at his pant leg. "Time to go?"

Levi glanced at the clock. With all his dawdling and daydreaming, he'd lost track of time. If they didn't leave now, they'd be late.

Leaving the last two plates and the casserole dish soaking in the sink, Levi dried his hands. He left the washed dishes draining on the counter. Betty would be appalled they'd walked out the door when the kitchen wasn't spotless.

If Jonah hadn't pointed to their lunch bags, Levi would have run out without them. He dropped Jonah off at the special school he attended. All the way to the center, Levi had to keep dragging his mind from the other day.

Working in the exercise room didn't help. His gaze strayed to the parallel bars. Pictures of Anna flooded his vision. The whole room seemed filled with her presence. Every time the door opened, he looked up expecting to meet her smile.

At a tap on the door, Levi swung around. Three-thirty. Too early for Anna. Jonah pressed his beaming face against the glass. The van had dropped him off after school.

Levi opened the door. "Do you have an aide?"

Jonah's forehead crinkled. "Diane's not here."

"But I am." An Amish girl who looked to be about sixteen waved to Levi. "I'm Kathryn. I'll be his aide until Diane comes back."

Amanda, the eight-year-old who rode in the same van as Jonah, came to the door. Levi waved good-bye to Jonah and Kathryn, and then stepped aside so Amanda could enter.

"Hi, Amanda." Levi tried to paste a grin on his face. As the day wore on, though, his facial muscles became less and less cooperative.

Instead of answering, Amanda tilted her head to one side and stared at him funny. Perhaps his attempt at a smile appeared more like a grimace. As he worked with her and the rest of the afternoon drop-ins, he forced himself to keep his instructions cheerful and upbeat.

After the last boy left at five, Levi's spirits plummeted. No final appointment. He'd finished for the day. Anna wouldn't be coming through that door. Never again.

Time to go. Levi shut the door to the exercise room and slogged down the hall to pick up Jonah. His brother jumped up and down to see him.

Jonah's greeting warmed Levi's heart. "How was he?" he asked Kathryn.

"He's so good." She turned to Jonah. "We had fun today, didn't we?"

Jonah waved the fistful of papers. "I did all this."

Once again, seeing the simple coloring pages with alphabet letters on them sent Levi into a downward spiral of guilt. Only, this time, he'd added another load. Guilt over his attraction to a married woman.

Chapter Seventeen

One eye on the clock, Anna shoveled cold leftover casserole into her mouth with one hand, while she jiggled Ciara with the other. Emily would be here soon, and Anna still needed to change her clothes.

But every time she set the baby down, the ear-shattering screams began. When she held Ciara, the shrieks calmed to whimpering. At least Anna could think if she cradled the baby. Although maybe she'd be better off with the distraction. Then her mind wouldn't keep wandering to Levi.

Emily poked her head in the front door. "Are you ready to go?"

"Almost. Could you take Ciara for a few minutes?"

"I'll take her over to *Mamm* and be right back."

Anna hurried into a fresh dress and black half apron. With all the one-handed push-ups she'd done, she managed to smooth the skirt under her a little at a time.

Emily returned. "Need any help?"

"I did it." Anna sat back in the chair, panting.

"Ever since you started exercising, you've been doing

so much more for yourself. Today's Monday. How come you didn't go to the center?"

Anna pretended to be busy checking her hair and adjusting her *kapp*.

"Because of Gabe?" Emily's soft tone was filled with sympathy. "You really shouldn't let that stop you."

"Levi said the same thing the other day."

When her cousin studied her, Anna wished she hadn't mentioned his name.

"You told Levi about Gabe?"

"*Neh*. Last week I told him I had an important meeting on Thursday, and that's why walking was so important. He asked how it went. I just said it didn't go well."

"How long was he here? Seems like you discussed quite a few things."

Anna fiddled with the brake on her chair to keep from meeting Emily's curious gaze. "We should go. Or we'll be late."

"Changing the subject?" Emily teased, but the determination behind her question made it clear she intended to ferret out the truth.

"Maybe," Anna mumbled.

Adopting a mock-stern frown, Emily put her hands on her hips and blocked the front door. "We're not leaving until you tell me."

"Come on, Em. We're already late."

"A minute or two won't make that much difference. They'll probably only introduce the instructors."

"This is my first class for certification. I don't want to miss any of it."

"Then why are you holding us up? It can be a two-second answer."

"Oh, all right. They stayed to have a piece of cake, so we talked for a while." A pretty long while once he got into his story about Jonah.

"So, what's going on between the two of you?"

"Nothing." *Absolutely nothing.*

Emily shook her head. "That's not true. I saw the way he looked at you. And with the way you keep evading my questions, I'm guessing you have feelings for him too."

"You're mistaken." Anna intended her clipped tone to end her cousin's prying. If Emily pushed much harder, she'd discover Anna's secrets. "Let's go."

"All right. But don't think you're escaping. I intend to find out all about this."

And Anna planned to block her questions. Right now, though, they needed to leave for class.

When they arrived at the firehouse meeting room, Anna let Emily push her across the parking lot and into the room to save time. If Anna had propelled herself into the room, she'd have stopped dead.

In the front of the room, standing next to the man giving the introductions, stood Levi.

His gaze had been fixed on the man at the podium, but when the door squeaked closed, Levi gazed in her direction. Their eyes locked.

All the air in the room seemed to have been sucked away. Anna's lungs collapsed from lack of air. Her chest ached, but she couldn't breathe.

Words vibrated through the microphone. "And our other first aid instructor this evening is Levi King."

His gaze stayed glued to hers. Good thing they had trained CPR instructors here because she was going to need one.

* * *

At a sharp jab in his ribs, Levi tore his gaze from Anna's.

Ron put a hand over the mike. "Umm, Levi? You planning to speak?"

"Huh?" Levi blinked and tried to bring himself back to the class, but questions swirled through his brain.

What was Anna doing here? Was she really here? Or had he imagined her? Heat rose to his cheeks as he remembered his fantasy of their lips meeting during CPR.

He longed to take another look, but Ron elbowed him again.

"You talking or what?"

In a daze, Levi stepped over to the microphone and went into his usual spiel. Thank goodness he had done this so many times, he'd memorized his whole speech. Otherwise, he would have been blundering through a mangled explanation. He avoided looking toward the back corner of the room for fear he'd lose his place and stumble to a stop.

When it came time to divide the room into two sections, he longed to take the right side, where Anna sat, but he waved Ron in that direction and took the left side. He couldn't prevent his gaze from straying in that direction more often than it should. Each time he did, she looked away.

He tried to tell himself he was only curious as to why she was taking the classes. And why had she come with her cousin instead of her husband? Amish couples usually did things like this together.

After the class ended, Levi agonized about speaking to

Anna. If he ignored her, she might think him rude. But if he chased after her, she might get the wrong impression. Politeness won. Or maybe it was the desire to be with her.

"Anna," he called as she headed to the door.

When she turned to look at him, his heart pounded out a rhythm that spelled danger. This hadn't been such a good idea after all.

Anna's cousin leaned down and whispered something. Then she steered Anna to one side, out of the crowds swarming toward the exit.

Levi walked toward them, wiping his sweaty palms on his pants. The easy friendship they'd shared in the exercise room had disappeared. Tension and uncertainty had taken its place.

"Hi, Levi." Emily's overly bright greeting contrasted with Anna's quiet hello.

His heart sank. She'd misinterpreted his friendly gesture. Or she'd sensed his hidden motive.

To defuse her suspicions, he directed his question to Emily. "What are you doing here?"

She laughed nervously. "Taking a class. Aren't we allowed to?"

Ach, he'd made a fool of himself. His question had come out wrong. "Of course. I didn't mean that the way it sounded. I just wondered why both of you were taking the class." He meant *together* instead of with their husbands.

Once again, Emily answered. "In case the children have accidents."

Her words stabbed him. They echoed Anna's words when she'd asked him about CPR. He tried not to reveal his attraction for Anna or his aching heart. "It's a good skill to have. You never know when you might need . . ."

He'd made the mistake of glancing at Anna, and the

sympathy in her eyes revealed she remembered his story about Jonah. If Levi wasn't careful, he'd get swept into an even greater blunder.

Anna's heart went out to him. His businesslike attitude didn't fully mask his deep-seated pain. His brother's tragedy must have spurred him to help others.

If they ever talked again, she'd use this as an example of another reason why Jonah's accident had been God's will. If it hadn't happened, would Levi have been motivated to teach first aid and CPR? How many lives had he saved by doing this?

Anna had been sitting tongue-tied while Emily and Levi talked. She broke into their conversation. "So, you teach these classes?"

A dead silence followed, and she berated herself. What an inane question. Obviously, he taught them. She'd just spent an evening listening to him talk and stealing surreptitious glances while he instructed the other group.

Levi blinked in surprise and focused on her. "*Jah*, I teach them here at the firehouse and at the local recreation center."

"That must keep you busy." What was wrong with her? She wanted him to see her as a witty and sparkling conversationalist. Instead, she kept babbling.

"Sometimes I teach four nights a week and on Saturdays."

"That's a lot," Emily exclaimed.

Anna tried not to let the tiny spark of jealousy kindle a blaze. Levi had made it clear there was nothing between them. What if he ended up liking Emily? The thought sent a stabbing pain through her heart.

Please don't fall for her.

It hurt to know Levi had no interest in her. Watching him court Emily would be devastating.

"It can be overwhelming sometimes. Especially right now when my *aenti*'s out of town." Levi stared down at the floor and confessed, "I left dishes in the sink when I came here tonight, and the dinner I made for my brothers . . ." He made a face. "Let's just say it was barely edible."

Emily stared at him with a puzzled frown. "You're doing the cooking and taking care of your brothers? What about your *mamm*?"

A look of sadness settled over Levi's face. "My aunt came to stay with us after *Daed* died ten years ago. *Mamm* passed away a few years later. Betty's cared for us ever since."

Poor Levi. He'd lost his daed *around the time of Jonah's accident, but he'd also lost his* mamm.

"I'm so sorry," her cousin said. "Anna lost both her parents too."

"I didn't know." Levi gave her a sympathetic glance. "It's not easy."

"*Neh*, it's not. I didn't know your *mamm* had passed too. I'm sorry." Those two words seemed inadequate for his losses, but Anna didn't know what else to say.

"*Danke*." His sorrow still shone in his eyes as he nodded to her and Emily.

Before her cousin could capture his attention again, Anna asked, "Will your *aenti* be gone long?"

"Twelve days." Levi's rueful laugh sounded a bit hollow. "When we planned it, that didn't sound like a long time. But now that I'm trying to take over all her chores, it's only been one day, and I'm struggling to keep up. I'd better figure it out quickly, or my brothers will starve."

"Anna's a good cook," Emily said.

"I know." Levi flashed Anna an appreciative smile.

Her heart sang, then sank as Emily stared from one to the other.

"You do?" she asked.

"I had some of her coffee cake. My *aenti* praised it, which is a huge compliment. Betty rarely does that for anyone's cooking." Levi's smile faded. A melancholy look entered his eyes.

Emily brightened. "Anna loves to help people. I'm sure she'd be happy to make you some meals."

Levi shook his head. "*Neh*, she has enough to do with the baby and—and all the rest," he added lamely.

"I wouldn't mind." It would be one way to pay him back for all he'd done for her. And she'd get to see him sometimes now that she wasn't going to the center. She hoped he'd agree.

His brows drew together, almost as if he were in pain. "You have too much to do."

Although he might be right with Ciara needing so much time and attention, Anna didn't want to lose this opportunity to be a tiny part of his life. "It's not quite two weeks, and it's no problem to double or triple recipes."

"*Gut*," Emily said. "It's settled then. If you can handle things tomorrow, we'll bring some casseroles to the next class."

Levi turned to Anna. "I really don't want to put you to any trouble."

"You won't be," Emily insisted. "But we'd better go so Anna can get Ciara into bed. See you at the CPR class on Wednesday."

* * *

The lights flickered. Ron glanced their way. "You almost done?" he called to Levi. "If not, can you lock up?"

"We're, um . . ." Levi didn't want to chase Anna and Emily away. Especially not Anna. But they'd said they needed to go.

Emily waved to Ron. "Thanks for the class. We're just leaving." She took hold of the wheelchair handles and pushed Anna toward the door.

Ron waited until they exited to turn out all but the safety lights. Then he waited for Levi to cross the floor.

"Well, well, well. Looks like someone caught your eye in this class." Ron cuffed Levi playfully. "About time."

"They're just, um, friends." That's all they could ever be. "Anna used to come to the center."

Emily's buggy was pulling out as Levi and Ron reached the parking lot. He stared after it, bereft. Now that Anna had stopped coming to the center, he'd never expected to see her again. But she'd be coming to Wednesday's CPR class. And her cousin had offered to bring meals.

As much as Levi enjoyed Anna's cooking, the thought that he'd be eating the same meals she'd share with her husband and children made him nauseous.

He pushed that from his mind as he drove home and took care of the horse. Normally, he could just flop into bed after teaching his evening classes. Tonight, he had a pile of dishes waiting for him, a sticky floor to mop, and meals to plan for tomorrow.

If Betty had known Levi had no girlfriend, she'd have left casseroles for a few days. But she'd wanted Anna to have a chance to demonstrate her homemaking skills. The only problem was Anna already had someone to practice on.

Chapter Eighteen

Anna faced Emily as they pulled out of the parking lot. "I can't believe you did that."

"Did what?" Emily's fake show of innocence didn't fool Anna.

"You know what. Telling Levi I'd make meals."

"Are you saying you don't want to help a family of boys who might go hungry for the next two weeks?"

Anna blew out a loud, exasperated breath. "I doubt they'll go hungry. I'm sure people in their church will help out. And if they get desperate, they can go to a restaurant."

"How do you know they can afford that?"

"I don't."

"See?" Emily sat up straighter, a triumphant smile on her lips. "Besides, you jumped right in and volunteered."

Anna pinched her lips together a minute. She had, hadn't she? "But—but what could I say? I wouldn't do it? That would be rude."

"And the only reason you agreed was to be polite?"

"Of course," Anna snapped.

Emily's piercing stare pinpointed Anna's fib. "You sure?"

Anna turned away, pretending to study the passing

landscape. She and Emily both knew perfectly well why she'd gone along with her cousin's suggestion. The nice thing about Emily was that she'd never force Anna to admit her underlying reason.

They approached a stop sign, and Emily slowed the horse. When the buggy was still, she studied Anna's face. "Did I make a mistake?"

"If I make meals for him, what will people think? What will he think?"

"That you have a kind heart. Besides, you're doing it for Jonah and his other brothers, not just for Levi, right?"

"*Jah*." But in her heart, she was doing it for him.

"So, there you are. You can say it's because you're worried about his younger brothers. They are younger, right?"

"I think so." Anna tried to remember what Levi had said. He had one brother a little older than Jonah. And the baby had been two years younger. His *daed* had already died, and his *mamm* passed away a few years later. Most likely she'd had no more children. Levi hadn't mentioned his *mamm* remarrying. If she had, his *aenti* probably wouldn't have stayed to help care for them.

"Perfect."

A car honked behind them.

"*Ach*, we can discuss this at home." Emily clucked to the horse, and it trotted off. "We don't need to get rear-ended by an impatient driver."

As soon as they passed through the intersection, Emily pulled onto the right shoulder, and the driver zoomed around them. "*Gut.* I didn't want him on our tail the whole way home."

They passed two farms before Emily spoke again. "Why don't we both make some meals for the family? That way, no one will think you're interested in him."

Emily's suggestion made sense, but once again a small shoot of jealousy took root. Suppose Levi ended up preferring Emily? And her meals?

With Ciara screaming in her arms, Anna collected ingredients and made casseroles. A small one for her. A large one for Levi.

A loud knock on the door signaled Emily had arrived. She popped into the kitchen dangling a padded baby carrier. "*Mamm* used this last night when she watched Ciara, and it seemed to help."

Anna appreciated her *aenti*'s thoughtfulness. "I'll try anything to comfort Ciara."

"You look exhausted." Emily held out her arms. "Why don't I hold her while you put this on? We can take turns holding her."

"That'd be great." She handed over the shrieking baby. "How does this thing go?"

With Emily's help, Anna adjusted the buckles and straps around her. Sliding the bucking baby into the carrier proved a challenge. Emily tried several times before she managed to secure both kicking legs in position.

After she'd tucked Ciara in, Emily stared at the heaving bundle, the flailing legs. "Good thing she's so small. Are you uncomfortable?"

"*Jah*. But it's easier than trying to hold a wriggling baby. This way, I know she won't fall."

"True. But you've had her for hours. Do you want me to take a turn?"

Anna shook her head and patted the baby's back. "I want her to get used to me."

"Did you get any sleep last night?"

"Sleep? What's that?" Anna tried to turn it into a joke, but it ended on a half sob.

At Emily's concerned gaze, she smoothed her face to project an air of calmness. But with fifteen-minute snatches of sleep three times last night, she wasn't sure she'd been successful.

"You don't have to keep Ciara during the day. She's *Mamm*'s responsibility. Take her over to the house."

Anna shook her head. She wanted to see if she could reach this nervous, restless baby. "Your *mamm* gave me a book about caring for babies born to drug-addicted mothers. I read that cuddling them helps a lot."

"But you need to take care of yourself too. *Mamm* has my sisters to help. You're here by yourself."

"I want to see if I can calm Ciara." Anna hoped she and this tiny baby might bond. Right now, Ciara's downy hair brushed her chin. Anna tipped her head and rested it against Ciara's. Wrapping her arms around the baby in the carrier, Anna hummed a hymn.

The kicks to her ribs slowed. Ciara pressed her head closer to Anna. Her shrill screeching quieted to hiccupping sobs.

"It would be a miracle if she goes to sleep."

Anna worried that breaking off her humming might disturb Ciara, so she only nodded. Keeping one arm tight around the baby, Anna went back to making casseroles.

Having Emily here made everything easier. Her cousin opened cans and jars, scooted around to get dishes and spoons, rinsed pots and utensils.

For an hour, Anna hummed and cuddled. Ciara's restlessness slowed, then stopped. Soon her chest rose and fell against Anna's. "I think she's sleeping," Anna whispered.

"Thank the Lord."

"I wish I could put her in the cradle, but I'm afraid it'll wake her."

"If it's not too uncomfortable, maybe it would be better not to disturb her."

"I know." Anna sighed. She could use some sleep herself. "I wish I had Jonah here to help."

"And his brother." Emily waggled her eyebrows.

Of course. Anna would never say that out loud. Seeing Levi last night had only increased that longing.

"Well, one nice thing about all these casseroles"— Emily paused for effect—"he'll have to return the dishes. It's a good way to guarantee you'll see him again."

"Em," Anna warned. Levi's rejection had cut deeply enough. She didn't need her cousin twisting a knife into that wound.

Her cousin's sly smile made it clear she didn't plan to drop the subject.

"Please stop," Anna pleaded. "He'd never be interested in me."

Emily stared at her in surprise. "Why not?"

"Because . . . because . . ." Anna's eyes filled with tears. Lack of sleep and the recent rejections made her overly emotional.

"*Ach*, Anna, I didn't mean to make you cry. We don't have to talk about him if you don't want to, but I hate to see you pass up a chance for happiness."

Happiness? More like heartbreak. Her cousin hadn't seen Levi's eyes filled with coldness. A coldness that turned Anna's insides to ice.

She and Levi had shared a few intimate glances. Then like a steel wall clanking down, his face had gone blank. The light in his eyes flickered out.

Emily stayed silent while Anna poured all her love into each casserole she made.

Levi spent all day Tuesday and Wednesday longing for the class to start. He arrived early and paced the floor.

"Would you stop that?" Ron said. "You're driving me crazy."

"Stop what?" Levi puzzled over Ron's request. He hadn't been doing anything, not even helping Ron set up.

"Back and forth. Back and forth. You're acting like a caged animal." He smirked. "You can't wait for those girls to arrive, eh?"

"What girls?" Even to Levi's ears that question sounded feeble. They both knew who Ron meant.

He laughed. "How many Amish girls do we get in these classes?"

"Not many," Levi mumbled. Too bad the ones that came were married. He didn't know about Anna's cousin, but Levi had eyes for only one girl. And that girl remained off-limits.

"And who spent hours after class on Monday giving them private lessons?"

"I wasn't giving them private—" He broke off at the grin on Ron's face.

"Aha, so you weren't talking about first-aid techniques?"

Levi ignored the peals of laughter. "Why don't we push the tables back and set up for class?"

"That would be more helpful than your pacing and fantasizing." Ron's eyebrows bobbed up and down in an *I-know-exactly-what-you-were-thinking* expression.

But he had no idea what Levi had been thinking or wishing. He wished he'd met Anna years ago so he could have courted her first. He would have loved being the one who'd worked with her from the beginning on her recovery. He would have loved seeing her joy as she conquered each new challenge.

"Umm, Levi?" Ron waved a hand in front of his face. "You planning to help with this class?"

"Of course."

"I'm wondering if you can even keep your mind on the material."

Levi had been wondering that himself. Teaching CPR to Anna filled his thoughts. If only . . .

"Hey, Levi, you didn't answer me."

"What?" Levi dragged his mind away from images of Anna's lips.

"Should I handle the class alone and let you work with the two ladies *privately*?" Ron closed his eyes and pursed his lips into a kiss. "Ooo, let me practice with you, Rachel."

"Her name's not Rachel. It's Anna."

Ron's eyes popped open. "Anna, huh?"

Levi couldn't believe he'd fallen for Ron's trap. If he hadn't been consumed by thoughts of Anna, he'd have been more cautious. "And Emily." He hoped suggesting another name might be a distraction.

"Sounds like Anna's your main interest, though."

"She's married." Levi had to keep reminding himself of that painful fact.

"You're going after a married woman?"

"Of course not." He'd never do that. He also needed to keep his mind from straying and his heart from leaping when she walked through the door.

But ten minutes later, when Emily and Anna arrived early, his mind and heart forgot his resolve.

Emily pushed Anna through the door because Anna

held a huge wicker basket on her lap. The meals she'd prepared for him. He'd pushed that from his thoughts, half hoping they'd been kidding. The other half hoped they weren't.

Although Emily waved, Levi focused on Anna's tentative smile. She seemed nervous and quickly glanced away. Had she realized his interest?

"Hope there's room in the refrigerator for all this." Emily gestured to the basket.

"I—I'm not sure." Levi could barely keep his mind focused on the food. He forced himself not to stare at Anna.

Emily brushed past him with the wheelchair and headed for the kitchen.

Levi trailed after them. "You seem to know your way around."

"I've helped at plenty of firehouse fundraisers." She lifted the basket from Anna's lap and set it on the counter beside the refrigerator. Then she opened the door and peered inside. "Hmm. We'll need to rearrange things to fit it all in."

"I can do that," Anna volunteered. She moved into place and started consolidating items on the lower shelves. "Why don't you hand me the casserole dishes?"

As Levi stared, Emily lifted dish after dish out of the basket and handed each one to Anna, who stacked them neatly on the top shelf.

"Anna included instructions for cooking each of them." Emily pointed to the neat, hand-printed labels pasted on each dish.

"Hey, Levi, you planning to set out the training manuals and masks?" Ron called. "I'm getting the videos set up. The mannequins are all set out."

"I'd better go." His face burning, Levi threw a quick

danke over his shoulder and headed for the cartons of books.

Ron sidled up next to him as he finished setting books at the last table. "I'm worried those girls may divert your attention. I'll take that half of the classroom."

As much as Levi wished he could work with Anna, Ron was right. Levi needed to be professional. "All right."

"Oh, and when I introduce you this time, will you pay attention?"

"*Jah*. I mean yes."

Ron laughed. "You don't need to translate for me."

The door opened, and other students flowed into the room in a steady stream. Soon, almost all the seats had been taken. Emily and Anna came from the kitchen and slid into place near the front of the room.

How would he concentrate with her so close to the podium? He opened the teacher's manual and pretended to study it, even though after teaching so many classes, he knew it by heart.

Ron stared at him. "You planning to do the intro tonight?"

Levi shook his head and stepped to the side. This time he paid attention to Ron's cues and responded on time. Then Ron stepped aside so Levi could go over the manual and answer any questions. He covered the differences between adults and children.

Once Levi had finished, Ron played a few videos with different scenarios. Then he smiled broadly. "And now the moment you've all been waiting for. Ta-da." He did a drumroll on the podium with his fingers. "The mannequins." With a theatrical gesture, he pointed to the torsos of adults and children as well as some diapered babies scattered around the floor.

While Ron knelt on the floor and demonstrated, Levi

explained the process. "These mannequins will click to show you've pushed hard enough. They also have lights to show your compression rate. Watch for two green lights. Red is too slow. Yellow is too fast."

"Use your face mask for breaths." Ron showed the trainees how to do that, then he jumped to his feet. "We'll be coming around to help you and answer questions. Once you've mastered the skills, we'll time you to make sure you can do at least two minutes of CPR. We'll expect five cycles of compressions and ventilations."

They assigned partners to work together and take turns. At first, Levi turned his back so he wouldn't be tempted. As he circulated among his trainees, he stole glances in Anna's direction, hoping she might need his help when she had to get out of the wheelchair and onto the floor.

After Levi took over the other side of the room, Anna tried to focus on the steps in the manual. First, call for help. Next, check the person. And last, do CPR.

Her mind kept floating back to the day she watched Levi helping Diane. He'd followed all three steps. Anna hadn't watched him long, but he'd told people to call 9-1-1, then he checked Diane before he began the breaths and compressions. Now Anna had to remember those steps and be able to do them.

Ron wove through the group, watching the first person. "Press harder," he said to most of them. "It takes more pressure than you think. You want two green lights."

He stopped beside them, and Emily, who was already kneeling on the mat beside the mannequin, went first. This was a refresher for her, so she did it perfectly the first time.

"Excellent." Ron checked her off the list.

"What about my cousin?" Emily asked him. "Could she do it on a table?"

He pursed his lips. "Hmm. It's fine if you want to practice on a table, but unless you do it on the floor, we can't certify you. I can give you a certificate of attendance to show you took the class."

Emily shook her head. "That won't work. She has to be certified for foster care."

Ron turned to Anna. "Can you get out of the chair and onto the floor?"

"I've never done that, but . . ." She glanced over to Levi, whose gaze seemed to be fixed on her.

He bent to say something to the man he'd been observing. Then he hurried over. "Do you need help, Anna?"

Meeting his caring expression left Anna tongue-tied.

"She has to get on the floor so she can be certified," Emily explained.

"You've never learned to do that?" Levi asked. "Usually they teach that in rehab."

Anna bit her lip. "That's my fault. I refused to waste time on that. All I wanted to do was learn to walk." Surely, Levi had seen her single-minded determination.

"I can help her do this," Levi said to Ron. "Could you work with Carlos?" He gestured toward the man he'd been working with a few minutes ago. "He's fine with the rate, but he needs to press down harder."

Anna's pulse sped up as Levi squatted in front of her. Some of it was nervousness, but the rest came from being so close to him.

"I'm sorry I never taught you this. Getting out won't be too difficult. You've built up your arm muscles and can support your weight on one side."

"Can I help?" Emily asked.

Levi touched the black kneeling mat beneath his feet. "Could you get another one of these from that closet?" He pointed to a door on the far wall. "Anna will have to sit with her legs out."

As Emily hustled off, Levi turned back to Anna. "Lock your brakes. Then slide to the edge of the seat. Once Emily gets back, we'll get the mats ready for you."

"I won't have mats in an emergency," Anna pointed out.

"You may end up with some bruises if there's an emergency. I had to have shards of glass picked out of my knees once, but it's a small price to pay for saving someone's life." His eyes filled with sadness. "Sometimes, though, you're too late."

Was he thinking of Jonah? Or had he lost someone he'd worked on?

"I'm sorry." Anna kept her voice soft so the others around her couldn't hear.

"I tell myself it's God's will, but those failures still haunt me."

That reminded Anna of something she wanted to tell him. "Remember when you asked why God had let Jonah's accident happen?" Without waiting for him to answer, she continued. "Maybe it was so you'd help all these people. Would you have taught these classes otherwise?"

"*Neh* . . ." Levi answered, slow and thoughtful.

"How many lives do you think the people you have trained have saved? Have you ever thought about that?"

His eyes brimmed with admiration and something deeper Anna struggled to name. "*Danke*, Anna. I—" He broke off as Emily appeared waving the mat.

"Can you set it at the end of this one? I want to make Anna as comfortable as possible."

After Emily placed the second mat against the first one, Levi flipped up the footrests and pointed to Anna's side. "If you shift your knees in this direction, you can grab the bar on the opposite side."

From here the floor looked so far away. Could she do this? With Levi and Emily both watching, she had to be brave. She'd deal with any bumps and bruises later.

"Now this will be a stretch, but reach your right hand down to the floor." He patted a spot far from the wheelchair. "Set it here. That arm will be your support." Then he scooted back. "I'm going to give you room to sit."

Anna stretched her arm down and swallowed hard. Too far from the floor. If she bent over any farther, she'd topple out onto her head.

"It's all right." Levi extended his arms. "I'm here to catch you if you fall, but your left arm should hold you. Reach a few more inches. Palm onto the floor."

When Anna hesitated, Levi nodded toward the wheelchair handles. "Emily, could you hold the chair so it doesn't tip? It shouldn't, but it might make Anna feel safer."

How did Levi know what worried her? Once Emily grasped the handles, Anna had no more excuses. The worst that might happen was she'd tumble. And land right in Levi's arms. Wait, why would that be bad?

She took a deep breath and tilted forward until she touched the place Levi had indicated. Her left arm shook as she clung to the bar for support.

"You did it. Now all you have to do is transfer your weight to your right arm."

Levi's reassuring tone gave her courage. She shifted and, for a moment, her body hung suspended in midair. Then her arm buckled, and she thudded onto the mat.

"*Ach*, Anna, are you all right?" Emily leaned over the chair.

The fright from the sudden thump had knocked all the air from her lungs. She closed her eyes and tried to draw in a breath. She'd only been a few feet from the floor, and the mat had cushioned her fall. Rather than being hurt, she was embarrassed.

"Hey, Anna," Levi whispered close to her ear. "You did it. You're sitting on the floor."

Anna glanced up at him. "But I fell there."

"Are you hurt?"

"Not really. Just my pride." Something she shouldn't be worried about anyway. At least, until she realized most of the other trainees had been staring at her. Anna's cheeks burned.

"Ignore them. You did fine." Levi beamed at her. "Now you can practice on the mannequin." He moved the adult torso into place. "You're lower than those who are kneeling, so sit up as tall as you can and lean over to keep your shoulders above your hands."

Emily stood over her. "And you definitely have to press much harder than you think."

Anna put the face mask on the mannequin and pressed down. Then she tilted the mannequin's head and practiced her breaths. Then she placed a hand on the chest and interlocked her fingers. Praying for extra strength, she lifted herself and slammed down on the chest.

A yellow light blinked on.

Emily giggled. "Wow, Anna. I hope you never have to give me CPR."

"That's all right." Levi shot Emily a *please-don't-tease-her* look. "Remember you've strengthened your arm muscles so you can support your whole body. You have a lot of power behind your presses."

It was difficult enough being the center of attention as others sneaked peeks at her or stared openly. It was even worse to have set off the warning light. Emily's comment had scared Anna into overreacting. She'd worried about being too weak.

If everyone would leave her alone, she could try to get the pressure right.

Levi must have sensed her discomfort. He moved so he blocked her from the view of most people. Anna lifted grateful eyes to thank him, but their gazes met and held.

Chapter Nineteen

Look away, Levi. You have a job to do. He was supposed to circulate around the room, checking all of the trainees. But they all faded into the background when Anna was present. He only wanted to spend time with her.

Behind them, Ron cleared his throat. Levi jumped to his feet. "Keep practicing, Anna. You'll get it."

"I'm sure she will," Ron said dryly. He dropped his voice so no one else could hear. "Especially with all the special attention she received from the instructor."

"She needed extra help to get down to floor level." The defensiveness in Levi's voice highlighted his guilt.

"I know." Ron pinned him with a pointed glare. "Once she got out of the wheelchair, though . . ."

"I tried to give her some adaptive techniques for sitting instead of kneeling."

Ron held up a hand. "We're wasting valuable time arguing when we should be paying attention to our trainees. I think it'd be best if you go back to the other side of the room." He handed Levi the list. "Those are the ones who've passed so far."

"Mine's over there." Levi pointed to his paper, which he'd left beside Anna's mat.

"Figures." Ron headed in Anna's direction.

The last thing Levi needed was to get his coworker upset. He and Ron did many of these classes. They'd always worked well together and been good friends. For the rest of the session, Levi concentrated on checking and assisting each of the students who hadn't yet passed and tried to keep his glances at Anna to a minimum.

Some students also did CPR on the children and baby mannequins. Anna remained on the floor for those. A quick peek at her working on the infant hit him hard. She had a baby at home, so he had no business pining for her.

That time, when he turned away, he didn't look around again. Although he wished he could coach her, he didn't even watch when it was time for her to return to the wheelchair. To make sure he didn't peek, he kept his back to that side of the room as he collected the kneeling mats and mannequins.

By the time he'd stored them in the closet and gone to the podium, Anna sat at her place at the table. Ron was still gathering the remaining training items. Levi debated about helping him, but then one of the trainees got up to assist.

"Great job, everyone," Levi said, struggling to keep his attention from lingering in one spot. "Once you take this multiple-choice test, we'll grade it right away. Those who pass both parts will leave tonight with their CPR certification cards."

He and Ron worked in tandem to grade the tests and hand out cards. The room slowly cleared. He let Ron check Emily's and Anna's answers, while the two of them headed to the kitchen.

Levi tapped his pen against the tabletop as he waited for the last stragglers to finish. *Click. Click. Click.*

Ron set a hand on Levi's arm. "Can you stop that infernal noise?" He kept his voice low. "We have people still taking the test."

"Sorry." Levi hadn't even realized what he'd been doing. He twisted his head, hoping to catch a glimpse of Anna in the kitchen.

At Ron's long, exasperated sigh, he whipped back around.

"Looks like she's done." Ron waved toward a girl near the back. "Why don't you check her answers? Then go on out to the kitchen before you drive me crazy. I'll handle these other two." He held certification cards for Anna and Emily. "Oh, and why don't you give these out?" Then he winked.

In record time, Levi finished looking over the other test. He handed the girl her card. "Congratulations."

Before she even collected her things, he headed off to the kitchen. Ron shook his head as Levi rushed past.

"There you are," Emily trilled as he walked through the doorway.

Levi held out their cards.

"*Danke.*" Anna barely glanced up as she reached for hers. She seemed more interested in her certification card than in him.

Emily smiled at him. "The basket's all packed up. You should have enough in here for five days or so."

"You didn't have to do that."

Emily handed him the heavy wicker basket. "Neither of us could bear to think of your younger brothers going hungry. Or you, of course. Anna was especially worried about that."

A horrified expression crossed Anna's face, and she glared up at her cousin.

That made it awkward. Levi didn't know how to respond. Better to ignore that comment. Or pretend he didn't hear it. "*Danke*."

"We'd better go." Emily started for the doorway. "On Monday, your friend looked upset that we stayed so long."

"*Jah*, well . . ." This would be the last time he saw Anna. He wanted to say something, anything to let her know— *Let her know what, Levi?*

"I hope you don't have any bruises from getting down on the floor," he blurted out. "I'm sorry I didn't teach you that."

"It's not your fault."

Anna's soft answer stabbed at the tender spot in his heart.

"I know," Emily said brightly. "Anna could go back to the center to practice that. She needs to know how to do it in case anything happens to the children."

Levi stiffened as he remembered her family, her husband. As much as he wanted to teach her, it might be better for him to refer her to someone else. "It would be good for you to know how to do that." He rushed on. "If evenings are better for you, Alisha handles the evening classes. She comes in at six."

Was it his imagination, or did Anna appear crestfallen?

"I'm sure Anna would rather work with you." Emily's face reddened. "I mean, she's comfortable around you and you know her and all." She stammered to a stop.

Levi couldn't look at either of them. "I'd be happy to work with her on it."

"Oh, good." Emily beamed at him. "Anna can get her

van ride to the center. *Mamm* will watch Ciara until she gets home."

"If you're sure?" Levi glanced toward Anna without quite meeting her eyes. He wanted to be positive she agreed with her cousin's plans.

"Are you sure it works with your schedule?"

Even if it didn't, he'd make it work. But her spot remained open and always would. No one else could ever take her place.

Anna held her breath as she waited for his answer. He could have already filled that time slot. She wished Emily hadn't interfered and put Levi on the spot like this. And even more, she wished Emily hadn't made Anna's interest in Levi so obvious.

Maybe that's why he hesitated to answer.

"If the five o'clock appointment is still convenient for you, it's fine with me." Levi tried to sound businesslike.

His coldness made it seem like Emily had pressured him into it. Before Anna could find a way to back out gracefully, her cousin jumped in again.

"Great. Anna can come on Friday then. I'll let the van driver know she's going back to her regular schedule."

"Em." Anna's low voice held a warning.

"What?" her cousin asked. "Everything's all settled. We should go."

Anna shot her cousin a look. "I can make my own arrangements."

"Fine. You can call the van then." Emily flounced out of the kitchen.

"If you don't want to come . . ." Levi started.

"It's not that. I just don't want her arranging my life." Anna's words came out edged with frustration. She hoped

Levi didn't think it was directed at him. "I'll see you Friday, I guess." She tried to give him a cheery wave before she wheeled after her cousin.

Just wait until she got Emily outside. She'd really let her cousin have it. How could Emily humiliate her like that?

Anna held her temper until they were pulling out of the parking lot. "I can't believe you did that."

"Hmm . . . didn't you say that to me two days ago?"

"I probably did," Anna fumed.

Emily stopped at a light and turned to Anna. "Someday you'll thank me."

"Levi obviously didn't want to do it."

"I didn't get that impression."

Anna crossed her arms. "You wouldn't. And you probably didn't get the impression that I'm annoyed with you."

The light changed, and Emily lifted the reins. "I can tell, but I also don't like watching two people who keep eyeing each other the way you two do being separated forever."

Anna didn't know whether to be embarrassed that her glances had been so noticeable or pleased that Levi might have been returning them. She opted for silence.

"Come on," Emily said after they'd gone several blocks. "Are you really that upset about going back to the center to work with Levi?"

"*Neh*." Anna had to be honest. That part thrilled her. If only Levi felt the same way.

"I don't want to push myself at him. For all we know, he might have a girlfriend."

"He sure doesn't act like it, the way he stares at you."

Anna hadn't seen that. "He does not." Although if she were honest, he had looked into her eyes that time . . . But he'd followed it up by shutting her out completely.

"Look, you enjoy spending time with him. He can teach

you a skill you need to learn. And if it's God's will, it'll develop into something deeper."

God's will. Emily had brought Anna back to the most important point. She'd never asked if Gabe was God's will, and now she'd fallen for Levi. Maybe it was time for some serious praying. She needed to ask God to guide her before she made another terrible mistake.

Levi arrived home to sticky floors, dirty dishes, messy counters, and stacks of laundry. Yet his heart was singing. Anna would be back for exercise sessions. Even if she only stayed long enough to learn to get onto the floor without hurting herself, he'd see her again.

Right now, though, he had to get control of the household chores. Somehow, he needed to dig out from under the clutter. Once he did, he and his brothers should divide these chores so they kept things neat.

First, he unpacked the wicker basket. On top, they'd placed packages of homemade bread and several desserts. Then he moved the casserole dishes into the refrigerator. Before he set the last one on the lower shelf, he ran a finger over the label. Anna had printed those directions. Had she made all of these or had Emily helped? He couldn't believe her generosity.

By midnight, Levi had the house in some semblance of order, except for the laundry. He'd see about tackling that tomorrow. He had no evening classes to teach, so he'd have more time.

He headed up to bed, but as soon as he lay down, he remembered he'd forgotten to pack lunches for tomorrow. That meant getting up even earlier than usual. At least they had some fresh bread for sandwiches. Levi mumbled his prayers and added one of gratitude for Anna's gift.

The next morning, after a breakfast of boxed cereal, he assigned everyone additional chores while Betty was away. They'd take turns doing dishes, sweeping, mopping, wiping counters, and putting things away.

Nobody looked happy about the extra work, but they did their jobs while he packed lunches. The kitchen looked semi-presentable when they left for the morning.

They managed to do the same the next day. Or maybe the house just seemed brighter and cleaner because he'd see Anna that afternoon. He packed two empty casserole dishes into the wicker basket and took it with him when he dropped Jonah at school and headed off to work at the center.

The day passed slowly. During his three-thirty appointment, Jonah tapped at the door, and Levi waved. Anna often rode on that same van trip. He hoped that meant she'd already arrived. He couldn't wait to work with her.

At five o'clock, as he said good-bye to Jensen, Anna waited outside the door. She seemed eager to get started. Levi tried to curb his enthusiasm.

After holding open the door for her, he dragged a thick gym mat to the center of the floor. "We can practice here."

Anna parked her chair at the edge of the mat. "I can't believe I'm going to learn to fall out of here." She patted the chair arms.

"It's not every day I get to tell someone to tumble out of their wheelchair." Levi wanted to be sure she'd be all right. "Did you have any bruising from the other night?"

"Not that I noticed."

"What does that mean?"

"When you have a screaming baby to care for, you don't have time to pay attention to pain, eating, or sleeping."

And just like that, the baby—and Anna's husband— came between them. "I'm sorry," he said stiffly. "I imagine it's rough."

"It's a lot harder than I expected."

"I feel the same way about keeping house with my *aenti* gone. It isn't as easy as I thought." It didn't compare with caring for a baby, but he had to change the subject so he didn't keep thinking about Anna at home. "That reminds me. I brought back two casserole dishes and your basket. They're over there on the table."

"*Danke.*"

"I'm the one who should be saying that. I can't imagine what my brothers would be eating this week without your meals."

"I hope they tasted all right."

All right? They were the best meals he ever had. "My brothers loved them. All three of them gobbled down the meals and asked for seconds."

"I'm glad *they* liked the food."

"I did too. It was delicious." He hadn't meant to imply he didn't. He'd worried he might give his feelings away by gushing. "We're all grateful for what you—and Emily, of course—did."

Her face scrunched up at the mention of her cousin. Had Anna done all the work and now resented Emily getting the credit? He needed to get off the personal topics. She'd come here to exercise.

Anna tried not to react when Levi mentioned Emily's name, but her cousin had only helped by gathering ingredients and putting them away. All the dishes were Anna's own recipes, prepared with love.

Well, maybe not love—at least, not yet—but definitely with a lot of caring. She'd hoped when Levi ate them, he'd think of her. Not Emily.

Anna brought herself back to the room. She'd come for a purpose. To learn to be a better foster parent. And she'd get to spend this time with Levi. Time to put Emily out of her mind and appreciate being with Levi.

"Will this mat be enough of a cushion? If not, I can get a few mattresses the kids have been making for the homeless. We could put those on top."

Anna didn't want to waste even a minute of their time together. "This will be fine."

"All right, then. Do you remember the steps from the other night?"

She locked her brakes, scooted to the edge of the chair, and got herself ready. She reached over but paused before putting her hand on the floor. The worst part was tipping so far forward and praying her hands and arms would support her when she let her body drop.

"You can do it."

As always, Levi's encouragement washed over her, giving her strength and determination. She put her hand flat on the spot he'd patted and swung her body to the floor. This time she landed more smoothly.

"That was great. Now comes the hard part. Getting back into the chair."

Anna groaned. "Can't I just stay here for a while?"

Levi studied her. "What happened to the person who never wanted to quit?"

Her eyes stung. Pressing her lips together, she turned

her head away. That part of her had suffered a blow. How much of it should she share with Levi?

"Anna?" Levi's caring tone revealed he'd understand.

"I made a promise seven years ago. I thought I needed to walk to keep it. That's why I worked so hard."

"And you found out you didn't?"

She shook her head. All the pain came rushing back. Why had she wasted all those years? Focused hard on a plan without asking for God's leading?

"I've always been stubborn. It's gotten me into trouble. And it's why I'm in a wheelchair."

"That personality helped you learn to walk, so it isn't all bad."

"You don't know the whole story. I ruined several lives, including my own."

"I can't believe that," Levi said, his voice soft and gentle.

"I did. We were seventeen. I was jealous of my friend Nancy's relationship with John. The two of them had already talked about getting married. I'd just started dating Gabe. I wanted to prove to Nancy that I had a better boyfriend, so I suggested a buggy race."

Levi drew in a breath. "Is that how you got hurt?"

Anna kept her gaze on her lap. How could she have been so foolish? So jealous? So prideful? "Gabe didn't want to do it, but I talked him into it. We were neck and neck as we neared the top of the hill. Then John pulled ahead. I didn't want to lose."

The whole scene came rushing back. The horse galloped around a sharp curve in the road, hooves thundering on the asphalt, metal buggy wheels clattering. Wind whistled past the open windows.

Adrenaline rushed through Anna, setting her heart

thumping painfully against her ribs. They had to win. They had to.

"Don't let them beat us, Gabe," she shrieked, but John edged past.

She reached over and grabbed the reins, intending to flick them. To spur the horse faster. But the buggy swayed, tossing her to one side. She accidentally jerked on the reins. The horse and buggy careened off the road. They jounced and bumped as they plunged down the embankment. Terrified, she'd dropped the reins. Gabe tried to control his runaway horse. Loose rocks and gravel pelted the sides of the buggy. They scraped through underbrush and toward the woods. She'd been thrown from the buggy.

Blessedly, she had no memory of that or of landing. She'd only learned those details when she came to, after three days of being unconscious. For several weeks afterward, her brain stayed fuzzy. She remembered little and recognized no one but her parents. But one thing she could never forget. The moment she'd yanked on the reins.

"It was my fault. All my fault."

"What was, Anna?"

"The accident. I—I jerked the reins." She squeezed her eyes shut, wishing she could block the terror sweeping through her. "The horse veered off the road and down the hill. I got tossed out."

Levi winced, and his eyes filled with sympathy. "*Ach*, Anna."

Despite the years that had passed, sometimes she woke, petrified and sweaty, her body rigid, immoveable, still trapped in a waking nightmare.

"They told me I'd be bedridden forever. They said I'd never walk."

"And you proved them wrong."

"I did. But the reason I did that was all wrong." She covered her face with her hands. Behind the darkness of her cupped hands, a picture of Gabe looking at that girl appeared. Why had she humiliated herself by walking across the floor to him? "I made a fool of myself."

"By walking?" Anna's statement confused Levi. Seeing her so distressed, he longed to reach out, to comfort her. Except he had no right. All he could do was listen.

"I made a promise." Her hands muffled her voice. "Once I discovered things had changed, I should never have walked to him."

To him? Levi's chest tightened. She'd made her promise to a man? But she was married. Who had she made that promise to?

She'd also lost Levi. He couldn't follow her story. "Did this happen in the past or was this recently?"

Anna lifted her head. "Last Thursday."

He clenched his hands into fists at the lines of pain etched around her mouth and eyes. If only he had a way to erase them. To protect her. To take away the hurt.

"That was the reason you stopped coming here?"

She nodded.

"I don't understand. What happened?"

A long, slow sigh escaped her lips. Levi stared down at the mat to stay focused on her explanation rather than other things. Things he should never be thinking.

"It's a long story," she said at last.

"It seems to me I said the same thing on Saturday. You listened to me. Now I can return the favor."

Anna drew circles on the mat with her finger as if reluctant to begin.

"I won't judge you."

She looked over at him, surprise written on her face. "I didn't think you would. It's just that . . ."

"That what?"

"Gabe asked me to marry him when I was in the hospital."

So, Gabe is her husband?

"I turned him down because I thought he pitied me, but he kept asking."

Until you said yes?

"Finally, I sent him away, but I told him I'd give him my answer when I could walk."

"That's why you were so determined to walk?" *So she could answer Gabe's proposal?*

Now he was thoroughly confused. Had she married someone else? Was she a widow?

"*Jah.* I never should have made him wait so long. I walked to him the way I'd planned. But I had to turn down his proposal."

She'd told him she'd married someone else? And had a family? Had this Gabe waited for her all this time only to have his hopes dashed?

"That must have been hard." Gabe must be brokenhearted. Levi had experienced that same sorrow at the sight of Anna holding the baby. And every time he was around her, he ached more.

"I had to," Anna repeated, "because Gabe had fallen in love with someone else." She looked bereft.

"But I thought you turned him down."

"I did. How could I marry him knowing he wanted to be with someone else?"

"But—but—" Levi could hardly stammer out his question. "You're not married?"

"Me? Who'd want to marry me?"

Plenty of people, including me.

"Whatever made you think that?" Anna demanded.

"You have a baby."

Her cheeks turned pinker than the rose-colored dress she wore.

Levi looked away. It never occurred to him she might be unmarried and have a child. But that would mean she'd been shunned. He'd just assumed . . .

"Wait. You thought Ciara was my baby?"

"She's not?"

"Of course not. She's my *aenti*'s foster child. I've been taking care of her to help out and to let the other children sleep at night."

"The way you looked at Ciara and cared for her, you just seemed so . . . so, I don't know, like her real mother." He stopped before he made a fool of himself.

Now that he thought about it, she'd been equally as caring toward Jonah. That loving sweetness seemed to be a part of her nature. She'd be a wonderful mother.

Anna had winced when he said the word *mother*. Did she think Gabe's rejection meant she'd never marry or have children? She'd asked who would marry her as if she didn't believe she was worthy of love.

Levi wanted to reassure her, but he had no idea if she'd be interested in him. He also needed to go slowly. She'd been hurt. Maybe it would be a while before she was ready for another relationship. He needed to find out if she'd ever consider dating anyone else or if her love for Gabe would last forever.

He gathered his courage. "Anna, do you think you'd ever—"

Chapter Twenty

A tap at the door interrupted Levi. Kathryn peered through the glass at them. Then she opened the door.

"Are you ready for Jonah?"

Not really. Not when he was about to ask the most important question of his life.

Kathryn ushered Jonah into the room without waiting for an answer. "Sorry, but I have to hurry to an appointment."

The clock showed Anna's session should be over. Yet she still sat on the mat. They hadn't even started on the hardest part of her session—getting back into the chair.

Levi couldn't continue their conversation with Jonah here. Anna waved at his brother, and Levi tried to make his smile as welcoming as possible. In case Jonah had noticed Levi's frown when Kathryn came to the door.

"Hi, Jonah. Are you ready to go home?" Anna asked.

Jonah nodded. "Can I come to your house?"

Levi would like to do that too, but he couldn't get away with blurting out that question.

"I want to play with the baby and the toys."

Before Anna could answer, Levi intervened. "We have chores to do at home. Lots of them." To be sure Anna didn't think he was avoiding visiting her, he explained, "With my *aenti* away, we have to do all the household jobs along with our usual chores."

Did she look disappointed? She dropped her head too quickly for him to tell for sure.

"Jonah, you'll get to spend some time with Anna now while I teach her to get back into her wheelchair." He turned to her. "If you want to, that is."

"I'd like to learn."

Jonah squatted beside Levi as he coached Anna back into the chair. It took her several tries before she could lift herself high enough and keep her legs positioned properly.

"You did it." Levi beamed at her, and beside him, Jonah clapped.

Her cheeks flushed and forehead damp, Anna smiled triumphantly. "Not very pretty."

"*Jah*, you are." Jonah's words rang with honesty and loyalty.

Levi agreed, but he understood Anna meant her attempt to get into the chair. "What matters is you did it. It'll get smoother the more you do it." Taking a deep breath, he added, "You're welcome to come back next week for more practice."

Anna didn't meet his eyes as she said softly, "I'd like that."

Maybe it was best she hadn't been looking because Levi broke into a huge grin. *JAH!!*

"I'd better go so I don't miss the van, but I'll see you tomorrow," Anna said as she headed out the door.

Levi stopped dragging the mat back into place. "You will?"

"Don't you teach Water Safety at the firehouse tomorrow?"

He brightened. "You're taking that?"

"It's one of the certifications I need. This area has a lot of ponds and creeks."

At the word *creek*, Levi's face and insides both tightened.

"I'm sorry," she whispered.

Levi waved a hand. "It's all right." But his gaze strayed to Jonah who'd taken his place and was trying unsuccessfully to tug the mat. "Let me help you with that," Levi said, rushing toward Jonah.

Together, they tugged the mat into place. By the time they finished, Anna had gone. But at least Levi would see her tomorrow.

He sprayed cleaner on the mat and wiped it down. And he cleaned several other surfaces from Jensen's session. He passed the windowsill and stopped. He'd forgotten to give Anna her basket. He'd put it in the buggy to take with him tomorrow.

When he ushered Jonah out to the parking lot, the van was pulling out. Anna seemed to be looking in their direction. Jonah waved, and Anna waved back. With joy in his heart, Levi joined his brother. Today, a huge weight had lifted. Discovering Anna was unmarried was a huge, unexpected gift. Now he only prayed she'd consider dating him once she was over her heartbreak.

Anna's heart soared when both Jonah and Levi waved. *Ach*, he had her basket. She'd been so overjoyed at being around him again, she'd completely forgotten to take it. But she could get it tomorrow.

Her heart pattered faster. She'd see him at Water Safety, and she'd committed to going to the center next week. She hoped learning to get back into the wheelchair would take a long time.

But she wished she'd hadn't told Levi about Gabe. He'd

been such a good listener and so sympathetic, she'd spilled the whole story. What must Levi think of her?

She'd been so selfish and determined, she'd caused a terrible accident. She'd paid physically, but others had also paid. Her parents, her church, and Gabe had footed the huge hospital bills. Gabe's family lost their buggy, and the horse had been hurt. And she'd kept Gabe tied to her self-centered promise for so many years. Even now, he probably still suffered from guilt.

Now that Levi had heard all this about her, he'd never be able to look past what she'd done. And although Anna prayed for God's forgiveness, deep inside she still wrestled with shame.

The van pulled in front of the house, and Anna waited impatiently to be lowered to ground level. She wanted to spend a little time alone dealing with the past before she collected Ciara.

But when she opened the front door, Emily sat on the couch, rocking the whining baby in her arms. "*Mamm* asked me to bring her over here so the other children could take their naps."

"I see." Anna tried to keep her disappointment from showing. "I'll take her."

Emily flicked her head in the direction of the kitchen. "Have dinner first. Today's my day off, so I can watch Ciara for a while."

"Did you get to eat?" Anna asked.

"*Neh*. I hoped to share your casserole. I put one in the oven to bake. But we may have to take turns eating. Rocking Ciara like this lessens her screaming."

"The children won't still be napping now. Why didn't you eat at home?"

"You trying to get rid of me?" Emily's teasing tone didn't quite hide her hurt.

"Of course not." Anna hadn't meant to upset her cousin. She'd only wanted a little time alone to remember Levi's looks, his words, his smiles.

"All right, I admit it. I wanted to find out what happened with Levi. How was class?" Emily followed Anna into the kitchen.

Keeping her back to her cousin, Anna checked the casserole. Almost done. She headed for the open shelves to get plates.

"Are you ignoring me?" Emily lifted Ciara to one shoulder and opened the silverware drawer.

"Maybe," Anna admitted. "It was just a class."

"He didn't say anything about the casseroles?"

"He said his brothers liked them." Anna set the plates on the table and continued, hoping to distract her cousin. "He brought the basket and dishes to the center. I forgot to take them home."

"Too busy thinking about him?"

Stifling a sigh, Anna shot her cousin an irritated look.

Emily put the silverware down and held up her hands. "Sorry. But don't worry. I'm sure he'll bring the basket tomorrow."

Of course he would. Anna had seen him carrying it in the parking lot. But she still felt foolish for forgetting it. She'd been so focused on herself and her story, she'd neglected to think about anything else.

Emily sat at the table. "Nothing exciting happened? I thought maybe the two of you might . . ." At Anna's glare, she trailed off.

"I don't know why you keep insisting Levi is interested in me. He treats me the same way he does anyone else."

"Sure, like he spent so much time with you on Wednesday night that his partner had to assign him to another group."

"He was only trying to help me get out of the wheelchair safely." Anna's tone ended up being a bit more snappish than she intended. "It's his job."

"Mmm-hmm." Emily didn't sound convinced. "How did the lessons go?"

"I did pretty well getting out." Anna rolled back to the stove to remove the casserole. "Getting back up will take a lot more practice."

"Did you want me to work with you?"

Anna hid her frown. She didn't particularly want to get good at that. Then she'd have no excuse to spend more time with Levi.

"Never mind," Emily said when Anna headed back to the table. "I assume your silence means you'd rather work with Levi."

"I can practice with you." Anna wanted to get Emily off the subject of Levi.

Unfortunately, she wasn't successful. Emily kept bringing him up. Anna finished her meal and reached for Ciara.

"You haven't had much time to eat yours." Maybe eating would keep Emily quiet for a while.

Her cousin stayed silent until she'd emptied her plate. "I'm disappointed. I was hoping for some news. You didn't do anything but get in and out of your wheelchair? No special glances? No secret smiles?"

Maybe there had been on Anna's part. Not Levi's. Although . . .

"Aha. I see that look in your eyes. Something did happen. What was it?"

"Since when have you gotten so nosy?"

Emily put on a hurt expression. "Me?"

Ciara squalled.

"Time for her bottle." Anna headed for the stove.

"I'll clean up." Emily raised her voice to be heard over the din. "Then once Ciara's quiet, you can tell me."

Anna resigned herself to telling Emily only a quick version, leaving out any glances and smiles. And especially avoiding any pattering hearts—on Anna's part, not Levi's.

With Ciara sucking on her bottle and the kitchen clean, Emily settled onto the couch with an expectant expression.

Anna sighed inwardly. *Please finish your bottle quickly, Ciara*. Her bedtime routine would put an end to Emily's inquisition.

"So?" Emily prompted. "What happened?"

"Not much. Levi asked me why I'd quit coming to the center, and I told him about Gabe."

Emily's squeal startled Ciara, and the baby let go of the bottle and wailed.

"Sorry." Her cousin waited until Anna comforted Ciara, and the baby took the bottle again. "I can't believe you told him about Gabe. What did he say?"

"Not much. He didn't have time. We had to leave."

"Well, you'll have tomorrow together. Who knows what will happen? I wish I didn't have to work. Not that I need to repeat the Water Safety class."

Anna tried not to let her relief show. She was already nervous about seeing Levi's reaction tomorrow. She didn't want to talk to him under the spotlight of Emily's curious gaze.

Levi carried the wicker basket into the firehouse the next morning. They'd added one more clean casserole dish, and his brothers each wrote a thank-you note. They had two more meals in the refrigerator he couldn't wait to try.

"You planning a picnic for two after class today?" Ron teased.

"*Neh*. Just returning the basket."

"Lucky you. I wish a few girls would make me some meals like that."

"I thought you had a girlfriend already."

"I do. Just joshing. Guess they'll be coming to class today?"

Levi wanted to avoid answering. His feelings for Anna were too serious for Ron's brand of teasing. Plus, his muscles had tensed up because every time he taught this class, he relived Jonah's drowning.

Ron raised an eyebrow, waiting for an answer.

"Anna will be."

"I guess it's good we don't need to break up into groups today. Try to keep your eyes moving around the room. Make everyone feel welcome. Know what I mean?"

"I always do."

"Yeah, you did until this past week."

Levi promised himself to avoid glancing at Anna. He could talk to her after class. But as soon as she came in the door, she drew his attention. He gave her a casual wave and then forced himself to do the same to everyone in the small group that followed her.

Ron did the introduction and stats on unintentional drowning and discussed possible hazards as well as household dangers like mop buckets, bathtubs, and even small puddles. Then Levi took over to discuss symptoms and steps to take for each one. Ron turned on a video that showed the symptoms caused by how long the person was in the water.

Levi never watched this part. Stealing a glance at Anna might distract him from thoughts of Jonah. Some people took notes, but Anna had set down her pencil and stared straight at him.

Poor Levi. As he went over the material, Anna could see how hard this was for him. Teaching these classes must be torture. She wished she had a way to ease his pain.

Once the video came on, Levi lowered his head into his hands. If they'd been alone, she might have hurried to his side, but here she could only pray for him.

When he looked in her direction, she sent him a silent, sympathetic message. He gazed at her as if clinging to a lifeline.

She tried to give him strength and support. He'd done so much for her, she was glad she could be there for him.

As the lights went on, Levi's sorrowful face smoothed into neutral lines. While Ron presented safety tips on drowning prevention and survival, Levi handed out copies of both papers.

When he held out Anna's sheets, he leaned close and whispered, "*Danke.*"

Her nerves fluttered at his closeness. He moved on, but her pulse didn't slow. She had trouble concentrating on Ron's talk. She'd have to review the important points once she got home.

After the program, Anna wanted to spend time with Levi, but she had no excuse. Reluctantly, she headed for the door.

"Anna, wait." Levi came running after her. "I have your basket. I forgot to give it to you yesterday."

She smiled up at him. They'd been in the middle of a

conversation when Jonah arrived. Levi had been about to ask her something. Something serious, judging by the expression on his face.

In some ways she regretted sharing her story about Gabe, but in another, recounting it had been a relief. Levi's reaction had taken some of the sting out of Gabe's rejection.

Talking about what had happened with Gabe had made it clear how much her human side, her stubbornness, and her self-centeredness had been driving her. Now she wanted to do God's will. Even if it meant she'd never marry. At the moment, God seemed to be leading her to be a foster parent.

All the classes she needed to take had been scheduled here at the firehouse, making it easy for her to get those certifications. She'd focus on everything she had to do to get ready to care for the children God sent to her and try not to let her heart or mind run away with fancies about Levi.

Levi stared at Anna, who seemed to be far away. "Are you all right?"

"Sorry. I got lost in thought."

"Good ones, I hope." He wished she'd been thinking about him.

"Mainly about doing God's will."

"Then definitely good thoughts." He smiled at her. Should he encourage her to share? Or was it too personal?

A chattering crowd jostled past. Now wasn't the time to have a deep conversation. He had to help Ron with the cleanup and be sure they had everything they needed for their classes next week. And Anna might have a ride waiting.

"If you wait here," Levi said, "I'll get the basket."

When he returned, he thanked her for the meals. Although he wanted to find a way to keep talking, even about everyday subjects, his mind had gone blank.

Ron came up behind him and clapped him on the shoulder. "Thanks for staying on track tonight." He grinned at Anna. "You two should go on a picnic with that huge basket."

Anna's cheeks colored, and Levi gritted his teeth. He'd already told Ron this wasn't a picnic basket.

Waggling his eyebrows, Ron said, "It's a lovely day out."

"I'm sure Anna has plenty to do. She has a baby to take care of." Levi tried to signal Ron to leave them alone, but his fellow teacher ignored the hint.

"Oh, you're the married one then. Sorry. Didn't mean to offend."

Anna's brow furrowed. "*Neh*, I'm not married."

"But you said she had a baby." At Levi's frown, he held up a hand. "Sorry. I didn't mean to judge. It's all okay with me. I just didn't think the Amish . . . Well, I guess everyone's human."

"It's not *her* baby," Levi said. "She's a foster parent. That's why she's taking the classes."

Now it was Ron's turn to look puzzled. "Don't you have to have the classes first?"

"I'm helping my aunt. She's already certified."

"Ron, don't you need to put away the video equipment?" Levi asked.

"Trying to get rid of me? Not very subtle, buddy."

And neither was Ron's remark. He'd made it clear to Anna that Levi wanted time alone with her. He did, but he'd hoped to do it without making it obvious.

Levi waited until Ron had left before saying, "Sorry. He likes to tease."

"That's all right." Anna peeped up at him shyly through her lashes. "I think you're very brave. For teaching these classes I mean. Especially this one. It must be difficult."

"It is. But I have to do it. If I can save even one life, prevent one drowning . . ." Levi swallowed hard.

"I could see how painful it was for you."

He didn't know he'd been so obvious. "I try to hide it. Guess I didn't do a very good job."

"You did. It only showed when the lights were out. Everyone else was watching the video. I doubt they saw."

The embarrassment over his feelings being so noticeable dissipated at another, more thrilling realization. Anna had been looking at him instead of the film. A frisson of excitement filled his chest. Was it possible she was interested in him?

Anna reached for the basket. "I'd better go. Emily's probably waiting for me."

Levi's spirits plunged. He'd hoped to have more time to talk to her. But he couldn't ask her what he really wanted to know. He had to save that question until they could talk in private.

"I'll see you Monday." Anna's cheerful voice warmed him. She sounded as eager to see him as he was to see her.

"I'm looking forward to it."

"Me too."

Anna's soft answer echoed in his mind long after Emily helped Anna into the buggy and stowed the folding wheelchair in the back. He waved to both of them as they pulled out of the parking lot, but his mind remained on Anna. Monday couldn't come soon enough.

Chapter Twenty-One

When Anna arrived for her session on Monday, she decided to focus on learning to get back up into the wheelchair smoothly. No more talking about Gabe or divulging personal secrets. And she would not, under any circumstances, reveal her growing attraction.

Levi, engrossed in working with one of his after-school students, didn't notice her head by his door. She carried the wicker basket filled with more casseroles on her lap. Getting time to cook on Saturday afternoon and this morning had been a challenge. Even with Emily's help. Ciara had been fussier than usual and rarely stopped crying, except for a few of the many times Anna tucked her into the baby carrier.

In the community center kitchen, Anna pushed aside a few lunch bags and plastic containers to make room for the five casserole dishes. She repacked the breads and desserts and covered them with a towel, so people wouldn't think they were snacks for everyone to share.

A few minutes before five, she headed back down the hall. Despite her resolve, Anna couldn't help responding to Levi's cheerful greeting. His broad, caring smile sent her insides cartwheeling. If only that smile were directed at her rather than at each person who walked through his door.

Something about his caring "how are you?" made Anna long to confide all her struggles and dreams. She pressed her lips together for a few seconds until she'd calmed herself enough to answer. "A little tired, but I'm planning to work hard today."

"I never doubted that. You always do."

"Not last week."

"That was my fault. I got you off track." Levi turned to pull out the mat they'd used last time. "You said you're tired. Baby keeping you from sleeping?"

"And eating and cleaning and—" Anna stopped before she mentioned cooking. She wanted the casseroles to be a surprise. Plus, she didn't want him to think making them had been any trouble.

"Don't skip eating. You need to keep up your strength." Levi stood and motioned for her to position her wheelchair by the mat. "As for making time for cleaning, I wish I had some tips for that. You should see our place with my *aenti* gone."

"I don't know how you find time for housework with working full-time and teaching almost every evening and part of Saturday."

"True. I tried to get my brothers on a schedule to do extra chores around the house, but Zeb's been working long hours at the farm to get some of the horses ready to take to an out-of-town horse sale this weekend. And Jonah tries, but he needs a lot of supervision."

"He's great with babies."

The quick flash of terror in Levi's eyes made Anna wish she hadn't mentioned that. He stared off into the distance for a bit with sorrowful eyes before shaking his head and focusing on her. "What were we talking about?"

"Your brothers and chores."

"Oh, right." Levi flipped up her footrests. "Daniel often leaves things worse than before he started. I'm trying to decide if that's accidental or on purpose."

Anna laughed. "If it is, that's a smart strategy."

"I guess. Most of the time, it's easier for me to finish it up than to call him back and teach him how to do it. Although often I don't even have time to do that, so I just let it go."

"I can understand that. I've been letting some chores slide ever since I started watching Ciara."

"That's a big job. Most moms have help from their families and older siblings or hire a teen."

"Emily does what she can, but my *aenti* needs her and her sisters. She has five little ones to watch. Two of the new ones have special needs."

"That's not easy. But you know that from Ciara."

Anna distracted herself from the kindness in his eyes by locking her brakes to signal she was ready to begin. She worried if she returned his look, her eyes would give her away.

Once again, Levi had wasted Anna's exercise time with conversation. "Sorry," he mumbled as he moved into position. He managed to keep his attention on the session while Anna got onto the floor and then struggled to get herself back into the chair several times.

Holly tapped at the door. "I have a phone message for you." She held out a small memo.

Levi waited until Anna was safely back in the chair to stand and take the paper. "*Danke*."

As Holly closed the door behind her, he skimmed the message. "*Ach*, no." What was he going to do?

"What's the matter?" Anna studied him with concern. "Is someone hurt?"

The alarm in his voice must have made it sound that way. "*Neh, neh*. It's from my *aenti*. She's staying an extra day and won't be coming home until later on Saturday."

"And that's a problem?" Anna asked it as if confused.

"I teach on Saturday until four."

The puzzlement on Anna's face cleared. "You're worried about having time to clean the house?"

That hadn't even entered Levi's mind. "My brothers might make messes." He had a much more pressing worry. "Zeb will be gone. What am I going to do about Daniel and Jonah? I can't leave them alone."

Anna's forehead knotted. "Why not?"

Levi sucked in a breath. "What if something happened to them while I was gone? It was hard enough to leave them with Zeb last weekend while I taught for a few hours. But to be away all day?"

"Isn't Daniel ten? My cousins have watched the little ones since they were seven or eight. I don't know Daniel, but Jonah will behave. Is Daniel a troublemaker?"

"That's not the problem. Neither of them will do anything bad. At least not on purpose. But accidents happen." Dangerous scenarios whirled through Levi's mind.

"Oh, Levi." Anna's soothing whisper brought him back to the room.

"Sorry. I'll figure something out." Maybe Ron could find a sub. Or someone from church could come in to stay with his brothers. Although he'd be ashamed to let anyone see the messy house.

Levi jerked his thoughts away from the dilemma. He needed to work with Anna.

Anna wished she could alleviate Levi's fears. He still blamed himself for Jonah's accident. She could do something to help. "I'd be happy to watch your brothers on Saturday."

"But you have Ciara. I don't want to add to your burdens."

"It's no problem. Jonah"—she stopped herself before she reminded Levi how his brother had held Ciara—"is so easy to take care of. And he enjoyed playing with the baby's toys."

"He did, but . . ."

Anna rushed on before Levi came up with any excuses. "I'm sure Daniel will be fine. My cousins would enjoy having company."

"I can't let you do that."

"You don't trust me?" Anna pretended to look hurt.

"Of course, I do, but—"

"Fine. Then it's settled. Do you want to bring them to my house, or should I ask Emily to drop me at your house on her way to work on Saturday morning? She has to be at the restaurant by eight-thirty."

Levi looked like he was about to protest. Then he sighed. "I don't like this idea."

"My house or yours?" Anna repeated.

"I'll drop them off," he said finally. "But only if you let me pay you back somehow."

"I don't need any pay. Besides, you working with me here has been payment enough."

"I'm falling down on that job." He patted the spot where she should put her hand. "Ready to try again?"

"I guess."

"You don't sound too sure."

Anna's hesitation had nothing to do with the teaching. When Levi asked if she was ready to try again, it reminded her of Gabe and their failed relationship. Was she ready to risk a broken heart? This time she had a lot farther to fall.

Anna's hesitation surprised Levi. "Has doing this hurt you? You seem to be coming down pretty gently, but if you're getting sore, we can work on something else."

"What else could I do?"

Did he detect some bitterness in her question? That was so unlike Anna. So was being reluctant to move ahead.

He probably shouldn't ask this, but he needed to know—both for himself and for her motivation. "Is your lack of enthusiasm because of Gabe's rejection?"

Her head snapped up. The way her chin jutted out warned him he'd crossed a line. But the initial flare of temper in her eyes faded to doubt and uncertainty. "Maybe. I had a goal. It might have been a foolish one, and now I know it wasn't God's will. But without that incentive, I have no reason to work hard."

"What about doing it for yourself?" Levi had tried suggesting something similar earlier, but maybe she'd be more open to hearing it now. "Also, don't you think the more mobile you are, the better you'll be as a foster parent?"

Anna nibbled at her lip. "You're right. If God's been directing me to do this, I should work hard to improve."

"Why don't you bring your crutches next time? We can

work on helping you get around, bend and carry, and do other tasks."

"I will." She brightened. Then she glanced up at the clock. "We have only ten more minutes. Let's see how many times I can get down to the floor and back up again."

That's the Anna he was used to. The take-charge, I-can-do-it woman who'd stolen his heart.

She practiced until she could do both movements rapidly and smoothly. Levi suggested several exercises she could do at home to strengthen both arms.

When Jonah peeked in, Anna was in her wheelchair, ready to go. "Will you be around for a short while?" she asked.

"I have to clean the exercise equipment before I leave." He gave her a questioning glance, but she didn't respond.

She headed out the door and down the hall. A few minutes later, she entered the room with the wicker basket on her lap.

"Oh, Anna, no. You can't keep feeding us."

"You didn't like what I—we sent?"

"It's not that. Everything was delicious, but I don't want you to spend your time making things for us when you're caring for a baby. You said you don't even have time to eat. You should take care of yourself."

"I made casseroles for myself at the same time."

Jonah hurried over and peeked in the basket. "Yum." He dug through the treats until he reached the brownies. Then he looked up at her as if asking if he could have one.

"Those are for you and your brothers." She turned to Levi. "Is it all right for Jonah to have one?"

When he nodded, she handed one to each of them.

"Mmm. Delicious," Levi said around a mouthful. He loved seeing the sparkle come back into Anna's eyes.

He'd also been grateful to hear her admit Gabe hadn't been God's will. *But what about me? Am I God's will for her?*

Levi didn't want to make the mistake of falling for the wrong person. He had a lot of praying to do.

Anna left with a smile on her face. She'd made two brothers happy. And Levi had helped her look at the setback with Gabe from a new perspective. Perhaps God had used her stubbornness and determination to answer Gabe to give her an incentive to walk. Not to walk to him, but to be mobile for the foster children.

That idea eased a lot of the sting of rejection. For now, she'd throw herself into getting around well on crutches. It also gave her a reason to continue her sessions with Levi.

Eager to learn and to spend time with him, Anna brought her crutches to the next sessions and practiced hard in between. She also found herself looking forward to Saturday.

She stayed up late cleaning so the house was spotless. For once, Ciara cooperated and slept much of the time, as long as she was cradled in the baby carrier.

Exhausted, Anna fell into bed, but she was too excited to sleep. She kept telling herself she might not even see Levi when he dropped off his brothers. But that didn't stop her from hoping. Not sleeping much had an upside. Rather than having to fight her way out of sleep, Anna was already awake when Ciara bawled.

She rose early to make a hearty breakfast. Soon, cinnamon buns were rising, and a cheesy breakfast casserole bubbled with hash browns, sausage, bacon, eggs, and onions.

While everything cooked, she dressed with care. Then

she changed and dressed Ciara, who wailed through most of it. She'd just settled the baby with a bottle when a tentative knock sounded on the door. They were here!

Ciara in one arm, she wheeled to the door. A miniature of Levi stood on the doorstep next to Jonah. She smiled at both of them before letting her gaze drift up to their older brother. Levi looked heart-stoppingly handsome this morning in his blue shirt.

He held out her wicker basket filled with empty, but clean, casserole dishes. "We really enjoyed every single one of these meals."

"They were good," Daniel said.

"I'm glad you liked them," she responded. Then she switched her attention to Levi. "Do you have time for a quick breakfast?"

Levi sniffed the air. "When it smells as good as that, I do." His enthusiastic smile and twinkling eyes brightened her morning.

Jonah stepped inside and stared down at Ciara.

"Once you've eaten," she whispered, "I'll let you hold her." She hoped Levi hadn't heard, or he'd worry. Then she turned to Daniel. "Hi, I'm Anna."

"I know. I'm Daniel."

"Come on in and sit down." Propping Ciara against her shoulder, Anna burped her, then she trailed the others to the kitchen.

"What can I do to help?" Levi asked.

Anna had already set the table and put out a pitcher of milk and a jar of applesauce. The casserole was staying warm on top of the stove. She slid the cinnamon buns out of the oven. After drizzling icing on top, she handed the pan to Levi.

"Can you put that on the table? I'll cut the casserole and bring it over."

Anna smiled to herself when he took the pot holders she extended and carried the cinnamon buns far out in front of him as if they were fragile. She cut the casserole and put the bottle back in Ciara's mouth so she could finish the rest of her milk and hopefully allow them to have a peaceful breakfast.

"Let me get that." Levi returned with the pot holders and picked up the casserole. "You have your hands full." He headed toward his two brothers, who were eyeing the dish hungrily.

"You haven't had breakfast yet, have you?" she said to the boys when they both attacked their full plates after the silent prayer.

Daniel piped up. "We had cereal. Dry cereal."

Levi looked embarrassed. "I didn't realize we were out of milk."

"It's an easy mistake to make."

"*Danke* for this." He gestured toward the table. "And for everything you've done." His eyes blazed with more than gratitude.

Was it possible he was interested in her? Anna lowered her gaze, but her heart sang.

Chapter Twenty-Two

After they finished breakfast and Levi left for his class, Jonah begged Anna to hold the whining baby.

"Of course." Without Levi's worried presence hovering in the room, she had no qualms about letting Jonah care for the baby. "I need to change her first, but why don't you sit on the rocking chair. She might like that."

She returned to the living room to find Jonah perched on the edge of the chair. He held out his arms.

"Once you slide back all the way," Anna told him, "I'll give you Ciara."

Jonah wriggled back into place, and she lowered Ciara into his waiting arms. He cradled the baby close and rocked back and forth, a contented smile on his face.

"She likes me," he said proudly.

"She certainly does."

Once again, Jonah had calmed the crying baby. Something about his touch seemed to soothe Ciara's agitation. Her eyes fluttered shut.

"You're putting her to sleep again, Jonah. *Danke*."

"Good job, Jonah," Daniel said. He looked over at Anna.

"Levi said we're supposed to help you with chores. What do you want us to do?"

Anna hesitated. Remembering Levi's description of Daniel's incompetence, she debated about taking him up on his offer. But maybe she could teach him to do some of them well, so he'd be more of a help.

"Jonah's already helping with the baby. You and I can do the dishes."

Levi probably would have had a fit if he knew Jonah was on his own in the living room with the baby. Anna debated about staying with him, but he and Ciara both appeared so content. And she did have work to do.

Although she understood Levi's reluctance to let his brothers out of his sight, he needed to remember that God was in control. As her *mamm* always said, *Fear is a sign you're not trusting the Lord.*

With one last smile at Jonah, Anna led Daniel into the kitchen and showed him how to fill the sink with dishwater.

"Not so high," she warned as the bubbles foamed and almost overflowed on the floor. "You need to leave room for your hands and the dishes."

After she showed him the correct order for washing and the best way to clean, she let him do the rest on his own. But she stayed close by to monitor. Once he'd washed and rinsed everything, she demonstrated using the dish towel.

Once he had the dish towel, Daniel rubbed vigorously. He rushed from one piece to another. Anna smiled at his energy. She debated telling him to slow down, but he was doing a thorough job.

Then a plate slid through his fingers. *Crash!* It shattered into slivers.

Daniel's lower lips wobbled, and he hung his head. "I'm sorry."

"Accidents happen." Anna should know. She'd had her share. Including the one that . . . She pulled her thoughts from her regrets.

"With accidents, the best thing to do is to fix up or clean up as much as you can." Some things could never be repaired. Like the plate that lay in shards.

A tear slipped down Daniel's cheek. "I didn't mean to do it."

"I know you didn't." Anna reached over and put an arm around his shoulders. "It's only a plate. It can be replaced. For now, why don't we clean it up?"

She gave lessons on sweeping gently and carefully. After every splinter had been scooped up, Daniel volunteered to clean the rest of the kitchen. He slid the broom under the tables and open countertops.

"You're doing a great job, Daniel," Anna said, as she finished drying the dishes and putting them away.

After she'd worked with him to clean the table and counters, they went into the living room. Jonah was still rocking and cuddling the sleeping baby. Anna eased Ciara from his arms and into her cradle. Then she suggested playing Uno around the kitchen table.

Ciara woke around noon, and Daniel asked for a turn to hold her. Anna settled him on the couch and sat next to him to give the baby her bottle. Jonah climbed up beside his brother and stared down at Ciara.

A few days ago, Emily had brought over a high chair her *mamm* had gotten at an auction. So far, Ciara had been too fussy to use it, but with the two boys to distract her, Anna decided to give it a try.

While they ate, the boys took turns giving Ciara bites of mashed potatoes and mushed peas. She loved the potatoes, but made faces and dribbled out most of the peas.

Jonah and Daniel laughed. Then, suddenly and sur-
prisingly, Ciara laughed too, and proceeded to spit out
more peas.

Anna couldn't wait to tell her *aenti*. That was Ciara's
first positive reaction.

Ciara had been quiet since Jonah had arrived that morning and only cried while being changed or waking up after
her nap. Anna wished she could keep the boys around all
the time.

After such a good morning, it only made sense she'd
have a fussy afternoon. Anna kept her in the baby carrier
while she did the dishes and mopped the kitchen with
Daniel's help.

Anna was wringing out the mop when Emily popped
in. "I'm done my shift at the restaurant. *Mamm* offered to
keep Ciara if you want a break."

"But the other children can't nap if she's crying."

"That's so." Emily nibbled on a fingernail. "*Mamm* feels
bad that you've been caring for Ciara more than she has."

"I don't mind." Despite her *aenti*'s warning, Anna had
gotten attached to Ciara. It almost felt as if Ciara had taken
the place of the baby she'd never have.

Daniel plopped onto the couch, looking glum.

"What's the matter?" Anna asked.

He'd been an enthusiastic helper. Maybe he needed to
be active and occupied.

"Our house doesn't look nice like this. When Betty's
there, it's clean. But now it's a mess."

Anna recalled Levi mentioning something similar.
"She's coming home tonight, isn't she?"

"*Jah*, and she won't be happy to see it."

Nobody should have to come home from a long trip to
a house in disarray. Anna turned to Emily. "You have anything planned for this afternoon?"

Emily's eyebrows shot up. "Are you planning what I'm thinking?"

"Probably. Daniel's done a great job cleaning today. If you and I help the boys, we could leave the house spotless for their *aenti*."

Emily grinned. "And make Levi realize what a wonderful catch you'd be."

"Em!" Anna flashed a warning glance at her cousin and indicated the two boys with a slight tilt of her head. "I was thinking about his poor *aenti* facing an untidy house."

Under her breath Emily muttered, "I bet you were." At Anna's frown, she followed it with a quick "sorry." But Emily didn't sound the least repentant.

To make up for her teasing, she agreed to help. "Let's do it. I'll take Ciara over to *Mamm* for the afternoon."

Anna's excitement grew. "We should be able to get it clean and get back here before Levi finishes his class for today and comes to pick up the boys. I made buttermilk baked chicken for their dinner. I can leave it in the oven."

"I thought you were doing this for his *aenti*," Emily pointed out.

"I am," Anna said defensively. "The boys need to eat."

"So does Levi."

Even Emily's sarcasm couldn't puncture Anna's good mood. She pictured Levi's surprised face when he arrived home to find dinner in the oven and a clean house.

Ten minutes later, they all piled into Emily's buggy.

"Awfully big basket for one dish of baked chicken," Emily said as she handed Anna the large wicker basket to hold on her lap.

Anna's cheeks heated. "I brought a few things to go with it." Her flushed face gave her away.

Emily peeked under the dish towel Anna had draped over the basket. "Hmm. Green bean casserole, scalloped potatoes, homemade bread, and snitz pie. Oh, and lemon bars."

"Jonah likes those."

"I see." Emily shook her head. "Anyone would think you and Levi are courting."

Anna sucked in a breath. "I'm just trying to be helpful. Neighborly. Kind."

"Riiight." Emily sounded like the *Englisch* teenagers who frequented the restaurant.

"Let's go, so we can get back before Levi comes to pick up his brothers."

"Are you going to tell me you aren't eager to be there when he comes?"

Pretending to ignore Emily's sly smile, Anna turned to look out the buggy window. Emily would probably tease her unmercifully for doing this, but Anna tried to tell herself she'd have done this for anyone who needed help.

While Emily took care of the horse, Daniel unfolded Anna's portable wheelchair and held the handles while she swung herself down into it. Then Jonah and Daniel helped tilt her chair over the low step onto the back porch and over the bump at the threshold. Anna rolled into the kitchen and blinked.

Breakfast dishes soaked in the sink. The stove was crusted with burned-on food. The kitchen floor needed to be swept and mopped. Someone had done laundry, but it still swung from the line.

"Daniel, why don't you take down the clothes and bring them inside? I'll put the food in the refrigerator and then start with the stove."

Emily entered the kitchen as Daniel exited. "What do you want me to do?"

Anna couldn't get upstairs. "Can you check the second floor?"

Maybe she should have Levi work with her on climbing steps using her crutches. That would give her a reason to keep going for sessions.

A few minutes later, Emily called down, "I found plenty to do up here."

After Daniel returned with the laundry, she had him take it upstairs and put it away. Then he joined her in the kitchen to practice his new skills of dishwashing and sweeping.

Room by room, the four of them set the house back in order. When everything looked spotless, Anna pulled the chicken, green beans, and scalloped potatoes from the freshly cleaned refrigerator and put them in the oven on low.

Emily, who looked hot and sweaty, sat at the kitchen table. "I think we should all stop for an ice cream cone on the way home."

Daniel cheered, and Jonah copied him.

"Do we have enough time?" Anna fretted. She didn't want to miss Levi. He might panic if he found nobody home.

"Relax. It's only a little after three. We'll be fine."

Anna sliced the bread, placed it on a platter, and covered it. She was unpacking a jar of her home-canned applesauce and the desserts from the basket when the front door banged open.

"I'm home." A woman's voice boomed through the house.

"Betty," Daniel squealed, and headed toward the sound. Jonah bounded after him.

Anna glanced at Emily, a question in her eyes. Should they stay or leave?

Emily shrugged. It was already too late to flee. Daniel and Jonah, each holding one of Betty's hands, dragged her to the kitchen, chattering all the way.

"Anna and Emily helped us get the house clean for you," Daniel said. "And I did all the dishes without breaking any."

Betty turned to him, a startled look on her face. "I should hope not."

His face flushed. "I did break a plate at Anna's house."

"I'm so sorry." Betty faced Anna. "I hope they weren't too much trouble when they were there."

"Not at all."

"It's nice to see you again, Anna. My nephews all rave about you. Well, except for Zeb, but he hasn't met you yet." Betty examined the kitchen. "You've done a wonderful job of keeping the house neat. It's not easy with all these boys."

She made it sound as if Anna had been there cleaning on a daily basis. Anna opened her mouth to correct the mistake, but Betty had already turned toward the table.

"You must be Emily. It's nice to meet you. Are you Anna's sister?"

"Her cousin. We were just getting ready to take the boys for an ice cream cone and to meet Levi."

Betty smiled at her. "That would be wonderful. I must admit, I'm a little tired from the trip. I could use some time to unpack and sip a cup of tea." She sniffed the air. "It smells like dinner is already cooking. *Danke*, Anna."

The smile she gave Anna made her feel as if she were one of the family. If only Levi would think of her that way.

Emily stood. "We'd better go if we want to meet Levi on time." She nodded at Betty. "Nice to meet you."

Anna echoed that sentiment and added, "I hope your trip went well."

With a beatific smile and a faraway look in her eye,

Betty sighed. "It was *wunderbar*. I'm sure you know the joys of being in love."

Anna swallowed and busied herself with picking up the basket. She knew all about being in love, but hers was unrequited. "I'm so happy for you." Anna forced the polite words past the lump in her throat.

"I appreciate everything you've done while I was away, Anna. I can tell I left my nephews in good hands. And thank you for bringing Anna," Betty said to Emily.

Emily had already risen from the table and started for the door. "You're welcome." With her back to Betty, Emily made a wry face. She must want some credit for all her hard work.

"I couldn't have done it without Emily. She helped a lot. I couldn't get upstairs."

"*Ach*, I didn't even think of that. This old farmhouse isn't easy to navigate." Then she murmured, "I suppose we'll be selling it." Betty made a shooing motion toward the boys. "You'd better hurry. And come straight back for supper."

"We will," Daniel promised as he rushed to the door.

A short while later, they were headed back to Anna's house, each holding a dripping cone. As they turned into the driveway, a familiar buggy stood to one side, the horse tied to a hitching post. Anna's heart thumped as fast and as hard as the horse's hooves hitting the pavement. She couldn't wait to see Levi. She only hoped he hadn't been waiting long.

Levi knocked at the door again. No answer. His mind raced with terrible possibilities. *What if—?*

He tried to pull himself together. She mentioned her

cousins might want to play with his brothers. Perhaps they'd all gone over to her *aenti*'s side of the house.

He strode in that direction as a buggy pulled into the driveway. His brothers tumbled out, ice cream cones in hand. But he had eyes only for Anna. He wanted to run over and take Emily's place, to help Anna into the wheelchair, but he froze.

Would he ever get a chance to speak to her alone?

"Levi, look!" Daniel charged toward him, Jonah in his wake.

They were all in one piece and seemed to be fine. And very happy.

Anna had that effect on everyone. She sowed joy wherever she went.

"We have to hurry home," Daniel said. "Betty is waiting for us. And so is dinner."

"Betty? I thought she wasn't coming until tonight." Then he frowned. "How do you know she's home?"

"We saw her. We went to—"

Emily placed a finger on her lips, then winked. Daniel smiled as if he'd gotten a secret message.

"There's a surprise waiting for you at home," Daniel said. "Well, more than one surprise. Not counting Betty. She's a good one."

Ach! He'd left the house a disaster, planning to clean it up after his class. Poor Betty would walk into a major mess.

"If my *aenti*'s back, we'd better hurry home," Levi said to Anna. "I would have liked . . ." He hesitated. "*Danke* so much for watching them."

His gaze locked on hers, and the softness in her eyes stirred something deep within. Levi might have stayed there, mesmerized, if Daniel hadn't tugged at his arm.

"Levi, come on," his brother begged, forcing Levi to break his connection with Anna.

Still, he couldn't leave without thanking her for all her help and meals. "You did so much for us while Betty was away. *Danke* for everything."

"I was happy to do it." She accompanied her words with a sweet smile.

A smile that made Levi want to stay and—

Daniel dragged him toward the buggy. "You're missing the surprises."

When they arrived home, Daniel offered to take care of the horse. What had gotten into his brother? He was usually the last to volunteer for extra work. Had spending time with Anna turned his brother around? That seemed almost impossible.

Levi headed toward the house, Jonah one step ahead of him. When he opened the back door, the aroma of cheese and onion and fried chicken wafted out. It would be so good to have Betty home to do the cooking, although her meals could never measure up to Anna's.

He stepped through the back door and stopped. How long had his *aenti* been here? The kitchen appeared spotless. Dishes done, floors mopped, dinner cooking. And come to think of it, the laundry wasn't still hanging on the line.

He turned to Jonah. "Who cleaned the kitchen?" He suspected the answer but wanted to hear it confirmed.

Jonah beamed. "Me, Anna, and Daniel."

"Anna? Did she clean other rooms too?"

His brother nodded. "I helped Emily clean upstairs." His eyes became sad. "Anna can't go upstairs."

If she could, Levi had no doubt she would have cleaned that too. As grateful as he was for her kindness, the picture of the disarray she'd cleaned made Levi ashamed. What had she thought of his sloppiness? Knowing Anna, she wouldn't judge, but Levi wished he'd stayed up all night to put everything in order. He'd gotten up at four to do laundry and make breakfast before doing his other chores.

Several dishes on the counter caught his eye. Sliced homemade bread, lemon bars, and snitz pie? Betty hadn't had time to make all that. Had Anna made the meal too? How could he ever thank her for all she'd done?

Betty entered the kitchen. "Are you almost ready for dinner?" From the glow on his *aenti*'s face, her visit had gone well.

Levi didn't need to ask, but he could see she was bursting to share her good news. "How did everything go?"

"*Wunderbar.*" Betty bustled over to the stove and peeked in. "Vern hasn't changed a bit."

"So, you're getting married?"

"We decided not to wait. The wedding will be the last Thursday in October."

October? Less than two months away? How will we care for the house without her? "Um, congratulations."

"*Danke.* I'm so pleased to see how Anna cared for the house. And Daniel raved about her cooking. I know you'll be in good hands here."

Good thing she hadn't seen the place this morning. But he wasn't marrying Anna. He hadn't even asked her about courting. If he did, what would she say?

"I hope the two of you will be as happy as Vern and I are. I can see how much she cares for you. She has that special sparkle in her eyes when she talks about you."

Really? Or was that just the love-light in Betty's eyes being reflected?

Chapter Twenty-Three

The truth hit Levi hard when he woke the next morning. He only had a short while to figure how he'd care for his brothers once Betty left. Anna had helped out while his aunt was away, but contrary to what Betty thought, he and Anna weren't dating.

Anna had done wonders with the messy house and with getting his brothers to do their household chores. The whole house looked and smelled fresh and homey. And the meal she'd left had been delicious. As usual. But he couldn't depend on her for meals or household chores. Even if they were courting, he wouldn't expect her to help. She'd been generous, but she had her own home and a baby to care for.

Those concerns stayed on Levi's mind as he and his family headed to the Eshes' house for church, but the second sermon hit Levi hard. The minister brought up the familiar topic of submission to God's will.

"We need to trust God in all circumstances, no matter how difficult," the minister said. "When we're in a state of *Gelassenheit*, we're in a place of yieldedness. We're willing to let everything happen without complaint, without worry."

Levi squirmed. He'd been fretting about the future instead of trusting it to God.

"If we find ourselves trying to figure out how things will work out, we're taking over God's responsibility. Ours is to humble ourselves and stop relying on our own limited human knowledge."

What had Levi been doing all morning? Using—or perhaps more truthfully, wasting—his time searching for solutions. Instead, he could have prayed and left the results up to God.

One other point the minister made kept echoing in Levi's mind as he ate the meal after church and drove the family home in the buggy. *Surrendering to the will of God removes all fear.*

His life had been riddled with anxiety—constant worry about his brothers, uncertainty about his relationship with Anna, agonizing over when and whether to ask her about courting. His so-called fears paled when compared to people living through life-threatening illnesses, poverty, injustice, wars.

How had he become so wrapped up in himself that he'd elevated his tiny concerns to major issues? All the energy he'd concentrated on his own problems could have been better spent doing something to help others.

Lord, please forgive me for focusing so much on myself that I failed to think about others. I turn my anxieties over to You. Help me to leave them there and to be open to Your will and to opportunities to help those around me.

Levi's spirits lifted as soon as he'd turned all his burdens over to his Heavenly Father. God had a plan and purpose for his life. He needed to remain humble and ready to serve.

* * *

Anna tucked Ciara into the pouch, cuddling her close as she completed her Monday chores. She'd grown so attached to the little girl she'd been keeping her almost every day. Ciara still jolted awake screaming at night, but she'd settled down a bit during the day. The constant closeness and touching seemed to be helping. Music also calmed Ciara, so Anna sang or hummed as she worked.

Emily knocked and peeked her head in the door. "I'm off to work, but *Mamm* asked if you could come over as soon as possible. The social worker wants to talk to you."

"I'm almost done mopping the kitchen. I'll go over as soon as I finish."

After Emily left, Anna hurriedly mopped the rest of the floor, changed Ciara, and prepared her bottle. She hoped Millie hadn't discovered how much time Ciara had been spending with Anna. Maybe they'd make Anna leave Ciara at her *aenti*'s house.

If they did, Anna would spend as much time as she could over there. And although she'd welcome some sleep, nights would be lonely. Anna tried to imagine not cuddling and feeding Ciara in the wee hours of the morning.

Her *aenti* had warned her not to get too attached to foster children because they were only temporary visitors. But Miriam hadn't always followed her own advice. Several years ago, they'd adopted two of their fostered teenagers, who were now out on their own, and they planned to adopt Xavier, whose mother had signed him over to the state.

With Ciara's mom facing drug charges, perhaps she'd decide to give up her little girl. Anna would love to adopt Ciara. That would be one way to fill the loneliness and make up for the fact that the accident had stolen her chance to have children.

Anna headed across the ramp to her *aenti*'s kitchen. Millie's car sat in the driveway. Maybe she should have waited and let Miriam change and feed Ciara.

"*Gut*, you're here," Miriam called when Anna entered the kitchen. "We're in the living room."

Millie smiled at Anna and Ciara. "She seems pretty contented." She turned to Miriam. "Looks like you both have been doing wonders with Ciara."

As Anna fed Ciara her bottle, Miriam waved toward the two of them. "Anna seems to have a magic touch with Ciara. She's calmed the baby down a lot."

With a brisk nod, Millie smiled. "Great job." Then she unzipped the briefcase beside her to pull out a clipboard. "It looks like the case against Ciara's mother is pretty airtight. Her grandmother petitioned for custody, and the judge granted it. I'll be taking Ciara to her new home today."

Anna sat shell-shocked. She was losing Ciara right here and right now? With no time to prepare? No time to say good-bye?

Noo . . . she wanted to scream. She wanted to protest. She wanted to run away and hide Ciara. But how could she keep the baby from her own family?

"Will her grandmother be able to get up all night with her?" Anna choked out the question as she held Ciara even tighter. "Will she cuddle her to calm her? Will she—"

Millie held up a hand to stop her. Her voice, when she spoke, was filled with compassion. "It's hard giving up a baby you've gotten attached to. I'll note any tips you have and pass them on to Ciara's grandmother."

Blinking back tears, Anna tried to think of anything and everything she'd done to quiet and soothe Ciara. She listed her suggestions for Millie. Then she emphasized a second time, "Most of all, cuddling and singing and humming work best. Ciara really loves hymns. It is—was—the only thing that calmed her fits at night. And carrying her around in a baby sling during the day helps."

Millie finished jotting down the notes, completed the paperwork, and tucked her clipboard back into her brief-case. Then came the moment Anna dreaded. Millie put the strap of her briefcase over her shoulder and stood. With her arms outstretched, she walked toward Anna.

Anna wanted to shield Ciara from those work-worn hands. "I—I haven't burped her."

With a laugh, Millie scooped up Ciara and set the baby against her shoulder. "I think I can manage that." She patted the baby's back.

"She prefers it if you rub in circles instead of patting." Anna tried to keep her voice steady, but her words came out tear-clogged.

"Thanks for the tip." Millie followed Anna's instructions as she walked toward the front door. "I'll be sure to pass that on to her grandmother."

Then before Anna could whisper a good-bye, Millie strode out the door. Anna stared out the window as the social worker buckled Ciara into a car seat and drove off. The world crashed around her.

Honking outside the window stirred Anna from her fog. Why didn't that noise stop? The horn sounded again.

She peeked out. The van waited on the shoulder of the road. She'd been so mired in her gloom she'd forgotten today was Monday.

Maybe she should wave them on. But she'd dressed in her half apron and *kapp* to meet Millie, so she was ready to go. At least outwardly.

She wheeled out the door and waved to the driver.

Getting out of the house would be good for her. And seeing Levi always brightened her day.

After Millie took Ciara, Anna followed her *aenti*'s advice to keep busy. Doing extra work around the house kept her hands busy, but none of it stopped her mind from spinning or her heart from hurting.

"Are you all right?" the nurse asked as she strapped Anna's wheelchair into place.

"I will be." Anna hoped that would be true.

"I hope so." The nurse sounded uncertain.

Even Anna herself wondered how long it would take to get over losing Ciara. Or would she ever?

Her other concern was Ciara's mother. If the grandmother had raised a daughter who took drugs and neglected her daughter, would the baby be safe there? Or would Ciara grow up to be like her mother?

Sometimes good parents raised a rebellious, troublesome child. It happened in the Amish community too. Anna shouldn't judge the grandmother. She may have done her best. The only thing Anna could do was to pray for Ciara every day and trust God to provide her with a safe, loving home.

By the time she arrived at the center, Anna had left Ciara in God's hands, but the ache of missing her still remained. To lift her spirits, she rolled past Levi's door while he worked with one of the school-aged children.

He caught sight of her, and his smile drew her closer to the window glass. Like a magnet, the pull kept her stuck to the spot. Levi seemed to be equally as drawn to her. Or was it only wishful thinking?

The boy he was working with said something to him, and Levi broke his connection with Anna to concentrate on the child. She should wait somewhere else, but she fought an internal battle. Although she wanted to keep watching, common sense won. She moved away, determined to avoid the room until her session, but her thoughts remained with Levi.

She wandered down the hall, peeking into other classrooms, until she ended up in the lunchroom. A few people sat at the tables eating snacks. Some smiled and greeted her. Anna replied, but she wanted to be alone with her daydreams. Focusing on Levi eased a little of her pain over Ciara.

She'd drifted so far away, she jumped when a voice behind her called her name.

When she turned her head, Levi stood there, smiling down at her. "Jensen's mother picked him up ten minutes early for another appointment. Do you want to start now?"

"Of course." Anna cringed inside. She sounded way too eager.

The smile blossoming on Levi's face erased her worries. He seemed happy about having extra time with her. And he'd sought her out to ask.

But Anna didn't want to get her hopes up. She'd just experienced having her dreams dashed twice. Once by Gabe. And today with Ciara. She wasn't ready to take another chance with disappointment.

Anna's enthusiastic reply thrilled Levi. Yet despite her upbeat answer, her eyes held sorrow. Was she still pining for Gabe?

Levi didn't want to ask because he dreaded hearing the answer. But he couldn't ignore the pain in her eyes. "Are you all right?"

"Not really." She took a deep breath. "The social

worker"—Anna's voice broke—"came for Ciara today. She—she'll be living with her grandmother."

"*Ach*, Anna, I'm so sorry. That has to be hard." Levi wished he could take her hands or wrap an arm around her.

"It is. I—I got so attached to her." Anna clenched the wheelchair arms. "My *aenti* warned me about that, but how can you hold a baby and not get attached?"

"I imagine that would be impossible." Especially for a warmhearted, caring woman like Anna.

Anna stared down at the floor. "My *aenti* says hard work helps with the pain of loss." She waved a hand. "I guess we should get to work."

"First, I want to thank you for all you did while my aunt was gone. And cleaning the house? That was so kind and generous of you."

"Your brothers helped. And Emily did the whole upstairs."

Levi laughed. "I know how much help my brothers are. They probably made extra work."

"That's not true. They both did a good job."

"Only because of you." Levi had no doubt who deserved the credit.

Anna shook her head. "I showed Daniel how to do some of the chores, and he picked everything up very quickly."

That had been Levi's mistake. Maybe if he'd demonstrated the jobs . . . *Neh*, he hadn't been an expert himself, so his instructions would never have made the impression Anna's did.

"I wish I had a way to repay you."

"There's nothing to repay. Besides, you've given me more in these sessions than I got in my previous therapy."

"I'm glad to know that, but still—"

Anna interrupted him. "If our barn collapsed, would you come for the barn raising?"

"Of course."

"And would you expect me to repay you for doing that?"

"Of course not."

"Then why would you feel you need to repay me for helping when you had a need?"

She had a point, but Levi couldn't help feeling obligated. He'd find some way to help her. Maybe he could do that today by easing a little of her sadness over Ciara by distracting her.

"I had an idea of something new we could work on if you'd like," he said.

Behind the unhappiness in her eyes, his words kindled a spark. A tiny flicker of interest.

Gut. He'd caught her attention. "It upset Jonah that you couldn't go upstairs at our house. I thought maybe you'd want to practice with crutches on steps."

"That's a good idea. I thought about that when—" She appeared flustered. "Well, I could be a bigger help to my *aenti* if I could climb stairs."

Whew! Levi had worried she might not want to try. Working on the steps would keep her here for a few more weeks of sessions. At that prospect, a different kind of fire flashed through Levi, setting his whole body—and spirit—ablaze.

He shouldn't ask Anna today about courting. Not now when he should be working. And not on a day when she'd suffered a loss. But soon. Very soon.

Chapter Twenty-Four

The next few weeks flew by, and Anna completed everything she needed to do for being a foster parent. Losing Ciara had left a gaping hole in her days and her heart. But she moved forward with the process. She'd steel herself against getting too attached to the next children she fostered. Anna wasn't sure that was possible, but she was determined to try.

She'd passed the home inspection, and her interview had gone well. Because she'd be under her *aenti*'s supervision, everything had moved ahead smoothly. She was ready and eager to get started.

She hadn't expected to have a placement so soon, though. On Friday as the van dropped her off after her latest session with Levi, Miriam came rushing out of her front door, her face creased with worry. Anna headed toward her *aenti*, hoping nobody was hurt.

"Millie called to ask if you and I could handle emergency care starting tonight. Immigration officers raided a plant near here and rounded up illegal workers. Some of them have children at home with no one to care for them."

Those poor children. And their families. Anna's heart

went out to them. She'd been heartbroken when she lost Ciara. How would she have felt to have her own children taken from her?

"I have two open beds," Miriam went on, "so I'm taking two of the children. Millie also has a sibling group of two brothers and a sister. I told her you could put the boys in the bedroom with the twin beds."

Anna nodded, but her mind whirled. She'd been expecting one child. Three at once? How old were they? How would she care for all of them?

"The Mennonite church gathered a bunch of portable cribs, cots, and rollaway beds for anyone who needs them," Miriam went on. "I'll ask them for one for the little girl. Are you all right with that many?"

"I—I guess so." No matter how overwhelmed she felt, how could she turn away any motherless child? Anna's own concerns paled in comparison to the agony these children must have experienced.

"Don't worry. You'll be fine," Miriam assured her. "And we'll all be here to help. We're taking two sisters who are six and seven. Your three are younger."

"How young?"

"I don't think any of them are school age. Their mother, who's Somalian, was caring for several of the workers' children, so they swept her up in the raid too." Miriam's eyes reflected her sorrow. "I don't understand all this."

Neither did Anna. It made no sense. Why would you arrest people who were working hard and contributing to the community? Why didn't everyone open their hearts to others who needed a place to stay?

"I wonder what would happen in this world if people truly followed God's command to love everyone and care for strangers." Miriam shook her head. "Even Jesus was born in a stable far from home."

As much as Anna wished she could change people's hearts and minds, right now she could only do her part and care for three children separated from their mother. "I'll go over and get some supper ready. They'll probably be hungry. We can all eat together."

That was one less concern for Anna to deal with tonight. "I'll come and help you get the meal ready."

"*Danke*." Miriam headed toward the house.

Anna wheeled toward the ramp and followed her *aenti* into the kitchen. She'd been expecting to have some time to get used to being a foster parent, but evidently God had a different plan.

Dear Lord, I don't know why You're sending three children to me at one time, but please help me to care for these little ones.

While a huge pot of spaghetti bubbled on the stove, Anna supervised the younger children in setting the table, and the older girls sliced and buttered bread. Tomatoes, garlic, and onion perfumed the air as Miriam stirred the thickening sauce.

The knock they'd been waiting for the past hour finally came. Hannah hurried to the door.

"Let's not overwhelm the children," Miriam suggested. "Anna and I will greet them. The rest of you stay in the kitchen."

Anna accompanied her *aenti* into the living room as Millie led five bewildered children, each carrying a bag, through the door.

Millie sniffed the air. "Yum. Smells delicious in here."

"You're welcome to stay for dinner," Miriam said.

Her eyes weary and sorrowful, Millie shook her head.

"The other workers and I have too many children to place tonight."

While Millie introduced the children, Hannah ran to the kitchen and returned with a plate of spaghetti and two pieces of bread. "Maybe you can eat this on the way."

Millie stared at the food. "You're an angel. I won't have time to stop for dinner."

Hannah went over to the girl who looked close to her age, who was staring longingly at Millie's plate. "Do you want to come and have some supper too?"

The girl nodded, and Hannah beckoned to the others. "You can come too."

Once the children left the room, Miriam moved closer to the social worker and lowered her voice. "What's happening to their parents?"

"I don't know, other than that they've all been transported to York County Prison." Millie turned to Anna. "Taban, Assad, and Jamilah's mother was married to a Somalian-American, but he died recently."

Poor babies. First their father, now their mother. Anna hoped they wouldn't be separated for long. "How long will it be before they get to see their mother?"

"I really can't say." Millie looked troubled. "In some cases, immigration agents realize they made a mistake and turn the parents loose or let one parent go home to care for the children."

With only one parent, that might mean the three little ones could be back with their mother soon. Anna wished for their sakes that would be the case. And for the other two girls as well.

"Lawyers are trying to help some of them, but I've had cases where one or both parents get deported or remain in jail for a long time while their cases make their way through the courts."

"And what about the two girls I have?"

"Both of their parents have been detained. Let's hope they let one go." Millie didn't sound too hopeful. "I need to leave, but you have my cell number if you have any questions." She lifted the plate of spaghetti. "Thanks so much for this."

After Millie left, Anna's *onkel* came in the back door, and they all sat down for supper.

To everyone's surprise, as soon as Anna helped serve them their food, all three children bowed their heads and recited a prayer together. The two older Somalian girls did the same.

Before they lifted their heads, Assad added, "Dear God, please keep Mommy safe and bring her back to us."

Anna's eyes filled with tears. When the three little ones looked up, their own eyes were damp.

"I miss Mommy," Jamilah wailed.

Taban leaned over to hug her. "Me too."

Assad's moist eyes held hope. "She promised God would take care of us."

The two older Somalian girls stared at them with wet eyes.

"I prayed my mommy and daddy would come back too," the younger of the two, Uba, said.

Her older sister stared across the table at Anna's three foster children. "And I prayed for your mom too." Bilan turned to Miriam. "Their mom"—she gestured to the three younger children—"takes care of us after school."

"She was our pastor's wife," Uba added. "But he died."

"She means the pastor was killed," her older sister said.

"Two men stormed into our church and shot him. Mom says it was a hate crime."

Anna sucked in a breath. Hate crime? How could anyone hate another human being? Especially a pastor?

Assad piped up, "The police said the men didn't want someone with our color skin talking about Jesus."

"They don't want us to live here." Taban's eyes held a sadness he was too young to bear.

"Yes." Uba's eyes squeezed shut, and her face screwed up as if she were in great pain. "They shot five people in our choir while we were singing hymns."

"My dad and some other men tackled them and held them until the police came," Bilan, the oldest girl said in a matter-of-fact tone that didn't match the distress on her face.

Little Jamilah's lips trembled. "It was scary."

"The ambulance came," Taban said. "With loud sirens."

"Nobody else died," Uba said. "But our aunt is still in a coma."

Anna's stomach clenched. What horrors had these children been through? And now to be separated from their parents. She wanted to hug each of them close, wipe away their pain, and dry the tears welling in their eyes.

"Daddy asked Jesus to forgive them before he died. And he told us to do that too," Assad reminded them.

Anna's *onkel* cleared his throat. "We will pray for those men and others who carry hate in their hearts," he said in a thick voice. "We should eat before the food gets cold, but we pray silently before we do."

"Patties down," Emily reminded Iris, and held her hands still.

Then they all, including their five Somalian foster children, bowed their heads.

Anna's prayers included a heartfelt plea that the children would soon be reunited with their families. She had no idea how many families had been affected by this immigration sweep, but she prayed for each and every one.

His heart singing, Levi woke on Saturday morning. He'd prayed about his decision for weeks. God seemed to be leading him in this direction, but every time he started to speak to Anna about it, the Lord urged him to be patient.

For the past few weeks, he'd avoided talking to Anna about his feelings because he wanted to give her time to get over her old boyfriend and to adjust to Ciara's loss. Although she missed the baby, she'd moved forward with the process of becoming a foster parent. And yesterday when she came to class, her eyes sparkled. She'd been certified.

Yet behind the joy, he sensed a lingering sadness. That might be permanent. She'd always miss the small baby she'd cared for and loved.

Levi had followed God's guidance about waiting. But today, on such a bright, sunny morning, his whole body seethed with impatience. Right now, before Anna got distracted with caring for another child, he wanted to let her know his intentions. He hoped she'd agree to court.

He had no trainings scheduled at the firehouse today, because they had a chicken barbecue. Usually, he helped with those fundraisers, but he hadn't volunteered, so he'd have the whole day free to spend with Anna. If she agreed to a date.

Maybe they could pick up a meal at the firehouse and take it to the park for a picnic. Levi dreamed of a day of picnicking, talking, and most of all, staring into each other's eyes.

But what if Anna didn't feel the same way he did? What if she turned him down?

Levi hated to dwell on that possibility. If that happened, he'd head back to the firehouse and offer to help with the fundraiser. Keeping busy wouldn't erase the heartbreak. But it gave him a backup plan for the day.

He rushed outside to feed and care for the horse and then returned to the kitchen, whistling. A skillet filled with crisp bacon and hash browns sizzled on the stove. Levi inhaled deeply, and his stomach growled. It was great to have Betty back. And she'd be here all day to keep an eye on his brothers. Before her trip to Fort Plain, Levi had never noticed or appreciated all she'd done for them.

"Breakfast smells delicious," he said as he passed through the kitchen, in a hurry to get cleaned up for Anna.

"You look chipper this morning." Betty smiled. "I'm guessing you plan to spend time with Anna today. Want me to fix some lunch for both of you?"

"*Danke*, but I'll get some barbecued chicken from the firehouse for both of us." If Anna agreed to go out with him. He tried not to dwell on the possibility that she'd say no.

At the foot of the stairs, Levi paused and called out, "I'll tell the guys at the firehouse to save meals for all of you. That way you won't have to cook dinner tonight." After making sure meals were on the table each night while Betty was gone—even if Anna had done the hard work of preparing them—Levi realized how much work it took to keep a house running and wanted to give Betty a break. She'd done it every night for years and years.

"Your brothers would like that." Then she added, "And don't take long getting ready. Breakfast is almost done."

Levi intended to get ready quickly. He wanted to spend as much of the day as possible with Anna.

In fresh, clean clothes, he sped through breakfast and hitching up the horse. But once he reached Anna's street he slowed. Doubts overtook him. What if she didn't feel the same way about him as he did about her? What if she turned him down?

By the time he pulled in the driveway and tied the horse's reins to a post, Betty's delicious breakfast had turned into a churning mess in his stomach. Each step he took toward Anna's ramp added another worry. Worry built to dread. A dread of rejection.

With a shaky hand, he reached out to knock. The answer to his whole future lay behind that door.

Chapter Twenty-Five

Anna woke, groggy, cramped, and sweaty, with her hand stiff but still wrapped around the small girl's. The sleepless night flooded back. Would every night of foster care mean no rest? So far, it had.

Last night, after the three children had been bathed and dressed in their pajamas, they'd knelt by their beds to say their tearful prayers, begging God to protect their mommy and bring her home safely.

Anna bent over so she could place her hands on Taban's and Jamilah's shoulders, wishing she had one more hand for Assad. Her heart went out to these three fatherless little ones, who desperately missed their mother.

From his bag, Assad pulled out a Bible. "Mom"—he choked and lowered his head—"always reads to us before we turn out the light." His shoulders shook as he held out the worn, leather-bound book.

The children had only been able to bring a few possessions and clothes, so the fact that Assad had chosen this revealed what a special place God's Word had in their lives.

Anna flipped through the Bible to find a passage of comfort. John 14:1 seemed fitting. "'Let not your heart be troubled,'" she read. When she got to the sixth verse, both boys recited it with her. Her heart thrilled to know that these three children had been taught Scripture from a young age.

With both of their parents so grounded in the Word, what could their mother have possibly done wrong that she needed to be arrested?

That question niggled at her mind as she crawled into bed after hours of comforting the two younger children through their heartrending sobs. Going to bed in a strange house for the first time in their lives without their mother, so soon after they'd lost their dad, proved to be disorienting and frightening.

Assad's eyes swam with unshed tears as he tried to help calm his younger brother and sister. His lower lip trembled. When he curled up in bed with his back toward Anna, she glimpsed a stream of wetness trickling down his cheeks.

Cradling Jamilah in her arms, Anna turned her chair so she could rub his back, which made him cry harder. But he kept his sobbing silent. Probably because he was trying to be the strong older brother.

His need to be the caretaker had been apparent in how he'd shepherded his brother and sister over to Anna's house. He checked on Jamilah's cot and dug her lovey from her bag and handed it to her. She cuddled it close and stuck her thumb in her mouth. Then he helped tuck Taban in bed and directed the Bible reading and prayers.

Something about Assad's care for his siblings reminded Anna of Levi. He watched out for his younger brothers, even worrying about leaving them alone when they were old enough to be on their own.

Jamilah's head lolled against Anna. She'd grown heavier

as she got sleepier. After giving Assad one last pat, Anna wheeled the little girl to her rollaway bed.

Anna lifted Jamilah to set her in bed, but the small girl wrapped her arms around Anna's neck, practically choking her, and held on tight. Jamilah had her eyes closed, so she might be dozing. Maybe she believed she was clinging to her mother.

Her heart breaking for the little girl, Anna held Jamilah until soft, even breathing indicated she'd fallen asleep. Anna struggled to lift the child and lean over without disturbing her dreams.

Once she did, Anna stayed for a while, one hand stroking Jamilah's dark, curly hair from her face. She prayed for the small girl and her brothers, their mother and the other parents rounded up in the raid. Then she added petitions for the men—and all those like them in the world—who'd allowed their hate to lead to violence and death. She prayed that God would touch their lives, leading to repentance and a change of heart.

She'd passed the children's bedroom on her way to her own room. Taban had curled up in bed with Assad, who'd wrapped his arms around his younger brother. Assad, the protector.

After she slid into bed, another older brother came to mind and filled Anna's dreams.

A shriek jolted her awake.

Jamilah!

She had to get to the little girl before she woke her brothers. But sleep had fogged her brain and sapped her strength. She fumbled trying to get into her chair.

The screams grew louder.

Please, Lord, help me comfort her.

When Anna reached Jamilah's bedside, Assad stood there, awkwardly patting his sister's back.

He was leaning over her, whispering in her ear, "Mommy will be back soon. God's taking care of us."

Assad looked relieved to see Anna. "She's not listening to me. I don't think she's awake."

Jamilah's eyes remained closed, but she clutched at the sheet. "Don't go, Mommy!"

Assad turned troubled eyes to Anna. "She's dreaming about Mommy." His lips quivered.

Anna transferred herself to the bed and scooped Jamilah into her arms. Then she patted a spot beside them, inviting Assad to join her. He hopped up, and Anna wrapped one arm around him, pulling him close.

Jamilah's cries subsided to hiccupping breaths. "Mommy," she choked out, cuddling closer to Anna.

"She thinks"—Assad said in a broken voice—"you're our mommy."

"I know," Anna whispered. "Maybe that will stop her nightmares."

Jamilah stuck her thumb back in her mouth and sucked hard. Assad tucked her lovey into that fist and then took her other hand.

"I'm here, Jamilah," he crooned in a sweet, low voice over and over.

Anna had no idea when she fell asleep, but when she woke, Assad lay next to her, breathing deeply and rhythmically. Pins and needles prickled the length of her arm from the weight of the little girl she held. And curled up by her feet, Taban whimpered in his sleep.

So much for the separate beds she'd been required to have for each child. And Anna hoped no one would ask where she spent the night. She hadn't intended it to be in this rollaway bed with all three children.

Maybe she could slip off to her own bed now. Gently, she laid Jamilah beside Assad and tucked a sheet around her, hoping it might keep her snug. She slid to the edge of the mattress. It would bounce when she got into the chair.

Please, Lord, don't let them wake.

As she settled into the chair, Assad sat up, his face tense with worry.

"Where are you going? You're not leaving us, are you?"

"I'll be in the other room. You can call me if you need me." Anna hoped her words comforted him. "Jamilah is right beside you," she pointed out.

Assad nodded. "Did you know my name means *lion*? Daddy always said that meant I needed to be strong and brave."

"You have been, but it's all right to cry when sad things happen. Even Jesus cried."

"He did?"

"We can read about it tomorrow." All Anna wanted to do was crawl back into bed, but she couldn't until Assad had closed his eyes. She yawned several times while waiting for Assad to settle.

He wriggled close to Jamilah and put an arm around her. Anna sang several songs in a soft voice. Assad gave in to sleep during her third repetition of "Jesus Loves Me."

Anna's bone-deep exhaustion kicked in as soon as her head hit the pillow. She didn't wake until Jamilah tugged at the sheet a few hours later, needing to go to the bathroom.

Afterward, Anna took the little girl back to her bed and

tucked her in. But even with her brothers beside her, Jamilah wouldn't let go of Anna's hand, so Anna spent the rest of the night dozing off, slumped in her wheelchair.

When she woke the next morning, sore and achy, she slipped her hand from Jamilah's, got dressed, and headed into the kitchen. She'd make a big breakfast to start the day, but she had no idea what they'd do after that.

Sausages sizzled on the stove as Anna poured scrambled eggs into another frying pan. Assad padded into the kitchen, his eyes sad and faraway.

"That smells good." His voice, small and scared, still managed a note of politeness. "Should I wake Taban and Jamilah?"

Anna took a deep breath and nodded. Her day was about to start. She said a quick prayer that she'd be able to comfort the children and keep them occupied so they wouldn't dwell on their sorrow.

A short while later, all three children sat at the table, hands folded. Anna waited until they said their blessing aloud, then she encouraged them to join in the silent prayer. They seemed eager to spend more time talking to God.

They ate quickly, their heads down, their eyes holding a world of pain. She expected protests when she assigned chores after breakfast, but everyone cooperated. They also did their jobs well, so they must have been used to helping around the house.

Taban stood still in the middle of the kitchen. "It's so quiet here. No cars or trucks or sirens."

Anna hadn't thought about how different this life might be for them if they were used to a city apartment. Maybe they'd enjoy seeing the horses, chickens, and cows in her *aenti*'s barn.

Glancing around the living room, Taban asked, "Don't you have a radio for music?"

Assad elbowed him and muttered, "Use your best manners."

But Taban ignored his older brother's warning. "Where's your TV?"

"We don't have TVs," Anna explained. "Without electricity, we couldn't plug them in anyway."

"No electricity?" Taban glanced around as if he didn't believe her. "But what if your cell phone dies? And how do you dry your hair? Or—"

Another sharp jab in his ribs from Assad stopped him.

Anna suspected these were only the first of many questions she'd need to answer. "We don't need those things. The air dries your hair. And I have a black box—a phone—that runs on batteries." As a foster parent, she was required to have access to a phone.

"So, we can't watch any of our shows on TV?" Taban's melancholy eyes grew even more downcast. "And no music? Not even hymns?"

"We can sing those," Anna suggested.

"It's not the same." Taban sank onto the couch. "When will Mommy be back?"

Anna wished she had an answer for him. "I'm not sure."

"Soon?"

She had no idea. "I don't know."

Assad sat beside his brother. "It'll be all right. God is taking care of her."

Jamilah wriggled up onto the couch next to him. "But I want Mommy now."

A huge sigh lifted Assad's chest, as if he were carrying a burden much too heavy for his young soul. "I know, Jamilah. I do too. But we have to wait."

Anna wanted to sweep them all into her arms and hold them tight. They were too young to be going through this. She needed to distract them and keep them occupied today and every day until their mother returned. If she ever did.

"Let's go get dressed and make the beds." Anna tried to sound upbeat and cheerful, but suggesting more chores could never replace TV or a mother's presence.

All three children cooperated, but the gloom on their faces made it clear that keeping them busy wouldn't distract them from their loss.

As Anna brushed Jamilah's tangled curls, her brothers stood beside her, each holding one of her hands. Tears dribbled down her cheeks and onto her cat T-shirt.

At a knock on the front door, hope flashed into both boys' eyes.

Mommy? Taban mouthed as if afraid to say the word aloud.

They let go of Jamilah's hands and raced to the door. Anna, hairbrush in one hand, clasped the small girl's hand and rolled toward the door at a three-year-old's pace.

Before they reached the living room, a deep voice asked, "Is Anna here?"

Levi? Anna's heart leapt. She wanted to rush to the door, but she stayed with Jamilah. When she reached the living room, the boys were peering around Levi, who stood on the porch.

"Come in," Anna said to him, surprised by the disappointment in his eyes. Was he hurt by the lack of welcome?

Both boys continued staring out the door. Then Assad turned to Levi.

"Did you bring Mommy back?"

Anna hated to dash their hopes. "I'm so sorry, but Levi

didn't bring your mother. He's my, umm"—Anna fumbled for a word to describe him—"teacher."

Levi looked hurt, and Anna wished she'd used the word *friend*. But that might have conjured up images of being her boyfriend. Something best left alone.

Teacher? Is that all I am to her? Levi tried not to let his dismay show. Maybe he'd been wrong about asking her on a date. But what excuse could he give for showing up suddenly on a Saturday morning?

And who were these children? They'd been expecting their mother instead of him. Perhaps Anna was babysitting them, and she'd soon be free.

With a hangdog expression on his face, the oldest boy closed the door. "When will Mommy be here?"

"I wish I knew, Assad. Maybe we'll hear more news today."

At Anna's answer to the small boy's question, Levi's plans for a day alone with her came tumbling down. Could these be foster children? She'd only gotten certified, and she had three little ones already?

When the two boys had answered the door, Levi's fears had kicked in the way they always did when he had to be around youngsters. Possible dangers raced through his mind, keeping his whole body tense and on alert. What if something happened to one of them? What if he failed them the way he'd failed Jonah?

"Are you all right?"

Anna's question startled Levi from those nightmarish scenarios. Instead, it drew his attention to her tired eyes. "I should be asking you that."

She laughed. "I'm fine. Or as good as I can be with

about three or four hours of sleep. The children had a rough first night."

First night? They must be foster children then. "I see." Now what? Should he tell her about his plans for the day or just leave? She had to be wondering why he'd come.

Levi cleared his throat. "The firehouse is having a chicken barbecue today. I came to see if you'd like that, but I didn't know you were busy."

Had her eyes lit up because he'd said "barbecue" or because he'd said he wanted to take her?

"What a fun idea! I've been trying to think of something to do with the children today. They might like to go to the barbecue."

Levi gulped. He hadn't meant to take three children. Panic filled him. Parking lots were full of cars and careless drivers. The firemen cooked the chicken over open flames. Not to mention falls or— He shuddered.

Anna must have registered his reaction. "I didn't mean we had to go with you. I only meant it might keep the children occupied. At least for a few hours."

So, she didn't want to go with him. She'd been excited about the barbecue or maybe about finding an activity to do with the three little ones. Not about spending time with him.

All three of the children had hopped up on the couch. They sat huddled together, looking dejected.

His heart went out to them. *The poor kids*. He didn't know their story, but he couldn't imagine what it would be like to be separated from their parents.

Anna pulled up next to the couch. She reached out to brush the little girl's hair with tender strokes. He swallowed hard. She'd make such a good mother.

Maybe for a different husband. She'd made it clear she wasn't interested in going with him.

Then Anna glanced up, and their eyes met and held. Shocks zinged through his body. Her eyes seemed to be sending a message that contradicted her words. Maybe he'd been mistaken about her reason for not going with him.

"How will you get to the firehouse?" he asked.

"I don't know. This is Emily's Saturday at the restaurant, and my *aenti* has too many children to keep an eye on."

"I could take you if you want."

"You would?" Her eyes shone. Then she looked troubled. "But I can't leave the children with my *aenti*. All three of them have to go along. And you . . ."

Anna's sympathetic look melted him. She must be remembering his reaction to Ciara and his story about Jonah.

His words, which stuck in his clogged throat, came out gruff. "It's all right." He tried to correct his tone. "I'd be happy to take all of you."

Anna glowed like a girl who'd just been given a special present. "*Danke*. That would be wonderful."

Levi's heart overflowed with joy. She'd said yes. Not to his original plan to spending time together. Instead, his invitation had been for all four of them. So maybe her excitement stemmed from having a chance to eat barbecue or to entertain the children, who definitely appeared to need some cheering up.

Perhaps this was God's way of reminding him to be patient.

Chapter Twenty-Six

Anna finished the last few brush strokes on Jamilah's hair, mainly to tear her gaze from Levi's. And to calm her racing pulse. She'd get to spend the day with him.

When he'd first mentioned the barbecue, she didn't know if he'd been offering to bring her a meal or if he'd intended to take her along to the firehouse. He might only be doing it to thank her for making meals, but her sensible mind couldn't convince her thumping heart to see Levi's invitation as repayment.

"Would you all like to go for chicken barbecue?" Anna asked the three children.

At first, they stared at her as if they didn't understand the question.

Then Assad raised a hesitant question. "You mean at Steak & Wings? Mom always says it's too expensive."

At the word *Mom,* tears spilled down Jamilah's cheeks.

Assad reached over to squeeze her hand. Taban bit his lip.

Anna wished she could gather them all up in her arms for a group hug. Her throat hurt to speak. "This is outside at the firehouse. You can watch them cook the chicken."

"They also let you climb into the fire engine and see one of the ambulances," Levi added.

Taban's eyes lit up. "We can see a fire truck?"

Levi nodded, and Taban slid off the couch. With a sigh, Assad followed and turned to help Jamilah to the floor.

As they traipsed down the ramp to Levi's buggy, he kept a close eye on all three children. Anna hoped he could relax and enjoy the time together. But with the way he constantly watched for accidents or problems, that seemed almost impossible.

When they reached the buggy, the children stopped and stared.

His eyes wide, Assad pointed. "Are we riding in that?"

Jamilah stepped closer. "Like a princess carriage?"

"A horse?" Taban moved forward to touch the horse's side. "Is it real?"

The horse stamped and snorted. Taban jumped back.

"A real horsey?" Jamilah sidled next to Taban.

Levi put a hand on each child's shoulder and led them toward the horse's head. "If you let her smell you first, she'll be less skittish." He showed them how to let the horse sniff them. "Now you can rub her nose."

Once all three of them had gotten acquainted with the horse, Levi boosted them into the buggy's back seat. Then he turned to Anna. "Shall I help you?"

Anna couldn't look at him, or she'd be tempted to ask him to lift her. "I can do it myself." She didn't mean to sound so curt. She'd only been trying to keep her runaway feelings under control.

"I'm sorry I sounded rude. It's just that I'm used to taking care of myself." And that she'd be afraid of her reaction if Levi touched her. Even if it was for assistance.

"Of course." He didn't sound at all perturbed. "It's important for you to be independent."

She should have known he'd understand. He'd been so in tune with her needs in every session. He had a gift for reading people.

Levi waited until she'd gotten situated in the passenger seat, then he slid the door closed, and folded the wheelchair to take along.

Assad felt all around the seat. "Where are the seat belts?"

"We don't have any," Anna replied.

"That's dangerous."

At Assad's panicked words, Levi, who'd been getting into the driver's seat, stopped and stared around anxiously. "What's dangerous?"

"Not having seat belts." Anna spoke in calm, measured tones, hoping to quiet Levi's concerns. She was glad she had because he turned in her direction with a grateful smile.

A smile that made her heart leap. A smile that added extra sunshine to her day.

Levi untied the horse and got in. When he clucked to his horse, the buggy jerked as it started down the driveway.

Taban squealed. Jamilah shrieked. Assad, seated between them, took his brother's and sister's hands. They seemed to be squeezing his fingers tightly. But Assad didn't flinch.

Before they reached the end of the driveway, a deep frown marred his brow. "What if Mommy comes for us? And we're gone?"

Anna doubted their mother would be back so soon. But Levi pulled the horse to a stop.

"Should we let your *aenti* know where we'll be? She

can call my cell if their mother shows up. I always keep a phone with me in case the EMTs need extra help."

Heat rose in Anna's cheeks. She'd been so excited about going out with Levi, she hadn't even thought to tell Miriam they were leaving.

"Why don't I run in to let her know?" Levi handed the reins to Anna. "I'll give her my number."

If Anna's cheeks had been hot before, they blazed when Miriam poked her head out the front door and craned her neck to see Anna in the buggy. Maybe Miriam was only reassuring herself that the children were all there, but her gaze held more than curiosity about the children's welfare. Anna hoped Levi didn't notice Miriam's raised eyebrows and approving smile.

She didn't want to make him uncomfortable or scare him off before they enjoyed their time together.

Levi headed back to the buggy, his steps and spirits both floating. He'd get to spend the day with Anna. That joy blotted out some of his worries over keeping an eye on three little ones.

Before he climbed into the driver's seat, he checked on the three wide-eyed children. He needed to concentrate on helping them rather than focusing on himself and his fears.

The Sunday sermon replayed in his mind. He'd gotten caught up in fretting rather than trusting God. He needed to believe that whatever happened, the Lord had a purpose.

Please help me to let go of my fears and my need to control the outcome of every situation and instead to trust You every step of the way.

Praying relaxed the tightness in his jaw and the tautness

in his muscles. Until he sat next to Anna. This time, a different kind of tension filled him. Their hands brushed as she handed him the reins, and a shiver ran through him. Would he be able to handle being this close to her? Especially when visions of courting filled his mind.

He'd dreamed of this date with just the two of them, but even this semi-date with three children for company made him deliriously happy.

"I'm so glad you could come." Levi winced inside. Had he gushed?

Then Anna beamed at him, and rays of sunshine dissipated all doubts. "*Danke* for taking us."

Even the word *us* couldn't dim his joy. Anna sat beside him in his buggy. *Jah*, the back seat held three others, but she was here with him.

Little gasps came from the back seat as the horse picked up speed and the buggy bounced along. Levi slowed his pace. These *Englischers* wouldn't be used to buggy rides, and he didn't want to scare them.

Anna shot him a grateful smile. "This is all new to them," she whispered.

Behind them, one of the boys said in a small, scared voice, "It's so bumpy and noisy."

"The wheels are metal, Taban," Anna explained. "That's what makes the clattering noise. Cars have rubber tires, so they sound quieter."

"And the horse's hooves clip-clop." Taban sounded frightened.

"Cars make noises too. So do buses," his older brother pointed out. "You're not scared of them."

"Nooo." Taban didn't sound convinced.

"I'm a princess." The little girl sat with her head held

high, but her eyes revealed her terror. "But I don't like the bumping."

"*Shh*." Her brother leaned over and, in a whisper loud enough for both Anna and Levi to hear, warned the other two, "You don't want to hurt the man's feelings."

Anna grinned. "I guess I forgot to introduce everyone." She leaned over the seat. "This is Levi." She waved in his direction, then she told him, "The oldest boy is Assad. His brother is Taban, and his sister is Jamilah."

While keeping his eyes on the road, Levi tried to mentally match the names with the faces. It dawned on him that if he and Anna started a relationship, he'd have to get used to a lot of different children coming and going. That would be a challenge to his recent decision to let God control his life and his fears.

When they arrived at the firehouse, Taban's eyes glowed. He pressed forward in the seat as if eager to jump out.

Levi laughed and echoed something he'd heard often from his friends at the firehouse, "Hang on, buddy." Anna needed to get out and situated first. Levi hurried to the back to get her wheelchair.

This time he didn't ask if she needed help. He just parked the chair, put on the brake, and stood close. Just in case. Once again, he found himself asking God to slow his worried thoughts as she lowered herself into the chair.

After she'd settled in, he expelled a long, slow breath. Now for the children. He lifted Jamilah to the ground, but Taban and Assad ignored his hand and jumped down.

Levi gathered them close. "It's crowded here, so we need to stay together. Why don't you all hold hands?" Once they'd done that, he took Jamilah's hand. "Can you hold on here?" He pointed to the arm of Anna's wheelchair.

She nodded and shrank closer to Anna. Her face was scrunched up as if she were about to cry.

"What's the matter?" The caring in Anna's question sent a longing through Levi.

"She gets scared in noisy and busy places." Assad answered for his sister. "Mommy usually holds her when we go out."

"Would you like to sit on my lap?" Anna offered.

Jamilah nodded, but her eyes grew wet. "I miss Mommy," she wailed as Levi lifted her and set her gently on Anna's lap.

Anna wrapped her arms around the little girl, who cuddled close, her small body shaking with sobs.

Levi set a hand on Jamilah's head and smoothed back the hair that had fallen in her eyes. "Do you want me to push you?" he asked Anna.

"That'd be great. Then I can hold her."

She looked up at him with such gratitude his blood thundered through him. Seeing her with a child in her arms was also doing strange things to his insides. He longed to pull her into an embrace as tender as the one she was giving Jamilah.

People pushed past them. The five of them were blocking the driveway down to the fire station. They should move out of the way. It might be better to have one boy on each side of the chair, but when Levi suggested it, Taban refused to let go of his brother's hand.

Both boys looked nervous in a strange place. Levi could see why they wanted to stick together. He'd just need to find large openings in the crowd to steer the wheelchair and the boys through.

Anna inhaled deeply. "Mmm."

Levi did the same. The aroma of grilling meat permeated the air.

"It smells delicious, but it's a little early for chicken," Anna said. "Maybe the children might like to climb into the fire truck first."

"Good idea." Levi headed in that direction.

Ron stood by the engine, keeping order in the long line of children waiting for turns. His brows shot up when he spied them.

He left his post and sidled up next to Levi. Staying behind Anna and the children, he mouthed, *You're out with a married woman?*

Levi frowned, but then he remembered he'd told Ron that Anna was married. The last thing Levi wanted was for Anna to hear him talking about her behind her back, so he mouthed back, *She's not married.*

Ron's eyes went wide, and he gestured toward the three children. *Are these kids hers? You planning on an insta-family?*

Levi had no way to explain that the children weren't Anna's with her sitting right here, so he only replied, *Maybe.*

Better you than me. Ron rolled his eyes. "I gotta get back to work." He rounded the wheelchair. "Nice seeing you again, Anna." After a brief wave in reply to Anna's greeting, he hurried back to supervise the line.

But he'd left Levi with a sinking feeling. Insta-family? If they married, would Anna keep taking in more and more foster children even if they had their own family?

He'd always wanted a large family. Most Amish men did. But courtship and marriage with a woman who had so many children would be a huge responsibility.

Jamilah had fallen asleep with her thumb in her mouth, and Anna cradled her close. Her brothers, hand in hand, wended their way through the line snaking past the food stands offering drinks, donuts, fry pies, soft pretzels, and funnel cakes. Their gazes glued to the fire engine, they waited patiently for their turn.

Levi stayed beside her, one hand resting on her chair handle. "I remember when I was young, fire trucks fascinated me."

"I can imagine." Anna liked picturing him as a small boy.

"Maybe once they're done there, Assad and Taban might like to see the ambulance. I know more about those."

"I'm not sure that's a good idea."

Levi stared at her. "You're all right with them climbing into a fire truck?" When she nodded, he gave her a puzzled glance. "An ambulance is much closer to the ground."

"You're worried about them falling, aren't you?" After what happened to Jonah, she understood his need to be vigilant.

"I see dangers everywhere, but I've been praying and trying to turn everything over to God."

"That's great." She could only imagine how hard it had been for him to take on responsibility for watching three children on an outing he'd consider dangerous.

Although Anna served as their foster mom and should be the one who was stressed, Levi's overdeveloped big-brother complex coupled with his guilt over Jonah would trouble him. He'd feel obligated to take care of the children and her.

"I wasn't worried about them getting hurt." She kept her tone gentle, so he wouldn't think she was criticizing him. "I'm concerned seeing an ambulance might upset them." Anna explained about the church shooting, and their father's death.

"Those poor kids. To see people shot and lose their dad like that." Levi's eyes filled with compassion. "I don't understand what would make people do that."

"I don't either. All I can do is pray God will soften their hearts."

"I'm guessing those men have been caught and are in prison."

"I don't know, and I'd rather not ask the children."

Levi studied Jamilah's face. "But what about their mom?"

"She's been swept up in an immigration raid. We don't know what's going to happen to her."

"Is she nearby? Will you take the children to see her?" His jaw tensed as if the thought made him nervous.

"I guess I should, but I don't know if they even have visiting hours." Would it be too traumatic for the children? Was it even safe to take them to a prison?

"I can find out if you want. Ron's brother works as a cop. Where are they holding her?"

"York County Prison. Miriam has two girls whose parents were caught up at the same time. They'd probably want to go too."

"I'll let you know—" Levi's quick intake of breath alerted Anna to a pending disaster.

First, she checked on the boys, but everything looked calm over there. They had two children in front of them. Shifting Jamilah on her lap to free one hand, she pivoted her chair slightly to keep Levi in view.

He raced over to a small boy who'd bypassed the line of children and hopped on the back bumper. He'd reached up and now hung from the short ladder attached to the back of the truck.

The boy dangled in the air, trying to pull himself up to the topmost bar. But his feet swung in wide circles. He let go with one hand to reach for the next rung, but he missed. Swaying one-handed, his face terrified, he fought to reach the bar above him.

Then his hand slipped.

Chapter Twenty-Seven

Adrenaline coursed through Levi's body as he raced across the parking lot. He had to reach the boy. He just had to. "Hang on," he called.

But his cry came too late. The boy's palm slipped off the rung.

Levi lunged forward, arms outstretched, and caught the boy as he plunged to the ground. The boy's weight over-balanced Levi, and he stumbled.

He struggled to keep his balance but managed to keep one arm wrapped tightly around the boy. Levi's leg banged into the bumper. He extended his other arm. His hand slammed against the back of the truck. His palm stung, but he'd stopped them both from pitching onto their faces.

"Oh, thank you!" A woman came running up to him. "He got away from me. I—I thought . . ." She clutched at her throat. "I don't know what might have happened if you hadn't been here."

She took the boy from Levi's arms, set him on the ground, and knelt to scold him.

While Levi had been preventing an accident, Assad and Taban had moved up in line. They'd be next.

"Excuse me," Levi said to the woman. "I have to take care of someone." Two children, actually.

He limped as quickly as he could toward the fire engine cab. His palm smarted, and his leg would be bruised and sore tomorrow. Even his ribs ached from being battered by the adrenaline-fueled pounding of his heart.

Levi brushed off the pain. He had another duty to attend to. He couldn't let anything happen to Anna's foster children.

Anna had sat stunned, unable to breathe, as the small boy hung suspended in the air. Then he tumbled down. Levi had been too far away to reach. Somehow, though, he'd dashed forward and caught the boy midair.

They'd been about to smash to the ground or into the back of the truck. Anna prayed hard. Levi took a hit to protect the boy. And he'd saved him.

Now he was hobbling over to help Assad and Taban. Her heart swelled. Levi assisted and encouraged people all day at the center, taught classes at night, and stayed alert on his days off to rescue others. In her eyes, he ranked as a selfless hero.

Now he bent down to boost Taban into the fire truck seat. Then he stepped back to let Assad do it himself. Levi seemed to be able to tell when to help and when to let people be independent. He'd done the same with her.

If his sensitivity and giving nature had impressed her before, seeing him today increased her admiration a hundredfold. *Admiration?* Anna needed to be honest with herself. Her feelings for him had long ago passed well beyond admiration. She had to admit she'd fallen in love.

A swift, sharp pain pierced her. Levi had brought them to the fundraiser, but that had been kindness. How could he not ask when she'd made it clear she wanted to go but had no way to get here? She'd practically forced him into it out of politeness.

As nice as he'd been today, he was too far from her realm of possibilities. Why would he choose to date her? And as for the future . . . Her only chance to have children was fostering other people's little ones temporarily. Even if he did express an interest, she couldn't give him a family. Sadness welled up, and she hugged Jamilah, hoping to ease some of the hurt.

Levi, holding the boys' hands, strode across the parking lot toward her. Their eyes met, and once again, his gaze set her insides skittering. She broke their connection before she gave away the love bubbling up in her heart.

Anna kept her attention on the boys' excited faces and let her love overflow to them.

Taban gestured back toward the fire engine. "That was so cool. I wish we could sit in it again."

"We have to let other kids have a turn," his brother reminded him.

"I know." Taban scuffed his shoe on the blacktop. "I wonder if Jamilah wants a turn. Maybe we could go with her." He turned pleading eyes to Anna.

"Let's see when she wakes up." Anna suspected Jamilah would rather not brave the crowds.

Taban bounced up and down on his toes. "I could stand in line for her."

Anna smiled to herself. "That's nice of you to volunteer. Right now, though, I thought we should get some—"

A piercing siren split the air.

The boys clapped their hands over their ears. Anna wished she could do the same. Jamilah woke, crying out. Anna cuddled her and covered her ears.

Several men in uniform raced toward the firehouse doors.

The siren wound down, then started again.

Firemen cleared a path from one of the doorways, and an ambulance rolled out, its lights flashing and siren whirring. People jumped back as it screamed out the driveway and toward the road.

Before the shrill noise trailed off, Taban and Jamilah burst into tears. Assad rocked back and forth, looking distressed.

They must be remembering the church shooting. Anna wanted to reach out to comfort them, but Jamilah took up her lap and arms. How did mothers manage three children?

Without asking, Levi squatted down between the two brothers. He wrapped an arm around each of them and drew them close.

Assad stood, his body rigid and his eyes squeezed shut. But Taban threw himself against Levi's shoulder, sobbing. Levi, his eyes filled with compassion, tightened his arm around the small boy.

Anna had thought it impossible to love Levi more, but her heart filled to bursting. Once again, he'd sensed what each boy needed. He'd let Assad keep his dignity and personal space but soothed Taban.

People all around them stared. Anna could only imagine how they looked to outsiders. An Amish couple, holding three wailing Somali children dressed in *Englisch* clothes. Did people see Levi and her as husband and wife?

In one fluid motion, Levi stood with Taban in his arms, but he kept a hand on Assad's shoulder. "Is anyone hungry?"

Taban lifted his head and gulped words through his tears. "I am."

"Me too," came Assad's strangled voice.

"Why don't we head over to see them cooking the chicken?" Anna suggested. In an undertone, she said to Levi when he headed over to push the chair. "Watching that might distract them."

He nodded. "Afterward, I'll get dinner for everyone."

Anna hoped he didn't mean he planned to pay. She couldn't let him do that after he'd brought them here.

But that thought flew out of her mind when Levi, still holding Taban, tried to push her one-handed. Anna laughed. "I think this'll need to be a team effort."

She used one hand on the wheel while Levi pushed on the opposite handle.

"I can help." Assad moved past Levi and grasped both handles. Together, they wove through the throngs of people to reach the far side of the parking lot, where several men were cooking.

Taban sniffled, wriggled out of Levi's arms, and pointed at the huge metal racks with rows and rows of chicken halves grilling over open flames. "Look at the fire, Jamilah."

She stopped crying and stared at the flickering flames that spit and danced as grease dripped down.

One of the men flipped the grill. Fire flared up, and smoke spiraled into the air.

Jamilah pointed toward it. "Pretty."

Levi's face tensed.

Maybe they should go, so he could relax. Anna backed her chair up a bit. "I'm sorry. I wasn't thinking about how hard this would be for you."

Anna's sweet, understanding words touched Levi. He'd been doing his best to remember God was in control. But catching that small boy had sapped some of his willpower. Seeing children near open broilers conjured up visions of them darting too close or falling or getting pushed or . . .

"You don't have to leave because of me." Levi tried to banish the worst-case scenarios from his mind and smooth his face into a neutral expression. Neither of his attempts ended up being successful.

"Come on." Anna beckoned to the boys. "Let's go get something to eat."

The boys held on to the wheelchair, one on each side, as Levi maneuvered around the long lines at the food stands. They passed a table full of homemade baked goods for sale, and Taban stopped to examine all the choices.

"You can stop back here after lunch," Levi told him, "and pick out one thing for dessert."

"Really?"

Assad frowned. "Mom says sugar is bad for your teeth."

"That's true." Perhaps Levi shouldn't have offered. He didn't want to override their own mother's wishes. And he should have checked with Anna first. The boys were her responsibility. He had no right to make these decisions.

"We could get something to take home," Anna suggested. "Then you could brush your teeth afterward."

Even Assad smiled at that. And Levi marveled at how Anna never let negatives stop her. She found a way to conquer them. She'd done it in her life after the accident. He'd seen it as she learned to walk. When she mastered getting onto the floor for CPR.

From the very beginning, he'd been attracted by her determination and strong spirit. The more he got to know her, the more he'd seen her recover from blows that might make other women give up. Instead, Anna found a way to get over the obstacles.

She'd even bounced back after her ex-boyfriend's terrible rejection. As much as Levi wished he could shake some sense into that man, in another way, he wanted to thank him for setting Anna free.

Levi frowned. Anna seemed to have gotten over Gabe. At least he hoped she had. But maybe she'd been hiding her true feelings.

She seemed to avoid Levi's eyes today. Perhaps she'd sensed his interest and his intentions. Maybe she wasn't ready for another relationship.

He had sensed God telling him to wait, and he'd ignored the signal.

Taban prattled in Anna's ear about everything they passed. Then he groaned when he noticed the long line. "Do we have to wait in that?"

"*Neh*," Levi said. "Why don't you all sit here at a table? I'll stand in line."

Anna appreciated his thoughtfulness. She could offer to wait in line but that would mean Levi would be stuck caring for three children. He did a great job with them, but they were her responsibility.

After he'd steered them to a table, she reached into her pocket for some money.

Levi waved it away. "You made me all those meals. The least I can do is treat you to one."

"But the children . . ."

"I'm happy to get theirs too. Should I get a meal for each of them?"

Anna tried to gauge how much they'd eat. "Maybe the boys could share one meal, and Jamilah can share mine. They'll need to save room for dessert."

Taban cheered. "I can eat lots and lots of chicken and lots and lots of dessert."

Assad poked his brother. "Don't be greedy."

"I'm not." Taban plunked down on the bench with a pout. His moping lasted less than a minute before a swooping bird distracted him, and he snapped back to his usual bubbly self.

When Levi returned, balancing five boxes, he shrugged at Anna's startled look. "They threw in an extra box because I work here."

"I thought we decided on three."

"I don't know how hungry the boys are. And you can always take home the leftovers."

Anna shook her head. "*Danke.*"

Levi raised his eyebrows when Assad reached for his sister's and brother's hands, and they bowed their heads to say grace. Anna smiled at his surprise. All three children kept their heads bowed during the silent prayers.

"Their father was a minister," she explained in answer to Levi's curious look. Then she turned her attention to helping the children open their takeout boxes, but her mind stayed on Levi.

She couldn't help taking quick peeks at him as he leaned over to help Taban open the packet of plastic silverware and cut his chicken half into more manageable pieces. Not only was Levi generous, he was kind and caring and good with children.

"What are you thinking?" he asked, interrupting her daydreams.

Scrambling for an answer that wouldn't give away her

true thoughts, Anna groped for a reply. "Umm, well . . ." What could she say? "It's been such a nice day so far." That sounded inane.

Levi leaned back and glanced up at the sunny blue sky. "It has, hasn't it?"

"Yes, yes, yes," Taban practically sang around a mouthful of baked potato. "Lots and lots of fun."

Anna breathed a small sigh of relief. Levi assumed she'd been talking about the weather when she'd been referring to being with him. She sawed at her chicken leg, intending to give that to Jamilah, but the box slid around.

Levi jumped up. "Let me get that for you." He rounded the table.

"It's all right." She'd been doing it one-handed, but she could free her other hand. She didn't have to keep holding Jamilah the way she did Ciara.

Before she could untangle her arm, Levi stood beside her. "Do you want me to hold the box? Or shall I just cut it?"

Jamilah, who'd been staring at her brothers gobbling down their meals, wailed, "Where's my box?"

"Right here," Anna told her. "I'm sharing my chicken."

The little girl thrust out her lower lip. "I want my own box."

Levi tore the lid from the box. "Here's one for you." He finished separating the chicken leg and set it in the lid. Then he reached for his box and added his plastic container of applesauce and his roll. He started cutting his baked potato in half, but Anna stopped him.

"Jamilah can have half of mine. And you can have my roll."

"I'm fine. The chicken's my favorite part."

Assad watched the two of them. Then he held out his applesauce. "Do you want mine?"

Levi waved it away. "You eat it, buddy."

Gratitude shone in Assad's eyes as he dug into his meal. And Anna's heart echoed that same thankfulness.

They all ate plenty but still had leftovers. Levi helped Anna pack them into two boxes to take home.

"Time for dessert." Levi ushered them to the baked goods table and told the children they could pick out one treat.

Assad stood back, deliberating, while Taban grabbed the biggest chocolate cupcake on the table.

Anna laid a hand on his arm before he bit into it. "We have to pay for it first. And let's take it home. I think you all had plenty to eat."

Taban's mouth drooped, but he didn't complain.

Jamilah reached for a cupcake covered in multicolored sprinkles.

The Amish woman behind the table smiled at her, then looked at Anna. "Should I put them all on a paper plate for you to take home?"

"That's a good idea." Anna thanked her with a smile.

Assad went back and forth between two cupcakes before settling on one with blue icing.

"Looks like it's cupcakes for dessert. What flavor would you like?" Levi asked Anna.

She chose lemon and reached in her pocket to pay. But Levi beat her to it. With one hand, he gave the lady some money and with the other he passed her another chocolate cupcake.

"Mine's the biggest one," Taban declared.

Levi laughed. "I won't forget." Then he handed the plate covered with plastic wrap to Assad. "Think you can handle this until we get to the buggy?"

With a broad smile, Assad took the cupcakes. "I'll be careful."

Levi set a hand on his shoulder. "I know you will."

When they arrived at the house, Levi helped carry the leftovers inside. Assad balanced the plate of cupcakes with great care, while Taban skipped along beside him, his eyes on the treats. Jamilah trailed behind to hold Anna's hand.

Levi opened the front door, then stood on the threshold uncertain whether to enter or to leave. He did have the food containers, but he felt uncomfortable walking in without an invitation.

Anna must have sensed his hesitation. "You're going to have a cupcake too, aren't you?"

Levi would love to, but he didn't want to impose. Once Anna flashed him a *you're-welcome-to-join-us* smile, all his internal protests disappeared. He followed them into the kitchen and set the boxes in the refrigerator.

Anna motioned for Assad to put the cupcakes on the table. "Have a seat," she said to Levi. Then she headed to the refrigerator for milk.

"What can I do to help?" Levi asked.

"Can you pass out the cupcakes? I'm sure you remember whose is whose." Anna laughed as she returned to the table with milk. "I'll get the glasses."

After she set one at each place, Levi held each one while she poured the milk. Then he sat at the table, deliberately choosing a place far from Anna. Otherwise, he'd never swallow a bite. But part of him fantasized about sitting beside her like a married couple.

The cupcakes silenced Taban's jabbering. He shoved most of his into his mouth, leaving a ring of icing around his lips. Jamilah had dots of frosting on her nose and cheeks as well as smears on her hands and down the front of her dress.

Only Assad had managed to stay spotless. He licked the frosting from his cupcake like ice cream from a cone. Once the top was clean, he took small bites and closed his eyes to savor them.

The contrasts between each child's personality amazed Levi, although it shouldn't, because his own brothers had different temperaments. Daniel and Taban both jumped into life with gusto. Jamilah was still young, but like Jonah, she seemed tenderhearted.

Assad, the worrier, the responsible one, reminded Levi of himself. Always watching out for others, making sure they stayed out of trouble, anticipating dangers and trying to avert them before they occurred. If only Levi had developed that side of himself when he was as young as Assad. Then Jonah's accident never would have happened.

Fighting his way out of the pit of old memories, Levi surfaced to find Anna studying him.

"Are you all right?"

He managed a smile. "I was thinking how each child is so different, so unique. Yet, I can also see similarities between them and my siblings."

Anna's face lit up. "That's so true." Then she giggled. "I know who's most like you."

The children all looked up from their cupcakes when she laughed. Then they followed her gaze to Levi.

"I do too," he admitted. "I only wish I'd started that young."

Anna gazed at him sympathetically. "I'm sure you did. Getting sidetracked once as a child can happen to anyone."

"Why did it have to happen then?" Levi couldn't keep

the anguish from his words. But even as he said it, a deep knowingness flooded over him.

Jah, he blamed himself, but at the same time, he also blamed God.

The minister's sermon came flooding back. *Humble yourself.*

It hit Levi in a blinding flash. He hadn't been humble; he'd been arrogant. Every time he demanded an answer, he was questioning God's will. He was insisting he knew better than God what should have occurred that day.

Forgive me, Lord, for my pride in assuming my way was best.

"Levi?" Anna stared at him.

Had she been talking to him? If so, he hadn't heard.

"Sorry," he murmured. "I was praying. I didn't realize how angry I've been at God for what happened to Jonah. I asked for forgiveness."

Anna's eyes shone. "That's *wunderbar*." She gazed at him thoughtfully. "Speaking of forgiveness, what if one of your brothers had been older and made that same mistake? Would you forgive him?"

"Of course." Levi answered with no hesitation.

"Then why can't you forgive yourself?"

Levi sat in stunned silence. Anna's soft question touched a chord deep within him. Not only had he needed to humble himself before the Lord, he also had to accept God's forgiveness for what he'd done.

Taban, who'd finished his cupcake in several bites, stared from one to the other as if trying to understand their conversation. But then his gaze fell on the uneaten treat in front of Levi.

"Everyone gets one cupcake." Anna stopped Taban's hand from snaking across the table. "That's Levi's."

If Anna hadn't intervened, Levi probably would have let Taban have it. After such deep spiritual epiphanies, Levi had little interest in food. His mind stayed focused on heavenly things.

"Anna, if it hadn't been for you—and these children—I wouldn't have learned this lesson today."

"God would have found another way." She discounted her role in it.

She was right. But Levi rejoiced that she'd been part of bringing him to this spiritual understanding.

Chapter Twenty-Eight

It thrilled Anna that God had touched Levi's heart. She prayed her words might open his mind to a new way of looking at his actions that day. He'd been young and fascinated by a fish, rather than a neglectful brother.

With a faraway look in his eyes, Levi rose. He picked up the cupcake. "I guess I should take this with me so I don't cause any fights."

"Makes sense. But you're not leaving already, are you?" Anna wanted to clamp her hand over her mouth to trap that plea. She sounded needy and desperate.

His head tilted to one side, Levi stared at her. "You wanted me to stay longer?"

"I—I, well . . ." Anna wanted to deny it, but that might hurt his feelings. Besides, if she did, she'd be lying. Unable to look at him, she focused on her fingers, pleating a small square of her apron into tiny folds. "We—I had a good time today. I hoped you could stay for supper."

She couldn't believe she'd just done that. Especially when she had no idea what they'd eat if he said yes.

Levi said nothing, only stood there looking startled. Was he still dazed from his spiritual insights, or had her

sudden invitation left him speechless? Or was he struggling to come up with a plausible excuse?

Please say something. Anything. At this point, she didn't
care if it was a yes or a no. Well, she did care, but she just
wished he'd break the awkward silence.

Taban shattered the quietness. He jumped off the bench,
setting it rocking. "What are we going to have for dinner?"

Leave it to Taban to expose that she was unprepared.
"I'm not sure." The leftover chicken wouldn't be enough
to feed all of them.

Luckily, Assad drew everyone's attention by pointing to
Jamilah. "She's eating the cupcake paper."

Anna reached over to wrestle the soggy paper from
Jamilah's mouth. She got a chunk of it before the little girl
fussed and clenched her teeth, refusing to let Anna take
the piece she'd bitten off.

Assad came over to help. He took the larger piece from
her hands. Then he pointed to Jamilah's mouth. "Yucky,
yucky paper. Spit it out."

His sister shook her head and chewed. Anna slipped a
finger between Jamilah's lips and dug around. She managed to extract most of the paper.

"I guess a little paper won't hurt her," Anna said as
Jamilah swallowed the rest.

The little drama had taken some of the heat off Levi.
And it had given Anna time to compose herself.

With her back to Levi, she said in measured tones, "I
suppose your *aenti* expects you home for supper."

Levi had made a fool of himself. The minute she'd
asked him, he'd gotten tongue-tied. His whole being
shouted, *Yes, yes, yes.* But he couldn't force air or words
from his constricted chest.

Anna's invitation hadn't seemed like mere politeness. She appeared to want him to stay. After all this time of wishing and hoping, had his prayers been answered? Or was he reading too much into a simple offer of a meal?

He'd waited too long to answer. Now she was giving him an excuse to leave. She must have taken his silence for a no.

Betty would understand if he didn't show up for supper. She'd expect him to spend as much time as possible with Anna. All he had to do was answer one simple—or not so simple, after the way he'd complicated it—question.

Levi cleared his throat. "Anna, I'd like to have supper here."

"You would?" She sounded uncertain. He couldn't see her face to see if she regretted the impulsive invitation because she remained facing away from him as she helped Jamilah to the floor. "What about your *aenti*?"

"She'll be fine with it. Betty's used to being flexible."

"If you're sure." Unlike her earlier, almost-pleading expression, Anna seemed resigned.

"I'm sure." *Very sure.* He'd like nothing more than to spend more time with her. Even if his plans for private time with her had been scuttled.

Assad took his sister's hand. "Should we brush our teeth now?"

"Good idea," Anna said. "Why don't I help Jamilah? Maybe I can get any bits of paper out of her mouth."

"Anything I can do to help?" Levi offered.

"You can help us." Taban took his hand. "Mommy always checks our teeth." A bleak look crossed his face.

Levi set a hand on his shoulder and squeezed. He wished he could do more to ease Taban's loss. First his dad, then his mom.

That reminded Levi he'd forgotten to ask Ron about

them visiting their mother in prison. He'd give Ron a call before dinner.

"So, what color is your toothbrush?" Levi asked Taban. Sometimes distraction worked with Daniel. Maybe it would with Taban.

"Red." He held up a see-through toothbrush, and a light inside blinked on and off.

"That's pretty fancy." Levi helped him with the toothpaste and handed it to Assad.

Near them, Anna coaxed Jamilah to open her mouth. Levi's heart thumped hard in his chest as he supervised the boys' toothbrushing. The intimacy of caring for children together raised fantasies of them doing this with their own family.

He stopped his runaway thoughts. Imagining a life together like this proved to be too dangerous.

When they finished, Anna glanced up at him, her eyes soft. "*Danke*. Taking care of them is so much easier with two par—adults."

Had she almost said "parents"? Maybe she'd been thinking the same thing he had. Levi didn't dare meet her eyes. If they held an invitation, he'd be powerless to resist.

A slow burn rose from Anna's neck to her face. She couldn't believe she'd slipped up like that. Had Levi guessed she'd been pretending they were getting their children ready for bed?

The thought plunged her into despair. She and Levi could never have children. Marrying him was out of the question.

Despite his fears about not being good with young children and his worries about them getting hurt, he was good with them. He also did great with the older kids who came to the center. He deserved to be a *daed*.

Even if he showed an interest in her, she couldn't reciprocate. She could never deprive him of a family.

With a heavy heart, she headed to the kitchen to plan and prepare a meal. Chicken-rice casserole would be easy, and she always kept cans of cream soups in the pantry. They had enough leftover chicken from the barbecue to make a casserole. She'd put some rice on to cook.

"Can I do anything to help?"

Levi's voice behind her made her jump. She hadn't heard him come into the kitchen.

"There's not much to do. I'll chop up the chicken for a casserole. First, I want to give the children something to do."

"That's a wise idea. If they're occupied, it will help keep their minds off their mother."

Anna only had baby toys from Ciara. "Card decks for Dutch Blitz and Uno are on the bookshelf in the living room. The boys might like one of those. Jamilah may be too young to play cards. I have a few picture books."

"I can keep an eye on them while you fix dinner," Levi volunteered.

"Are you sure?"

"It will do me good to face my fears. It'll help me learn to trust God more."

Anna couldn't argue with that. "That would be a big help. It won't take long to get the casserole ready."

"Take whatever time you need. First, though, I want to call Ron"—Levi lowered his voice—"about visiting. I'll go outside so the children don't overhear."

"I appreciate it."

While Levi made his call, Anna gathered the picture

books and two decks of cards. "Want to play Uno or Dutch Blitz?" she asked the boys.

"What's Dutch Blitz?" Assad studied the cover on the pack of cards.

"It's a card game." Anna showed them the four colors and explained the rules.

By the time Levi came back in, the children were engrossed in the game.

"Ron called his brother to check," Levi said. "Children's visiting hours are from three-thirty to five-thirty on Wednesdays. Randy emailed Ron the application you need to get approved. Ron will print it out and get it to me. I can give it to you on Monday."

"That's so kind of him. And of you."

Levi waved off her appreciation. "Oh, and Randy said it could take two to four days for approval."

"Will the application cover the children?" Anna would rather not have this conversation in front of them, but she had no place to go for privacy.

Assad glanced up, listening intently to their conversation.

Levi, who had been talking quietly, dropped his volume even lower. "You'll need to contact their social worker. Supposedly, many of these parents turn their rights over to the social workers. She should have their documentation, so she can fill out their paperwork."

"I'll call Millie on Monday."

"You'll need to see if she can go next Wednesday. Ron said she'd need to be there the first time."

"*Danke* for finding that out."

"Happy to help." Levi turned to the boys. "You look ready to play. Can I join you?"

When they nodded, he settled on the floor with them and called to Jamilah, "Do you want to play too?"

She came over and settled beside Levi.

"I'll be on your team," he assured her.

From time to time as Anna prepared the meal and set the table, she peeked into the living room. Levi appeared to be enjoying the lively game of cards as much as the boys. Jamilah giggled with delight when Levi helped her beat her brothers.

Misty-eyed, Anna longed to be a part of their tight circle. They looked like a family. More than anything, she yearned for a family. A family with Levi. A family she'd never have.

Anna moved back and forth in the kitchen, once again reminding Levi of being part of a family. His wife fixing a meal while he played or did chores with the children. What if that could be his reality?

Once she finished the casserole, Anna came into the living room. The sad, faraway look in her eyes puzzled him. She'd seemed so happy while they were at the firehouse.

"What's the matter?"

A startled, wary look flashed across her face as if he'd intruded into a private area, tramping past signs saying CAUTION. STAY OUT.

Anna only shrugged. Her lopsided smile offered little reassurance. "You know how you said earlier you realized you needed to accept God's will?" At his nod, she continued. "I do too. Only, it's not always easy."

Levi could sympathize with that. "I know." Anna had listened to him talk about his problem, and her support had helped. Maybe he could return the favor. "Do you want to talk about it?"

Her cheeks flamed, and she looked away.

"It's your turn, Levi," Assad pointed out.

Levi helped Jamilah choose a card. By the time he returned his attention to Anna, her blush had faded, and her angst had flattened into a neutral expression. One that walled her off from him.

"I put the casserole in the refrigerator. I'll bake it an hour before we eat."

Even by saying ordinary, everyday things like that, Anna could make Levi's heart flip over in his chest. He hoped she'd move to a place where he didn't have to crane his neck to see her. "Did you want to join us in the game?"

Taban groaned. "I'm winning. I don't want to start over."

Levi grinned at him. "We don't have to do that. Maybe Anna would want to be on your team." That would put her almost directly across from him.

Assad sighed.

Anna moved until she was behind both boys. "Why don't I take turns working with each of you?"

Assad looked up and gave her a grateful glance.

Of course, Anna had noticed Assad needed attention too. Everyone expected him to be mature, but he was still a child. It must have seemed unfair to him that his younger siblings each had an adult partner. Anna had picked up on that.

She reached out with quiet, behind-the-scenes help, like she had with meals for Levi's family and her surprise cleaning before Betty came home. Anna's care for others made Levi even more determined to do something for her.

Like figuring out what had made her so depressed about doing God's will.

Anna's position allowed her to keep an eye on both brothers' hands. An even greater benefit was being directly across from Levi.

She nudged Taban twice to put down a different card. Her strategy worked, and he laid down his last card.

"I won, I won," he crowed.

Assad's shoulders slumped as he handed his leftover cards to Levi.

"Must be your turn to win next, Assad," Levi said as he passed out the cards. While the boys' heads were bent to pick up their cards, Levi winked at her.

Winked. He only meant to signal her to help Assad more this game, but that didn't stop the fluttering in her chest.

Anna nodded to show she'd gotten the message. Then she forced her gaze down to Assad's cards. She had no business wishing for things she couldn't have.

After several uncorrected errors on Taban's part and what Anna assumed were deliberate mistakes by Levi on Jamilah's part, Assad held only two cards. After the next two rounds, he held his last card aloft before placing it on the pile. "I'm the winner," he declared.

Over the children's heads, Anna met Levi's eyes and smiled. Their strategy had worked. Once again, Levi winked. This time, it wasn't a sign of their conspiracy. This wink was more deliberate. Almost saucy.

Flustered, Anna lowered her gaze. Had she misinterpreted Levi's meaning? Maybe it had only been to show a shared triumph.

But whatever he'd intended it to mean, it started a spark inside Anna that only blazed hotter as they ate their supper together and Levi helped the children get ready for bed. His every action, every look, fanned the flames higher. By the time they said good night, no amount of caution or common sense could extinguish the out-of-control inferno.

Chapter Twenty-Nine

On Monday morning, Anna took the three children over to Miriam's to play with her cousins and the other foster children. She pulled her *aenti* aside to explain why she needed the phone.

"Millie called this morning," Miriam said. "Immigration is releasing Uba and Bilan's mother today, so they'll be going home."

"That's *wunderbar*. What about their father?"

Her eyes sad, Miriam shook her head. "He'll be deported, because he shoplifted some groceries as a teenager. I'm not sure how the girls' mother will support them. Their dad worked two jobs. They barely made it, even with the mom's job."

"Maybe we can do a fundraiser for them," Anna suggested. "But that will only help temporarily." Her heart ached for another family who would lose a father.

Her *aenti* nodded in Assad's direction. "Their mother's case is much more complicated. You'll need to talk to Millie about it."

"I will." Anna took the phone and headed into another

room. She didn't want to get the children's hopes up and then dash them.

It took a while to get connected to Millie, who agreed to process the children's forms. "The kids are all U.S. citizens, so it shouldn't take long. I'll let you know when they have their clearance to go."

"Thank you for doing this."

"You're welcome. You'll need to take their birth certificates along the first time you go to the prison. I have my clearances, so I can go along and present them. I'll also make sure you're designated as their caretaker. That way you can go in with them."

Anna dreaded that. How would the children react to seeing their mother in prison? "We're hoping to go next Wednesday, if that'll work for you. I can have Levi call you to confirm."

"Let me check my calendar." After some paper shuffling, Millie said, "I'll have to rearrange one appointment, but let's plan on it."

That reminded her. "My *aenti* said there might be problems for the children's mother."

Millie sighed. "Some snafu with DACA."

"DACA?"

"It stands for Deferred Action for Childhood Arrivals. Maybe you've heard of Dreamers in the news?"

Anna shook her head, then realized she couldn't be seen. She so rarely talked on the phone, she forgot. "Not really," she said.

She didn't have time to read the newspapers. If she did, she'd read *Die Botschaft*.

"Dreamers were brought to our country illegally by their parents when they were children. They've grown up here, so they know no other home."

"I see," Anna said, unsure what all this had to do with the children's mother.

"Yasmiin, the children's mother, is a Dreamer. She claims she reported her new address when they moved from Minneapolis to Lancaster. Immigration officials insist they received no forms recording the change of address."

"That should be easy to fix, shouldn't it?"

"I wish." Millie's long, drawn-out sigh made it sound awful. "They also didn't get the check she claims she sent, so she lost her DACA."

Anna didn't really understand what that meant, but she'd read up on it later. For now, she had one main concern. "What does that mean for the children?"

"As U.S. citizens, they're all right. And Yasmiin signed them over to Children & Youth, so they'll be taken care of, whatever happens."

"Why would she do that? Doesn't she want them?"

"It's just a procedure we recommend to immigrants who are arrested. It makes it easier to get their children back if and when they're released."

It made no sense that signing your children over to the government made it easier to keep them. Anna struggled to understand all this confusing new information.

"Anyway," Millie continued, "the children may be with you for a while. A lawyer from her church is trying to help her prove her case, but these things take time."

The longer the children stayed with her, the more time it gave Anna to get attached. That might not be such a good thing.

After their Saturday together, Levi couldn't wait to see Anna on Monday at five. He'd picked up the paperwork she needed, and he hoped she'd stay for a short while after her session so he could discuss their relationship.

He'd spent the past two days replaying her every look and gesture. Her excitement about going to the barbecue. Her invitation to stay for dinner. Had those been because she wanted to spend time with him? Her blush and flustered look when he'd winked at her. Had that affected her as much as she'd affected him?

He'd never gotten a chance to ask the question burning inside. Maybe today he'd get a chance. Would she let him date her?

He pushed aside all his thoughts and questions to concentrate on the children and adults who came to each session. But every spare minute, he returned to visions of Anna. Until she showed up for her session.

Just seeing her outside the door set his pulse racing. And when she smiled . . . How would he bear it if she said no?

"I have papers for you," he announced as soon as she walked in. "I hope you can stay for a bit after the session."

"Of course."

Did she seem as eager for that as he was? Or was that only wishful thinking?

Levi alternated between willing time to fly faster and worrying that it moved too quickly. While Anna practiced using crutches on the therapy steps, she told him about her call to Millie that morning. As usual, she worked until she was breathless and exhausted.

When she sank back into her wheelchair after the session, he brought her the application form and told her Ron had rechecked to be sure the children's visiting hours hadn't changed.

"*Danke.* I planned to find out about that. You've saved me a lot of trouble."

Levi thought he read more than gratitude in her eyes.

He knelt so he'd be at her eye level. "Anna, I have something I'd like to ask you. This isn't really the place I'd have chosen to do it, but with you having the children, well, it's the only spot where we might have a little privacy."

Her eyes opened wide at the last word, but Levi couldn't tell if it was in alarm or anticipation. He hoped it was the latter.

"I've enjoyed our sessions and getting to know you," he started.

"You're not going to be doing them anymore?" Anna sounded upset.

"*Neh*, that's not what I meant." He was making a mess of this. His nerves had frayed from being so close to her and from wrestling with what he wanted to say.

The most important moment of his life, and he couldn't get the words to come out properly. Maybe he should skip the warm-up and plunge in.

He reached for her hand. "Anna, I care for you." He took a deep breath. "And I'd like to court you."

Levi wanted to date her?

All of Anna's dreams had come true. His hand, warm and tender, clasped hers, and her whole being burst into song. He'd just said the words she'd never expected to hear from the man she loved.

Every cell joined the chorus of *jah, jah, jah*.

Anna pinched her lips together to keep those words from flowing through. *Neh, neh, neh*. She'd already made that decision on Saturday. He'd soon get over her and find another woman. One who could give him children.

"I—I can't."

Levi stared at her as if he were having trouble comprehending her answer. "Is it because of the children?"

Anna almost said yes before she realized he was talking about her foster children.

Without waiting for her answer, he continued. "I understand they're your first priority and you can't leave them much. We can do things together that they'd enjoy. Picnics, parks, and . . . even prison. I'll help you take them there. Whatever you need, whatever they need."

Ach, could he rip her heart out more?

"If you're concerned about my fears, my constant worrying about possible accidents, I'm working on turning all of that over to God."

"Oh, Levi, it's not that." She didn't want him to blame himself for her no.

"Then what?" Levi rocked back and let go of her hand. "You're still in love with . . ."

"Gabe? Definitely not." *I'm only in love with you.* "That relationship never would have worked."

Levi shifted farther away from her. "Forgive me," he said stiffly. "I should never have brought this up." He rose and turned his back to her. "I hope we can still be friends."

What did she say to that? She didn't want to lose him. Even if they couldn't date, she still valued his friendship. "I'd like that."

She'd hurt him. She'd never meant to do that. Now she had to find a way to let him know her reluctance had nothing to do with him.

And after this, she'd have trouble thinking of him as only a friend. And she'd wrestle with keeping her feelings for him hidden. Even worse, visions of what-might-have-been would haunt her forever.

As Anna headed for the door, Levi kicked himself. Why hadn't he waited? Given her more time? God had seemed to be urging patience, but once again, he'd charged ahead without waiting for the Lord's leading. Levi prayed he hadn't destroyed his chances.

"I had something else to tell you before you go."

Anna's wheels slowed, then stopped.

He couldn't turn around to face her. Not until he controlled his disappointment. *Neh*, it was much more than that. His heart and spirit had been crushed.

"What is it?"

He kept his tone as neutral as he could under the circumstances. "I checked with people here at the center, and they recommended a driver who has a van with a lift. I scheduled it for children's visiting hours next week. I figured the paperwork would be done before then. If not, I can reschedule."

"I can't believe you did that."

"Sorry. I should have asked first."

"*Neh*, I'm not upset. I'm grateful. I hadn't even thought about how we'd get there."

"I'm glad I did it then. I figured you might not get clearances this week. Ron said it would probably take forty-eight hours, maybe more."

"That's perfect. Once we have permission to go, I'll tell the children."

"I, um, told the driver I'd be going along. We made plans to do something during the two hours you're in the prison. I can change that if you want."

"I'd like to have you along," she said almost shyly.

So, she didn't despise him. She could even tolerate his company. Maybe he had a chance after all.

Anna could have hugged him. She nixed that thought right away. But her mind wouldn't let go of the image. If she'd said yes to courting, she'd have the right to do that someday.

Instead, she'd turned him down. Although she was positive she'd done the right thing, the only thing she could do, it left her with a hollow emptiness inside.

The next few days dragged until she received her authorization. Then she waited to hear from Millie about the children's clearances. She'd planned to tell the children as soon as they all had permission to see Yasmiin.

But they'd have to wait until next week to visit. Children, especially those Jamilah's age or with Taban's personality, found it hard to wait. Anna decided to tell them a short while before they left. That day finally came.

"I have some good news. I'd like you all to get dressed in nice clothes. Levi will be here soon to take us to see your mommy."

"Mommy?" Jamilah squealed.

Taban jumped up and down, clapping and cheering.

Assad's face shone. "We're going home?"

Anna should have anticipated his question and prepared them better. She had never been to a jail before, so she had no idea what to expect or what to tell the children about what they'd face.

"Your mom isn't home yet. She's in prison."

"Why?" Taban stood, legs akimbo, hands on hips. "Mommy never does anything bad."

"I'm sure she doesn't." Anna hoped their mother's arrest had been in error. Since Millie had told her about the Dreamers, Anna had read about them as well as articles in the local paper about citizens who'd been rounded up in these sweeps.

"Then why's she in jail?" Taban demanded.

"I'm not sure. All I know is that she and some other parents were picked up by Immigration." And that it had something to do with Dreamers.

"What's im-great-son?"

How could Anna explain that? She barely understood it herself. "I think you have to have permission to come into the country. Immigration agents arrest people who don't have permission. Sometimes they make mistakes." For the children's sake, Anna prayed that would be the case with their mother.

"They made a mistake with Mommy," Taban insisted.

"I hope so."

Assad looked nervous. "Mom was scared of getting taken away."

That didn't sound good. What if the whole family had been here illegally? Would they take the children away when they went to see their mom? Maybe this wasn't a good idea.

"She said we'd always be safe," Assad said with conviction, but his eyes reflected doubt.

"If your mom said that, then she must be right." But how safe were they if they had to be left with strangers like her?

Assad stared at Anna as if assessing her truthfulness. "What if she made a mistake?"

Millie would have alerted Anna to any irregularities. "The social worker filled out all the papers for you to visit your mom. She would have told us if there were any problems."

"You're sure?" Assad glanced around at his sister and brother. "We can't take them there if it isn't safe."

Anna agreed. "When Levi gets here, we'll ask him to call Millie. We can check before we go."

With a grave expression on his face, Assad nodded.

For as young as he was, he seemed wise beyond his years. He'd taken on the role of a parent to his siblings. Anna wondered if he'd always been that way or if he was trying to take his father's place.

If they didn't hurry, though, Levi would arrive before they were ready. "Can you two get dressed in nice clothes while I take care of Jamilah?"

"Come on, Taban." Assad ushered his brother to the bedroom.

They emerged a short while later in dress pants and collared shirts. Taban's had been buttoned crookedly, and his collar had rolled inside his shirt. Assad sighed and fixed the shirt while Anna brushed everyone's hair.

While they waited for Levi, Taban leapt up and down, and Jamilah broke into a huge smile. "Mommy. We get to see Mommy," she sang at the top of her lungs.

Assad didn't share their excitement. He seemed downcast.

"Are you all right?" Anna asked him.

He didn't meet her eyes. "I thought your good news would be that Mom was coming home. But she's still in prison."

"I'm sorry." Anna longed to hug him, but his rigid back made it clear he didn't want to be touched. Maybe he'd be more open to an embrace after he saw his mom. For now, she'd respect his need for space.

When Tom arrived, Levi came inside to assist Anna with getting the children into the van.

Taban thrust out his lower lip when he saw the van. "I want to ride in the buggy."

"It's too far for the horse to travel," Levi explained.

"We have seat belts." With a look of relief, Assad buckled Jamilah into the car seat.

Taban climbed into one of the booster seats, and Assad clicked his brother's belt, before he got into the other booster seat and secured his own seat belt.

"Wow. You have an elevator." Taban leaned over to watch the lift move Anna up into place.

Even Assad seemed fascinated. "Do you have a seat belt?"

Levi pointed to the wheels. "Anna's chair is strapped in here. See?"

Assad examined the security features. "But she could fall out of the chair."

"I'll be all right," Anna assured him. "I'll hold on tight." She patted the chair arms.

Assad's skeptical look made it clear he didn't consider that sufficient protection.

Once again, Anna prayed he'd relax and act more like a child than a miniature adult. But he'd been through a lot in his few short years, and it had sobered him.

To get Assad's mind off her chair, she asked Tom, "How did you know to have all the car seats?"

"Levi told me the ages." Tom started the engine. "I often transport Amish families, so I have an assortment of car seats and boosters in case I need them."

Levi leaned over to check that all the children's belts and buckles were snug and secured. "Good job, Assad."

For the first time that day, Assad beamed.

Anna tucked his response into her memory. He seemed to respond to praise. But perhaps the fact that it had come from Levi made a difference. His encouragement always made her feel special too.

When they arrived at the prison, Millie was waiting for them with the children's birth certificates. The boys stared in awe at the metal detector, but Jamilah shrank back against Anna. After much coaxing, her brothers convinced her to walk through the archway to them, so the guards could inspect Anna.

Getting through was an ordeal with the wheelchair, which had to be thoroughly examined. Anna also had to endure being patted down. They made her take the hairpins from her bun and get her long, thick hair checked by a female guard to be sure nothing had been concealed in it.

After Millie presented the children's documents, and they'd been scanned in, Anna presented the ID she used to write checks. With a quick pat on Anna's shoulder, Millie left. Jamilah crawled onto Anna's lap. The little girl wrapped her arms around Anna's neck, barely allowing her to breathe.

"It's all right. We're going to see Mommy now," she whispered, but Jamilah only clung more tightly.

The guard escorted them into the room. Despite all the noise and commotion in the room, the two boys only had eyes for the thin woman the guards led into the secured space behind a Plexiglas window.

"Mommy!" Taban raced toward her, only to be stopped by the clear barrier. "What is this?" He pounded on it.

Anna hurried toward him and caught his arm. "*Shh,*

Taban," she whispered. "They'll make us leave if you're not quiet."

"But I want to go to my mommy."

Anna wished she'd better prepared him for the visit, but she hadn't known what to expect.

Yasmiin had the same large brown eyes as her children, but hers were wet with tears. She clamped her teeth on her trembling lower lip as if holding back a cry.

"Oh, Taban."

At his mother's low, husky voice, he looked up. "Mommy, why are you in there? Are you coming home with us now? Why do they have this here?" He knocked on the Plexiglas.

"Don't do that. Please, Taban." Yasmiin tried to calm him by speaking in gentle, calming tones. "The guards won't let you stay if you don't behave."

"But I want you to come with us. Are we going home?"

Yasmiin closed her eyes. "Not today."

"When then?" he demanded.

"I don't know," she answered brokenly. "I hope you're being a good boy."

"I am."

"Assad? Can you come closer? Are you taking care of Taban and Jamilah?"

He nodded and took a few steps closer.

"He does a wonderful job with them," Anna said.

For the first time, Yasmiin focused closely on Anna. Her eyebrows rose. "You're the foster parent?"

"I am. You have three wonderful children."

"But you're so young. And—and I wasn't expecting you to be Amish or—" Yasmiin gestured to the wheelchair. "Can you handle them?"

Anna wanted to calm Yasmiin's fears. This poor mother

had enough to worry about being in prison. Anna hoped to reassure her about her children's care.

"I share a house with my aunt," Anna said. "She's very experienced and has taken in foster children for the past twenty years. The social worker wanted to keep your children together, and I have more room in my part of the house."

Assad spoke up. "Don't worry, Mommy. Anna does fine, and she's a very good cook."

Such a little man. Anna wanted to hug him for trying to lessen his mother's worries. And it did seem to help. Yasmiin smiled at Anna.

"Thank you for taking care of them." Then Yasmiin's brows drew together as she studied her daughter, who still had her face buried against Anna's shoulder. "How is Jamilah doing? Ever since she saw her father . . . Since the"—Yasmiin swallowed hard—"shooting, she's had nightmares."

"She's had a few. It helps if I stay with her. Sometimes her brothers do too."

"Yes, I'd often find them curled up in the same bed. Like little puppies." Yasmiin's smile didn't reach her eyes. "Or they'd all pile in with me, especially after—"

She didn't need to finish. Anna nodded to let Yasmiin know she understood.

"Jamilah," her mother crooned. "My precious baby."

The little girl still had her face hidden against Anna's shoulder, but she turned toward the sound of her mother's voice with a plaintive "Mommy?" She held out her arms to be picked up.

With a sob, Yasmiin twisted her head away. Her shoulders shaking, she seemed to be struggling to get her feelings under control.

"Mommy wants to hold you, Jamilah. And she's sad that she can't," Anna explained.

"I'm sorry." Yasmiin faced them again. Tear tracks on her face revealed the pain of separation. "This is so hard."

Anna could only imagine.

For the rest of the visit, Yasmiin's struggles to hold herself together remained obvious, but although her eyes stayed misty, she didn't cry again until visiting hours ended and they had to say good-bye.

As the guards led his mother away, Assad asked, "Is this a hate crime?"

Puzzled, Anna asked, "What do you mean?"

"You know, like what happened to my dad. Did they lock Mommy up because they hate her?"

To a child, seeing his beloved mother in prison with guards watching all of them, it must look that way.

"Oh, Assad." Anna opened her arms, and he came to her and let her embrace him and Jamilah.

"Me too," Taban said, so Anna made room for him.

"Time to go," a guard said. "Move along."

Both boys stayed close to her as they headed out to the parking lot. Levi waited outside for them, giving them a sense of normality and relief.

Chapter Thirty

One morning, Anna and the children had just started cleaning up after breakfast, when Emily knocked and stuck her head in the door. "Hey, Anna, Millie called. Yasmiin wants to see you during visiting hours today. It's really important."

"But children's visiting hours aren't until tomorrow."

"I know. She only wants to talk to you."

"What does she want?"

"No idea. But Millie emphasized it's urgent." Emily started to leave, then poked her head back in. "I have off today, so I can watch the kids. *Mamm*'s getting a new child today, so I'll keep your little ones over here. The new boy will have enough people to adjust to when he walks in."

"I need to call Levi to see if he can arrange the van."

Emily came inside. "I'll keep an eye on things while you go do that."

Going to the prison meant missing her session with Levi this afternoon. Anna pushed aside her disappointment. Taking care of the children meant tending to their needs. And if Yasmiin needed her, Anna had to go. Maybe Yasmiin had gotten news that she was being released.

Anna imagined the children's excitement at that news,

and her own joy overflowed. Then reality sank in. She'd miss them so much. Without them, her life would be empty.

She slowed as she reached her *aenti*'s back door. She warned herself not to build up stories in her mind. Until she talked to Yasmiin, Anna had no idea what the children's mother wanted.

Besides, worrying and stirring up all the negative possibilities in her mind meant she'd forgotten who was in charge of her life. God had a plan for her. All she needed to do was trust Him.

With a less fearful heart, Anna left a message for Levi with Holly in the office. When she got back home, the kitchen sparkled. Anna thanked her cousin.

"I'll come over whatever time you need me," Emily promised.

"Levi doesn't have a break until noon, but Holly promised to give him my message. I hope Tom can take me today."

"Leave it to God," Emily reminded her.

Anna shook her head. Would she ever get out of this habit of fretting over small things? Levi worried about possible accidents, but she stewed over the future. God had control of both.

Twenty minutes later, Emily ran over with a message from Levi. "Tom will be here in an hour. Oh, and I canceled your van ride to the center this afternoon. I figured you wouldn't make it back in time."

"*Danke.*" Anna appreciated her cousin doing that, but she regretted missing her afternoon session with Levi.

"I'll stay now so you can get ready." Emily waggled her eyebrows before hugging Jamilah.

Anna put her hands on her hips. "I can finish the cleaning. Besides, it'll only be Tom. Levi has sessions all afternoon."

Emily laughed. "You walked right into my trap. So, you

would try to look special for Levi?" Emily dragged out his name in a breathless voice.

Anna frowned at her. "I do need to change my work dress and apron before I go."

Taking Jamilah's hand, Emily shooed Anna toward the bedroom. "Get ready in case Tom's early. Jamilah, the boys, and I will finish cleaning."

By the time Anna changed, Tom was pulling into Miriam's driveway. Anna cruised down the ramp and hurried toward him. The passenger door opened, and Levi stepped out.

"Levi? Don't you have to work?"

"Your message sounded urgent, so I asked Holly to call in a sub."

"You didn't have to do that." But it thrilled her that he cared enough to miss work.

"I wanted to." He bent to strap her chair into place, and he stayed beside her as Tom raised the lift. With a smile that didn't reach his eyes, Levi waited until her door closed before getting into the passenger seat.

Levi had never taken off work like this in the middle of the day, but God had seemed to be urging him to go with Anna today. Despite the fact that she'd turned him down, they were still friends, and if she received bad news, he wanted to be there for her.

Besides, if he hadn't come along, he'd never get to see her today. Emily had canceled Anna's session. That had spurred him to spend this time with her.

Anna left her purse in the car and only clutched her ID card. Levi prayed for her each step of the way.

Tom interrupted him. "Hey, buddy, mind if I head out

to get a burger and fries? I'm not going to get another chance to eat today."

"I don't know how long Anna will be. Why don't I wait here?" Levi felt burdened to pray for her, and he wanted to be there when she came out the door.

"You sure? It won't take long."

"It's a nice day. I'll be fine." He only prayed Anna and Yasmiin would be too.

Anna went through the metal detectors and waited patiently while a policewoman probed the bob under her *kapp* and patted her down. At least, they didn't make her take it out this time. They seemed to recognize her.

Then she waited for Yasmiin to appear behind the Plexiglas.

"Oh, Anna, I'm so glad you could come."

Yasmiin's face was drawn and pale.

"What's wrong?" Anna asked her.

"I lost my case, and they refused an appeal. They're deporting me back to Somalia."

Anna gasped. "*Ach*, no. What about the children?"

A sickish look came over Yasmiin's features. "I wrestled with this all night. I can't take my babies back there. They might be killed or kidnapped."

Neh, any mother who loved her children couldn't put them at risk.

"But how can I give them up?" Tears dripped down Yasmiin's cheeks.

"Oh, Yasmiin." Anna had no words to lessen Yasmiin's sacrifice.

"God reminded me of Solomon and the mother who gave up her baby to save him."

Except unlike that mother, whose reward was to keep

her son, if Yasmiin gave up her children, she'd never see them again.

"God gave His only Son for us." Although her voice trembled, Yasmiin's words carried a deep conviction. "How can I refuse to release my children? God knows what's best for them. I must trust Him."

Anna wanted to reach out and embrace Yasmiin, but the barrier stood between them. Who would hold her, comfort her when she left behind all she'd ever known? Who would ease her sorrow? Only God could do that.

In a choked voice, Yasmiin said, "I couldn't have asked for my babies to have a better caretaker, especially in the circumstances. I prayed so hard that they'd be with someone who would teach them about the Lord. God answered those prayers."

"You've taught them well. They pray at meals and bedtime, and Assad often reminds the others about God. He insists we read the Bible every day, and they like to listen to my children's Bible storybook."

"You don't know how happy that makes me." Yasmiin extended her hand as if to squeeze Anna's. Then she dropped it onto the table in front of her, a hopeless gesture that wrung Anna's heart.

Her voice shaky, Yasmiin continued. "Christians are persecuted in Somalia. That's why my mother escaped to America. In Somalia, we met in secret in people's homes. But every day brought new dangers. To our lives and our faith."

Anna had been derided for her old-fashioned clothing and Amish ways, but she couldn't imagine being forbidden to go to church or to speak about God's Word.

"I can tell how much you love my children, and they seem happy and comfortable with you. I'd been thinking about asking you to adopt them."

Chapter Thirty-One

Adopt them? Anna sat there, stunned. Yasmiin would give up her children to someone she'd known such a short while? And that she'd even consider Anna?

"But . . ."

That word pierced Anna's heart and dreams. Yasmiin had considered her, but she'd changed her mind. Anna's spirits had soared like a balloon until the sharp pinprick deflated them.

Yasmiin stared off into the distance and twisted her clasped hands. Around the two of them, other conversations and arguments buzzed. Anna willed Yasmiin to speak.

When she finally did, Anna wished she could stop up her ears.

Her voice so low and shaky she could barely be heard, Yasmiin pushed out each word. "I spent months as a single mom. It's a hard life." She lifted her head and gazed into Anna's eyes as if willing her to understand. "I want my children to have a mother and a father."

She had given Anna the most precious gift—entrusting her to care for her children forever, granting Anna's deepest desire to be a mother—and had taken it away with one word. *Father.*

"I—I'm not married." And not likely to be. Ever.

"I know." Yasmiin's face, which had contorted in pain, smoothed into something resembling compassion. "This Levi the children often mention, is he your boyfriend or fiancé or whatever you call it?"

"Special friend." The words trembled on Anna's lips. Along with having children, her sleeping and waking dreams revolved around dating Levi. And though she often went further than that to imagine him as her fiancé or husband, all of those titles would remain fantasies.

"Levi's your special friend? Does that mean you'll be getting married?"

If things were different, *jah*, Anna had no doubt she'd be marrying him. But she had to be honest. She shook her head. "No, I don't plan to get married."

The pain in Yasmiin's eyes seemed to well up from her soul and spill out of her. She bowed her head and neck as if the burden she carried had weighed her down too much to go on.

"Then I'll have to see if someone from my church can take the children. Most of them already have families of their own. I prayed about this all night and felt certain . . ."

"I'm so sorry," Anna said. "I love all three of them deeply, and I'd be happy to adopt them."

Yasmiin shook her head. "My boys need a father. A godly man who'll set an example for them."

Anna couldn't give them that. Inside, she cried out to God. *Why? Why did I come so close, only to lose my only chance at having a family?* She'd lost her heart to the three little ones. Now they'd be taken from her too.

Yasmiin rose, her head bowed, and started to shuffle off.

"I'll only be here a short while. Tomorrow will be the last time I can see my children. Will you bring them?"

"Certainly." Anna had been so wrapped in her own sorrow. Hers paled in comparison to Yasmiin's. She'd never see her children again. "We'll be here as soon as visiting hours start, and we'll stay until the end."

Without another word, Yasmiin whirled on her heels. Her shoulders shook as a guard escorted her out.

Her eyes blinded by tears, Anna almost collided with someone as she wheeled herself out the door. Levi stood there waiting for her.

"Anna, what's wrong?" He steered her over to a quieter area of the parking lot and got down to her level.

"I . . . I can't . . . talk about it." She choked out each word. Miriam had warned her about getting too attached to foster children. She'd done it again. This time, though, they'd be given away to a stranger. Not a family member. And they could have stayed with her, if only . . .

Why, God, why?

Anna bowed her head. She couldn't blame God for her own foolishness. She'd been the one who caused the buggy accident. All the pain and loss she'd suffered since had all been her fault.

"Tell me, Anna." Levi's gentle, caring command brought her back to the story.

A few tears trickled down her cheeks. "Yasmiin's being deported."

Levi sucked in a breath. "Oh, no."

"She can't take her children with her. Not into a dangerous country." Picturing the perils Yasmiin faced, Anna cried out to God. *Please protect her, Lord.*

"What a horrible decision to have to make."

"I can't even imagine it." Losing children she'd come

to love ripped Anna's heart into shreds. How could their mother bear to give up her children?

"So, the children will stay with you?"

Anna tried to stop the torrent of tears threatening to overflow, but Levi's question opened the floodgates. She couldn't answer; she only shook her head.

Levi waited quietly until most of her sobs had subsided. "What's going to happen to them?"

"I don't know." Her voice broke. "Yasmiin's going to ask people at her church to take them."

"You wanted to adopt?"

"*Jah*, but I can't."

"Why not?"

All of Anna's heartache gushed into her answer. "Because I'm single." *And I always will be.* She'd lost the children and her only chance at marriage. Lonely years stretched ahead of her.

Levi wished he could wrap his arms around Anna and comfort her. "Lots of single people adopt nowadays."

Anna shook her head. "Yasmiin wants her children to have two parents."

The words Levi had been about to say died on his lips. Was God giving him another chance with Anna?

It might be a marriage of convenience for her, but he'd love her with every fiber of his being. Maybe in time, she'd come to care for him too.

"Anna," he said softly, "if you want, I'll marry you."

Her headshaking grew even more violent. Each movement of her head added another wound to his bloodied heart.

"I don't want someone to marry me out of pity."

"*Ach*, Anna. I didn't ask you because I felt sorry for

you." Her negative reaction to his proposal made him wary about revealing the truth. He'd told her he cared for her when he asked her to date him, but he hadn't been totally honest. He'd fallen totally, hopelessly in love with her.

She dashed at her eyes with her fists as if trying to stem the tears, and Levi fought to pull himself from his own pain to concentrate on hers.

God seemed to be nudging him to admit his true feelings. Remembering her rejection when he'd asked about courting her, Levi hesitated. Telling her about his deeper feelings might ruin their friendship. He didn't want to do that.

"I can't believe I'm going to lose the children."

Every anguished word she spoke increased Levi's agony. "Anna, we could get married so you can have the children."

Why was God giving her everything she'd always dreamed about—marriage to Levi, the chance to be a mother to three children she already loved—only to snatch it all away?

Levi had offered to give up his life and future to help her. She'd always been impressed by his selflessness. But she couldn't let him do this.

"I wish I could marry you, but I can't."

"Why, Anna, why?" The anguish in Levi's eyes and words tore at her soul. His grip tightened.

He'd captured her hands and hadn't let go. Now she disentangled her fingers from his and clutched the edges of her apron.

"Because"—she lowered her head—"because I can't . . .

have children." Each word wrenched from her lips carried oceans of pain and shame. Once Levi understood, he'd leave her, walk away, and never come back.

They fell into dead silence. Levi didn't move or speak. Around them leaves rustled, a bird cawed. In the parking lot behind them, horns honked, people shouted.

"Look at me, Anna." When she didn't respond, he reached out and, with a gentle finger, tilted her head up until he could look into her eyes. "Is that the reason you don't want to marry me?"

He read the truth in her eyes. "If I told you that doesn't matter to me, would it change your answer?"

"I can't do that to you."

"Anna," he said urgently, praying he wasn't mistaken about the feelings her eyes had revealed, "are you turning me down because you don't love me?"

"Of course not." Then she jerked her head away and gazed off into the distance.

"Do you love me?"

Anna bit her lip. Levi stopped breathing. Waited for her answer.

"More than anything in the world, but—"

He put a finger over her lips. "Then that's all that counts. Nothing else, except God's will, should come into this decision."

"But—"

"No 'buts,' Anna. I want to marry you, children or no children. Will you promise me to pray about it?"

Hope fought with wariness in her eyes. She closed her eyes as if concentrating on her internal struggle. Or maybe she was praying. Right here. Right now. Her lips moved silently.

When she opened her eyes, Levi didn't need to ask her decision. Her face shone. And the love-light in her eyes filled him with joy.

"Anna, I'm only going to say one more thing about children. How many we have is up to you. If you want to adopt twenty or more, I'm fine with that. I'm also happy with having three children. If that's the number you choose, it's a big enough family for me. I'd want to marry you even if it meant having no children. Besides . . ." Levi stopped short.

"Besides what?" Anna asked.

"*Ach,* I should have mentioned this before I asked you to marry me. If you want to change your answer . . ."

Anxiety gripped Anna. Had Levi changed his mind about getting married?

"You can still say no. I'll understand."

Levi had just reassured her he didn't mind that she couldn't have children. Did he regret it? Had he come up with an excuse to back out?

"My *aenti* is leaving soon, so I'll be responsible for my three brothers."

"Are you hoping that will make me say no?" She couldn't resist teasing him a little after he'd made her worry he wanted to call off the wedding.

At the sharp, swift pain in his eyes, Anna regretted making him suffer. "When you asked me, I assumed your brothers were included."

"You really don't mind expanding our family by three more?"

"Of course not. I love your brothers. Well, the two I've met already. I'm sure I'll love Zeb too." She smiled at him. "Looks like both of us are package deals."

"I guess so. I'm happy with the package I got."

Anna laughed, but then she sobered and her eyes stung. "I can't believe this. For years now, I've asked God why He didn't let me have children. I never thought I'd end up with six." *And a man who loves me.*

"Or more," Levi added.

His words filled her heart to overflowing. "I can't believe I wasted all those years pining for the wrong man."

Levi took her hands in his. "But if you hadn't, we never would have met."

Anna stared at him. She'd never thought about that. "You're right. God even had a purpose for that." Why had she fretted so much about her future when she could have been walking forward in faith?

Chapter Thirty-Two

"*Ach*." Anna pulled her hands from Levi's.

He looked startled and hurt.

"I have to see Yasmiin before she finds another family for the children."

Levi stood and spun her chair around so she could rush back into the prison. She hurried through the door and tried to go around the metal detectors.

One of the guards blocked her way. "You have to go through the metal detectors and be patted down."

"But I already did that. I was just in here. I need to tell Yasmiin something. Something important."

A weary expression on his face, the guard enunciated each word. "How do we know you didn't get a knife or gun or drugs while you were outside? Besides, whoever you visited has already gone back to their cell block."

"But . . . but . . ." She needed to talk to Yasmiin now. What if Yasmiin made arrangements to give the children to someone else?

"It's only a short while till visiting hours end. You'll have to wait until next time." The guard's cold, unsympathetic voice chilled Anna all the way to her bones.

Next time might be too late.

The guard made a shooing motion with his hand, and Anna turned and headed back out into the fading sunshine. As she wheeled through the door, she almost mowed Levi down again.

"Tom's not back yet. He went for a meal." Levi motioned her to the spot where they'd talked before. Then he squatted and took her hands in his. "What happened?"

The warmth of his fingers melted some of the iciness inside. "They won't let me see Yasmiin. I have to come back for the next visiting hours."

"I'll check with Tom, but I'm sure that won't be a problem."

"But what if Yasmiin finds someone else before then?"

Levi smoothed his thumb across the top of her hand, sending tingles through her body. "Anna, if this is God's will for you, for us, then it will all work out. Why don't we pray about it?"

Some of Anna's tension leaked away. Levi was right. She needed to put this in the Lord's hands.

They both bowed their heads and turned everything over to their Heavenly Father. Something Anna should have done years ago. If God intended for her to have Levi and the children, He'd take care of all the details. And if not, she could trust Him to lead her down a different path.

Assad opened the door when Levi knocked. Levi had come a little early in case she needed help getting the children ready for visiting hours. *Neh*, if he were honest, he'd come early to be with her.

Anna hadn't heard him come in. She had her head bent over as she frowned at a paper in front of her. Then she closed her eyes for a while, and soon a smile blossomed on her lips. She opened her eyes, picked up her pen, and let her fingers fly across the page.

Levi enjoyed watching her. Her eyes sparkled when she sat back and tapped the pen against her mouth. Her very kissable mouth. Levi dragged his thoughts away from that temptation.

They had too many spectators. The children were playing cards and looked happier than he expected. Perhaps Anna hadn't told them about their mother.

He tiptoed out to the kitchen and set his hands on her shoulder. "Surprise," he whispered in her ear.

She jumped a little at his touch, but then she relaxed back, and smiled up at him. "I like surprises."

"You were really absorbed in your writing." He wanted to peek at what had held her attention, but he forced himself to sit down at the table without looking.

"I've had this on my heart for a while. I'm writing a letter to Gabe."

"Gabe?" A tinge of hurt colored his question. Yesterday, Anna had agreed to marry him. Had she changed her mind?

"*Jah*, Gabe." She nibbled on the end of the pen. "I'm struggling with how to sign it."

"Not 'Love,' I hope."

Anna's head snapped up, and she studied him. "You aren't jealous, are you?"

"Well . . ." Truth be told, he was. Why would she be writing to her ex-boyfriend?

"*Ach*, Levi, you're the one I love." Anna's radiant smile soothed some of Levi's hurt. "As soon as I'm done, I'll let you read it." A sparkle in her eye, she lifted her pen. "I know how to end it."

With a flourish, she glided her pen across the paper.

Her lips tilted up in a sly smile. "Don't worry. I didn't sign it 'Love' or 'Very truly yours.'"

"Glad to hear it."

"Just so you know, Gabe's getting married. I decided to send them a wedding gift—kitchen tools for Priscilla and a toolbox for him. Something you said yesterday gave me the idea to write him a letter." She slid it across the table to him.

Feeling a little guilty for intruding, Levi skimmed her message.

Priscilla and Gabe,

I hope these tools help as you start your new life together. I wish you only joy and happiness as you follow God's will for your lives.

Sometimes what appears heartbreaking is only God's way of moving us to a new and better place. The Lord has blessed me in so many ways, and I know He has even more exciting plans for me in the future. I thank Him for bringing the two of you together so He could lead me in a new direction.

With many prayers,
Anna

Levi had a lump in his throat by the time he finished. "That's kind and generous of you."

"I think Gabe feels guilty about not keeping his promise. I'm so blessed now that I don't want anything to spoil his happiness."

He'd picked a woman who was beautiful, inside and out. One who had a generous and caring spirit. What more could a man want? And he couldn't help smiling at Ron's comment. His friend had been right. Levi had ended up with an insta-family.

"What's so funny?" Anna asked as she folded the letter and slipped it into an envelope.

"When we were at the barbecue, Ron thought all three children were yours. He asked me if I really wanted an insta-family. I certainly never expected that to come true."

"Neither did I." Anna met his gaze.

Levi could stare into her beautiful eyes all day. But Tom would be here soon. "We should get ready to go."

"I know. I usually wait until the last minute to tell the children we're going, but today I've been putting it off because . . ." Her voice trailed off.

"They don't know yet?"

Anna shook her head. "I dread telling them, but I don't want to leave that to Yasmiin. Saying good-bye will be hard enough for her."

Levi couldn't even imagine how heartbreaking it would be to leave her children behind, knowing she'd never see them again. That had to be one of the greatest sacrifices a mother could make.

With Levi here for backup, Anna could no longer put off telling the children. They were all in the living room, laughing and talking as they played a game. How could she destroy that happiness?

Anna entered the room, and Levi took a chair beside her and held her hand. She appreciated the strong, warm fingers entwined with hers. His touch gave her much needed emotional support.

"When I went to see your mommy, she had some bad news." How did she explain *deported*? Would they understand?

Assad's hands stilled. He set down his cards and turned his full attention to Anna. The other two copied him.

"They're sending your mommy back to Somalia." Anna's words dropped like heavy stones.

"But she doesn't want to go there. Not ever," Assad burst out. "It's scary and dangerous."

"Yes, it is. That's why she'll be going alone. She doesn't want any of you to get hurt."

Taban jumped up. "She's our mommy. We have to stay with her."

"She can't take you with her," Anna explained again. "It's too dangerous."

"But I want to go with Mommy," Taban cried.

Jamilah glanced from Assad's tension-filled face to Taban's angry one and started to wail. "Want Mommy."

Only Assad didn't participate in the crying. A frightened look in his eyes. "But what will happen to us?"

Levi got down on the floor and put one arm around Jamilah, his other around Taban.

"Your mommy asked us about adopting all of you." Anna hoped that was still the case. She'd been praying nonstop all last night and today.

Assad stared at her through narrowed eyes. "You'll never be my mommy." His voice flat and cold, he crossed his arms.

"I can't ever take your mommy's place. But we'll give you a home and do our best to take care of you." If we get custody.

Anna pushed the thought of losing them aside. The children needed all her attention to deal with their distress.

Tom honked outside.

"Remember, your mommy will be very sad," she told all of them. "Maybe you can try to cheer her up by telling her some of the fun things we've been doing."

Was she asking too much of children who were about to lose their mother?

Anna also needed to let them know they could express their feelings. Especially Assad. "It's all right to cry. We all feel sad."

Jamilah sniffled and gulped most of the way. Taban's tears transformed into anger. He kicked the back of the seat in front of him.

Tom remained undisturbed by the kicks and drove to the prison without saying a word. Levi must have explained.

Levi got out to help her and the children. Then he walked them to the door. "I'll wait right out here," he whispered to her. "And"—he swallowed hard—"I'll be praying."

Used to the security routine, the children stayed stony-faced and endured the wait during Anna's lengthier process.

Soon after they entered the room, Yasmiin, her face stoic, was brought in. Her eyes revealed how desperately she wanted to embrace her children. But, trapped behind the Plexiglas shield, she couldn't even hug or kiss them good-bye.

Taban rushed to the window and pressed his face against the barrier. "Don't go, Mommy!"

Anna expected the guards to drag him away, but they had tears in their eyes.

Swallowing down the lump blocking her throat, Anna removed Taban from the glass and wrapped an arm around him to keep him close to her chair and to comfort him.

Anna needed to speak, but she could barely get words out. The weight of Yasmiin's grief fell over all of them, and they sat in silence, while she memorized each child's face in turn, and they tucked their last picture of her into their hearts.

When Yasmiin broke her gaze and lowered her head, Anna prayed for her and the children. She waited until

Yasmiin looked up to broach the question burning on her heart.

"Yasmiin, I don't know what arrangements you've made with your church, but yesterday Levi asked me to marry him. He loves the children as much as I do and is also willing to adopt them. If you'll let us."

Anna sucked in a breath and waited for the answer. An answer that had the power to shape her whole future.

Chapter Thirty-Three

Whispering a prayer that she'd be able to accept God's will in this situation, whatever Yasmiin's answer might be, Anna sat with an arm around Jamilah and Taban. Assad had edged closer to her chair. Anna wished she had another arm to draw him to her.

Yasmiin hesitated. "A friend at church called several people in the congregation. A few are willing to take in one child or maybe two at most."

Terror flared in Assad's eyes. "No."

"Don't worry, honey. I want you all to stay together." Yasmiin pinned Anna with a searching gaze. "If you're willing to take all three of them . . ."

"We are. I promise I'll love them as my own." Anna lowered her eyes as she spoke of her own inner ache. "I can't have children, so Assad, Taban, and Jamilah will be especially precious to me."

She rushed on, trying to reassure Yasmiin she and Levi would be the best choice. "Levi has come to love all of them. He'll be a good father." Anna hoped it would help Yasmiin to realize her little ones would be cherished.

Relief flared in her eyes. "I can tell they'll be loved."

Jamilah, who was sitting on Anna's lap, reached her arms out for her mother to hold her. Yasmiin pressed her lips together and took a shuddery breath. Then she managed, "I love you, baby. I'll always love you." She said the same to each boy in turn.

Assad shoved his hands deep into his pockets before he met his mother's eyes. In a choky voice, he promised, "I'll take care of Taban and Jamilah."

"I know you will, honey. You've always been my dependable helper."

Yasmiin looked at each of them in turn. "Be good for Anna and Levi." Her voice broke.

"Please keep us posted as to where you are," Anna said to Yasmiin.

Her tear-clogged, cynical laugh made Anna ache for her.

"I have no place to go," Yasmiin said. "No job. No friends. No relatives."

Anna couldn't even imagine going to another land where she knew nobody. She'd always been grateful for her Amish community and the support it provided. Yasmiin would be a stranger in an unfamiliar land.

"I was only eight. I don't remember anything. All I know is the country's dangerous."

A memory of Yasmiin's face, when she recounted the terrors her children would face if they returned to Somalia with her, haunted Anna. "We'll be praying."

"I'll need God every step of the way. I don't remember the language. Without that, I have no way to get a job." Yasmiin shook her head. "Our church members, despite how poor most of them are, raised a little money to keep me going. But I'll be depending on God to see me through. Maybe someday . . ."

She shook her head. Her face revealed the agony of leaving her home and losing her children.

"When you can, write or contact us. I'll be sure the children answer," Anna promised.

"I'll do my best." Yasmiin's mouth moved silently, but Anna read Yasmiin's lips.

If I survive.

Anna prayed God would protect this young mother, and that someday she'd get to see her children again.

Squeezing her eyes shut, Yasmiin said, "I will pray for them and you many times every day."

"And we will keep you in our prayers."

What more could you say to a mother who might never see her children again?

And even worse, how did you comfort children who were losing their mother so soon after losing their dad?

Levi paced outside the building. Back and forth, he walked, praying the whole time. First, for Yasmiin, who had to give up her children. Then for the children. And their future. Most of all, he wrapped Anna in prayers and love.

Please, Lord, help us both to accept whatever Your will is for our lives.

He'd become attached to these children, and Anna loved them so much, she'd be devastated. But whatever the outcome, he'd be beside her to protect her. And they'd always keep the three children in prayer.

When they finally emerged from the prison, the children had bowed heads and tears streaming down their cheeks. Anna met his gaze with tear-filled, but radiant, eyes.

"They're ours," she said.

Levi knelt and opened his arms. He longed to embrace Anna and dry her tears, but two sobbing boys flung themselves at his chest. Anna held Jamilah, whose eyes were wet with tears. She cuddled her lovey and sucked her thumb hard, appearing more confused than sad.

Levi met Anna's eyes over their heads. *I love you*, he mouthed as he hugged the boys close, *and our new family.*

Her eyes shone as her lips formed *I love you too.*

God had given him the desires of his heart. He was about to marry the woman of his dreams and get an insta-family.

Taban lifted his head and looked Levi directly in the eye. "Mommy will come back, won't she?"

His soon-to-be son had asked him the first question he'd have to answer as a father. "Let's pray about that." That would be his answer to many of the thorny questions they'd ask over the years.

He and Anna had taken on a tremendous responsibility, but if they put God first, He'd lead them every step of the way.

Epilogue

As autumn weather turned the trees overhead gold and russet, Levi thanked the Lord for a lovely crisp day for their wedding. He and Anna had talked to the bishop about marrying quickly because they wanted to give the children a stable home.

Members of the church, along with many of Levi's friends at the firehouse, had completed an accessible addition to the *dawdi haus* with enough room for their large—and hopefully growing—family. Levi and Anna had decided to continue fostering children and to increase their family size through adoption.

Anna had teased Levi about his insistence that he'd be fine with twenty children. They hadn't settled on a final number for their family. They'd leave that up to God.

Both he and Anna had learned many lessons about trusting the Lord's leading in their lives. Even during the darkest times, they'd found God had a special plan. Levi's soul filled with gratitude for His many blessings as he and Anna recited their promises to each other and before the Lord.

When the whole congregation gathered around to support them at the end of the wedding, Levi's heart soared.

He would be part of this *g'may* now, and they'd made him and his brothers feel so welcome. And now before God and all these witnesses, Levi had sealed this sacred bond for life with a woman he loved, adored, and cherished.

And she had brought three adorable children into his life. Together, they celebrated the rest of the day. Their lives couldn't be any fuller.

Or so he thought until a few weeks later.

Anna had just headed into the kitchen to fix breakfast when Emily knocked and stuck her head in the door. "I came over early to take the three children and Levi's brothers for breakfast and to help them get dressed. That way, the two of you can have a little alone time."

Just her and Levi? How heavenly that would be. "*Danke*, Emily. That's so thoughtful of you."

Just before Emily closed the door, she said over her shoulder, "I'll bring them back in an hour."

Anna and Levi barely had time to enjoy a leisurely breakfast together and get ready before Emily knocked again. "Are you two ready? The vans are here."

"We'll be right out," Anna called.

Tom and one of his friends were taking the extended family to the courthouse. Levi offered to push her down the ramp, and Anna appreciated the break. They'd get there faster too.

Before they reached the van, Levi stopped suddenly. Anna glanced up to see what had arrested his attention.

Assad, Taban, and Jamilah stood beside the van waiting for them.

Anna's eyes filled with tears. All three of them had on Amish clothes.

"It was their idea," Emily said. "They wanted to surprise you."

Levi shook his head and swallowed hard. Then he reached for Anna's hand and squeezed.

Assad's cheeks reddened. "We wanted to look like a family today."

Anna could hardly get the words out. "We are a family. I can't tell you how happy you've made us." She had hoped to convince them to give up their *Englisch* clothes in a few months, but she didn't want to push too hard, knowing it was their last tie to their mother.

Today, on the most momentous day of Anna and Levi's lives—aside from their wedding—the three children had reassured them they wanted to be part of their family.

For Anna, it was a sure sign that this was God's will.

Thank you, Lord.

They all piled into the vans. Miriam, her family, and her foster kids climbed into one van. Levi, Anna, his brothers, and the three children piled into the other. Betty and Vern and his boys had driven down from Fort Plain and planned to meet them at the courthouse.

Assad supervised his siblings, being sure they were safely belted in, and Daniel looked out for Jonah. Levi strapped Anna's wheelchair in last and stared into her eyes with a special smile until she'd been lifted into place and the van door slid shut. Then he hopped into the front seat, and they started their journey to the courthouse and to parenthood.

Inside the courtroom, Anna sat by the end of the bench beside the three children, while Levi and his three younger brothers sat on the other side of Assad.

A man came in and stopped beside Anna. "Many of our church members are here today to represent Yasmiin and

Dihoud. He was our beloved minister, and we love their children as our own."

Anna shook his hand, and Levi leaned over to be introduced. The children rose from their seats to hug him. Then he handed Anna an envelope. "This has been on a long journey after being smuggled out of Somalia. Yasmiin asked me to give it to you on adoption day."

He laid a hand of blessing on Anna's shoulder. "I have taken over as pastor, and we will keep all of you in our prayers."

"Thank you," Anna whispered. "We pray for Yasmiin every night."

"As do we," the man assured her. "God be with all of you."

Before the judge entered the courtroom, Anna opened the envelope and slipped out one thin sheet of paper. Her eyes blurred as she read:

Dear Anna and Levi,

On this special day, I wanted to thank you for making my children a part of your family. They will always be my babies, my little ones, and my arms ache to hold them, but I believe God has a purpose for even the greatest heartbreaks, and I look forward to reuniting with all of you in heaven, if not before.

God has blessed me with many needy children here, although none can take the place of my three precious darlings, who stay forever locked in my heart.

I work as an aide in a hospital. It is hard work because the hospital is short-staffed. We care for many children who have been wounded by bullets or maimed in explosions.

I am so thankful my boys are not here. If they were not in the hospital, they would soon be taken to be trained as soldiers. Children as young as nine are forced to fight.

I am entrusting this letter to a friend who will smuggle it out of the country to mail it, otherwise I would not, could not, write this without putting other people's lives in jeopardy.

I have found an underground church, a small group of believers who meet for worship. We share a New Testament, which we keep hidden. I am so grateful for the Scriptures I memorized over the years. They may find and destroy our Bible, but no one can take those passages from me.

I pray that the children are growing in health and a knowledge of the Lord. Please tell them that I love them. Not a day goes by that I don't miss them. I keep them always in my prayers. I pray they are growing to love you and that God will give you both the strength and wisdom to raise them. I ask God's blessings on all of you, each and every day.

> *With love and many, many prayers,*
> *Yasmiin*

P.S. Please send any correspondence to the address below. I don't trust letters to arrive in Somalia, so Khalif has promised to bring them into the country whenever he returns here on business. It may take months for mail to get to me, but he can be trusted.

Anna's eyes stung. She fought to hold back tears as she passed the letter to Levi. When he had read it, he met her gaze, his own eyes as damp as hers.

"We'll read it to them later," she said after he'd handed it back. She tucked it back into the envelope. And she'd help the children write back.

Even Taban remained subdued by the solemnness of the occasion when the judge entered. They sat quietly, waiting to be called.

Millie sat near the front because she was handling two adoptions today.

After Anna and Levi were called and sworn in, they answered the judge's questions about why they wanted to adopt and about their ability to provide a safe, stable, and loving home. Following a few questions for Millie, the judge signed all three adoption decrees.

Chills ran through Anna as Levi reached for the papers officially declaring them to be the parents of Assad, Taban, and Jamilah. Even his hands shook a little as he studied the papers and then handed them over to her.

Anna ran her fingers over the names. These were now their children.

They all slipped out of the courtroom. Anna's and Levi's families along with Yasmiin's church members gathered around Anna, Levi, and their brand-new children.

"Let me snap a few pictures for Yasmiin," the *Englisch* pastor said.

Anna looked pleadingly at Levi, who held up a hand. "We prefer not to be photographed."

"Oh, sorry. I forgot about that." The minister looked contrite. "I just thought Yasmiin would like to see . . ."

"Tell you what. Why don't we get together in a group, and we'll put our hands on the children's shoulders? Could you take a picture that doesn't show our heads?"

"Sure, sure." The minister waited until they'd set up the shot. Then he snapped a few pictures. "I have an idea. What about one with the five of you facing the courtroom seal, holding hands? Okay to photograph your backs like that?"

"Perfect," Anna agreed. They also posed the same way and included Levi's brothers.

"Yasmiin will love these, I'm sure." The minister shook Levi's and Anna's hands. "We'll be praying."

"We appreciate that."

Assad and Taban didn't let go of Levi's hand until after the church members had departed. Jamilah crawled up onto Anna's lap. Jonah came over and took Taban's hand. Daniel ruffled Assad's hair.

Zeb smiled at all of them. "Welcome to the family."

Everyone started for the vans. Miriam had a special meal and cake waiting for them to celebrate. Levi's brothers, excited about the food, rushed out with Anna's relatives.

But Assad tugged on Levi's hand to hold him back. Anna stayed beside Levi.

"I have a daddy in heaven." Assad looked pensive. "And one on earth." He slid his hand into Levi's. "And I have two mommies. One who lives far, far away who loves me very much, and one right here." He reached for Anna's hand.

"Who also loves you very, very much," she finished.

He grinned. "I know."

"And I have three of the most precious children in the world." Anna looked at each one in turn and thanked God for this wondrous gift.

Then she met Levi's eyes. His smile lit that familiar spark in her heart. A spark that flamed into a blaze. A blaze that would continue to burn throughout their years together.